BLACK CAT

V.C. Andrews® Books

The Dollanganger Family Series
Flowers in the Attic
Petals on the Wind
If There Be Thorns
Seeds of Yesterday
Garden of Shadows

The Casteel Family Series
Heaven
Dark Angel
Fallen Hearts
Gates of Paradise
Web of Dreams

The Cutler Family Series
Dawn
Secrets of the Morning
Twilight's Child
Midnight Whispers
Darkest Hour

The Landry Family Series
Ruby
Pearl in the Mist
All That Glitters
Hidden Jewel
Tarnished Gold

The Logan Family Series
Melody
Heart Song
Unfinished Symphony
Music in the Night
Olivia

My Sweet Audrina
(does not belong to a series)

The Orphans Miniseries
Butterfly
Crystal
Brooke
Raven
Runaways (full-length novel)

The Wildflowers Miniseries
Misty
Star
Jade
Cat
Into the Garden (full-length novel)

The Hudson Family Series
Rain
Lightning Strikes
Eye of the Storm
The End of the Rainbow

The Shooting Stars Series
Cinnamon
Ice
Rose
Honey
Falling Stars

The De Beers Family Series
Willow
Wicked Forest
Twisted Roots
Into the Woods
Hidden Leaves

The Broken Wings Series
Broken Wings
Midnight Flight

The Gemini Series
Celeste

V.C. ANDREWS®

BLACK CAT

POCKET BOOKS

New York London Toronto Sydney

and

Following the death of Virginia Andrews, the Andrews family worked with a carefully selected writer to organize and complete Virginia Andrews' stories and to create additional novels, of which this is one, inspired by her storytelling genius.

This book is a work of fiction. Names, characters, places and incidents are products of the author's imagination or are used fictitiously. Any resemblance to actual events or locales or persons, living or dead, is entirely coincidental.

 POCKET BOOKS, a division of Simon & Schuster, Inc.
1230 Avenue of the Americas, New York, NY 10020

Copyright © 2004 by the Vanda General Partnership

ISBN: 0-7434-2867-6

First Pocket Books hardcover edition October 2004

10 9 8 7 6 5 4 3 2 1

V.C. ANDREWS and VIRGINIA ANDREWS are registered
trademarks of the Vanda General Partnership

POCKET and colophon are registered trademarks of
Simon & Schuster, Inc.

Manufactured in the United States of America

For information regarding special discounts for bulk purchases,
please contact Simon & Schuster Special Sales at 1-800-456-6798
or business@simonandschuster.com.

BLACK CAT

Prologue

Our Family History

♊

I have never doubted that the day my daddy died my mother knew about it long before his construction business partner, Mr. Calhoun, came to our house with the dreadful news. Earlier that day she had swooned and had remained unconscious long enough to terrify my brother, Noble, and me. Afterward, she would tell me that the spirit of a cat as black as Death itself had passed right through her heart.

When she spoke about these things, her eyes were wide with amazement, an amazement that nearly kept my heart from beating. I know I was holding my breath while she talked. My chest wanted to explode, but I didn't dare take a breath and risk interrupting her.

"I saw it come out of a shadow in the corner of the ceiling where it had nested in anxious anticipation. I swiped at it when it descended and came at me, but my hand didn't push it aside, and in seconds it had done its dark deed," she said, and then her eyes grew small and she told me of a similar event her grandmother had experienced on the occasion of her grandmother's brother's accidental death. He had fallen from a horse and hit his head on a boulder.

"The sound of a horse's hooves pounded through her head, and when she looked up, a black cat leaped through the air, its paws set to claw right through her chest. She actually fainted on the spot, and when she woke up, the first words out of her mouth were 'Warren is gone.' No one had found his body yet, but everyone knew someone soon would," Mama added in a deep whisper, the sort of whisper that passes through your heart like the black cat she described.

Our family history on my mother's side was rife with example after example of someone being able to see the future, sense an upcoming tragic event, or read signs in nature that foretold someone's sickness or death. It was a gift of prophecy she believed would be handed down through her to Noble and me, but most likely to Noble. Why she believed that so strongly, I do not know, but I do know it was the main reason why he could never be permitted to die.

Often at night after Baby Celeste was born, Mama would sit in Grandpa Jordan's old rocker with her cradled in her arms and rock her to sleep while she told me these family stories. I felt as if she were wiping away the cobwebs and dusting off the past that lingered in every nook and cranny, under every shadow. She would look out at the darkness that draped our house like a heavy satin veil, and she would talk about that dreadful day when my daddy died and all the days of her past with such vivid recollection, as if she were able to look back through a microscope for time seeing the smallest of details. She would speak not to me as much as to herself and to the spirits that she said sat with us, uncles, aunts, and cousins, all joining us to hold what now seemed to me to have been an eternal wake.

There was indeed so much to mourn.

I didn't have to have the gift of prophecy to know that there was so much more yet to come before that dark veil would be lifted from our home and our lives.

1

Noble's Pleas

♊

"Noble," Mama called with urgency resonating in her voice.

I turned to see her waving at me from the front steps of the porch. Her hazel brown, shoulder-length hair fell straight alongside her cheeks. She had a radish-red bandanna tied across her forehead, which she said would ward off recent curses whenever they were thrown in her direction, so I knew something had spooked her today.

She was standing there with Baby Celeste beside her, which was quite unusual. Mama never brought her out during the daytime for fear someone, even from the distance in a passing car, might see her and learn that she existed. This secrecy had existed from the moment Baby Celeste had been born, a little more than two and a half years ago.

Today was one of those summer days in July when clouds seemed hinged to the horizon, not a single sliver of one interfering with the orange disk of sun sliding gracefully over the icy blue toward the mountains in the west. I was on my hands and knees pruning weeds in the herb garden. The redolent aroma of rich, wet soil filled my nostrils. Worms, lubricated and shiny from the night's rain, slipped through my muddied fingers. A wisp of a breeze teased me with a promise of some relief that had yet to be fulfilled. I was already quite tan, the farmer's tan, Daddy used to call it, because my arms were dark up to the edges of my sleeves and my neck down to my collar. It was evident only when I was naked.

Mama took another step toward me and away from the house to call again. Through the hot, undulating air that lay between us, the house seemed to shimmer and swell up around her and Baby Celeste as if it were determined to block them from the view passengers in cars along the highway would have. The house would always protect them, protect us. Mama believed that. She believed it was as sacred as a church.

Anyone looking at the house might readily accept that it held some special powers. It was large and unique in this area of upstate New York, an eclectic Queen Anne with a steeply hipped roof, two lower cross gables, and a turret at the west corner of the front facade. The turret room was a fairly good size round room with two windows that faced the front. Mama told me that her grandfather had often used the room as a personal retreat. He would spend hours and hours alone in it, reading or simply smoking his pipe and staring out at the mountains. Perhaps because of that story or simply because the room was so private and hidden at the top of the small stairway that led up to it, I used it as a retreat, a secret place, as well.

Sometimes at night after Baby Celeste was asleep

and Mama was distracted, I was able to sneak up to the turret room, where Mama had put all our mirrors except the ones on the bathroom walls above the sinks. There were many antiques and boxes of very old things stored there. She put the mirrors there because she said our good family spirits avoided them, especially full-length mirrors like the gilded-framed oval one with a rose carved at the top.

"Despite the eternal joy they share in the other world, they do not like to be reminded that they are out of their bodies, that their bodies are long decayed into dust. What they see of themselves is more like an image captured in a wisp of twirling smoke," she explained.

I thought that made good sense. While we were in this world, nothing held our attention or was as important as our bodies. Who didn't look at his or her body often during the day, whether it be in a storefront window, a mirror, pictures, or even in the eyes of someone else? What was more intriguing than yourself?

Denied the common opportunities to do so, I would stand before the oval mirror in the turret room, undress, and gaze at my uncovered and now undisguised female body, turning to look at myself from every angle like someone who was trying on a new dress. Often, I would feel as if I were looking through a window at someone else and not in a mirror at myself. That made the mirror seem magical to me, and that in itself turned the turret room into a special place. It not only held secrets of our past in old dresser drawers and cartons, it provided a pathway of escape, a place where dreams were unrestricted, and after all, it was in dreams only that I could be who I was.

For nearly ten years now, I had had to deny the existence of whom and what I saw standing before me.

There was no doubt in my mind that no night in my life would ever be as traumatic as the night Mama took me out to the small, old family graveyard to say good-bye to myself in a funeral so private even the stars were kept hidden behind clouds.

Lying there in the open, freshly dug grave with his hands crossed over his chest was my twin brother, Noble, wearing my dress and even my amulet, the Mystic Star with its seven points. I hadn't even realized she had taken it off me during the night. Noble's eyes were so tightly closed they looked stitched shut. I had let Mama down, disappointed her so deeply, I made her very soul cringe. I hadn't protected my twin brother and therefore I had to be the one buried and gone. She transformed me into Noble like some wizard waving a wand, and then she told the world I had been kidnapped. The community pitied her, pitied us when search parties found one of my shoes in the forest and concluded she was right: someone had taken me.

Dozens of people traipsed through the property and crossed over to our nearest neighbor, an elderly man named Gerson Baer, who lived alone. He had nothing to offer, but because he was a loner and a neighbor, he fell under some suspicion for a while. He was wise enough to permit a full search of his house and property, and eventually the police left him alone, but Mommy predicted nasty, stupid people would always suspect him. She sounded as if she really did feel sorry for him, but she also mentioned that it helped us.

A week went by and the story stopped being published in the paper. Occasionally, one of the sheriff's patrolmen appeared. The detective returned and went back over the story. Mommy looked terrible. She didn't eat. She didn't do anything to make herself attractive. Some people, old friends of Daddy's, and his former partner, Mr. Calhoun, sent over flowers and candy with good wishes. The detective offered to contact any family to assist us, but Mommy thanked him and told him we would be all right. He promised to keep us up-to-date on any new developments.

In the beginning, whenever I heard people talk sadly about me, it was truly as if I were invisible, a ghost listening to people talk about her and what she was like when she was alive. Mama said nice things about me, things that made me ache to return and again be that responsible, bright, and intelligent girl. Visitors who had come to sympathize would shake their heads and look at me sadly.

"I bet you miss your sister very much," they would say. Or they would say, "How lonely you must be, all by yourself now."

Mama would agree we had been inseparable, truly twins who could think each other's thoughts. Her eyes would gloss over and she would look as if she couldn't take another breath. The visitors would blanket her in sympathy.

I had to nod or wipe a drummed-up tear from my cheek because Noble, being a boy, wouldn't show his sadness so readily. He would be tougher. Slowly, in small ways at first, Mama had me imitate Noble, even take on his bad habits. Nothing angered her as much as my resisting or failing to succeed at such forgery. I wanted so to please her, but for me, every little action, characteristic, habit, I successfully simulated was like another shovelful of dirt I cast on my own grave. Sometimes, at night, I would wake up feeling as if I were suffocating. I would be all in a sweat, the redolent aroma of cool, dark earth about me. I thought I even felt it on my face and brushed my cheeks frantically before settling down and trying again to sleep.

Every night I fell asleep thinking I might never wake up or I would wake up in a grave. There was only one way to stay above it, to keep out of it, to remain alive.

Mama had always loved Noble more than she loved me, and now as Noble I could have all that love for myself, so I worked hard at becoming my brother. I took on chores girls my age would never assume like chopping and splitting firewood, changing tires, and greasing lawn mowers and other engines. I repaired a shed roof, hammered and sawed, painted and varnished. My hands developed calluses. My thicker forearms looked more like a boy's than a girl's, and when I walked, I strutted with a masculine gait that even took me by surprise when I became aware of it. It was Mama's smiles of satisfaction that made me aware. Her smile of approval countered and overcame any hesitation, any self-consciousness I might have.

Growing hard and lean, remaining in home school and rarely confronting girls my age, I succeeded to the point where I even dreamed Noble's dreams, saw the spirits I imagined he would see, such as cousins his age who had had similar tragic deaths, impish, naughty little boys who teased their sisters and like him went running and shouting through make-believe battlefields and jungles, or I would see strong uncles with muscles built out of hard farm work or carpentry. Our dainty, female family spirits seemed to avoid me the way they would avoid Noble. It was as if they were really and truly a part of Mama's plan or at least afraid of contradicting it.

For as long as I could remember, Mama had communicated with her family spirits. She had promised both Noble and me that we would be able to do the same, and although our daddy shook his head and

didn't believe in any of it, he didn't really try too hard
to force her to stop believing. There was no doubt in
my mind that she wouldn't have under any circumstances anyway. It was a major part of whom and what
she was. She would tell Daddy he couldn't love her
without loving that. Even as a little girl, I could see he
knew that and he accepted. How great was his love, I
thought, and like every little girl, I dreamed I would
find someone as wonderful as my daddy to love me.
However, I was terrified I wasn't as good and as beautiful as Mommy and would never find anyone like
Daddy.

Mama always thought Noble would cross over, as
she called it, before I did, but Noble never had as pas-
sionate an interest in our family spirits and the world
beyond as I had. It frustrated Mama. She tried everything, including teaching him how to meditate, but
nothing worked, so she concluded that something evil
was standing in Noble's way. That was why she made
me truly my brother's keeper and why she was so
upset when he died in the accident in the creek. He fell
off the big rock from which he was fishing. I wanted
him to come home, but he wouldn't, so we had a tug-
of-war with his pole. Was Mama right? Was it really
my fault?

He couldn't die; he wouldn't die. His spirit would
enter me, and that was how it would be forever and
ever. But neither Mama nor I understood how powerful
the woman in me would become. Years later in my
solitude I couldn't hold her back. I couldn't prevent
her from reemerging. At my private, secret place in the
forest, I uncovered myself and let myself breathe as
Celeste, and it was during one of those episodes that
our new neighbor's son, Elliot Fletcher, discovered the
truth and blackmailed me into having sex with him.

Now, when I think of that, when I permit myself to remember those secret rendezvous, I hear a voice inside me that tells me I wasn't blackmailed as much as I would like to believe. I wanted what had happened to me to happen. It was a way of denying what I had become and returning to whom and what I was.

Baby Celeste was born as a result of all that, but I had to keep my pregnancy secret as long as I could, knowing how Mama would be devastated. I couldn't even tell people that I had seen Elliot drown that day he lost control of himself while crossing the creek to go home. I felt sorry for his father, who was a pharmacist in a nearby village, and who had to bring up both Elliot and his sister, Betsy, after his wife had left him. Betsy was a constant source of trouble, promiscuous and wild, and now he had lost his son and would probably never know he had a granddaughter.

I hid my pregnancy for as long as I could, and when it was impossible to do so any longer, I was terrified. Mama's reaction was to deny it had ever occurred. She kept it well hidden and her way of greeting the birth of my child was to declare to me and to herself that my baby was a miraculous creation, a spiritual creation, the return of Celeste. She so named her, and then, to my shock, she dyed the baby's hair so she would look like me and not have Elliot's red hair, not yet or perhaps not ever.

Now, when I looked at my baby even from this distance, seeing her beside Mama, holding her hand and looking in my direction, I saw myself as a little girl. I couldn't help believing at times that Mama was right. Celeste was my resurrection, my returning, my rebirth, a true miracle. She had my gestures, my laugh, my way of sleeping with my lips pursed and my left hand pressed flatly against my cheek.

All these thoughts, these memories, these feelings, ran through my mind like the creek that ran through our property, rising and falling not with the rain and the melting snow as did the creek, but with the storms and changes that showered on our very private world.

Today was yet another.

"Hurry up," Mama ordered when I put the garden tools aside and started toward the house.

She turned, lifted Celeste into her arms, and went into the house quickly, fleeing with her as if the sunlight were deadly. I trotted back and took off my muddied shoes. She was waiting in the hallway.

"What's wrong?" I asked, seeing the urgency in her face.

Had she seen some curse floating around us, around me? Was that why she wanted me inside quickly? It wouldn't be the first time. Too often as I grew up on the farm, and even when Noble was alive, Mama's call to us was like an alarm bell, an alert to hurry back into the safety of our home to avoid being caught in a gust of cold, dark wind, what she called the "icy breath of Death, himself." How could we not shudder and rush into her waiting warm embrace?

Baby Celeste stood there with her thumb in her mouth gazing up at me. Usually, when she was with Mama for a while, she would reflect Mama's moods and look more like her than me.

"Mrs. Paris is coming right away for some Nufem," Mama replied.

"Oh," I said, my fears eased.

Nufem was the name Mama had given to her secret herbal supplement to relieve women of the discomforts of the menopause. I knew only that she combined things like red raspberry, passionflower, black cohosh, wild yam, and some motherwort to create her remedy.

I think she added some vitamin supplements as well. She had given it to the mayor's wife, who had heard about it from Mrs. Zalkin, wife of the egg farmer who lived a few miles east of us, and now apparently Mrs. Paris, who was the wife of one of the biggest landlords in nearby Sandburg, had been talking to the mayor's wife.

Over the past year and a half, Mama had developed a number of customers for her herbal remedies and had even begun to supply herbal plants and products to a health food retail outlet in the bigger city of Middletown. She had begun this little business through her friend Mr. Bogart, the owner of an estate jewelry and spiritual gem store where she had bought Noble and me our amulets. It kept us busy, me in particular, cultivating and growing her plants and herbs and helping her grind and mix ingredients.

Mama wasn't just selling these herbal remedies, however. She would offer the customers, people she called her clients, instructions about meditating and tuning in to a peaceful coexistence with the spiritual world of nature. More and more people seemed to be interested in such things, and Mama and I, who were usually thought unusual if not downright strange, had at least become positive in some people's eyes. I know it made Mama happier.

"I want you to take Baby Celeste up to the turret room and keep her quiet," she said.

It was what I always had to do whenever anyone came to our house—hide Baby Celeste, occupy her so she made little noise and attracted nobody's attention. Nothing was more important than keeping her existence a secret.

As if she herself understood how important it was, Baby Celeste did not cry or complain whenever I had to hide her away. If anything, my taking her up to the turret room amused her and she always kept relatively quiet. She would gaze at all the old furnishings and antiques like someone lovingly looking at religious icons in a church. I was sure any other child would have been bored, but not Baby Celeste. Her patience amazed me. Mama, of course, was not surprised by Baby Celeste's behavior at all. She believed Baby Celeste was the true heir of all the family's spiritual powers.

"She'll be even greater than I am someday," Mama had told me.

"Don't just stand there looking stupid, Noble," she snapped at me now. "I told you. The woman is on her way here. She could be coming down the driveway any moment. Hurry!"

"Okay, Mama." I scooped up Baby Celeste.

The gravity and criticality Mama had whenever she wanted Baby Celeste hidden away frightened me. I had nightmares of her being discovered and then taken from us for one reason or another. After all, what sort of people keep a baby hidden from the world? Where did the baby come from anyway? they'd wonder. Why was her hair being dyed? If I expressed my fear about this, Mama would shake her head at me as if I were too stupid to ever know anything.

"Don't you understand that they would never let that happen, Noble?" she asked. "I would have thought you did by now."

The *they* in our lives were the spiritual family members who hovered about our farm and home, in and out, watching over us always. I didn't disbelieve her. I had seen the way they looked at us and watched over us, warning Mama of things from time to time. The way Baby Celeste looked in the direction of a family soul, and the way her eyes grew small and interested, convinced me she had already crossed over. Perhaps Mama was right about her. Perhaps she came directly from them and didn't need to cross. She was never away from them. Birth had simply been another doorway in the spiritual world for her and not as it was for the rest of us, a doorway to a lesser place, making it necessary for us to find our own way back.

"Up we go," I sang, and ascended the stairs.

Baby Celeste smiled at me and lay her head on my shoulder. I kissed her little forehead and brushed back her hair. How could anyone who saw us together not know instantly she was my child? Maybe Mama was afraid of that more than anything and that was why she grimaced whenever I did show Baby Celeste too much affection.

"You can love her, but as a brother would love a sister, as a sister," she would constantly remind me. Baby Celeste was truly locked away in the world Mama envisioned for us.

I wondered how being so confined, so isolated, would effect Baby Celeste. How long could it go on? When would it end? Or would it never end?

Rarely feeling the sunlight on her face, rarely smelling the aroma of spring flowers, hardly ever luxuriating in the soft touch of the breeze, Baby Celeste would surely be disadvantaged in ways I couldn't imagine.

And yet, when I sat with her in the turret and listened to Mama and her customer's muffled voices below, I realized how similar my plight was to my baby's. Wasn't I as trapped and shut away in the prison of Noble's identity? Rarely did I look out as I would if I were permitted to be myself. A woman's world was as distant to me as playing and being in daylight was to Baby Celeste.

"We're alike in so many ways, Celeste," I told her, whispered to her while we waited in the turret room.

She glanced at me, the tiny dimple in her cheek flashing like a small Christmas light as she tightened those sweet, small lips. Often when she looked at me or listened to me, she seemed so much older. She wore the face of someone who understood things far beyond her years. And then, an instant later, she was Baby Celeste again, laughing and giggling at the most insignificant little things.

A ray of sunshine trapped the floating dust and she marveled at the way the particles glittered. She reached out to touch them and then laughed and looked at me to see if I had the same wonder.

I smiled.

A long time ago so many things were full of wonder for me. Stuck in the dark places now, I closed my eyes, I lowered my head, I plodded along afraid of stepping too far to the left or too far to the right. Nothing frightened me as much as disappointing Mama. More often than ever these days, she made me feel it was only the three of us, floating on some raft in a sea of turmoil. We needed each other. We had to keep our world tightly guarded, behind tall, thick protective walls. It was only then that we would be safe.

Baby Celeste played quietly with one of her dolls while we waited. Shortly after Baby Celeste had been born, Mama had brought out the dolls Mr. Taylor Kotes, the owner of the biggest lumber company in the community, had given to me. He had courted Mama after Daddy's death, and there was a time I thought he would become our new daddy, but he was killed in a terrible car accident when a drunken teenager in a truck rammed into him on his way home from our house. I had really begun to like him, too. Even Noble, who was resistant and angry about Daddy's passing, had started to accept him.

His death reinforced some of the rumors about Mama, especially because Mr. Kotes's sister spread them. Back then she had people believing that anyone who got too close to us was in some sort of danger. Mama was beautiful and still striking. She could have had one man after another romancing her, but she didn't seem to mind our isolation. In fact, she welcomed it, especially after my supposed kidnapping. Being a former schoolteacher, she continued my homeschooling. Back in those days, I could count on the fingers of one hand how many visitors we had a month, not considering our spiritual visitors, of course.

She played our piano at night, raised her herbs and vegetables, and walked the farm with her ancestors at her side. Before I had crossed over and could really see the spirits if only occasionally, I would watch her stroll with her head slightly bowed, nodding, pausing, and gesturing to someone standing beside her. I remember straining, studying the air, searching desperately for a vision. I so wanted to be like her to see what she saw, to hear what she heard.

At dinner she would tell me things she had been told, stories from our past, episodes of sickness, accidents, love affairs, fights, an anthology of our heritage. There were young women who had had their hearts broken in love and women who had died young, as well as men who were killed in wars or suffered fatal accidents. There were many stories about my great-great-grandfather and grandmother who were buried on our property along with their unborn child. In that small square of fieldstone were three tombstones and of course Noble's or my unmarked grave long ago covered with new grass. No one but me and Mama knew it was there.

Sometimes, I would sit on the grass in the small cemetery and think about Noble lying below. I would think about our days together before the tragedy. He had had a wonderful imagination, and like Mama he never seemed lonely. His dragons and knights occupied his days. I used to be jealous of that. I thought it surely meant he would cross over long before I did, which was what Mama always expected, but the ghostly figures Noble saw were manufactured in his own mind and did not come out of the world beyond.

I didn't think Mama would like me visiting the unmarked grave, so I did it when I was confident she was too occupied to see or when she was on one of her shopping trips. I used to think how horrible it was for him to be buried and forgotten this way. Lately, I have heard him pleading from beyond, asking to be acknowledged. Until he is, he is caught in some limbo. He can't be with our daddy and he can't come back to us.

However, just the thought of telling Mama this terrifies me. I know she will see it as some sort of betrayal, and whenever she thinks that, she assumes something evil has entered the house or me. She would lock me away, make me fast, give me some secret herbal cure that would make me sick to my stomach. It didn't matter. In her mind it purged me of the evil.

My only hope is she will hear Noble's pleas herself one day, but she hasn't yet, not yet.

One of the first words Mama taught Baby Celeste was Noble. That is all Baby Celeste ever calls me. It's on the tip of my tongue when I'm alone with her to have her call me Mommy, but I'm afraid of what Mama would do to her if she ever looked at me and said such a thing in front of her. Surely, she would think evil had contaminated her and she would probably lock her away and feed her some herbal medicine designed to purge her of the darkness, too. How she would suffer. I wouldn't be able to stand it, so I don't dare put any ideas in Baby Celeste's mind.

And yet, especially when we're alone as we are now in the turret room, I catch her looking at me differently. Perhaps it's only wishful thinking on my part, but it seems to me she gazes at me the way a child lovingly gazes at her mother. She loves to throw her small arms around me and press herself to me. She can lie beside me for hours without becoming restless, and she loves falling asleep with me in my bed, whenever Mama permits her to come to my room and do so.

The Noble in me tries desperately to remain a little aloof, but he is quickly swept aside. I stroke her hair. I kiss her cheeks and forehead. I hum a lullaby. I hold her tightly and rock and close my eyes.

And I hear Noble arguing and pleading, "You can see you should stop being me. It's not fair to the baby. Get Mama to let you stop. I'm cold and it's dark and I'm afraid. Please, Celeste. Help me."

I'm crying now just thinking about it.

The tears streak down my cheeks and drip from my chin, but I do not make a sound. I hold my breath and bite down on my lower lip. An ache in my heart is growing larger and lasting longer every passing day, but what can I do to stop it? What do I dare do?

The front door opens and closes below. I hear a car's engine start and I stand up and peer out the window to watch Mrs. Paris drive away with her bundle of herbs and her newfound wisdom. She will spread the word even more and there will be additional customers. I'll be hiding up here with Baby Celeste again and again and again.

Soon after Mrs. Paris's car turns and is gone, Mama comes up the stairs and opens the turret door.

"How are my children?" she cries.

Baby Celeste smiles up at her. I hide my final tears and take a deep breath.

"We're fine, Mama," I tell her.

She picks up Baby Celeste and we descend the stairs with her listening to Mama talk about Mrs. Paris, how the woman was mesmerized by the things Mama told her. Mama reinforces and confirms what I suspected.

"She'll be happy and she'll tell others and we'll have more customers for sure, Noble. We have a lot to do. They're starting to appreciate me around here," Mama says proudly. "Your father never thought that would happen," she adds, looking out the window. Then she laughs.

I'm sure she's right about all of that and I'm happy for her. Somehow, I still can't say I'm happy for us. Perhaps I never will. There are times when I feel so terribly lost, but I can't say it. She would not understand. She would even get angry at that.

I return to the work in the garden. The sun is sliding down the sky now. It's almost to the tip of the mountain range, and its rays thread through the woods around us, lighting up the green leaves, turning them into emeralds dangling off branches. I can almost hear the shadows stirring and unfolding like charcoal cellophane in the darkest corners.

Something takes shape and soon I am sure I see a pair of female cousins who had lived nearly two hundred years ago come out of the woods and walk toward the house. They are barefoot, but it's all right because their feet don't quite touch the ground. I see they are chatting excitedly. They want to tell Mama something, something new, or perhaps something they had forgotten to tell her the last time they had spoken. I'm sure I will hear about it at dinner tonight. They don't look my way until they are just about to the house. Then they turn and both wave. I wave back.

"Tell her to let Noble go," I whisper. "Please. If you tell her, she will listen."

They don't hear me, or if they do, the idea frightens even them. They go into the house, and for a moment or two it is as quiet as a graveyard. Then the scream of a large crow spins my head around. It rises out of the woods as if it's being chased and then veers toward the descending sun and disappears in the glare.

I cover my eyes quickly before the hot, bright light burns them. Too often these days I welcome darkness.

My brain is jumbled, mixed images rush through like visual static: Noble falling backward off the rock; Elliot waving foolishly at me; as the water carries him off, his laughter dying away; Daddy coming home from work and scooping us up into his arms and crying, "My twins, my right arm and my left"; Mr. Calhoun in our front doorway, his hat in his hands, his head bowed; Mama walking out into the darkness to speak with her spirits; and Noble smothering his cries in his pillow, his anger in his pillow.

Something has brought us here, something, as Mama often says, far greater than us. We cannot challenge or defy it. We must be who we are. It's our destiny. It flows along like the creek. I dream of it, of our blood flowing, our faces floating on the water's surface like discarded pictures.

The sound of Mama's piano flows from the house, out of any opened window, and snaps me out of this reverie. I close my eyes and listen to the melodies. Most of the time they are sad and heavy, but sometimes, she plays light, happy tunes. Sometimes, she even sings along. She's doing so tonight. She has a wonderful voice, a voice Daddy used to call angelic. It could fill us with happiness and hope and make us wonderfully content with each other, with ourselves.

Those cousins, I think, surely they must have come to her with something good, something wonderful. She'll be happy tonight. She will chatter continuously at dinner and laugh at everything Baby Celeste does or says. All the dark shadows will be swept away. It will seem like everything is really all right.

These nights, these times are special gifts, aren't they? Aren't they? Shouldn't you be grateful for every one, every hour and every minute? I ask my reluctant self.

I do not answer. There is only silence around me. Even the birds are mute and the small breeze has stopped. The whole world has been put on pause.

I suck in my breath and work on until it is time to go in to wash up for dinner and help Mama with Baby Celeste. Noble's pleas die down behind me and get carried off in the breeze, carried into the shadows in the forest.

I cannot help him, although it makes my heart ache so. Once again, another night, I leave him buried in his unmarked grave with my name on his lips and his name branded invisibly on my forehead.

2

Mama's Voice

$$\text{II}$$

I can tell just from the way Mama has prepared dinner tonight that she is going to declare something important. The spirits have spoken, just as I suspected.
She works quietly, hardly saying a word to me, and
from time to time she glances at an empty chair or at a
doorway and nods slightly. I see nothing, but that
doesn't surprise me.

Mama once explained that there were levels and
levels of existence in the spiritual world and it took
years of devotion and faith to reach them all. It was her
way of accounting for why I could still not see spirits
and hear spirits she could see and hear and why I did
not know things she knew.

Even when I was just a little girl, I realized that
Mama travels on different highways. When she plays
her piano, the music carries her off. I can see it in her
face. She might have her eyes turned toward me, but
she doesn't see me. She plays but she is really like

someone in a trance, and when she stops playing, she often has new things to tell me. She is truly returning from a journey where she had gone to places inhabited by wise souls.

It is often the same when she works in such deep silence as she is working now. She is there in the room with me, but I don't feel she is really there. She is so distant it is as if she has left her body behind and gone off somewhere. I do not interfere or try to get her attention. I wait and I keep Baby Celeste occupied so she doesn't disturb Mama.

Baby Celeste helps me set the table. I watch her work and see how serious she is about her assignments, how carefully and determinedly she folds the napkins, arranges the forks and spoons. It is like looking back through time at myself again and it brings a smile to my lips. I was so like that, so intense, so concerned about doing it all perfectly. I remember how that annoyed Noble, who didn't want to take any of these household chores seriously. He would be satisfied eating right off the table. How many times had he come to the table without washing his hands and been sent back? Dozens if one. Mama tried sending him to bed without eating, too, but he was insufferable and stubborn.

Now of course I try not to be so interested in what Noble called sissy things, but I can't help but love handling our old china and running my fingers over the embossed golden design along the edges of each plate, dish, and bowl. They were Mama's great-grandmother Jordan's dishware and the old, heavy silverware had belonged to Mama's great-great-grandmother. Heirlooms are important in our home because Mama believes that possessions like that are still tied to the spirit of those who possessed them. When we used them, when we sat in her great-grandfather's rocking chair or slept in the beds our ancestors slept in, we were more connected with them.

"Everything has spiritual importance," Mama told me. "Think of it as you would think of indelible ink. When someone from our family touched something, his or her prints became forever a part of it, and now we can feel them, see them easier."

She told me these things when I was very young and it left a deep impression on my mind and fostered the belief that our home was a living thing. Everything in it felt and saw and heard. It all breathed and was sacred. The walls were like sponges absorbing and holding on to the laughter, the words, the cries, of all who lived here or visited. Nothing was lost and forgotten.

"If you put your ear to the wall," Mama once told me and Noble, "you can hear them."

Noble did it a few times, heard nothing, and thought it was just a silly story. I did it and I did hear voices, muffled mostly, but voices. Sometimes, I woke to the sound of a laugh or even a scream and my little heart would pound. I would look over to see if Noble had heard anything, but he was in a deep sleep, undisturbed. I waited and listened and then slowly lowered my head to the pillow, but it wasn't easy falling asleep again. In the morning when I would tell Mama I thought I had heard something, she would nod and say, "Of course you did."

Footsteps above us, shadows that glided across walls, whispers that flowed in and out of rooms like tiny birds, were all expected and never feared.

"We're loved," Mama would say. "We're surrounded by great love."

Occasionally now, Baby Celeste would stop playing with a doll or her teacup set on the floor of the living room and look at something in the room, usually a chair or the settee. Mama would study her and then smile.

"What, Celeste?" she would ask. "Did you see someone, hear someone?"

I would hold my breath and wait for her response, for I had seen or heard nothing.

Baby Celeste would simply smile and go back to her play. Mama would give me that all-knowing look and nod, and I would stare at my child and wonder, does she really have that vision, and if she does, will all this really make us safer, happier? Where are the three of us going? What do the spirits really intend for us? Perhaps tonight I would learn that and then I would truly begin to understand who we were.

We sat at the table and began our dinner. Baby Celeste sat in a booster chair and ate with the quiet concentration of someone far older. I was nervous, but tried to hide it. In the hallway the grandfather clock chimed. The breeze had become a wind and the house began to creak, especially right above us. It sounded more like those footsteps on the roof I often heard. I watched Baby Celeste and saw her eyes lift toward the ceiling and then back to her food. Was I like that when I was her age, so accepting?

Mama ate quietly, once again looking as if she was in a trance.

Toward the end of our dinner, she put down her knife and fork and sat a little forward. I could feel her eyes were on me. When she was like this, it was not good to stare back or blurt out a "What's wrong?" It was better to just wait. I finished eating and put down my fork. Baby Celeste clapped her hands and I smiled at her anticipation.

"As you know, Noble," Mama began, "we cannot

keep Baby Celeste hidden from the world forever. It is a strain on us all and I appreciate how well you have done with your share of the responsibility. I know how hard it is for you to never go anywhere with me because you have to remain behind to care for Baby Celeste.

"Our extended family," she continued, which was another way of including our spiritual ancestors, "believes we are quickly approaching the day when we cannot and should not keep her locked away from the outside world any longer."

She smiled at her and Baby Celeste nodded her head as if she were commenting on Mama's statements. Mama stood up, lifted her out of her booster seat, and set her down. She immediately ran around the table to me and crawled up onto my lap. I held her and waited for Mama to continue.

She returned to her seat.

"Naturally, people will be surprised and will wonder how she could simply just appear. There are so many busybodies, so many snoops. It could bring us undesirable attention.

"Therefore, we have to prepare for that day, prepare for the questions and the curiosity, especially when people see her and see how extraordinary she is."

Baby Celeste lay back against me and listened to Mama attentively.

"At first, the community, the gossips, people with no lives of their own, I should say, will obviously conclude that she is my child, the product of some illicit affair. Accusatory eyes will fall on each and every male who could possibly be her father. There will be noisy chatter all around us. Wives might even suspect their husbands, especially those who have come here for one reason or another. I'm sure you can see that it would not be nice for us."

"What will you do, Mama?" I asked. How I wished she would reply with "Why, tell them she is yours, unmask you, permit you to be who you are, to return."

But to do that, she would have to admit that Noble is gone and she would have to bury him for real this time.

"I have been told what to do. I want you to understand that whatever I do now, it is for us all, and I must ask you to be cooperative," she replied.

I nodded and waited, holding my breath. What was it she expected me to do?

She smiled and rose.

"Take Baby Celeste into the living room, Noble. I'll clean up myself tonight."

I started to shake my head and stopped. I couldn't believe she wasn't going to tell me any more.

"When will all this happen?" I blurted.

"You'll see." She started for the kitchen.

"But . . ."

She turned and looked at me with those piercing dark eyes. I had learned a long time ago that when and if I ever contradicted her or challenged anything she said, her first assumption was that I had been compromised by something evil. Our protective wall had been broken somewhere and it was my fault. I wanted to dispute that, but I was afraid, even more afraid now that I had Baby Celeste to care for as well as myself.

I picked up Baby Celeste quickly and left the dining room. For the next hour, I sat quietly and watched her play. Then I heard Mama go upstairs. She was gone so long, I couldn't help but wonder what she was doing. It was close to Baby Celeste's bedtime anyway, so I had her put away her toys and I took her upstairs. I heard Mama in her bedroom and I went to the doorway.

She was unpacking cartons and bags, taking out some of her prettier dresses and shoes, things she had put away for what I thought was going to be forever and ever. I also noticed that her vanity table, which normally had little more than some of her herbal creams on it, was now covered with makeup and brushes, tubes of lipstick, eyeliner pencils and pads. She had brought down the full-length mirror from the turret room, too.

"What are you doing, Mama?" I asked.

She stopped and blinked as if she just remembered us. "Oh, is it that late?" She glanced at the clock. "Yes, get her washed and changed. I'll be right in to put her to bed."

"But why did you take out all those cartons? What are you doing with all that?"

"I'm picking out what is still nice."

"And the makeup and the mirror?"

"Don't stand there cross-examining me, Noble. Just do what I ask."

"I'm not cross-examining you, Mama. I just wondered. That's all."

I thought full-length mirrors made our spirits feel uncomfortable. Why had she brought it out and put it in her room of all places, a room our spiritual family visited more frequently than any other in the house?

"I'll let you know when to wonder," she replied, and returned to her inspection of her wardrobe. Some of the clothing she hadn't worn since Daddy's death. She hadn't even worn it for Taylor Kotes.

She held up one dress and looked at it as if someone were in it.

"That expression 'it's so old it's new' certainly applies to my wardrobe," she muttered, turning the dress. "Besides, a woman who wears classic things will stand out in this world. She will catch the eyes she wants just like some fisherman catches the fish he wants."

Was she talking to me or to herself or perhaps someone I couldn't see?

She stopped talking, so I quickly left her and took care of Baby Celeste. Afterward, she came to the room and put her to bed. I waited, hoping to hear more of an explanation, more details about what had to be done.

Smiling at me, she kissed my forehead and said good-night. I couldn't help but be worried. Whatever she was about to do, to begin, was something that would have a major effect on Baby Celeste. What could it be and why wasn't I told, too? What if it was a big mistake and resulted in our losing Baby Celeste? I needed the comfort of spiritual voices. It had been so long since I had felt and seen Daddy near us. Did that have to do with Noble and his situation?

Mama was being secretive, I thought, and I was frightened of secrets. Secrets could lead to betrayal. It was always difficult to keep anything from Mama, and even if I did, I wasn't confident. I believed she truly had the power to see into my heart. The only thing I had not told her lately was what I believed about Noble, about his suffering and his need to have his name returned to him, but I also knew that for me to listen to him, to help him, was to change everything. Mostly, it meant Mama had to accept he was gone.

Would we ever dig up his grave and take my dress and amulet off him?

In nightmares I saw us both in the cemetery at night. I was digging and Mama was crying so hard. When the grave was uncovered and we could see him, he opened his eyes and reached up toward us. Mama screamed and I fell forward into the grave.

This recurrent nightmare always woke me. I would

sit up in a sweat and calm my thumping heart while I listened for anything in the house. I longed for Daddy's
voice and the touch of his hand. If I longed hard enough,
he would come and he would tell me it was all right.
Everything was going to be just fine. Go to sleep.

Would he be here tonight? I wondered. Does he
know about Mama's secret plan?

The grandfather clock chimed below. It sounded
like the countdown to doom. I lowered my head to the
pillow and I waited and listened.

But I heard only silence. Even the house was holding its breath.

Tomorrow, I thought, tomorrow will bring answers
and hopefully not just more questions.

Mama said nothing more the next day, however. We
all went about our daily routines. She left for town late
in the morning so I had to come in and be with Baby
Celeste until she returned. When she did, she had more
than just groceries this time. She had gone to a department store and bought other things to wear, including
new shoes. She didn't unpack them in front of me, but
brought them up to her room and closed the door.

It made me more nervous and I could hardly do my
work in the garden without stopping every few minutes to
look toward the house and wonder what was happening.

Just before the end of the afternoon when she usually
called to me to come in and wash up for dinner, I heard
the front door open and close and saw her come down
the steps. She was wearing a bright blue, off-shoulder
dress and she had her hair brushed back and tied behind
her head with a white and pink ribbon. It amazed me
how quickly she could look younger when she wanted
to do that. She looked my way so I gathered up my tools
and quickly hurried back to the house.

As I drew closer, I saw she was wearing earrings as

well and she had a necklace of pearls I had not ever seen. She was wearing lipstick and some rouge.

"I'm going for a walk," she said. "Baby Celeste is still napping. When she awakens, you can finish setting the table. I have a meat loaf all done."

"Where are you going?"

"I just told you Noble. I'm taking a walk."

"But . . ."

"But what?" she asked, her eyes searching my face, scrutinizing me.

"It's getting late and it will be dark soon."

"So? Don't you think I'm aware of that?"

"Yes, but . . ."

"But what? What?" she screamed.

I swallowed back my question: Why would she dress up and put on makeup to go for a walk? She didn't put on makeup to go to town or to stores.

"Okay," I said.

She nodded and walked down our long driveway. I watched her from the porch until she reached the road and turned left.

Where could she possibly be going? And why?

A movement to my left caught my attention. I turned and saw what looked like Daddy walking into the forest. I started to call to him, but he was gone as quickly as he had appeared.

Something had called him back into the shadows. Did it have something to do with Mama, with her plan? On the lower thick branch of the tree he had just passed sat the large black crow I often saw. He stared back at me and was so still he looked stuffed. A sense of great anticipation hovered over everything. It made me feel as if I were in the eye of some great storm.

I hurried inside to check on Baby Celeste and wait for Mama's return.

To my surprise, she didn't return for so long, I actually began to worry that something might have happened to her. What could I do? I couldn't leave the baby and go looking for her. Baby Celeste and I set the table and I finally had to take out the meat loaf and serve the vegetables and mashed potatoes. Although we had never had a dinner without Mama present at the table, Baby Celeste ate well and didn't seem half as nervous or confused about it as I was. My ears kept listening for the sound of Mama's footsteps on the front porch or the sound of the front door opening. I fidgeted with my food. My stomach tightened so much that I could barely swallow anything.

Where was she?

It had grown darker and darker just as I had predicted, too.

I looked at Baby Celeste. She smiled at me and tapped her fork. I shook my head and she stopped. Why didn't it bother her more that Mama wasn't here?

"Just eat, Celeste," I said.

Finally, I heard the distinct sound of an automobile approaching the house. Why was there an automobile here? I wondered. No one ever came here without first calling, and Mama hadn't mentioned any customer coming. I couldn't answer the door, not without her here. Oh, where was she? I moaned to myself.

I rose quickly and went to the front door. Opening it slightly, I peered out, and to my utter surprise I saw Mama emerge from a car. After she was out, she turned and laughed at something. It was a different sort of laugh, too, different from her amusement at something Baby Celeste had done or said. This was the light, flirtatious laugh of a young girl. I strained to see who was driving the car, but with the sky moonless tonight, the shadows were undiluted, thicker, masking the identity of the man. In fact, his silhouette was so dark, he looked more like one of our spirits. Could it be that?

I saw Mama lean in toward him before she closed the door. Although I couldn't make out any words, I knew something was said, something that was followed by another laugh and then her closing the door. She stood there as the driver backed up and turned to go down the driveway. She waved and then lowered her head and started for the house.

I closed the door softly but quickly and then scooped up Baby Celeste, who had followed me and was standing at my side.

"Let's finish eating," I told her, and put her back on her booster seat as Mama entered the house.

I looked back when she reached the dining room door.

"Everything all right?" she asked. "Is the baby eating?"

"Yes, Mama. But where have you been?"

"I'll be right down," she said instead of replying to my question, and went to the stairway.

I took my seat and waited for her. Baby Celeste finished eating and crawled out of her seat. She came around to me as Mama descended the stairs. She had changed into a housecoat and went right to serving herself her dinner. Both of us watched her quietly and waited.

"It's probably cold by now, Mama. Do you want me to heat it up for you first?"

"Why would I want you to do that? Since when do you heat up food for me?"

"I just thought . . ."

"It's fine," she said.

She ate quietly for a few moments, gazing at the

two of us. Baby Celeste was so still and quiet sitting on my lap that it was as if she had turned into a life-size doll.

"Just look at the both of you," Mama began, "staring at me like this. Anyone would think I had been away for days, weeks, even months."

"I was worried about you, Mama. It had gotten dark and you never miss dinner. I didn't know what to do," I said, unable to keep the panic out of my voice.

She grimaced. "I need to know you have more grit in you than that, Noble. You've got to have a man's heart, courage. I don't want to see you grow into one of these namby-pambies I hear these people complain about when they come here to buy their remedies. From now on I might be gone more often and you'll be more and more in charge of things. I need to know you are capable of being responsible and strong."

"I don't understand. Why would you be away more and more, Mama?"

"Oh . . ." She waved her hand. She looked to the side and shook her head at someone standing there listening to our conversation.

Baby Celeste turned and with her tiny right forefinger traced the shape of my right ear.

"Put her down," Mama ordered gruffly.

I lifted her out of my lap and set her on the floor. She stood there confused for a moment and then just sat at my feet. Mama took a deep breath and blew the air between her lips. She was obviously annoyed and I had no idea why or what I had done to make her so.

She ate a little more of her meat loaf and mashed potatoes, then paused and suddenly, as if nothing had been said before in a testy tone, smiled.

"You'll never guess whom I just met during my walk today," she began.

"Who?" I asked quickly.

"Mr. Fletcher," she replied.

For a moment I thought I had imagined hearing it. That name, that family, their very existence, had been erased from the pages of our memories and censored as vigorously and firmly as profanity. Once—well, more than two years ago—I mentioned seeing Betsy Fletcher with a boy parked at the beginning of our driveway. Mama went into a rage, forbidding me even to think of the Fletcher family. I was never to go anywhere near their property line.

I said nothing. I stared and waited, holding my breath.

"He was sitting on his front porch reading his newspaper when I reached the front of his property," Mama continued. "I heard him greet me and I paused and looked his way. The moment I did so, he rose and bounded off that porch like someone who hadn't seen a living soul for decades. His boyish enthusiasm actually made me laugh."

"What did he want?" I asked in a throaty whisper.

"Oh, he was very nice. He wanted to see how I was, how you were. He spoke so quickly I had no time to respond to one question before he asked another. He told me he had been hearing good things about my remedies and wanted to assure me that even though he was a pharmacist dispensing chemical medicine, he had a great deal of faith in what he called old-time panaceas. He told me his mother had a cold cure in fact that had been passed down from generation to generation. Its ingredients included nutmeg and honey, milk and old bourbon."

"But why was he so friendly? Wasn't he still angry about my not telling the police when I had last seen El-liot? You remember how angry the police were at me."

"No, no, nothing unpleasant came up in the conversation, except of course, his problems with that dreadful young girl."

"What do you mean?"

"His daughter, Betsy. You know what I mean, Noble. You know what kind of a girl she has turned out to be and how she has brought her father nothing but heartache. I actually felt sorry for the man. A man needs the sympathetic ear of a woman when he wants to confide in someone about the troubles he has with his children. If he has no wife, as Mr. Fletcher doesn't, he will look for the first sympathetic female face.

"And besides," she continued, "we can comfort each other for we have both lost a child."

But this was Dave Fletcher she was talking about, Elliot's father, I wanted to blurt. This was the man and the family you often told me were surrounded by dark evil. These were the people you had forbidden me to speak to, to know. This was the man you told the police was at fault for the problems of his own children. How could she say and believe one thing for so long and just as suddenly change?

More important, why?

"Don't look at me like that, Noble. It's sinful not to have compassion for others who are in pain. Besides, I never really met the man before, spoke to him long enough to appreciate his wit and intelligence."

I glanced at Baby Celeste. What about her? What about the fact that she was Dave Fletcher's granddaughter, a granddaughter he had no idea existed, a granddaughter we were keeping from him?

"He's a very polite man, too. He was so concerned about my walking back in the dark that he insisted over every objection that he drive me home. He practically begged me to permit him to do it.

"I can't imagine why his wife deserted him. You would have thought a man like that would have found another woman by now, wouldn't you?"

She made her eyes smaller and leaned toward me. "Why do you suppose he hasn't, Noble?"

I tried to swallow, but couldn't. I shook my head. "I don't know, Mama."

She nodded, smiled, and sat back. "I do. I do."

She looked off, her eyes drifting toward someone else.

"What do you mean, Mama?"

"What do you mean, Mama?" she mimicked. "The first Celeste was so much brighter than you are, Noble. I used to be surprised at her insights and how fast they were coming as compared to your own, but I'm not surprised any longer. You don't concentrate enough. You question too much."

Tears came to my eyes, tears that were so confused they didn't know which way to travel on my face. Was I crying as Noble, his feelings hurt by the comparison, or was I crying for myself, lost forever in Mama's mind, buried forever in that grave?

"I don't mean to question too much, Mama. I just . . . don't understand."

"You don't have to understand. Just do what I tell you to do and accept what I want you to accept," she snapped, and stood. "Take the baby into the living room. I want to be alone." She began to clear the table.

I rose slowly, scooped up Baby Celeste, and carried her out of the room quickly. While she played, I listened and heard Mama's murmuring. At one point I heard her laughing and then grow quiet. When she was finished in the kitchen, she went upstairs without even looking in on us. It was very unusual. Even Baby Celeste realized that something was very different by now. She stopped playing and came to me, lowering her head on my lap and then raising it to look into my eyes.

I listened for Mama's return, but she didn't come back down the stairs, so I picked up Baby Celeste and went up. Once again, Mama was in her bedroom. This time the door was closed. I stood there listening. She was talking softly. I knocked and she stopped.

"What is it?"

"Should I put Baby Celeste to bed?"

"Yes, yes. Make sure her face is washed," Mama said impatiently. She didn't even mention that she would be out to tuck her in as she would do every night.

I went ahead and prepared Baby Celeste for bed, then I tucked her in myself and kissed her good-night. She clutched one of her dolls, her favorite one actually, in her arm and smiled at me.

"Celeste," she said.

"What?" I asked her, my heart stopping and starting. "What did you say?"

"Celeste."

I thought she meant me. I thought she was breaking through a cloud so thick and dark that no one could pierce it. What a wonderful thing. It was truly a message from beyond. My heart filled with joy and then she lifted the doll and said, "Celeste."

She didn't mean me after all. She had named her doll after herself.

"Oh," I said, my voice dripping with disappointment. I smiled through it. "Yes, Celeste."

I touched the doll lovingly and she embraced it again and smiled. I kissed her forehead, fixed her blanket, said good-night, and left her.

For a moment or two I stood in the hallway undecided as to where to go and what to do myself. Then I returned to Mama's door and knocked again. This time she opened it.

"What?"

I was speechless. She was wearing an aqua blue, form-fitted light sweater blouse and a matching skirt, but the skirt was far shorter than any she had worn since Daddy's death. I also noticed that she wasn't wearing a bra and the V-neck of the sweater revealed more of her cleavage than she had ever revealed. With her hair back, the teardrop gold earrings with a tiny ruby in the middle of each were visible. They were her mother's. She had made up her face with rouge and eyeliner and a bright red lipstick.

"What is it?" she demanded. "Don't stand there gaping at me like that when I ask you a question, Noble. Well?"

"Baby Celeste is in bed," I told her.

"Oh. Good. Very good, Noble." She started to close the door.

"Why are you so dressed up?" I asked.

She paused and looked as if she was deciding whether to bother to answer.

"I'm going out," she said.

"What? Where? Now?" I fired at her. Her glare made me feel uncomfortable, but I wouldn't just turn away.

Her face softened a bit. "I decided to accept an invitation. He had asked earlier. He wanted to take me to the Lodge, a small hotel on a lake in Greenfield Park. I was there once with your father years and years ago, and I remember the restaurant and the bar had windows that looked out on the lake. On an evening like this it should be very pleasant. I just called him."

"Him?"

My mind was reeling. Did she mean Daddy? Who had asked her earlier?

"Mr. Fletcher, Dave. He's feeling particularly low tonight. His troublesome daughter, Betsy, has run off again. The best thing would be if she would stay away for good, of course, but she doesn't do that. She goes off with one worthless man or another and returns when she has exhausted her interest in him or has run out of money." She paused and smiled. "I knew that was going to happen today, of course. It's what I would call a moment of opportunity."

I was as speechless as someone who had just been struck in the head with a rock.

"Opportunity for what?" I finally managed to ask.

She shook her head. "Go to sleep, Noble," she shot back, and, before I could say another word, closed the door in my face.

I went to my room and sat on the edge of my bed, dazed and confused. About ten minutes later, I heard her come out and descend the stairs. Rather than follow her, I looked out my window. Sure enough, I saw a car coming down our driveway. The front door opened and closed below and Mama was visible. As soon as she approached the car, Dave Fletcher got out and hurried around to open the passenger's door for her. She got in and he got in and they drove off, the taillights diminishing and then disappearing around the turn at the entrance to our property.

I had no idea why but my ribs felt as if they had turned into a cage of ice.

I heard voices clamoring inside me, one in particular complaining.

I thought it was Noble.

"She's not even thinking about me at all anymore. She's not," he said.

Or was it my own voice?

After all, we were both dead and buried. He was in a grave outside.

And I was in a body no longer permitted to be my own.

She wasn't thinking of either of us anymore.

3

Baby Celeste's Gift

♊

I waited up for Mama for as long as I could, but I kept drifting off and finally fell into so deep a sleep, I never heard her come home. My eyes snapped open before dawn and I sat up in bed realizing I had fallen asleep in my clothes. I was surprised Mama hadn't looked in and woken me to ask me why. Could it be that she was still not home?

Practically tiptoeing out of my room, I saw Mama's bedroom door was open. She usually left it open so she could hear Baby Celeste if she called out during the night for any reason. She rarely did. In fact, I rarely saw her cry and complain. She was born contented, Mama says.

I approached Mama's doorway as quietly as I could and then peered in and was relieved to see her in bed. However, her clothes were cast sloppily over a chair and it looked as if she had simply kicked off her shoes not caring where they fell, which was quite unusual.

She hated anything to be out of place in the house because it would upset the balance of energy. She looked dead asleep so I returned to my room and tried to go back to sleep myself. I tossed and turned and went in and out of dreams filled with people I had never met. Was our home a haven for all wandering spirits? Mama never spoke about any but our own family, and those I saw when they wanted to reveal themselves to me, I had seen before in a picture in our house.

The morning light startled me like a bell rung right by my ear. I rose just as Baby Celeste was calling. To my surprise, Mama hadn't risen, and when, with Baby Celeste in my arms, I looked in on her, I saw Mama was still in a deep sleep.

Baby Celeste thought it was funny and laughed. Mama stirred, but didn't awaken. She didn't get up even by the time I had washed and dressed Baby Celeste. I took her downstairs and made breakfast for the two of us. Mama came down while we were at the table eating.

"I can't believe I slept so late," she said. "It's been a long time since I've been out on a date. Dave wanted me to try his favorite cocktail. Something called a cosmopolitan. It made me a little giddy. I can't recall laughing as much for years, or at least since I was with your father."

She kissed Baby Celeste and looked at me. Mama never drank alcoholic beverages, except for some elderberry wine. Why had she done so now and why was she acting so casual about it? Imagine if I had done such a thing, I thought. She would lock me in the turret room for days.

"My God, Noble, speaking of your father, you have his angry face on this morning. It's like a mask you found among his old things in the attic."

I looked down, then raised my eyes at her slowly.

"Why are you doing this, Mama? Why now and why with this man?" I asked timidly.

She sighed deeply, thought a moment, looked into the right corner of the room, then nodded.

"Haven't I told you many, many times that nothing happens to us without a reason, without a purpose, Noble?"

"Yes, but what does that have to do with this?"

"Sometimes it takes a while to understand, but nevertheless, we do finally understand. Sometimes it happens with the help of our family, which was what happened in this case."

"What were you told?" I asked as boldly as a police investigator.

"I was told, as you so bluntly put it, that the Fletchers were brought here for a purpose."

"The Fletchers? What purpose?" Did she mean the birth of Baby Celeste?

She stared so hard at me I didn't think she would answer, but she did.

"To protect us."

"Protect us?" I shook my head. How could she even think such a thing considering all that had happened between me and Elliot Fletcher? "I don't understand, Mama."

"You will," she promised. "Be patient and cooperative and you will. Now I'm going to make myself some soft-boiled eggs and then start on a rhubarb pie. That's Dave's favorite pie. I don't suppose you remember me telling you rhubarb pie was my grandfather's favorite, too, do you?"

"No." I felt sure she never had told me and I didn't want to permit her to lead me away from the topic.

"Well, it was. So you see, everything means something, Noble. Nothing just happens by coincidence. I've been teaching you that for as long as you could hear, I think. What you have to imagine," she continued, turning to her teacher's persona (she could take it off and put it on like a coat), "is the world is full of lines, invisible strings, all intersecting, connecting, running parallel for a while and then touching. Every action, every word spoken, every birth and every death, is another line, even every thought, and when you can understand that and you have the ability to see that, you will know what to look for, as I do. You simply have to have more faith in me and yourself and try harder. Then it will come to you just the way it came to me. I can remember the exact moment."

She paused, closed her eyes, and then with her hands over each other and pressed to her chest, breathed in the way she would over a bed of wildflowers. When she saw how I was staring at her, she stiffened like someone caught doing or thinking something illicit.

"It looks like it might rain this afternoon, Noble, so get to your work as soon as possible," she ordered, and went into the kitchen.

I rose, lifted Baby Celeste out of her chair, and watched her hurry to join Mama. Then I went out to the garden.

I was troubled all morning, convinced that somehow what Mama was now doing would eventually lead to a disaster that would hurt Baby Celeste more than anyone else. Every once in a while, I stopped working and searched the dark corridors of the forest hoping to see a vision, to get a message from Daddy or hear his voice offering me a solution or an understanding that would calm my taut nerves.

Everything I did, every move I made, caused me to

vibrate inside as if some invisible hand had reached into me and strummed those nerves. From time to time, I realized I was holding my breath so long, my lungs ached.

"Oh, Daddy, where are you?" I whispered, and looked for him in the pockets of darkness here and there in our forest, but I saw nothing, felt no one's presence near me.

Finally, just before lunch, I heard the front door open and the screen door slap shut. Mama hurried down the steps toward her car. She was carrying her pie. When she opened the car door to put it gingerly on the front seat, she turned to call to me.

"I have to be gone awhile, Noble. I want to bring this pie over before Mr. Fletcher starts his shift at the drugstore. Go inside and look after Baby Celeste. She's in the living room. Make her lunch. Everything you need is set out on the kitchen counter, and don't make a big mess for me to clean up when I return," she warned.

She got into her car and drove off.

The sky had become fully covered with clouds promising rain, just as Mama had predicted. An unexpected cold breeze rubbed across the back of my neck like a hand that had been dipped in ice water first. I spun around.

Without the sunlight now, the gloomy, dark places in the forest that surrounded our property deepened. Even the songbirds were blanketed and hooded like hawks. An eerie stillness fell about me. It was so quiet I could hear the pulsating throb of my own heavier heart. My vision blurred and then I thought I saw Fletcher's face take form under the branches of a sapling. It was a face I had seen many times in dreams these past two years. It formed, faded, and reformed

like a face rising and sinking in the water, just the way
I imagined it had that dreadful afternoon.

I could barely hear him at first, but his whispering
imitated the rhythm of the thumping that rose up my
body and settled in my head. His voice grew louder,
stronger. He was calling out to me. I wanted to turn
and run into the house, but I was mesmerized by the
sound of his voice, by that undulating cry that rose and
fell with the wind.

"You never told her the truth," he said. "You never
told anyone the truth about what you saw and what
you knew had happened to me."

I stepped back, shaking my head.

Was he speaking to me or was my own conscience
rising like a thick-skinned bubble out of the inky
depths of my troubled soul.

"You'll drown in the lies just like I drowned in the
creek. The deceptions are too heavy. They'll bring you
down. They'll bring you both down. I'll see to it. I
will . . . I will . . ."

"No!" I shouted, or at least I thought I had. The
sound reverberated through my bones like some
trapped explosion.

Mama's too powerful, I thought with confidence.
Our family is too powerful. His spirit can't come here
and harm us. He could never touch us. We won't give
him the opportunity. We won't weaken our castle of
faith.

"You're forgetting the lies," he whispered like an
eavesdropper on my thoughts. "The lies are like cracks
in your great wall of protection. If she doesn't let my
father be, I'll come. I'll come. I will," he threatened.
From the very first time Mama had mentioned Mr.
Fletcher, I had been afraid of such a thing.

I turned and ran to the house, charging up the porch

steps and then stopping at the door to look back. The first drops of rain had begun, an almost invisible drizzle, intensifying with every passing moment. Fletcher's image was gone from beneath the branch of the sapling. Surely, it had all been in my active imagination. I caught my breath and was now ashamed of my fear and cowardice.

Mama was too smart to permit anything serious to occur between her and Dave Fletcher anyway, I thought. She was just doing what she said, being compassionate, commiserating with someone who had suffered a similar loss in his life and who needed a sympathetic ear. It was nothing more. It could be nothing more. Our spiritual protectors would surely warn her, dissuade her against going too much further. My fears were silly and selfish.

I hurried into the house and discovered Baby Celeste had crawled up and onto Grandpa Jordan's chair. She sat there with her Celeste doll in her arms and looked at me with a face that seemed to age before my eyes into the face of an old woman, one of the elderly aunts captured in a sepia photograph in one of the family albums.

As quickly as the vision appeared, it disappeared. I chastised myself for permitting my imagination to play such foolish games again.

"Come on, Celeste," I said. "Let's make lunch."

She slipped off the chair quickly and scurried like a puppy to my side, reaching up with one hand while she clung to her doll with the other. Thinking of a puppy brought back pages of memories of Cleo, the golden retriever I had had. He was a beautiful, loyal animal that had never left my side. Mama eventually gave him away because she had come to believe something evil entered our world through him like a Trojan horse. It broke my heart but there wasn't anything I could do.

When Mama made a pronouncement that was stamped with spiritual authority, there was no way to oppose it or contradict it.

"Some day I'll tell you about my dog, Celeste. How he would have loved you, loved to protect you. If he were here now, he wouldn't leave you alone for a moment, I'm sure."

"Dog," she said.

"That's right, my dog. Cleo," I told her.

"Cleo," she repeated, and she let go of my hand and ran ahead of me down the hallway.

"What are you doing?" I called.

She stopped at the hallway closet and struggled to open the door.

"What is it?" I asked, helping to open it.

As soon as I had, she got down on all fours and pulled aside a carton on the floor of the closet. Behind it was Cleo's egg-shell-white bowl. She brought it out to show me and I stood there with my mouth agape. The bowl had Cleo written on two sides of it. I remembered the day Mama had bought it.

"How could you . . ." I reached down and took it from her. I held it as I would some fragile jewel. Baby Celeste looked up at me, smiling. "I'd forgotten all about this." I smiled at her. "I guess you saw it when Mama moved things around in here and she told you what it was."

It didn't surprise me Baby Celeste would remember. She had a photogenic memory. All Mama and I had to do was tell her something once and she never forgot it, no matter how slight was our reference to something.

"Maybe someday Mama will let us have a dog again," I said, stroking the bowl as lovingly as I would stroke Cleo. Then I put it back behind the carton and closed the closet door.

I made us our lunch. Mama didn't return until late in the afternoon. The rain had come in periodic downpours so there wasn't much for me to do outside anyway. I spent the time with Baby Celeste. Mama had decided she was such a precocious child it would be a waste to spend all our time with her just playing with toys.

Consequently, she had gone out and bought what she considered were appropriate educational children's books and spent hours with Baby Celeste reviewing them. To my surprise, Mama had even been able to teach her some elementary reading. Mama, having been a teacher and having taught both Noble and myself at home all our lives, had great patience and concentration. Noble was never a great student, but he always did well enough on the exams we had to take at the school to meet the state's requirements for homeschooling. Obviously, Mama was preparing Baby Celeste for the same life and education.

I suppose I shouldn't have been at all amazed at Baby Celeste's abilities. I was always an exceptional student and had actually achieved my high school equivalency at fourteen. I loved reading and had read practically every book we had in the house, many of them old leather-bound classic editions. Baby Celeste's learning ability was just another way in which Mama reinforced her belief that my child was a spiritual resurrection. Watching her work with my baby did bring back my own childhood memories of our schooling at home. It was truly as if I was looking back in time.

We both looked up when we heard Mama return. She stepped into the living room doorway.

"How is she?" she asked, shaking the rain out of her hair. "Did you have lunch?"

"Yes, Mama."

"She should be taking a nap."

"She isn't tired. I'm the one who's tired," I muttered. "She's full of questions."

"That's how you learn, Noble, you ask questions, but I don't mean stupid questions," she added quickly.

Baby Celeste stood up and pointed. "Bowl."

"What?" Mama asked, turning to me.

"Oh. I mentioned I had a dog named Cleo and she showed me Cleo's bowl in the closet. I guess she saw you arranging things in there and didn't forget."

Mama smiled that soft, small smile that lifted the corners of her mouth and brightened her beautiful light brown eyes.

"She never saw me do anything in that closet, Noble. What's there to do?"

"But, how would she know then, Mama?"

"She knows," Mama said, nodding. "She knows every nook and cranny in this old house. She has the gift. I've told you that many times. Maybe now you'll start believing me and stop this doubting-Thomas business you've been conducting lately."

"I haven't been conducting any doubting-Thomas business, Mama."

"Sometimes, you don't see yourself as well as I do, Noble. This is the time when I need you to have more faith, not less. Come on, Celeste," she beckoned. "Time for a nap."

Obediently, Baby Celeste went to her and Mama lifted her in her arms.

"Put all this away neatly, Noble. I'm thinking about doing some redecorating in the house," she added, gazing at the living room and nodding. "We need to freshen things up a bit, perhaps get some new area rugs, do some painting, lots of polishing and whitewashing."

"But I thought it was important that we never disturb things, Mama."

"We're not disturbing them, Noble. See! This is exactly what I mean. Every time I make a suggestion lately, you come up with a stupid, contradictory remark," she snapped. "Don't you think I know what I'm doing and I have reasons for changing things when I change them? Well?"

"Yes, Mama."

"Yes, Mama," she mimicked. She stared at me so hard I had to lower my eyes. "When your father was alive, nothing was neglected long. I was hoping you would take after him more in that regard and I wouldn't have to be chasing after you to fix this, mend that, all the time. You should show some initiative, Noble. You spend too much time with the baby and not enough on the house and the property."

"But . . . every time I suggested changing anything you got angry at me, Mama."

"I'm not talking about changes. I'm talking about maintenance!" she screamed. She took a deep breath, looked up for a moment, then looked at me. "I don't want to get myself upset these days, Noble. I want to look fresh and happy and as attractive as I can. I spend hours and hours explaining to my clients how stress can add years to their appearance. I certainly don't want to be a bad example. Who would believe me then?

"Beauty and strength come from in here," she said, slapping her left hand over her heart while she held on to Baby Celeste with her right arm. "All the herbal remedies in the world, all the creams and lotions, can't contradict that. Harmony, harmony is what we should strive to achieve. Do you understand?"

"Yes, Mama."

"Good. Now do what I asked. I'll be down in a little while and we'll begin an inspection and analysis of the house from top to bottom."

It was on the tip of my tongue to ask if this had anything to do with Dave Fletcher, but I was afraid of what such a question would bring on. Usually Mama saw my fears in my face and attacked them, but she either didn't see them or did and chose to ignore them this time.

She walked off with Baby Celeste and I began to put all the toys and books away. She returned with a pad and pen and immediately decided that we needed to replace the curtains and drapes in the living room. Years and years of sunlight had faded them. Why it had taken her so long to notice and suddenly care was beyond me, but she dropped a heavy hint as we walked through the room, focusing closely on everything in it.

"I saw what nice things Dave has done in that old house since he's been there. He has good taste. You would never think a man forced to live like a bachelor with a daughter who couldn't care less about their home would have such a good eye for domestic beauty, but he does. He even understands balance. Oh, not as deeply as energy balance, but nevertheless, maybe out of some natural instincts, he has achieved quite a bit of that.

"Anyway, it made me think twice about our home, Noble, and how we've neglected it these dozen or so years. I know you've been good about basic repairs here and there on the outside," she said, contradicting what she had accused me of before," but the inside of a house is like the inside of a person. It has to be healthy and strong, too.

"Besides, when Dave comes here, I don't want him thinking we're living like people lost in their past. People often judge each other by their possessions. I know it's like judging a book by its cover, but nevertheless, it's how most people think and we can't ignore it."

"Mr. Fletcher is coming here?" I asked as softly as I could. I didn't want it to sound like another challenge or disapproval.

"Of course he's coming here. Why shouldn't he come here? I didn't raise you to be afraid of meeting people, Noble."

"When is he coming?"

"When I'm ready for him."

I thought I heard the sound of a laugh.

I spun around and heard the raindrops tapping against the windowpanes like fingers with long nails. This is so wrong, I thought. Mama is making a big mistake turning down this path. How could I make her see without raising her ire? I would have to tell her everything perhaps, especially about the vision I had had earlier and the threats that had followed.

Experience had taught me not to blurt out anything like that, however. I had to be careful, so very careful.

"You know it really is foolish of us not to have a microwave oven," she said suddenly. "It makes us look so backward and out of touch. There are other things I'd like to do in the kitchen. It's not that we don't have the money for these things. We do. I've just been distracted by other things, but some additions and small changes have to be made, Noble. We have to prepare for the future."

"What future?"

"What future? Our future, but most important, Baby Celeste's future. You can see yourself what she is, what she can do and will do. Nothing must stand in her way, especially some stupid prejudices. I want her to have all the opportunities to develop fully. Just like you've had," she added, stinging me with her gaze, "opportunities I don't think you've taken advantage of or fully appreciate yet."

"I do, Mama."

"We'll see. Time will tell. All right. Let's move on to the den. I'm thinking about recovering that floor, and it needs new lamps and I want to touch up the woodwork. You'll do that. We'll try to do as much as we can ourselves so we don't have people marching in and out of here all day. Tomorrow, I'd like you to start stripping off the paint around the window frames. We're going to repaint them all, freshen up the outside appearance of the house as well.

"I want anyone to look at our home and see the beauty that's in it and think, 'This could easily be my home, too.' Understand?"

I couldn't speak.

I couldn't swallow.

Who was *anyone?* Where was she taking us?

I managed to nod and she continued through the house, rambling off a catalog of improvements that even involved her own bedroom.

The rain slowed. The drops changed from finger-nails to tears on the panes, and in one, the water seemed to form the outline of a head, Elliot's head. I hurried away.

I thought perhaps that Mama had just been talking and didn't mean half the things she had said, but in the days that followed, Mama pursued this new and relent-less determination to spruce up our home. She was often gone for a good part of every day shopping and visiting with decorators.

In the evening she would spread out the samples of carpets, wallpaper, and paint colors on the living room floor and analyze not only the combinations, but what she called the aura of colors. White, for example, had an aura of high spiritual energy. With pink she felt pure love. She found nature and natural health in brown.

"How do you know all this, Mama? How do you see it?" I asked her as she studied the variations and combinations.

"I don't see it through my eyes. I see it in my mind. I can see colors around a person and that tells me their emotions, their thoughts. Energy flows in and out of us every day, Noble, and what we contain, absorb, and reflect tells a great deal about us.

"Each color has its own vibrations. Someday, you'll be able to feel them as I do." She paused and looked at Celeste, who was drawn to the whites and the pinks. "As, I believe, Baby Celeste already does," she added in a soft whisper.

"When will I be able to do that, too?"

"When you are not distracted by other, far less significant things," Mama replied with criticism in her voice. "When you can concentrate and meditate and take the time to experience them with the concentration they require."

What did she mean by distractions, by far less significant things? What had I done or said to let her make these statements, these accusations? Did she see something in me that I couldn't see in myself?

"Let me concentrate," she said before I could ask. "I need to make the right decisions. Seeing how well Mr. Fletcher has done in his own home has inspired me."

Despite how she made that sound, from the way she spoke about her choices and the ones Dave Fletcher had made in his home, I began to believe she was thinking in terms of setting some sort of spiritual trap.

What's more, the prospect of people coming to work in the house in the near future first put some panic in me. Then I thought, What about Baby Celeste? Did this mean we would finally reveal her? I'd like that and so would Baby Celeste. Perhaps all this wouldn't be bad, after all.

She answered that question the night before the drapery man came to measure the windows she wanted redone.

"What will we do about Baby Celeste when he comes to work in the house, Mama? And when others come?"

She paused and smiled.

"Remember that book Celeste read aloud to you, the one that disturbed you so much?" she began.

I had read only a few books to Noble. He never wanted to sit still long enough to listen, but Mama made him, hoping that he would develop an interest in learning and become a better student. He didn't, but the one book that did keep him mesmerized and did disturb him was *The Diary of Anne Frank,* and that was because he couldn't imagine being so locked up and made to be so quiet so much of the time.

Noble was truly like a wild creature when he was outside. He hated coming in to eat, to do our studies, and to sleep, and if he was sick and had to stay inside, he was unhappy. He would sit by the window and stare out like a prisoner in a dungeon. Neither rain, nor sleet, nor heavy snowfalls deterred him. Mama used to think he was tuned in to the spiritual energy in nature more than I was, but that proved to be a disappointment.

The length of time Anne Frank and her family were locked away and their restricted lifestyle both terrified and intrigued Noble. He had so many questions. How do you choke back a cough, a sneeze, a cry?

"Yes, I remember," I said.

"Well, that's how it will be when they're here, Noble. Obviously, it will be for a longer time than when I have a customer stop by. You might be up there with Baby Celeste all day."

"All day?"

"I'll bring you lunch, but you'll have to keep her especially quiet when they're working on my bedroom. I'm having a few things done, including new carpet. I would say you could come down when she's asleep, but if she wakes up and you're not there with her, she would be upset. It's a small sacrifice for you to make."

I was quiet.

"What is it, Noble? I can see your mind spinning like a leaf caught in the creek."

"You told me they said we cannot keep Baby Celeste locked away from the world too much longer."

"I know what I said. Don't you think I remember what I say?" she snapped.

"I didn't mean you don't remember. I meant maybe we could let her be seen finally."

Blood rushed into her face, but she closed her eyes and with the power she could will like a fairy goddess waving her wand, she forced the blood back.

"When the time is right, when the time comes, we will," she said slowly, punching out her words like my hammering nails. "The time is not yet right." She shook her head.

"I just thought it would make it easier for us all and . . ."

"Don't . . . think," she ordered. "Just listen and do what you're told. Do you understand? Do you? Because if you don't, if you feel like something is preventing you, some dark force is clogging your ears and mixing you up inside your head, I want to know right now. I don't want to put Baby Celeste in any unnecessary danger," she added, the heaviness of the underlying threat not lost on me.

"I understand, Mama. I understand."

"Good. Good."

Afterward, she went to her piano and played a musical piece I had never heard her play. Mama had very
little sheet music. She once told me the music, all the
notes, melodies, were already in the piano. When she
sat on the stool and brought her fingers to the keyboard, she had no idea what she would play until she
heard the first note. Then, she said, it all came up to
her through her fingers, into her arms, into her heart.

All of the women who had lived in our house had
played this piano, and cousins had often played when
they had visited. I remember Mama talking about them
when I was little, and about the piano never forgetting.
She made it sound magical, a conduit through which
she could reach back in time. Perhaps that was why
she often had new thoughts, new revelations, to announce after she had finished playing.

When I was younger, many nights I awoke and
heard the piano being played. Noble never did and
slept through it always. I would get up and tiptoe to the
top of the stairway to listen. I knew Mama would be
angry if I went downstairs and snuck up on her. Daddy
used to say she played in her sleep. She rose, went
downstairs, and played, then returned to bed and denied having done it.

"It wasn't me, Arthur Madison Atwell," she would
tell him. She always pronounced his entire name when
she wanted to stress something or when he made her
angry.

"Right, Sarah. It was your great-great-aunt Mabel,"
he would joke.

"I had no Aunt Mabel and you know very well I

didn't," she would say. Mama had no sense of humor when it came to her spiritual family.

Daddy would shake his head. If I was standing nearby and heard the conversation, he would wink at me and point to his ear. He once told me that when Mama talked about her spirits, you had to listen with half an ear.

Sometimes when she finished playing, she looked exhausted, drained, and sometimes she looked revived, even younger. This night she played with an intensity I had rarely heard. Her hair fell about her face and her face became flushed, her eyes bright. Even Baby Celeste stopped doing what she was doing and stared up at her in awe.

When she was finished, she lowered her head to the piano for a long moment, then sat up and smiled at us.

"It will all be well, Noble. I am confidant now. I have seen Baby Celeste."

"You have seen her?" I looked at her and then at Mama. "What do you mean? She's been here beside me all the while."

"I have seen her older, much older, and she is everything I dreamed she would be.

"Tomorrow," Mama declared, rising, "tomorrow it will all begin again."

She lifted Baby Celeste into her arms and carried her off toward the stairway.

With wonder I looked at the piano and then I followed her. We put Baby Celeste to bed and then we both went to bed ourselves.

Hours after I had fallen asleep, I woke just as I often had as a young girl, and I heard the music below. It was the same music Mama had played earlier. I rose, confused, wondering why she had gotten up and returned to the piano. However, when I went out to the hallway, the music stopped and I could see through Mama's open door that she was in bed. But I had heard the music. I had. To the day I died, I would swear to it. I wished Daddy would appear so I could confirm it, but he didn't.

I returned to my room and called for him in the darkness, but he didn't come.

Something's wrong, I thought. There's a reason he's not coming to me anymore. There's a reason he fled into the woods and he stays in the dark places.

Surely it had to do with these dramatic changes in Mama, I thought. How I need him now.

I fell asleep again, hoping at least to find him in my dreams.

But I found nothing but deep darkness.

4
Never Be Resurrected

Ⅱ

Right after breakfast the following morning, Mama told me to take Baby Celeste up to the turret room.

"I'll come for you when the drapery man leaves," she said. "He'll be here soon."

This first time we weren't locked away that long. He was only coming to measure the windows, but two days later, Mama had the carpet people scheduled and they would be at the house most of the day because they were doing three rooms. She had decided to have my room done as well as hers and the living room, and she had picked out the carpet, a rich almond color.

Baby Celeste had always been good for the short stays, but this first seemingly unending one was far more difficult for both of us. For one thing, Mama and I had forgotten we would be locked away for too long without going to the bathroom. The turret room had no bathroom, so we would have to go down a flight and the carpet people might be working on my room or Mama's. I began to panic as soon as I realized our oversight.

Baby Celeste had been toilet trained before she was quite two. She was truly advanced in every which way. Just before lunch, she asked to go potty. I opened the door and waited at the top of the short stairway in anticipation of Mama coming up with lunch. As soon as she saw me, her eyes flared with anger.

"What are you doing? Where do you think you're going? I told you to stay inside until I came for you. They are all still here," she cried in a loud whisper.

"Baby Celeste has to go potty, Mama. We forgot about that. I'll have to sneak her down."

I could see from the expression on Mama's face that she had truly forgotten herself. She thought a moment, then shook her head.

"No, you'll use one of the old chamber pots," she decided. "I'll get it."

"Chamber pots?"

She handed me the tray of food, entered the room, and went directly to a large trunk.

"Take it, Noble," she insisted when she found the pot. "Our ancestors did it this way before there was indoor plumbing. You and Baby Celeste certainly can."

"What about toilet paper, Mama?"

"Use the napkins I gave you on the tray."

I shook my head and looked back at Baby Celeste, who was standing anxiously, expecting to be carried down to the bathroom.

"She won't understand," I said.

"Then make her understand and keep it quiet. Go on," Mama said. "Just do it and don't contradict. And keep from looking out the windows. The carpet men are having their lunch outside and we don't want them to see you peering out and asking me all sorts of questions."

She practically pushed me back into the turret room. This time, she made sure the door was locked, too.

I turned to Baby Celeste.

"Potty," she said.

"I know." I set the chamber pot down. "You go potty in there," I said, pointing.

To my utter surprise she turned, lowered her panties and piddled in the pot. She did it like someone who had done nothing else all her short life.

Later, I had no choice but to do the same.

I had never seen a chamber pot before, and that piqued my curiosity about the rest of what had been brought up here and stored away over the years. I was always afraid of disturbing anything, but with all this time on our hands, I sought new ways to keep us both distracted.

Beside the mirrors and old dressers and tables, cartons of clothing were packed in mothballs. I found baby clothes, too, baby clothes I knew hadn't been mine or Noble's. Baby Celeste stood looking at the garments, touching whatever I touched. There were even old shoes and boots, and in one carton we found all sorts of hats. I amused myself and Baby Celeste by putting on some of the boots and hats. She wanted to wear them as well, and we had a good time with them along with gloves and belts bedecked in costume jewelry.

Suddenly, Baby Celeste turned as if she had heard something. Her eyes grew small the way Mama's did when she was concentrating. I watched her work her way in between an old dresser and some cartons. She stopped when she found something that caught her in-

terest and called to me. I followed and leaned over the
dresser to see what she was up to, and I saw she had
found a small ebony wood box with gold trim. She
held it up so I could see it better. It had been hidden
behind everything else so long that a layer of dust covered it. I took it gently from her.

"What have you found, Celeste?"

I turned it around and saw that it had a key to turn
on the back of it.

"It's a music box," I explained.

Her eyes brightened. We had one downstairs on a
table in the living room. Atop it was a ballerina who
danced to the music. Baby Celeste was so taken with
it, Mama thought she would wear out the mechanism.

I blew some of the dust off the little wooden box,
then squatted beside her to open it. Amazingly, despite
how long it had been up here, it began to play a piece
of a Mozart piano sonata that Mama often played.
Even Baby Celeste recognized it and said, "Mama.
Piano."

"Yes," I told her, then I realized it might have been
heard below. I held my breath and listened hard. Baby
Celeste saw the look of apprehension on my face and
froze as well. Their work made too much noise, I
thought confidently, and released my lungs. Then I
smiled at her and looked into the box.

All it held was a small lock of golden blond hair
tied with a thin piece of faded pink ribbon. It was certainly not Mama's hair, nor was it Noble's, mine, or
Baby Celeste's. It couldn't be my daddy's either. His
was raven black. Whose was it? Why had it been left
up here, hidden away in a dusty corner? This was
something people usually did with their baby's hair,
but pressed into family albums.

The music box stopped playing. I studied it further,

turning it over and every which way to look for some clue, but I found nothing else. Baby Celeste wanted to hear the music again, so I turned the key and let it play. We brought it back to the center of the room and spent the remainder of our time occupying ourselves with other things: her picture books and coloring books mainly. She fell asleep on my lap and I dozed off myself. In fact, we were both asleep and didn't hear Mama come up the stairs and open the door at the end of the day. Her gasp woke me.

She was standing over us, her eyes wide, her hands pressed over her breasts.

I stirred and Baby Celeste woke up, sat up, and rubbed her eyes.

"Where did you find that?" Mama asked, nodding at the small ebony wood box beside me.

"Baby Celeste found it," I said. "Something made her want to go exploring behind the old dresser. It was as if she knew it was there."

That seemed to disturb Mama more. Her right hand fluttered up to the base of her throat like a struggling baby bird. She took another deep breath.

"When did she find it?"

"I don't know. About two hours ago, I guess. It was back there." I pointed to the rear of the room. "What is it? Whose hair is that in it? Why is it up here? Why couldn't it be downstairs in the living room?"

I lifted the box and Mama backed away as if she expected it would explode.

"It's very pretty, and it plays that Mozart piece you play. See," I said, and started to open it so it would play.

"No!" Mama screamed. "Leave it be. Don't open it. Put it back where it was. Go on."

"You mean back on the floor behind the dresser?"

"Yes, just put it back there," she ordered.

"But whose hair is in it?"

Mama looked at Baby Celeste, who sat there gazing up at her as if she expected to hear the answer, too.

"It's . . . it doesn't matter. Just put it back."

"How come you want it left up here?" I rose to do what she wanted.

"I just do. I just do. Stop asking me and do what I tell you," she said angrily.

I had never seen Mama so visibly shaken. Her body trembled and she was pale. I hurried to put the box behind the dresser in the corner.

"You opened it," Mama said more to herself than to me. She looked about the room fearfully, then scooped Baby Celeste into her arms. Had the little music box called to some spirit she feared?

"Everyone's gone," Mama said. "You can come downstairs now. Bring the chamber pot to empty, too. Quickly!"

She turned and fled the turret room. I glanced back at the small box and then got the chamber pot and followed. My heart was thumping from Mama's reaction. Why couldn't we touch it, open it? Nothing in this house frightened her. If anything bothered her, she got rid of it or washed it in candle smoke.

I heard her descending the stairway quickly, more like someone fleeing. She was already down to the main stairway when I reached the second-floor landing. I went into the bathroom, emptied the pot in the toilet, then placed it on the floor. After that I paused to look into my room to admire the new rug. It did make the room brighter, and the rug in Mama's room gave it a new, fresh look as well, as did the new carpet in the living room. It made it look warmer.

"All the rugs are very nice, Mama," I said.

She had put Baby Celeste down and was standing by the window gazing out. She acted as if she hadn't heard me. Baby Celeste plopped on the rug and smiled up at me, pleased with the feel and the color.

"With the new curtains you're getting and the other things we're doing, the house is going to look so much better, Mama. You were right about that," I told her, hoping to get her to stop behaving so strangely.

"What?" she finally said, turning.

"The rugs are very nice. I was just saying how warm and wonderful the house is going to be when you're finished with your redecorating."

"No." She shook her head. "It's not warm and wonderful. We're in some danger."

"Danger? In our house?" How could we be in danger in the house? The house was our sanctuary.

She hurried past me and out of the room. I heard her rummaging about in the kitchen, then I heard her start for the stairway.

"Mama?" I said, stepping into the hallway. "What are you doing?"

She paused and turned to me. For a moment she just stared at me, her eyes blinking rapidly.

"Take the baby out for a while," she said.

"Out? Take her out?"

"It's dark enough. Take her over toward the shed, away from the front of the house. Go on. Do it, Noble. Her little sweater is on the sofa. I'll call you when I want you to come back inside with her."

"Okay," I said, and watched her charge up the stairway.

Baby Celeste couldn't be happier. She clapped her hands with joy when I carried her out of the house. I walked toward the shed and the gardens just as Mama had commanded, and then I set Baby Celeste down, folded my arms over my strapped-down bosom, and looked back at the house.

Twilight draped a dark gray veil around us. To me this time of day always looked sad. It was as if the sun were caught in indecision. Should it go? Should it stay? Reluctantly, it would soon blink and sink below the mountains. Did it drown every day and was it resurrected every morning?

Baby Celeste tugged on my hand. She realized we had a limited time in the softened light and she was hungry for everything she could see. I walked about with her, talking and showing her plants we were growing, wildflowers, and even milkweeds. Her curiosity was limitless. She was so taken with insects that she almost grabbed a bumblebee.

Periodically, I paused and looked back at the house. All of the rooms were still in darkness. What could Mama be doing? More and more stars appeared in the night sky. It was getting cooler and cooler. The wind came in from the north. I could hear it threading its way through the forest, rushing toward us. When would Mama call to us? I was trembling now from both the cooler air and her strange behavior.

Suddenly, I saw a glow building in the living room. It grew brighter and brighter, but not as it would if Mama had turned on the lamps. This was different. The light flickered, too.

Candles! I thought. She has lit candles.

But so many in one room? Why?

I lifted Baby Celeste into my arms and slowly walked back to the house. Just as I reached the porch steps, Mama came out, closing the door behind her. She leaned back against it. Although we were standing right before her, her gaze went past us or even through us. Actually, she looked like a blind woman.

"Mama? What are you doing? Shouldn't we go in for dinner? It's getting late for the baby. Mama?" I said in a raised voice when she didn't respond.

She blinked rapidly and looked at us. When she shifted a little to the right, the illumination was enough for me to see how flushed her face had become. She continued to stare without speaking.

"Mama?"

"Take her inside but don't go into the living room until I tell you. Now," she said, stamping. I felt myself jump inside as if I had another whole body under the one people saw.

She stepped aside and I opened the door and carried Baby Celeste in. I hesitated just enough at the living room doorway to look in. I had never seen Mama do something like this as extensively. Set up all over the living room were pictures of all the ancestors we had, at least two dozen pictures. Before each picture, she had placed a black candle. I realized she had formed a circle with the pictures, but what surprised and even shocked me more was seeing the small ebony wood box in the center of the floor.

"Go into the kitchen," Mama ordered, and I moved quickly, not saying a word. Her voice sounded on the verge of hysteria. Even Baby Celeste looked speech-less.

Mama said nothing about what she had done in the living room and I was afraid to ask her about it. Seeing the small candle illuminating the photograph of each family member gave me an eerie feeling. I knew she had performed some ritual meant to draw out their spiritual power to overcome something terrible re-leased by opening the small black wooden box. Since I had done it, I was afraid I'd be blamed for whatever she believed had happened and could happen.

Mama worked on dinner in that deep silence she could reach, a silence that seemed to take her away. She came up out of it occasionally to give me an order to do this or that with the bread, the vegetables, or to set the table.

Dinner was almost as quiet. Although I did get her talking about some of the other changes she was making in the house, I avoided any reference to the living room or the wooden box. I saw the way her eyes drifted toward the living room from time to time. Apparently she was waiting for something, some signal, herself. Just before we finished eating, that signal obviously came and her expression brightened. Her whole body, stiff and tense for the last hour or so, relaxed.

"I have to put things away, Noble," she told me. "Clear off the table and carefully stack the dishes. Keep the baby occupied, too."

She rose and went to the living room.

One of the truly wondrous things about Baby Celeste was the way she could tune into the mood of the moment and become a part of it. When Mama and I were light and happy, she was. If Mama was melancholy and quiet, she was. If something had made Mama angry, Baby Celeste avoided doing anything that could bring chastisement.

Throughout dinner, she was as quiet and as patient as a panther. She was even careful about how much noise she made clinking her silverware and dishes, and when she was finished, she didn't plead to get down from her chair, but instead sat and waited like an adult.

Before I finished getting things in order in the kitchen, Mama returned. She had been going around the house, upstairs as well, to put those pictures back where they were. She looked pleased with everything and cheerfully told me we could go into the living room now.

Everything was gone. The scent of the burning candles lingered, but she had opened windows as well to rid the room of that as quickly as possible. I sat on the sofa and opened one of Baby Celeste's books for her. She leaned against me and watched as I turned the pages and permitted her to identify everything on them.

Mama came in and went to the piano as usual. She played two Mozart sonatas for solo piano, but avoided the sonata captured in the wooden music box. It wasn't something she played every night, but more than not, she would end with it.

Baby Celeste became drowsy, so Mama took her upstairs to put her to bed. I went outside and sat on the porch. I was still feeling nervous from all that had transpired. I wanted to be alone and relax. Now wearing a light jacket, I could enjoy the night air. The sky was cloudless. The wind I had heard earlier had carried the remnants of clouds away, sweeping the heavens clean so that the unblocked stars twinkled with a brilliance not often seen.

On evenings like this, melancholy would unfold itself inside my heart like a newly hatched bird spreading its wings within the confines of a nest, bringing with it the realization that flight loomed in its near future. It was a promise surely to be realized, a promise so strong it filled the mind of the baby bird with images of itself gliding, turning, rising, and floating on the wind. These were memories it had inherited, memories that were part of who and what it was, memories that could not be denied or buried long in its dark unconscious.

Likewise for me, the melancholy that unfolded

brought with it memories, too, girlhood memories, an impressive nostalgia for things dainty and feminine. Fantasies came galloping back onto the field of my dreams. During a time in my life that was so long ago and now seemed to be truly someone else's life, I could imagine myself falling in love with a handsome and mysterious man. Once, I could see myself as a mother who could unashamedly love her child and did not need to hide her maternal emotions. Scents of perfume filled my nostrils. Dresses and shoes, scarves and ribbons, danced before my eyes.

Noble used to imagine knights and dragons, monsters and heroes, coming out of the forest. He filled his days with stories and games he created in his active boyish imagination. Sometimes, Mama made me play alongside him so he would have companionship. I never once even thought to ask him to play with my teacup set or my dolls with me, not that he would want to do it. My playtime was too calm for his bursts of energy. I used to think he would go shouting through the house all the time if Mama didn't stop him. Were all boys like him? I wondered. Were they all afraid of softness and the little silences that invaded our daily lives? Did all of his visions and dreams have to roar and crash against the walls of his imagination? Was reality such a threat?

But I, too, had had fantasies, and just because I was older and life and the world were so different for me now, I didn't stop having them. Even now, tonight, I envisioned my own version of a handsome knight coming out of the forest that ringed our property, about to do battle with all the demons that chained me to this dark and dismal existence. I longed to be swept away, to be carried afar where I could let my hair grow again, where I could unstrap my bosom and permit my breasts to breathe, and I could once again experience and enjoy all the dainty and beautiful things in a woman's world.

I would have clothes and dolls and perfumes. I would have jewels and my laughter would be untethered and melodic, instead of guarded and short. Somewhere and sometime, I would be able to flirt with my eyes, blush, and sigh, and I would be unafraid of the sound of my own name perched on the lips of a handsome young man.

Do I dare wish for such things? I wondered. Will I be cursed for eternity? Will all our family spirits hate me and stop protecting me?

Most important, would Mama hate me as she has never hated anyone or anything?

I was so lost in these thoughts that I almost didn't hear the front door open slowly. Mama emerged carrying the small ebony wooden box cupped in her right hand like an offering she was going to make to some angry god. I didn't speak. I barely breathed, and incredibly, she didn't look at me or notice me sitting there. I could only watch her, amazed at how she moved. She stepped down the porch stairway like someone walking in her sleep. When she turned, I saw that in her other hand she carried a small garden spade.

I started to stand, to call to her, but she walked faster and went directly toward the cemetery. Both intrigued and a little frightened, I followed far behind her, walking as softly as I could. She went into the cemetery. When I reached the entrance, I saw she was on her knees, digging in front of Infant Jordan's small tombstone. I stood there quietly, watching her dig. She became more and more determined about it, working faster and more intently. Finally, she concluded that the hole was deep enough and she placed the wooden box in it. She covered it quickly, smoothing the earth as best she could and replanting the clumps of grass.

Then she stood up slowly, stared at the tombstone a moment, stepped up to it, and placed her hands on the embossed baby hands. I remember how she used to tell Noble and me that she could feel those hands move. We tried, but felt nothing, or at least Noble never did. I couldn't be sure.

Mama stood with her hands on the tombstone so long, I wondered if she would ever leave. I heard her whimper. Crying was something I rarely heard Mama do, and it was surely something she wouldn't want me to hear. Now I was terrified of being discovered watching her. I had no idea how she would react, but the very fact that I hadn't made her aware I was doing so would surely anger her. She would accuse me of spying on her. Her rage could very well have something to do with why she had just buried the box and the fact that I had opened it.

Slowly, as quietly as I could, I stepped back into the shadows. The more I did that, the more I did look sneaky, but it was too late to reverse my action. I had committed myself to not being seen. I continued to retreat, and then I froze in place when she turned from the tombstone and started out of the cemetery. Her eyes were down and she was walking quickly. She paused to flick errant tears from her cheeks, then she continued walking. I held my breath and watched her hurry back to the house.

As soon as she entered, I walked into the cemetery and gazed down at the place where she had buried the black box. Why was she burying it here? Why did it have to be buried at all? What did all this mean? What deep, dark secret had Baby Celeste uncovered when she found the ebony wooden box? What had happened when we had opened it?

In deep thought I walked back to the house and stood just outside the door listening. I didn't hear her moving about so I entered as quietly as I could, barely closing the door behind me. When I looked into the living room, I saw Mama sitting in Grandfather Jordan's rocker. She didn't look up at me even though I felt she knew I was standing there, which made me wonder if she had realized I had been outside all this time and if she was now furious at me.

"Mama?" I finally said. "Are you all right?"

"Of course I'm all right," she snapped. "I'll always be all right."

"Are you angry at me?"

"No, I'm angry at myself."

"Why?"

She rocked in the chair. I thought she wasn't going to answer.

"I forgot about it," she finally said. "I should have remembered."

"About what? The wooden box? The lock of baby's hair?"

She spun around so fast that she almost cracked the arm of the rocking chair.

"How do you know it was a lock of baby's hair?" she demanded. Then she relaxed, nodded, and smiled. "He told you, didn't he? Your father whispered it into your ear. Yes, I'm sure."

She threw her head back and rocked harder.

"No, Mama."

She brought her head down again and glared at me. "If you lie to me, I'll know. I'll always know when you tell lies, Noble."

"I'm not lying, Mama. I haven't heard Daddy for quite a while now."

"Um," she murmured. She rocked and thought. Then she let out a long, deep breath. "I should have known she would find it someday. I should have known." She stopped the rocking abruptly and spun her head around at me again. "Do you see how special she is?" she asked, flashing her eyes at me. "Do you?"

"You mean Baby Celeste?"

"Of course that's who I mean. Why do you stand there and pretend to be so stupid all the time?"

"I'm not pretending to be stupid, Mama."

"No, you're really stupid, is that it? Oh, the burden, the burden," she wailed, rocking on.

"Sometimes, you have to help me understand things, Mama," I said as calmly as I could manage. "Why is that so terrible?"

She thought and rocked.

"Was the lock of hair Infant Jordan's?" I asked.

She smiled. "Yes, it was."

"Why do you blame yourself then? Why was it wrong to keep a lock of her hair? You kept ours and pasted it in the family album."

"This was different."

"How?"

"Questions, questions, since when are you so full of questions? Your sister was always full of questions, but not you, not you," she added with her voice drifting.

"I just wondered how this was different."

"It was different because she was never alive," Mama said in a tired voice.

"Oh, I know that."

"No, you don't know. She was never alive."

I smiled at her. Now she was the one forgetting and

sounding stupid, I thought, although I would never dare even suggest such a thing.

"But you told me, Mama. You told both of us. You told us she was stillborn. Isn't that what *stillborn* means?"

"She was *never* alive. Even on the other side she was a dead thing. We live first there. I've explained it to you many times, haven't I? We are born and we die many different ways and eventually return to what we were, return to where we were created in the first place."

"I know."

"She was a dark dead thing. She was born of evil, and opening the box was like opening Pandora's box. That's why I had to do what I did tonight. The evilness was set loose in our house. It had been sleeping up there all this time, just waiting for an opportunity."

"Is that why you put out all the family pictures and lit the candles?"

"Yes. I had to bring them all here, have them all help us, and they did.

"But it's all my fault," she added, rocking. "I shouldn't have taken a lock of her hair in the first place. I did it when no one could see. I had to have it. I just had to have it. I should have known. You see, I wasn't as powerful as Baby Celeste is. If anything proves it, that does."

What did she say? She had to have it? That made absolutely no sense.

"You did it? You took the lock of hair from her head?"

Now I was really confused. She remained silent, rocking, staring at the wall, her lips tight with rage.

"But how . . . you weren't even born yet, Mama."

She turned to look at me, and in her expression I

could see that she had said more than she had wanted. She actually looked frightened for a moment and turned away.

"Mama?"

She shook her head. "I don't want to talk about it anymore and I don't want you to talk about it. Ever."

"But how could you be there to do it?" The question wouldn't swallow back. It was a bubble that wouldn't be denied no matter how I tried to keep it from reaching the surface. How could she be there to cut the lock of hair from a stillborn baby born to her great-grandparents?

The answer was in the heavy silence that fell between us. It wasn't a stillborn baby born to her great-grandparents. Was it her mother's baby? Why wouldn't she ever have told us? Why would she say it was her great-grandparent's child? My heartbeat quickened and a feather made of ice brushed over the back of my neck.

"Was it your mother's baby?"

She turned back to me ever so slowly, and when she did, her eyes seemed to have sunk deeper into her skull. Her lips became tight and thin.

"No."

"No? Then I don't understand."

"She came out of me," she said in a deathly whisper.

"You?"

"I wasn't much older than you are. I hid it from my mother until I could hide it no longer and she drew it out of me so it would be stillborn. It was wrinkled and ugly. Only its hair was pretty, only its hair. Its hair was like spun gold. I couldn't resist."

"Your baby? How did your mother know it was evil?"

She looked away and rocked. "Every family has a dark spirit in it, a blemish. He was my father's younger brother. He wasn't here often or long, but it was enough. I was seduced, and afterward he was punished."

"What happened to him?"

She smiled. "Yes, something happened to him. My mother put a curse on him and he died a horrible death, his insides rotted out with cancer. But he was a handsome man, a charming man. Evil always is, you know. 'The devil hath a pleasing face,'" she quoted.

She looked at me. "That's why it's so important to be careful, to be guarded, to be good. That's why you must listen to everything I tell you and do what I tell you, Noble."

She turned away again and rocked. "If she had lived, if she had been alive, she would have been the first Celeste. She knew that and she worked and worked at returning until she entered my Celeste, and that is why I had to bury her forever and ever. Now all the evil is underground and we're safe. We're safe," Mama chanted.

She had entered the first Celeste? Had Mama always thought me evil? Was that why she so readily believed Noble's death was my fault?

"We're safe," she chanted. "She's dead and gone. Buried and gone."

She looked at me again. "And she'll never be resurrected." Her words fell like small explosions on my ears and echoed.

And echoed.

"Never be resurrected . . . never be resurrected . . . never . . ."

I turned and ran out and up the stairway.

5

I'm Beautiful

♊

All my life I had grown up believing that our house was truly sacrosanct, that we really lived within a castle protected by our family's spiritual wall as Mama had described, that we were safe and that the only evil that could come into our lives had to come from without, and only if we ourselves weakened and permitted it to happen. All of our family spirits were good. They hadn't had perfect lives. Some weren't productive and had caused their own problems, but their hearts were pure. That was what had made us special, what gave us the power to cross over, to see them and hear them. We had been given the gift because we had this pureness in our blood.

It was shocking to hear otherwise, to learn that someone so close to us had been dark, depraved, and unholy and that his seed had entered our world like something infectious, a disease of evil that could contaminate us. Was Mama then right about me? Was the wickedness my grandmother aborted able to resurface within my heart, in the first Celeste's heart?

Mama's revelations resurrected my memories of that fateful day Noble died, a day not only Mama denied, but I did, too. Despite my reluctance to remember, my attempts to dam them up and keep them away, the images came flooding back over me. It was like someone pinning my eyelids back and forcing me to see, to look upon the ugliest and most frightening things. I wished I could shake the pictures out of my head, drink one of Mama's wondrous elixirs and forget forever, but that could not be.

Instead, I recalled Noble standing on the big rock in the creek. I had come to get him to go home. Mama was upset he was out there alone. He was stubborn so I grabbed his fishing pole, and then he and I had a tug-of-war with it. Once again I saw him losing his balance, only now I saw myself deliberately shoving that pole into him, driving him off the rock. Anger and jealousy had taken control of my arms. The dark thing had truly come to life within me. He fell off and hit his head on smaller rocks. I had to admit it. It was my fault, my fault. Mama was right to bury me and I had to stop fighting it. I vowed to put away my childhood fantasies.

I would dream no more of handsome young men, of being a beautiful young woman, and having children of my own. I had to pay for my sin and remain forever incarcerated in my brother's identity. This was my prison. This was my fate. I would not cry and moan about it either. All that was feminine, gentle, and tender within me would be pushed aside and forgotten. I didn't deserve it. Anything that tried to revive it in me was surely evil, the evil Mama battled daily.

I pledged to myself that I would join her struggle

and fight beside her. I would put away the memory of that small black wooden box. I would forget that strange night and I would think no more about the golden curls, the pink ribbon, and Mama's sobs in the cemetery that hid so many of our family secrets. All graveyards, it occurred to me, were like gardens. They contained beautiful souls, flowers of the purest spirits, but they also contained the remains of the most sinister hearts, weeds that could choke the flowers.

The effort it had taken Mama to drive the malevolent spirit from our home seemed to reinforce her determination to follow the new plan she had been given, a plan I did not yet fully understand and was now more afraid of questioning. Was she right? Did my questions rise out of a pool of inky evil still within my troubled soul?

Mama continued to go out on dates with Dave Fletcher, and each time she did, she came home late and slept late. I was still afraid of what this could lead to, but I made no comments and I put on no disapproving faces. For one thing, she did seem to be happy. She was looking younger and younger and her revival along with the way the house was being revived brought new sunshine into our lives.

It encouraged and inspired me to look past the dark and the gray. Like Mama, I wanted to put a new shine on the surface of our world. I whitewashed our fences, repainted shutters and doorjambs, cleared the weeds away from the sides of our driveway, pruned and trimmed our bushes and trees. The worn, tired, and droll look our house and property had was dramatically changed. Mama decided that even the shed had to be repainted and a new roof put on it as well. The only disadvantage to all this that she saw was that it would attract more gawking eyes. Cars passing by did slow down and some even stopped so the curious could get a longer, better look. Baby Celeste had to be kept even more secluded. Twilight was now too early for any sort of outing.

The work I did was hard, especially in the hot summer sun, but I didn't complain. My hands developed calluses on their calluses. Many nights my muscles ached and I was so exhausted, I couldn't wait to finish dinner and get to bed, sometimes as early as Baby Celeste went to bed. However, I was up early and on to my chores often before Mama was up and at her own, especially after one of her dates with Mr. Fletcher.

And then one afternoon she told me she was going on a special date with him that very evening and she needed me to take complete charge of things for nearly twenty-four hours. I didn't understand what that meant until she added, "I won't be home tonight."

"Why not?" I asked.

"Dave's taking me to a special bed-and-breakfast place eighty miles or so away from here. It's near Albany," she said, "and it wouldn't make any sense to go there to eat and enjoy the surroundings if we had to hurry back.

"You'll have to take care of Baby Celeste. Be sure she eats well and goes to sleep early. I'll call you in the morning and let you know about what time I'll return."

"But I was going to get up early to finish the shed roofing tomorrow, Mama. It's easier to work in the morning now."

"It will wait," she said firmly. Then she smiled at me. "I'm very proud of you, proud of the way you've gone about your work on the farm, Noble. Your father would not have done much better. He's proud of you as well. Has he told you so? Have you heard his voice lately?"

I shook my head.

"You will," she promised. "It will all come back to you. We're in a transition period. Everything waits on everything, but we'll be fine. We'll all be fine." Then she hugged me and held me longer than she usually did. "Everything I've been told would be will be," she whispered. "You'll see."

More than ever now, I wanted to know exactly what that meant, what she had been told would be, but I still didn't dare ask. Sometimes, it was better not to ask, I thought. Sometimes, I didn't want to hear the answers, but it was on the tip of my tongue to warn her about Elliot, to tell her what I had seen, to warn her about his anger, about the threat a vindictive spirit like that could bring to us, especially after I had seen her do what she had done with the black box.

But I couldn't bring myself to do it, for after all, it had been I who had brought Elliot into our world. I was responsible for everything that had happened as a result and that could happen in the future.

"What about Mr. Fletcher's daughter, Betsy?" I asked instead. Of course, I wondered if she knew anything about Mama and her father.

"What about her?"

"Is she still gone?"

"Yes, and it breaks poor Dave's heart to worry about her so each and every day. My grandmother used to say that sometimes children are rained down upon us as a punishment for past sins. I'm afraid it's so in Dave's case. His children were never any source of pleasure and pride for him.

"Unlike mine," she added, running her fingers through my hair. "My beautiful children."

As if she sensed she was being referred to, Baby Celeste cried out for us. She had woken from her daily nap.

"I'll see to her and then I have to get myself ready,"

Mama said. "Go finish what you're working on today. I'll have your and Baby Celeste's dinner prepared. All you will have to do is warm up things. Baby Celeste will be excited about helping you without me supervising. She will have more to do, more responsibility. It will be an adventure for her. You know how excited she gets over new things."

Mr. Fletcher had yet to set eyes on Baby Celeste and, like everyone else in the community, had yet to learn of her existence. When and how would Mama deal with that? I wondered.

When I returned to the house, I found Mama all dressed and ready to go. She had her hair brushed and styled beautifully. Two days earlier she had gone to a beauty salon for the first time in ten years and had it cut. When she came home that day, I almost didn't recognize her. However, it wasn't only the use of makeup now, the change in her hairstyle, and the updated wardrobe that surprised me. A new brightness was in her face, a new life in her eyes, that truly made her look younger and more vibrant. Did this come from being in love? Could she be in love?

I was actually a bit jealous. Despite all the pledges and vows I had made to myself, I couldn't help but imagine what I would look like with longer hair, with makeup on my face, and with jewelry and new dresses and shoes. This overwhelming fantasy revived feelings and emotions I had experienced years ago in the forest in my special place where I had gone to be alone, to explore my inner self and feel the freedom of being who I really was, even if only for a short while. These thoughts, my curiosity, was titillating, tantalizing, drawing me to the edge of some precipice, tempting me with simply leaping off and sailing into the wind of my driving desires.

I said nothing about it to Mama, of course. She remarked about the flushness in my face and thought it was a result of my hard work in the hot sun. She had packed a small bag and waited by the front window for signs of Dave Fletcher's approaching automobile. When he turned down our driveway, she kissed and hugged both me and Baby Celeste and made us promise we would behave and follow all her rules, the most important one still being to keep Baby Celeste from being seen and discovered.

"I'm sorry you have to stay inside all morning tomorrow, Noble," Mama said, "but I'll try to get back as early as I can. Remember to clean up after dinner," she called back from the door, going out as soon as Dave Fletcher drove up to the house.

I peered out through a curtain and saw him get out to take her little overnight bag and give her a kiss, this time smack on the lips and a little long, too, like a kiss in a movie full of passion and surrender, a kiss that lingered in sighs of contentment, a kiss I would never know. I heard her laughter and watched her hurry around to get into his car. He had opened the door for her, bowing like a gallant gentleman out of a romantic novel. After she got in, he came around and looked at our house. I pulled back from the window and waited until he was into his car, too. Then I watched them drive away.

Baby Celeste stood by watching me quietly. I shook my head when I turned to her.

"Mama's making a mistake," I said. "I don't understand what she is doing. How can this be good, be part of some wonderful plan for us?"

Baby Celeste smiled at me as if I were the one who didn't know what she was doing and not Mama, or as if she knew I was drawing my words mostly from a well of envy. Then she hurried out of the room.

"Kitchen, Noble," she cried. She knew we were going to work on our own dinner, and as Mama had predicted, she was excited about doing it all.

Before, during, and after dinner, I felt this trembling inside me. I told myself it was simply because I was worried so about Mama, but deep in my heart of hearts, I knew that wasn't the reason. It wasn't trembling born out of fear. It was from a tickling that began in my heart and emerged around my breasts, tingling at my nipples and warming through my body, down around my thighs.

Every once in a while, I would stop and think about Mama all dressed up and I would see her kissing Dave Fletcher and think about that kiss. I saw myself being kissed, not by Dave Fletcher, of course, but by someone young and handsome, and I could almost feel the touch of his warm lips on mine. I shifted and squirmed in my dining room chair almost as much as Baby Celeste.

For a while she was a good distraction, filling my hours, demanding my attention, but finally, she grew tired and lay limply against me. I carried her upstairs and dressed her for bed. She hugged me around the neck and held on to me for a few moments longer than she had ever done, perhaps because she knew we were going to be alone for a long time, that Mama was far away from both of us. I put her doll in her arms and she closed her eyes and fell asleep almost immediately.

As I stood there looking down at her and admiring how beautiful she was, I realized Mama hadn't been on top of dying her hair as she usually was. Her natural red color was climbing up through those soft strands. For as long as Baby Celeste had been alive, Mama was careful not to let the tiniest spot of red return. She couldn't have missed this, I thought. Something new was about to happen, something important.

I left Baby Celeste's bedroom and hesitated in the
hallway. I should just go downstairs and read or go to
bed myself, I thought. I should. I even started for the
stairway, but stopped at the top. My heart was pounding. I closed my eyes and bit down on my lower lip,
hoping that the pain would drive the feelings and the
urges out of me, but it was too hard, too hard to fight
it, to drive it away. I couldn't help myself.

I turned and headed for Mama's bedroom. At the
doorway I hesitated, battling with myself one final
time and losing. As soon as I entered the room, I knew
I would not turn back. There was only one vanity table
and one vanity table mirror and one full-length mirror
outside the turret room, and they were here. I gazed at
myself and then quickly took off my shirt and my
jeans. I unstrapped my bosom and lowered my under-
pants.

It was truly as if I were reemerging to the surface
of my own body, maturing instantly into a young
woman. I tingled all over. My breath quickened. I sat
at the table and began to experiment with Mama's
new makeup, trying on different shades of lipstick,
eyeliner, facial powders. All I had to go by were pictures I had seen in the few magazines we had in the
house, what I caught on television when Mama permitted it to be turned on, and of course, what I had recently seen her do.

I tried brushing my short hair so it took on some
style like hers now had, and then I went to her closet
and began to try on her skirts and blouses, her dresses
and even her underthings. I had never worn a bra, and
the way it shaped my breasts, especially under one of
Mama's pretty pink or white sweaters, fascinated me.
I tried on different earrings, necklaces, and bracelets.
With every completed outfit, I imagined a different

occasion: a date, a dance, attending a theater, or just going shopping in a mall. I strutted about and pretended boys were looking at me, smiling, flirting, beckoning with their eyes.

"Don't go too close," I warned myself as if I were with a far more sophisticated girlfriend. "Don't answer them. Don't look back. Don't smile."

But wasn't there always one to look back at, one handsome boy who held my attention and my imagination? I had to smile back. I closed my eyes and dreamed of our conversation, of our meeting and walking together. He would ask me on a date and I would agree to go.

As quickly as I dreamed of it, I returned to the closet and sorted through the garments for something appropriate. What do you wear on your first date with a boy you like? You can't be too obvious now, but you have to be attractive. It's not wrong to emphasize your attributes, is it? Just a little. Oh, how I wish I had a real girlfriend, someone with whom I could talk for hours and hours on the telephone, talk about the absolutely silliest, most insignificant things that so filled our lives and dress them up like balloons and crepe paper at a party.

I'm missing the party, I thought with some panic. I'm passing it by forever and ever. Shaking the sadness out of my head, I continued.

I found a light blue dress that could be worn off-shoulder. It had a deep V-neck collar that exposed the depth of my cleavage, and it fit me snugly around my waist. The sight of my feminine self took my breath away. I am pretty; I could be sexy, I thought.

"Stop giving me those reprimanding looks, Mama," I said to the face I imagined in the mirror. "You had the same thoughts and did the same things when

Daddy came to take you out on your first date, didn't you? You fell in love with yourself, too. And don't try to tell me that was different because that was then and this is now. It's always different for you. Older people always say that."

I looked through the earrings for a pair that I thought fit my dress, and then I found the necklace Daddy had once given Mama a long time ago, a necklace of real diamonds. She never wore it anymore. For me it was the most forbidden thing to wear, but I did anyway.

Because I imagined this to be so special a date, I returned to the vanity table and changed my lipstick color, again to fit my dress, my look. I kept the eye shadow and brushed my lashes. Once, Mama had considered trimming my lashes, but in the end she'd decided they were all right. "After all," she said, "think of how many women are heard saying 'I wish I had his eyelashes' when they see a boy who has naturally long ones."

Yes, think of that.

I finished by spraying myself with one of Mama's colognes, and then I stood up and spun around, laughing at my image in the mirror, at my wonderful transformation.

What now? I thought when I stopped.

I looked at the bedroom doorway. Do I dare? It had been years and years since I'd worn girl's clothing in this house. Only in the turret room in secret or in my own room and bathroom had I uncovered my female body since those days in the woods, at my secret place.

My excitement gave me courage, but my heart pounded as I started toward the doorway. What if Mama suddenly appeared and caught me? What if she had changed her mind, was too worried about us, or had even had an argument with Dave Fletcher and was on her way back? What if she walked through that front door and confronted me? The very possibility nailed my feet to the floor. I couldn't walk out. I couldn't.

Then I looked back and saw myself caught in the vanity table mirror.

I'm beautiful, I thought. I truly am. I shouldn't be hidden away.

More firmly determined, I left the room and went to the top of the stairway. After all, I imagined, hadn't I just heard our doorbell? It was my date. Mama had let him in and he was standing down there and looking up in anticipation of my descent. I started down slowly, a soft smile on my lips, the same soft smile I recalled on Mama's when Daddy was alive and they were alone and didn't know I was watching.

There he would stand, my imaginary handsome boyfriend, standing at the doorway and looking up at me.

"You're beautiful," I would surely hear him tell me in a breathless voice of admiration.

"I am not," I would say, and blush to keep my veil of innocence and humility over my face.

Mama would step back. In fact, she would disappear into the wall because she couldn't prevent this. It would be like standing in the creek and trying to hold back the water with your bare hands. I flowed around her and finally over her.

My boyfriend would hold out his arm for me to take and we would walk out and get into his fine sporty, flashy, red automobile.

It was all there, all happening right before me if I only let it happen.

I descended the stairs.

Then I turned and walked into the living room and sat on the sofa as if it were the front seat of that car. I was in his car. I was.

"You drive carefully," we heard Mama call from the house.

His smile, my excitement, our anticipation, was an umbrella that kept the rest of the world away, kept it out there. Mama's words fell like rain and disappeared in the ground. We could hear only our own voices. He reached out and took my hand into his and squeezed it gently.

"I'm so happy you decided to go out with me. Thank you," he said. Of course he would say that.

All I did was smile and look down, thinking, be modest, be coy.

We drove off. Where would we go? A fine restaurant? A movie? To a dance club? Just somewhere beautiful where we could walk and be alone? No matter where we went, we longed to be alone. I could feel the need building inside me and I could see it building inside him, too.

We'd park, just as people on dates always did. He knew a place, a secluded place where no one would disturb us. When we drove in, he turned off the lights.

I did the same in the living room. I was sitting in the same sort of darkness now.

"I really like you, Celeste," he would say. "I've admired you for a long time and worked hard at getting up my courage to ask you out. If you had refused, it would have broken my heart, cracked it like an egg."

"Sure it would," I would say cynically. I was supposed to say that and then he was supposed to protest and vehemently assure me and reassure me that I was truly someone special in his eyes, the girl of his dreams.

"Not a night has gone by when I haven't closed my eyes and seen you and fantasized that you and I were together like this. I've waited for this night and for this kiss," he would say, and he would kiss me, and yes, it was wonderful and even better than Mr. Fletcher and Mama's kiss. It tingled down inside me, deep, into my very soul so that I softened in his arms and let his hands explore my body, a body I turned into him eagerly. It was as though I had been waiting for him for a thousand years. My surrender excited him more, and the more excited he became, the more I did.

I felt myself sliding down on the back of the sofa just the way I would in the car. I felt his hands behind my back, unzipping my dress, lowering it until my breasts were uncovered and he could bring his lips to them, to my nipples, to nudge them and moan and swoon over me.

It was like sinking slowly into a warm bath. I didn't stop his hands from moving under my skirt to my panties. Soon naked beneath him, I heard him whimper with delight and I heard him say, "I love you."

Our lovemaking was gentle and then our passion seized us and made us frantic with the need to please each other as well as ourselves. I cried out many times and he kissed me so many times, I felt he had left his lips on my cheeks and on my mouth. When it ended, it was like closing the covers of a wonderful book, a book about us. I was satisfied and yet disappointed that it was over.

"Love like this is so intense and so demanding, Celeste," he told me when I complained about it ending, "that if we didn't stop, we would destroy ourselves, explode, burst our hearts because of how full we filled them."

"Yes, yes," I would whisper, did whisper.

I closed my eyes and embraced myself, just realizing then that I was naked, that I had somehow taken off Mama's clothes as I had imagined in my fantasy. Then I heard a snicker and my eyes snapped open.

He was silhouetted in the doorway. I blinked and rubbed my eyes, but the shadow didn't go away. There was just enough light when he moved to the right to reveal his red hair.

"How did you get in here?" I whispered. Even though he stood in the darkest places, I could see his smile.

"You let me in," he said. "When you're like this, you let me step across. Don't you know that?"

I shook my head. I knew it, but I didn't want to know it, to believe it.

"If you didn't change, if you remained like this, if you would be who you are, your troubled little brother could come in, too. Instead, he's trapped out there in the darkness. Go to the window and look. Open it and listen."

"Get away," I cried.

"I'm not going to go away, and if your mother continues to do what she's doing, I'll be back many, many times." After a moment he added, "How's my baby?"

Then I heard him laugh. I hurried to gather up Mama's clothes.

"Or should I say *our* baby?"

As fast as I could, I turned on the nearest lamp. He was gone in the instant, decimated in the light, and I caught my breath. Then I hurried out of the living room and up the stairs, returning to Mama's room. As quickly as I could, I put back her clothes and I sat at the vanity table and wiped off the lipstick and rouge and eyeliner. My heart was thumping so hard, I thought I would faint and Mama would find me here the next day, still unconscious.

When I was done removing the makeup, I made sure the room was how I had found it, taking care to close every jar and tube on that vanity table. Afterward, I went into a hot shower and let the water practically burn my skin. I looked in on Celeste and saw she was quietly sleeping, undisturbed, that soft, little smile still on her lips. Her dreams were all good, I thought, and breathed easier.

This night I crawled into bed like someone lying down in her own coffin. I folded my arms over my stomach and pressed my hands together.

"You have to die again, Celeste," I whispered. "You have to go back."

It was truly as if I could press my female body back inside me. When I looked at my window on my left, I saw Elliot's face and hands pressed to the pane. He was on the outside looking in again. I had to keep him that way, keep him away from us. How could I get Mama to understand?

"Daddy," I whispered, "please come back to me. Please tell me what to do."

I waited to hear his voice.

The silence was painful. It made my ears ring. I turned over and buried my face in the pillow.

Tomorrow, maybe, I thought. Tomorrow he will come and I won't feel as alone and lost.

When I looked up again, Elliot's face was gone. Between two dark purple clouds, a star gleamed.

Daddy used to tell Noble and me that every star in the sky was another wish, another promise.

"How come there are so many?" Noble asked him.

"People wish for so many things. Aren't you wishing for things all day long? How about you, Celeste?"

"Yes," I said. "Lots of things."

"Mommy says the old well is a wishing well," Noble told him.

Daddy smiled. "Yes, that's about all it's good for now."

"I throw a rock in it every day and make a wish," Noble told him.

"Do you? What about you, Celeste?"

"She doesn't," Noble answered for me. "She thinks it's silly."

"I never said it was silly."

"Well, you don't do it."

"I wish on the stars like Daddy says instead," I said.

Noble looked angry but frustrated. "I don't care."

Daddy laughed. "What did you wish for today?"

Noble pressed his lips together and folded his arms tightly around himself.

"You don't have to tell," Daddy said, running his fingers through Noble's wild hair.

He looked up at Daddy and then looked at me. "I don't have any good friends. I wished Celeste was a boy."

I fell asleep envisioning a rock falling forever down the wishing well.

When it hit bottom, I woke with a start. I felt someone's presence and sat up to see Baby Celeste standing in my doorway with her doll in her arms.

"Celeste, what are you doing up?"

I swung my feet around to get out of bed.

"Woke me," she said.

I paused and smiled at her, then knelt down to look into her face. "Who woke you?"

She nodded out the doorway. Was Mama home?

"Mama?"

She shook her head.

"Then who woke you, Celeste?"

"Daddy," she said, and ran back to her room.

Like a person frozen in a chunk of ice I rose and heard the air crackle around me.

Then I followed her and watched her put her doll back in its little bed.

"Daddy woke you?" I asked her.

She smiled at me.

"Where's Daddy?"

She went to the window. I followed and looked out with her. I saw no one.

"You see Daddy, Celeste?"

She shook her head and raised her arms. "Gone."

I looked out again. Did she mean my daddy or did she mean Elliot?

Deep in my heart I understood that it wouldn't be long before I knew.

6

Thanksgiving

♊

Mama didn't return until late in the afternoon. She called in the morning to say she was on her way back, but they might stop for lunch, and if they did, she would do some shopping.

"You need some new things to wear, Noble. I expect you will be getting out and about soon and I want you to look good," she added.

What did she mean by out and about? Out and about where and for what purpose? Wondering about it made me nervous all day. I kept Baby Celeste occupied with games and reading, and then for lunch we pretended to have a picnic on the living room floor. I set out a blanket and played the radio. It was something we had done and she loved. Someday soon we'll have a real picnic out in the bright, warm sunshine, I thought, although I didn't know how or when.

I remembered the picnics we used to have when Daddy was alive. Noble loved them, as did I and even

Mama. We were all so happy then. It was hard to believe it could ever change, that anything evil could ever touch us or harm us, and that there would be a time when we wouldn't be together. How does that feeling, that wonderful feeling, ever get captured again? Maybe it never would.

After I put Baby Celeste in bed for her midday nap, I sat on the porch with the door open and the screen door closed. I would be able to hear her if she called to me. I regretted not being able to do any work around the farm. It was sunny, but a cold front had made its way south from Canada and the afternoon temperatures were unusually low for the time of the year. It was more like a beautiful fall day, a perfect day for the kind of work I had left to do.

About four o'clock, I saw Mr. Fletcher's car turn into our driveway. I rose quickly and went into the house. Baby Celeste was still asleep. I crouched by the front window in the living room and watched as the car came to a stop in front of the house. Mr. Fletcher hopped out instantly and ran around to open Mama's door. They were both laughing at something. He opened the rear door and took out some shopping bags. I could see he wanted to carry everything into the house for her, but she told him she could manage. I knew she wasn't sure if Baby Celeste was upstairs asleep or not.

They kissed again and Mama started for the house.

"I'll call you later," he sang out, got into his car, and backed it up. She stood on the porch watching him turn the car around and drive off before she entered the house. I met her in the hallway.

"Is everything all right?" she asked immediately.

I didn't want her to know I had been spying on her through the window, but I was sure she saw it in my eyes. Sometimes I believed that what I looked at remained on the surface of my eyes and Mama could see it. It was futile to deny having looked at something forbidden.

"Yes, Mama."

"Where's the baby?"

"She's still taking her afternoon nap."

"Good. Here." She held out one of the shopping bags toward me. "There are some very nice new shirts for you, socks, and two pairs of jeans."

She started for the stairway.

"Where were you? I thought you were coming home much earlier," I said, following.

She turned, smiling down at me.

"You sound like my father, Noble. 'Where were you?' he would ask in a similarly grouchy tone. And he would stand just like you're standing with your hands on your hips. The men in this family are surely cut from the same cloth."

I lowered my hands quickly. "I was worried."

"Worried? I called. You knew I was coming home about now. Stop being such a . . . a nervous Nellie." She laughed to herself and continued up the stairway.

I looked back at the doorway as if Mr. Fletcher were still present and then I hurried up after her. Despite how I had cleaned up and reorganized her things, I couldn't help being afraid that when she went into her bedroom, she would know I had been there and I had done what I had done with her makeup and clothes.

But she wasn't behaving like my insightful mother, my perceptive, gifted mother. She was acting more like a teenage girl, giggling over the events of her date, babbling to me nonstop about the way Mr. Fletcher and she had enjoyed this wonderful dinner and slept in what was often used as the honeymoon suite. She raved about the beautiful grounds.

"The place had a lake. As soon as we finished breakfast, we went for a rowboat ride. I can't remember the last time I did something like that. It was like being in a Venetian gondola. There I was lying back with a wildflower in my hair and he was rowing and singing in Italian. He has a very nice voice, you know.

"I hated to leave the place, but we went to this enormous mall. I felt like someone from another planet, or at least another country. I couldn't get over the size of the place. Dave found it amusing, but believe me, you could spend weeks there without seeing it all, Noble, and there were so many nice restaurants from which to choose for lunch. I had Mexican food. I hadn't had that since your father courted me.

"Anyway, I wasn't bored for a second, not a second," she said, unpacking her bag.

She looked at herself in the vanity table mirror, and for a long moment I thought she was going to realize I had been at the table, but she was really just looking at her own hair and face.

"Dave thinks I have remarkably young-looking skin. I guess I do. Of course, that's no accident. Look at what I bought myself," she quickly added, and took a sheer, pink negligee out of her bag. She held it up against herself. "Well? Don't just stand there like someone unconscious with his eyes open, Noble. Isn't it exquisite?"

"Yes," I said, but from the smirk on her face, I knew I didn't sound excited enough for her.

"Why don't you go try on your new clothes? I might have to shorten your jeans. Go on. Put on a pair and come back here," she said with some annoyance.

She turned back to her bag, but after another pause, she continued to talk to me as if she had immediately forgotten her disappointment.

"Do you know what Dave's favorite love song is, Noble? 'La Vie en Rose.' Isn't that remarkable? It was your father's favorite love song, too. I haven't played it since he died, but I will play it again. I'll play it for Dave the first chance I get when he comes to the house."

"You're inviting him here?"

"Of course I'm inviting him here. Don't you understand anything?"

I shook my head. How was she going to manage all this, manage Baby Celeste? Or did she expect me to hide upstairs with her?

"Just go try on those jeans, Noble. I don't have the patience for your stupidity at the moment. Go on," she ordered, waving me off.

Dazed, I went to my room and did what she asked. Before I could return, she came to my room. She had put all of her things away and changed into one of her housecoats. Now she looked more like herself with the makeup gone, too.

"Just as I thought," she said, kneeling to pin up my cuffs. "I need to raise it about an inch and a half. Okay. Take them off. I'll do it as soon as I can."

Baby Celeste, hearing her voice, cried out.

"Oh, good, she's up," Mama said, and hurried to her room.

I took off the new jeans and put on my old ones. As I was doing so, I heard Mama running a bath in her bathroom. Why was she doing that? I wondered. It was too early to give Baby Celeste her bath, I thought, but when I peered into the bathroom, she was doing just that. She had the baby in the tub.

"Why are you giving her a bath now, Mama?"

Baby Celeste looked up at me and smiled.

Mama didn't answer. She poured one of her herbal

shampoos over Baby Celeste's head and began to scrub the dye out of her hair. I watched astonished as she rinsed it and the full rich color of her red hair was restored.

"Why are you doing that, Mama?" I asked breathlessly.

"Because it's time." She turned and looked at me with a harder, colder, more determined expression on her face. Her eyes were dark, too. "It's time. Time to greet tomorrow."

Time to greet tomorrow? What did that mean?

"You can go back to work now, Noble. There is still a lot of daylight left. Go see to your chores."

I didn't move.

She spun on me. "Well?"

"Okay, Mama."

I walked down the stairs slowly. I couldn't help having troubled thoughts. So much was changing, and quickly, too. Our world was going through some sort of upheaval. In so many ways, I should be happy about it, I thought, but I wasn't happy as much as I was frightened. Tomorrow suddenly felt like a threat.

I worked outside until Mama called me in for dinner. Seeing Baby Celeste with a full head of rich red hair was startling, but Mama didn't skip a beat. It was almost as if she didn't notice what she had done.

"We're going to have a little dinner party a week from tonight," she announced when we sat at the table.

"Dinner party? What do you mean, Mama?"

"I'm going to bring out the best china and use my grandmother's linen tablecloth. It will be a very special night. It's time Dave got to know you, Noble."

I felt my throat close up and fought to get it open so I could speak.

"You're inviting Mr. Fletcher to dinner here?"

"That's the idea of a dinner party, Noble. You invite guests. In this case we'll just have one." She leaned over to wipe some cranberry juice off Baby Celeste's chin.

"But what about Baby Celeste?"

"What about her?"

I shook my head slowly, fear building inside me. What was it she wanted me to say, to think? What truth was I to ignore? Should I come right out and ask her if she wasn't worried he would see his son in Baby Celeste's face? The way Mama talked about her, she had no genetic makeup but that which came from our family, and her side of it to be more exact.

"I mean, he'll see her," was as much as I dared say.

Mama turned from me to Baby Celeste and shook her head sadly.

"Oh, yes," she said as if just remembering it all. "Poor little Celeste. How dreadful."

"What?" I asked, and held my breath.

"My second cousin on my mother's side, Lucinda Heavenstone, and her husband, Roger, killed in a car accident, and both so young with so much to live for. As you know, Lucinda's parents are both deceased," Mama continued, turning to me and reciting. "Roger's father had that bad stroke two years ago, remember? And his mother, of course, died giving birth to Roger. His stepmother wants nothing to do with caring for Roger's father or poor little Celeste, now left all alone in the world.

"Except for us. How could we not take her in?" Mama asked me. "And how she has taken to us. Such an exceptional child, don't you think?

"Anyway, what's family for if we can't do a good Christian thing like this? We can't let her go off and live with strangers, be farmed out to some foster care, now can we, Noble?"

I stared at her. Would Mr. Fletcher believe such a story? Would anyone? On the other hand, would anyone care whether it was true or not?

Mama looked so confident, and yet the way she smiled made her face look more like a mask. She had something else to say, something else in her mind.

As if on cue, as if she knew how precisely to time everything, Mama turned toward the kitchen just as the phone rang.

"I'm expecting a call," she told me, and got up.

I listened as hard as I could.

"Oh, Dave," I heard her say, "something terrible has happened. I won't be able to see you tomorrow. I have to go to Pennsylvania. A young cousin of mine and her husband were killed in a terrible car accident. They were hit head-on by one of those dreadful tractor-trailer trucks. They're both dead, but miraculously, their child escaped serious injury. . . . Yes . . . No, I'm not going just for the funeral. I'm going to bring their baby back here. A little girl barely three years old. There's no one else. . . . Yes, yes, it's a horrible affair. I know you understand. I appreciate that. . . . No, I'll be fine. Thanks for offering. I'll call you as soon as I return. . . . Thank you. I'll be fine, Dave. Please. . . . Yes, I know, but what does family mean if I can't do this? . . . Me, too. I'll call you as soon as I can."

I heard her hang up.

When she returned to the dining room, both Baby Celeste and I looked up at her.

She smiled at us. "Don't look so worried, children. Everything is going just the way I was told it would."

Baby Celeste clapped her hands as if she understood every word. My eyes met Mama's and held. For the first time ever, it was she who shifted away first. She busied herself with clearing the table.

"Take the baby into the living room," she ordered. "I'll be there soon. I want to practice 'La Vie en Rose,'" she added, threw a smile my way, and went into the kitchen.

I lifted Baby Celeste out of her chair and took her into the living room. I felt so weak and frightened inside, I thought I might drop her, so I put her down quickly. Tonight she wanted to look at pictures in albums. A collection of them was on a shelf of a side table. Some of the pictures were so old they were faded nearly to the point where nothing could be clearly seen. Baby Celeste would sit with an album opened on her lap and look at the photos for hours if we let her. How she could be so interested in people she had never met or seen intrigued me. She loved to point out babies and children.

There were some photographs of Noble and me, and when she looked at them, she invariably pointed to Noble and said, "Noble." I could never tell if she saw him or saw me in the pictures, but she did stare with greater interest at my picture.

"The first Celeste," I would whisper to her. She wouldn't speak. She would look at me and then back at the picture.

What went on in that little head of hers? I wondered. What did she think when she heard the name and looked at me? What was she really capable of knowing?

When Mama came in, she went right to the piano and began to practice the song. After a while, she began to sing it, too, sing it in French. She had a beautiful voice. Why wouldn't Mr. Fletcher fall head over heels in love with her? Why wouldn't anyone?

Before she was finished, she looked to one of the front windows and then back at me, expectantly.

"I knew the song would bring him, Noble," she said.
I stared at the window.

Bring him? Bring whom? Daddy? Her smile told me that was whom she saw.

But there was just darkness there for me. I waited anxiously for his smiling face, but the face I saw when I finally saw one take shape was not Daddy's. It was Elliot's. I turned sharply to see if Mama saw him, too, but she was singing again and quite lost in her own thoughts.

Tell her, I thought, tell her before it's too late. If she looks up quickly enough, she will see, too, and she will believe you.

I didn't cry out. I just didn't have the courage, and moments later there was only darkness in the window. When I finally went up to bed, I couldn't stop the trembling. I had a terrible case of the chills and thought I might be coming down with something, but eventually I fell asleep, and when I woke, I was fine.

The following day Mama remained secluded. She didn't set foot out of the house. After all, she was supposed to have gone to Pennsylvania to get Baby Celeste and bring her home to us. At dinnertime she received a phone call from Mrs. Zalkin, who was bringing a friend the next day to purchase some herbal skin creams Mama had created.

"This is perfect," she told me after she hung up. "It's all going so perfectly."

I had no idea why until I realized Mama did not ask me to take Baby Celeste up to the turret room when they arrived. The moment they set their surprised eyes on her, Mama looked at me and winked. She began her story and they listened with faces full of sympathy and understanding, but also with some underlying skepticism, which to my surprise didn't bother Mama at all.

They left praising her for her wonderful act of charity, but they looked at each other and practically winked.

With Baby Celeste in her arms, Mama stood on the porch and watched them drive off. Then she smiled and turned to me.

"It's only a matter of days now before the whole community knows," she said. "It wasn't just a coincidence that one of the busiest busybodies came to see us today, you know. Oh, how the rumors will fly. It will be like an attack of locusts." She laughed strangely.

My heart should have been singing with joy. Baby Celeste was freed, released from the prison of nonexistence. She could burst onto the world, play in sunlight, go on trips with us, come alive.

But my second self was full of warnings. It was truly like waiting for the second shoe to fall, and fall it would. That night Mama called Dave Fletcher and invited him to her special dinner as she had planned. From what she had told me, I knew that people in the community were already buzzing about her romance with Mr. Fletcher. Slowly she had filled the trough of gossip, implying to her nosy clients that this affair had emerged from secrecy, that it had been going on for some time. Some people even claimed to have known, which amused Mama even more.

"They wondered how I could be so disinterested in men, and they wondered why Mr. Fletcher never had any romantic interest with all the available widows and divorcées floating about the community. Now, they all think they have the answer. Are you beginning to understand, Noble?" she asked.

Of course, I did. All of it had been running like an underground stream below my conscious thoughts. Mama believed our spiritual family had planned and arranged it, and they were still actively at work on everything to follow. Anyone who looked at Mama, Mr. Fletcher, and Baby Celeste together now would come to the conclusions Mama wanted./She didn't have to worry about anyone discovering that her story about cousins in a tragic accident was fictitious. Not only would she never have to face the truth, no one would ever know the truth. No one would ever know who I really was. In another way, an effective and admittedly clever way, she had buried me even deeper.

So my joy for Baby Celeste was tempered and short-lived. Her coming out was my eternal burial. I tried to be happier, be the way Mama wanted, especially in front of others, but it was like being draped in a dark cloud and looking at the world through eyes veiled in gauze.

All that following week, Mama had both Baby Celeste and me accompany her on every shopping trip. Once she had kept Baby Celeste hidden from the very sun, and now she wanted as many eyes to see her as possible. She deliberately attracted the attention of the women she knew were gossipmongers, whether we were in one of the malls, department stores, or on the streets of the nearby village.

She had a wonderful spiel and rattled it off with great dramatics.

"When my cousin had her child," she told the mayor's wife, "she called me immediately to ask if I minded her naming the baby after my poor lost Celeste. Of course, I thought it was a wonderful gesture and told her to please go right ahead. So here she is," she said, bouncing Baby Celeste in her arms, "my Celeste. It's all a tragedy, but look at the beautiful, blessed child that has been born of it."

She nearly brought them all to tears.

Afterward, she smiled and told me, "No matter what they think about Dave Fletcher and me, they'll keep it locked up like some very deep secret. They love my story too much. They're so full of confusions that they'll never spread bad gossip about Baby Celeste. She won't have to hide her head when she is older. If anything, she will be on the receiving end of their pity."

When I looked at the faces of these people, I saw Mama was right. How well she knew them. How could I ever question anything she did or thought?

"And the baby has taken so to Noble," she told them. "It's as if she has been with him since the day she was born. He's very good with her, too," she added, looking proudly at me. "It's been just as lonely for him as it has been for me, but you have your Celeste again, don't you, my son?" she would ask me in front of them.

"Yes," I would say.

You see, I was already a part of it all, already in the web she had woven with her spirits.

But no moment was more terrifying for me than the night Mr. Fletcher came to our house for the dinner party, the night he would set eyes on his own grand-daughter and not know it, and the night he would set eyes on me again.

Mama was more nervous than I had ever seen her about her cooking, about the table, and about our home and how it looked. I wasn't sure which of us was more anxious about Mr. Fletcher's impending arrival. Only Baby Celeste seemed unchanged. Even the days full of travel and shopping, being outside and meeting other people for the first time in her life, didn't seem to have had as dramatic an impact on her as I had anticipated it might. It was truly as though she had expected it would all happen just this way. No one could tell she had been sequestered all her life.

Mama had decided to roast a turkey. It was like a Thanksgiving dinner, and not by accident either.

"Dave didn't have a Thanksgiving last year," she told me. "His daughter wasn't home and he didn't feel like traveling to New York to visit with his relatives. He's not that close to his family anyway, which is what I expected. It all works so well for us, you see. It's truly our Thanksgiving, Noble."

She prepared all the fixings as well. She stuffed the turkey, made creamed onions and sweet potato pudding. She had cranberry sauce and homemade bread. For dessert she made another rhubarb pie, but this time she would have vanilla ice cream for it. The house was filled with wonderful aromas and my stomach churned in anticipation, almost driving out the butterflies.

The table had been set since midafternoon. Every once in a while, Mama would step into the dining room and change something, replace a glass, move a plate, fix the flowers, and inspect the silverware. She was undecided as to whether I should sit across from Mr. Fletcher or beside him, and she changed the seating arrangements twice before concluding I should sit beside him.

"I don't want you staring at him and making him feel self-conscious," she said. "I know you, Noble. You can do that without even realizing what you're doing."

Maybe she was right. The only time I could recall being as nervous in front of strangers was when I had had to go to the school to take the high school equivalency test. I was putting Noble Atwell down as my name. The teacher who monitored the exam seemed to stare at me with intense scrutiny from time to time. I did my best to ignore him, but sometimes my hand shook as I wrote.

The hour before Mr. Fletcher was to arrive, I sat in

the living room and kept Baby Celeste occupied.
Mama relented on her usual televison restrictions, too,
and permitted us to watch some children's shows.

"My cousins would certainly have let her watch
television endlessly," she remarked from the doorway
as we watched. "I know how young parents are today.
They use the idiot box as a babysitter. They don't want
to spend all that much time teaching and instructing
their children. They're too selfish."

She spoke about the fictitious cousins as if she
really believed they had existed. It made me feel as if I
were an actor in a play, especially when she wanted
me to reinforce everything she said. After all, it was
still a drama we had to perform for Mr. Fletcher.

"You remember how they were when they visited us
a year ago, Noble? Remember?"

She waited for my reply.

I nodded. "Yes, Mama."

"Right," she said, pleased. And then, before Mr.
Fletcher's car pulled up in front of our house, she declared, "He's here. Just be yourself and don't make
him feel a bit uncomfortable."

Don't make him feel uncomfortable? Was she
blind? Couldn't she see how I was shaking inside, or
did she simply want to ignore it?

I heard the car door shut. Baby Celeste looked up
and away from the television set.

"Shut off the television and get her up to go into the
dining room," Mama instructed.

She went to the door before Mr. Fletcher had time
to use the knocker.

"Welcome," I heard her cry.

I lifted Baby Celeste into my arms, took a deep
breath, and walked into the hallway just as they finished embracing. She turned to us.

"You remember my son, Noble," she said.

"Yes, of course. Hi, Noble," Mr. Fletcher said.

If any painful memories were clouding his brain, he kept them well hidden. He smiled warmly at me. It had been nearly three years now since I had really looked at him. His reddish-brown hair had some gray streaks. I didn't recall that, but I did recall how similar his build was to Elliot's. He looked a few inches more than six feet, slimmer perhaps. I couldn't forget those turquoise eyes, eyes Elliot had inherited. Baby Celeste's were more a cerulean with tiny green specs. Like Elliot, Mr. Fletcher had a slight cleft and even some fine freckles about the bridge of his nose and across the crests of his cheeks.

"Hi," I said.

"Hi," Baby Celeste said without any coaxing. She had a wide, happy smile, too.

Mr. Fletcher laughed. "What a delightful child. I guess she feels at home here already."

Mama nodded. "She makes it easy for us. You'll be amazed at how sweet and loving a personality she has. Come in, come in."

She closed the door and I stepped back. He smiled at me again.

"Let me show you some of the house. I've been doing some redecorating," Mama told him. "Noble, would you get the baby situated in the dining room. We'll be right there."

"Yes, Mama."

"Yes, this is nice," Mr. Fletcher declared as soon as he looked into the living room. "The piano looks like a real antique."

"It is, but I keep it tuned. I'll play something for you later," I heard her promise him.

I brought Baby Celeste into the dining room and set her in her booster chair. I could hear them talking as they walked through the downstairs. Occasionally, Mama's laughter floated back.

"I thought I had an interesting old house, but this place is fascinating," he told her in the hallway.

"We think so. We always did," she told him.

"Well," Mr. Fletcher said, stepping into the dining room with her, "this is absolutely beautiful. What a nice table. I'm overwhelmed, Sarah."

"It's nothing." Then, indicating the chair beside me, she said, "Here is where you should sit."

He nodded. "Is there anything I can do to help?"

"Yes," she said. "Enjoy the meal."

He laughed. "I don't expect that to be very difficult," he said, and turned to me.

I couldn't help cringing inside, but his face was full of warmth and friendliness.

"You've gotten pretty tall, Noble. Your mother is very proud of the work you do around here, too. Your ears probably were itching all the time she's been with me."

Mama smiled. "Dave's grandmother, it seems, was full of superstitions and old ideas."

"Whose wasn't?" he said. "If your ears itch, someone's talking about you. If your palms itch, you'll be getting money."

"If a knife falls off the table, you'll have visitors," Mama chimed.

They both laughed like two conspirators who had been rehearsing their lines for days. When they laughed, Baby Celeste laughed.

"She is a delight," Mr. Fletcher declared. "And after all she's been through."

"Yes, we were afraid she'd be up all night with nightmares, but fortunately, she's taken to us quickly. Why, she's even calling me Mama," Mama told him.

"Really?" He was impressed. "Well, that will make

things easier for you, Sarah, although"—his face
soured with his personal problems—"it's not easy
bringing up young people these days." He looked at
me and nodded. "Not everyone is as fortunate as you
are. You probably made a brilliant decision when you
decided to homeschool your children and keep them
away from all the bad influences out there."

"Exactly. Now, when Noble goes out in the world,
he will have a sensible, strong way about him. He's responsible, honest, and very loyal," Mama added with
her eyes on me.

Mr. Fletcher shook his head in admiration. "I envy
you, Sarah. A woman alone and you've made such a
beautiful home and now a nice little business with your
herbal remedies and all. You live in an early twentieth-
century home, but you're a modern day woman to me."

Mama blushed at the compliment. I couldn't remember when I had last seen her blush. Could it be
that she really liked this man? Could their love be so
strong as to overcome even the secrets we kept locked
in our hearts?

Mr. Fletcher looked at Baby Celeste so intently, I
was sure he was seeing Elliot's face. My heart
pounded. Mama looked to be holding her breath as
well.

"Da da," Baby Celeste suddenly said.

Mr. Fletcher's eyebrows nearly leaped off his face.
His eyes widened with surprise.

My heart stopped beating. I was sure of it.

Then he laughed.

"See," Mama cried, "she's adopted you already. I
hope you feel like you are with family."

My mouth fell open. Did she dare tempt the truth, a
truth poised to leap out at us all and bring down everything in what would be total destruction?

Mr. Fletcher beamed. He looked around the table, smiling at Baby Celeste, smiling at me, then nodding.

"It really does feel like Thanksgiving, Sarah," he said. "I can't thank you enough."

He doesn't know, I thought. He doesn't understand. Mama looked at me, and in her face I saw her pleasure and her confidence.

Her eyes shifted toward Baby Celeste, who was looking at her with a face that had a remarkably similar expression.

It was the tomorrow Mama had predicted.

I had no idea where it would lead us, but I felt like someone caught in a strong wind or an ocean wave. All I could do was surrender to the future.

7

The Weakened Walls

♊

Mama outdid herself. It was her best dinner ever. Mr. Fletcher's mouth was as filled with compliments as it was with the succulent turkey and delicious stuffing, and when she brought out his favorite pie, he looked ready to give her whatever she wanted. That adage embroidered on a small plaque in the kitchen, *The way to a man's heart is through his stomach,* never looked truer.

He took a forkful of pie, put it in his mouth, and closed his eyes with pleasure.

"And I thought I was a half-decent cook," he told me. "Nothing lets you know how much of a bachelor you are as when you actually believe you enjoy your own cooking, Noble. Beware of that." He laughed.

When the dinner ended, he insisted on helping Mama clear the table. She refused. She wanted him to adjourn to the living room with Baby Celeste and me. I was terrified of being with him without Mama.

Thankfully he insisted. "I do it every night for myself, Sarah."

"But you are our guest."

"I'd rather like to continue to feel I'm part of a family rather than just another guest," he countered, in magical words.

"That's very nice of you, Dave. Noble, take the baby into the living room. We'll be in as soon as we finish here."

Relieved, I quickly did what she asked. Baby Celeste occupied herself with her doll and teacup set, but I noticed she kept looking to the doorway in anticipation of Mr. Fletcher and Mama. We could hear them laughing in the kitchen.

Afterward, they came into the living room and Mr. Fletcher sat on the settee to listen to Mama play. To his surprise and mine, Baby Celeste crawled up beside him and leaned against him. He looked at me, smiled, then put his arm around her.

"Hello there," he said, and she looked up at him, her eyes twinkling. "What a special child she is, Sarah. No wonder you didn't hesitate to take her into your home. I'd take her in myself in a heartbeat."

"I'm sure you would," Mama said, throwing me a conspiratorial glance. It made my heart freeze. Surely he would soon realize who Baby Celeste really was. Mama always said blood was thicker than water.

She began playing some of her Mozart sonatas, and then she played "La Vie en Rose." I watched Mr. Fletcher's face soften, and his eyes fill with love and appreciation. I had expected it and seen hints of it, but somehow, being in the same room with the two of them and feeling the heat in the air between them, I was truly amazed at how palpable the emotions between them were. The past seemed to have been completely erased, forgotten. Mama truly could do whatever she wanted, but more important perhaps, she could get other people to do what she wanted.

When Baby Celeste fell asleep to the music, Mama asked me to take her up and put her to bed. I lifted her in my arms, and when I leaned over to do so, my eyes met Mr. Fletcher's. He looked at me with new interest, his gaze seeming to reach down into my heart, reaching inside me. I had to move away quickly, fearful he would see all the deception and fear in my eyes.

After I put Baby Celeste asleep, I started down the stairway, and midway I heard their conversation.

"Noble looks like such a sensitive, gentle young man," he told Mama. "That's rare these days. The teenage boys I see all look unwashed, lazy, actually bored with life, and certainly not gentle enough to care for a little girl."

"Yes, he's a wonderful son," Mama said. "A very unselfish young man."

"But doesn't he get lonely here though, Sarah? A boy that age should be out among his peers, even though I don't approve of the way teenagers conduct themselves these days. A boy this age still needs to socialize, don't you think? He should be thinking more about girls, too. I don't mean to poke my nose in where it doesn't belong. I'm just impressed with him and want what's best for him, for both of you."

"You're not poking your nose into any forbidden places, Dave. Yes. Noble should get out more. I suppose it's my fault. I don't encourage it enough, but he's been introverted ever since we lost Celeste."

"Yes, I know how devastating that must have been. The police never found any clues?"

"Nothing. It was like a ghost had taken her."

"How horrible for you, for you both."

"Yes. You have to remember Noble lost his father at a young age, too. They were so close. I can see him to this day standing on that front porch for hours waiting for my husband's truck to appear, and when it did, the joy in his face was electric. Those eyes lit up like stars. He absolutely idolized his father, and to see him die when he appeared so strong . . . well, it shook Noble up something terrible."

"I understand."

"The combination of those losses was very, very traumatic, Dave. The only time he started to emerge was when he met your son. I was tempted then to permit him to attend public school. He was making such an improvement. I wanted it to continue."

That was a lie. Why was she telling him such a thing?

"I know. I wish I had encouraged their friendship more. I see that now," Mr. Fletcher said. "I was a fool to listen to all the gossip about you."

"It's understandable. You were new in the community and you had just been through a bad marriage. Here you were with two teenagers. Why shouldn't you be extracautious?

"Anyway," Mama continued, "the tragic death of your son, his one real friend, was another devastating blow. I had my hands full just to get him to go out and tend to his chores, much less return to the stream to fish or walk through the forest. He went through a period when he did believe the nasty gossip about us. We only could bring harm and catastrophe to anyone with whom we had contact. It turned him into a real introvert, made him afraid of getting too close to anyone. I did the best I could, the best I could."

I heard her sigh deeply.

"I know he belongs in some sort of professional therapy, but for now I'd like to keep trying to help him myself. There's enough of a stigma on him just being my child, much less to add all the connotations that are acquired when a person goes into therapy, and don't think it would be kept secret. Not in this community of busybodies."

"I understand. Maybe, if you permit, I can get him out and about, take him fishing perhaps, go on hikes."

"I'd like that, but we have to move slowly."

"Yes, of course. You're a terrific woman, Sarah. I haven't met anyone with as much understanding, tolerance of people, and sympathy for them as you have. You have such a contentment about you, such a spiritual balance."

"I am who I am."

"Well, I for one am glad you are who you are."

They were quiet for a long moment. They couldn't be just sitting there looking at each other.

They're kissing, I concluded. It was as if I could see through the walls. They had embraced. She put her lips close to his and they kissed.

I turned and as quietly as possible went back upstairs to my room. I closed the door and, with the lights off, went to my bed and lay there staring into the darkness.

In the room below, Mama and Mr. Fletcher were probably still embracing, kissing, perhaps doing much more by now. Such imaginings sent my mind reeling back through time. I was in the forest again. I was alone and I was free to be who I was. I had taken off my brother's clothes and unstrapped my breasts. The cool air was refreshing and my body tingled with such pleasure, I nearly came to tears.

Then I heard a branch crack.

It was more like a clap of thunder.

I opened my eyes slowly, and when I looked up, I

saw Elliot standing there gazing down at me, his
mouth twisted, his eyes wide. I felt every muscle in my
body freeze. His lips moved, but for a few moments
nothing came out, no words, no sounds. He looked to
be having trouble swallowing. I was still, deathly still.
Finally he spoke.

"You're a girl?" he asked, to confirm what his eyes
were saying.

All of it, all that followed, returned with a vividness
that made me moan aloud. I could feel him inside me,
his hands all over me. I was helpless, trapped in the deception my mother had made me assume. She had put
me in harm's way, I thought. It wasn't my fault. None
of it was my fault. It would never be my fault.

"No," I heard Daddy whisper. "It's not your fault,
princess."

I turned and I saw him standing there. He caressed
my face. He leaned down and kissed my cheek.

"What she's doing is wrong," he said, nodding at
the floor and what was happening below. "She's making a big mistake. Try to stop her. Try."

"She won't listen to me," I moaned.

"She will if you try," he insisted. "You must do it
for all of us, Celeste, all of us."

"I'll try," I promised.

He began to back up. "Try," he urged. "Try."

"Daddy!" I called, but he was absorbed into the wall
and in a moment was gone. Was he there? Did I wish
for him so hard that I imagined him there and heard
him say the words I wanted to hear?

Below I heard the sound of the piano. Mama was
playing again. It was soft and lovely, the sort of music
that would beguile an unsuspecting soul. I drifted off,
then woke to Mama's calling up to me.

"Come down and say good-night to Dave, Noble,"

she told me when I rose and went out to the top of the stairway. "It's not polite to withdraw without saying good-night to our guest," she added with firmness.

I scrubbed my cheeks to wake myself and descended the stairs. Mama waited a moment to be sure I was coming, then she went back into the living room.

"Oh, she didn't have to disturb you, Noble," Mr. Fletcher said, standing when I entered.

"It's all right. Good night. Thanks for coming," I told him, unable not to sound mechanical, rehearsed.

Nevertheless, he smiled. "Maybe one of these days you and I can do some fishing. Doesn't have to be in the creek. I hear Masten Lake is pretty good for bass. What do you think? Do you know it?"

I looked at Mama and then nodded.

"Great. I'm going to have all of you over to my place soon. Of course, we'll arrange it so your mother does all the cooking." He laughed.

He started for the doorway and I stepped back. He paused and extended his hand.

"Night, Noble."

"Good night," I said, shaking his hand.

"Man, those are callused palms. You're working him to the bone, Sarah."

Mama laughed and followed him out. She stepped onto the porch and closed the door behind her. I was just about to the top of the stairway when she returned.

"Noble," she called.

I looked back and she walked into the living room. What did she want? I started down again.

"You did well," she said, sitting on the settee. She smiled. "It wasn't as hard as you thought it would be either, was it?"

I didn't know what to say, so I just shook my head. She leaned back and looked up at the ceiling.

"You know what he said to me tonight? He said two people like us don't belong alone. Together, we could make a whole new life for ourselves, for the children."

"What did he mean?" I asked, unable to hide my fear.

"What did he mean? What did he mean? How can you be so clever at times and then so stupid at others? It was as close as he could come to asking me to marry him. That's what he meant."

"But . . . what did you say?" The very idea of it was terrifying.

"I didn't say anything, Noble. A woman doesn't leap at a man's first offer. She doesn't make herself sound desperate or even that interested. Instead, she fills him with doubts so his own confidence dwindles."

"Why?"

"So he knows that when a woman says yes, if she does, it's a woman's decision, fully, and it's a woman's gift. That way," she added, turning her tone darker and gazing down at the floor, "no matter what happens, it's his fault."

"You're not thinking of saying yes ever, are you, Mama?" I asked, thinking of my promise to Daddy.

"Of course, I am."

"But I thought all you wanted was to have him blamed for fathering Celeste. You said people are thinking that already. Why do you have to carry this any further?"

"What did I tell you about challenging my decisions, *their* decisions," she emphasized, her eyes wide and full of gathering rage.

"Maybe it isn't their decision, Mama. Maybe you're hearing the wrong voices, evil voices pretending to be good." Never before in my life had I dared make such a suggestion to her, but it seemed a reasonable way to disagree.

She lifted her head and turned her eyes toward me so slowly, it made my blood cold. Her eyes grew smaller as she scrutinized me.

"What are you saying? Who have you heard? Who has been visiting you, Noble?" she asked quickly.

I took a deep breath and sat on Grandfather's chair. How careful my words had to be.

"I've seen Elliot," I said. "I've heard him, too. He's warned me that if you continue with his father, he will have more power to do us harm."

For a long moment she looked as if she was considering what I had said. Some hope filled my heart. Then her expression of suspicion returned and she looked at me hard again.

"Did he come into this house?"

I started to shake my head, but my eyes were already saying yes.

She nearly jumped at me. "He did, didn't he? When?"

"When you were away with Mr. Fletcher."

She smiled, but it was not a warm smile. The smile was carved out of ice.

"What did you do, Noble? What did you do to give him entry into our world? Tell me!" she screamed.

"Nothing."

She shook her head. "You might as well wave a flag with the words *I'm lying* written on it in my face," she said softly. "You know that. Well?"

It was suddenly hard to breathe. I felt as if the walls were closing in on me, and as they moved toward me, the air thickened and thickened, squeezing my ribs. I looked about frantically.

Daddy, I thought. Daddy, where are you? I need your help. Why aren't you here? Daddy? You came to me so quickly before. You told me what to do. Please, Daddy. I need you. She'll listen to you. Please.

I looked about frantically.

Mama's eyes darkened. She turned and looked toward the windows where I was looking, then she fixed her eyes back on me.

"Whom are you looking for, Noble? Who is supposed to help you?"

I didn't want to tell her about Daddy's visit and what he had said, too. She would accuse me of lying to get out of being caught in a lie.

"Nobody," I said quickly.

"Then answer my questions, Noble. What did you do to weaken our walls?" she demanded.

"Nothing."

"You're lying again. I repeat, what did you do? I'll find out anyway. It's better if you tell me, better if you begin to purge yourself, Noble. Well?"

She was right. I couldn't lie to her, not now, not with her bearing down on me with those eyes.

"I . . . I was just curious."

"About what?"

"About your makeup, your clothes."

Her face brightened with the blood that rushed up her neck and into her cheeks. There was so much fire in her eyes that I couldn't look at her. I shifted mine toward the floor and waited like someone anticipating a whip snapping on her back.

"You used my makeup again? You put on my clothes?"

I didn't reply. When I was younger, I had experimented with her makeup after spying on Betsy when the Fletchers had first moved next to us.

She nodded, a new look of calm on her face, but calmness in her now was even more threatening.

"I want you to go up to your room and remain there until I tell you to come out again," she said.

I knew what that meant. Oh, how well I knew.

"No, Mama, please."

"I'll help you," she said, continuing her reasonable tone of voice.

I kept shaking my head.

"I don't want you touching the baby, talking to her, even looking her way until I say it's all right to do so, even after I let you come out again."

"Mama, no, please . . ."

"Go upstairs, Noble. I'll bring you something soon."

I had to tell her; I had to tell her everything and take the chance.

"Mama, listen to me. I didn't see only Elliot. Daddy came to me. He came to me tonight. He told me you were making a very big mistake."

She smiled again, that same chilling grin.

"That wasn't your father. Haven't I told you many, many times that evil can assume a pleasing identity to get us to put down our guard?"

"It was Daddy. It was."

"You're such a fool, I do worry about you. Without me, what would happen to you?" She leaned toward me and in a hoarse whisper said, "It was your father who brought this whole plan to me."

She sat back again, nodding.

"What?"

"That's right. This didn't just come out of thin air. He was the one."

I shook my head, but she continued to smile at me as if I was the one very, very mistaken.

"I wondered why you weren't seeing or hearing him for so long. When I asked him, he told me not to worry

about it, but this explains it. You had darkness in your
heart. You had doubt. Without the faith you cannot
cross over, Noble. You cannot be with our good family
spirits.

"It's my mistake," she said. "I have been concentrating on all this so hard, I missed the signals."

"Mama . . ."

"Go upstairs. It will be all right." Then she smiled
again, but warmer. "Think. If this wasn't right, would
Baby Celeste have been so charming, so delightful and
loving toward Dave?"

"That's because he's her—"

"What?" she cried, again nearly leaping at me, her
eyes stretched so wide, I thought they would tear at the
corners. "What?"

I shook my head and looked down.

"Go upstairs. Now!" She stood up and hovered over
me.

Tears streaked down my cheeks, but I didn't realize
it until they began to drip from my chin. I tried to
swallow, but my throat felt as if the sides of it had
turned to rock. The strapping around my bosom tightened.

"I can't . . . breathe, Mama."

I tried to stand, but as soon as I did, the room began
to spin. I reached out to steady myself, but nothing was
there to take hold of. Mama didn't grab me either. She
let me fall back. I thought I was falling through the
chair, through the floor, through the very foundation,
falling into that grave that haunted me so. The last
thing I remember was her glaring at me hatefully.

Then I blacked out.

When I woke, I was in my bed. How had she gotten
me up the stairs? I wouldn't have been surprised to
hear her tell me my daddy had brought me to my

room. I was still dressed but the blanket had been tucked in the sides of the bed so firmly, it was like a straitjacket. I struggled with it. The effort made me nauseous and I had to stop and lie back awhile. A black candle burned in the window, throwing a wavering glow over the walls and the shut door. Shadows wiggled like worms on the driveway, stuck and desperate to move on. There was nothing to do about my situation at the moment, nothing to do but sleep.

The darkness flooded over me again. I slept so deeply that I was beyond the reach of dreams. It was the sleep of the dead with only the muffled sound of footsteps on the surface of graves.

Hours and hours later, the morning light confused me, and for a minute or so, I just lay there gazing at the blue sky and the clouds I could see through the window. I looked down and saw the chamber pot Mama had given me for Baby Celeste and me in the turret room. The sight of it put the panic back into me. I tried to bolt upright and struggled to throw the blanket off me. I was still dressed in what I had worn the night before. I turned to look at my clock and saw it was gone.

I rose and went to the window. From the way the sunlight washed over the forest and grounds, I concluded it was late in the morning. I hurried to go out. It didn't surprise me to find my door locked. I rattled it and called for Mama. Then I listened hard. The house was too silent. I rushed back to the window and opened it so I could see where our car was always parked. It was gone.

I stepped back from the window and recalled everything that had happened, all that I had said to her and she to me. Mama was purging me again. I saw she had left me water, but nothing else. Where had she gone?

How long would she keep me in here? What ceremony would she put me through now, what herbal panacea?

There was nothing for me to do but wait. I didn't want to drink the water. I didn't trust anything, but I was too thirsty and eventually relented. I had to use the chamber pot as well. I had no idea of how many hours went by, but the sun's movement and the shadows below told it was considerable. Finally, I heard our car approaching the house and rushed to the window to see Mama driving with Baby Celeste in a car seat beside her. I waited until she had entered the house, then I called and pounded on the door.

She didn't come up immediately. She remained below doing whatever it was she was doing. Finally, I heard her ascending the stairway with Baby Celeste, talking to her softly.

"Mama!" I screamed. "Please, let me out now. I promise I'll be good."

She paused, then she went on to Baby Celeste's room. I listened, and when I heard her footsteps again, I knocked on the door.

"Stop making all that noise. The baby's taking a nap," she said. "I'll bring you something in a few minutes and we'll empty your chamber pot."

"I want to go outside, Mama."

"Of course you do." She was standing right outside my door. "But it's not you so much as what's inside you, Noble," she added in a loud whisper.

"No, Mama, no. I'm all right. I promise."

She didn't reply. I heard her walk off and descend the stairs. Pounding on the door and crying out would do no good. It would make it all worse. I knew that from the times before when she had done this to me. I had to find the patience and convince her she had corrected whatever it was she imagined had gone wrong.

I knew she would put me through a fast. I tried to sleep to conserve my energy. I did drift off from time to time, but woke often. The sun's descent deepened the shadows in my room. My stomach growled, demanding something. Finally, I heard my door being unlocked. I sat up quickly. Mama entered with a glass of something in her hand.

"Drink this," she told me.

I shook my head.

"You must. It won't hurt you, Noble. It will strengthen you."

"What is it?" I knew it was fruitless to ask. She would never reveal her secret formulas because she believed to do so would reduce their effectiveness.

"Never mind what it is. It will strengthen you." She held it out. "The faster you cooperate, the faster this will all end."

I thought about jumping up and running out, but I was afraid. Why hadn't Daddy come to me all this time? Why hadn't he spoken to her as well? Was she right? Had something evil taken on his appearance to fool me?

"You know in your heart that I know what's best for you, for all of us, Noble," she said softly. She reached out and caressed my cheek. She hadn't done it so lovingly for so long. I closed my eyes, enjoying the touch of her hand on me and all that it brought. "Go on," she urged.

I reached out and took the glass. Whatever was in it was yellow. I was sure at least it was some combination of herbs. I knew what she thought about the protective powers of ivy, juniper and garlic, milkwort, and ragwort, among others. Mama expected that someday I would take over producing her remedies, so from time to time she explained them and showed me how she mixed them. There were, however, so many, and so many that carried mystical and spiritual authority.

As usual, I hated the taste and had to close my eyes to drink. I did it as fast as I could. She explained again as she had explained before that it wasn't meant to be tasty. It was meant to be thought of as medicine. Just as there was medicine for the body, there was medicine for the soul. Mama saw spiritual qualities in everything. It was how she had taught me to see the world around us as well, even the world outside our house.

My stomach gurgled and I sat back on the bed.

She took out my chamber pot, emptied it, and then returned.

"Can't I go out now, Mama?"

"Soon. Sleep first."

"Where's the baby?"

"The baby is fine. Worry about yourself for now," she told me, and left.

I heard the door being locked.

Even though the darkness thickened, I didn't bother putting on a light. I lay back in my bed. The drink was already making me feel hot and dizzy. Nausea came and went, and suddenly I felt that I was sinking in the bed, but as I was sinking, I was rising, too. The spiritual part of me was lifting out of my body. I was hovering over myself.

And then I thought I saw our family spirits come into my room and walk slowly around my bed, circling and circling. I recognized many from their pictures. Everyone's eyes were closed. No one would look at me. I cried out. I begged, but no one responded.

Slowly they filed out until they were all gone. Then I sank back into my body.

And I slept.

In the morning Mama opened my door. She had Baby Celeste in her arms and she was smiling.

"See," she told Baby Celeste, "Noble is fine again."

I rubbed my eyes and, using my elbows, pushed myself up to sit. I was still groggy and a little dizzy.

"Rise and shine. You have to get up now, Noble. We have a lot to do. I want everything to look as nice as it can. We have work to finish.

"Dave came over last night while you were asleep, and he formally proposed to me.

"And I said yes." She held out her hand. The large diamond glittered in the light as if the light originated with it.

"He gave you a ring?"

"Of course. It was his mother's, too. It has a nice energy to it. For now anyway."

"You're formally engaged?"

"Yes, Noble. We're formally engaged," she said, smirking. "Sometimes I think thoughts sink into your head like a stone in thick mud. An hour later you realize what you had heard."

She shook her head at me and then smiled.

"We're going to have a real wedding, too, and here on our farm. So you see, there is a lot to do. Now you understand why I had begun.

"Wash up and come down to breakfast." She turned and left.

I sat there, still feeling dazed. Then I started to get up, slipping my feet into my shoes. He gave her a ring. There was going to be a wedding. It was really happening.

I thought I heard a loud sobbing and went to my window.

Below, I saw Noble standing and looking up at me.

Then I heard Elliot's laugh.

Noble lowered his head, turned, and started for the forest.

A cloud drifted over the sun and dropped a long, dark shadow around him. It seemed to swallow him up until he was gone.

Leaving me feeling even more alone.

8

Patience and Faith

♊

If I was ever afraid to ask Mama any questions about her and Mr. Fletcher, I was now. I didn't want to do anything to lead her to believe I hadn't been purged of the evil she thought had entered the house and me. Fortunately, she was too involved in her relationship with Mr. Fletcher to notice my nervousness. At breakfast she went on and on, bragging about the sacrifices Mr. Fletcher was willing to make for her.

"No, not just for me, for *us*," she emphasized. "He's putting his house up for sale immediately."

I looked up quickly. Immediately? When did she intend to get married?

"It takes time to sell a house, especially one like that," she continued as if she had read my thoughts. "However, Dave knows there is no way I would agree to move from here, and he's quite happy about moving in with us. He's selling all of his furnishings as well, and if his daughter doesn't return home, he'll put all of her things in storage. He might even give much of them away to needy people, who would appreciate it more than she does.

"You look surprised, Noble. What is on your mind?" Mama asked with a smile. "Go ahead, tell me."

"When will you be getting married?"

"We're discussing the exact date soon. I want the wedding to be held here. He wants to have it catered by some well-known company in the area, but I explained that I don't want any strangers who have no real interest in us other than money to be part of our joining together. Besides, it's not going to be a big wedding party by any means. I can certainly handle the number of guests we'll have, and you'll do a great deal to help me set up for it.

"I've already talked to Mr. Bogart about it. He has suggested the minister to perform the ceremony. It's someone who appreciates our way."

"There'll be no honeymoon as such," she continued. "Sometime later, when events permit, we'll take a holiday. All of us. Just like any other family."

"What about your work?" I ventured.

"Oh, my work. I've told you how much Dave respects my herbal remedies, and as for spiritual things . . . well, you'll be surprised at how much he believes. He's not capable of what we're capable of doing, of course, but his beliefs aren't at great odds with ours. In time, because of his love for me, he will accept everything, especially when I show him a world he never imagined existed right around us. He's always complimenting me on my temperament and voicing aloud how much he wants to learn so he can escape from life's worries, especially"—she made a disapproving face—"the worries he has about his daughter." Mama laughed. "He calls me a 'fresh drink of water.'

My grandfather used to use that expression. Still does," she muttered.

What did all this mean? I wondered. Had she ever told Mr. Fletcher about our family spirits, about crossing over, or was their talk only about spiritual harmony, peace, meditation? Would he become like Daddy, tolerant, understanding, or would he run for cover the first time Mama told him someone else was in the room beside us?

She didn't seem a bit concerned, and that both worried me and made me curious. The biggest question was yet to be asked: What about me? What would she ever tell him about me? And as a consequence of that, what would she ever tell him about Baby Celeste? How could we keep our secret world from him if he was living here? Or would we? Was his love for Mama so great that she believed she could trust him with everything? What did she know that I didn't?

"Please wipe that look of worry from your face, Noble. I promise you nothing will change, nothing will interfere with our spiritual balance. What we do now, we do for Baby Celeste," she added, looking at her. "She's our future, and therefore, she's everyone's future. Do you understand? We must protect her, protect everything that has been entrusted in our care. I'll be depending on you."

"Yes, Mama."

"When a precious little girl like Baby Celeste grows up in a world without a real mother and a father, she's always at a disadvantage. People will mark her as an illegitimate child. There are so many stupid prejudices floating about out there. Of all people, you and I know that too well. I want to make sure our Baby Celeste has no disadvantages.

"You'll see," Mama said, patting me on the hand.

"In time everything becomes clear, Noble. It just takes patience and faith, the cornerstones of our lives. I should have named my children that, Patience and Faith." She laughed. "Maybe Baby Celeste will name her children Patience and Faith." Mama looked at her again.

At the sound of her name, Baby Celeste looked up quickly and smiled.

"You will, won't you?" Mama asked her. "You'll marry the right person and you'll be a blessing to all you touch and all who touch you. Won't you, my dear, dear child?"

Baby Celeste nodded as if she truly understood. I was beginning to believe she did.

"And as to you," Mama said, turning back to me as if I had done something wrong already, "you need not worry about Dave interfering with you or trying to change you. He will be here to do whatever we ask. Whatever suggestions he makes to you, you can accept or reject. Be with him as much as you like or as little as you like. Just don't insult him or give him any reason to think you don't appreciate him. Do you understand?"

"Yes, Mama."

"Good. I'm so happy for you, Noble. I'm so happy I've been able to help you see things, the right things. In time"—Mama turned her head slowly toward Baby Celeste—"our Baby Celeste will help us see even more. There is so much left to discover through her."

I looked from her to Celeste. What did she mean? How could a baby help us to see more, discover more? Who did she think Celeste really was?

"Oh, Noble, I'm so happy. So happy for us all that I've decided the three of us are taking the day off," Mama declared with a bounce in her seat. "We're going shopping and to lunch at the big mall in Middletown. Wear something nice," she told me. "I want to buy you some more clothes, too, and some prettier things for the baby, as well as myself," she added with a slight blush. "We need to get the baby some new books as well. What would you like? Is there something you've been thinking about lately?"

"No, Mama."

There really were things I dreamed about, but I could never mention them. How often had I snuck a look at a new style in a magazine, new shoes, or jewelry? For a while months ago, I had some magazines hidden in my room the way a teenage boy might have *Playboy* or some other such magazine hidden in his. Eventually, I was so frightened of the possibility of Mama finding them that I snuck them out and buried them behind the house. We both had our private graveyards, I thought.

"Well, you'll think about it some more. I'm sure you'll see something you want when we walk about the shops and look in the windows and at the displays. Sometimes, it's fun just to look at what's new."

Fun? Since when did she think that was any fun? How changed she was. I couldn't recall a time when Mama had been as buoyant and energized as she was now. As she moved through the house, she hummed and sang. She primped and preened in front of the mirror for almost an hour, experimenting with different ways to wear her hair, different outfits and jewelry and shades of lipstick. Every time I suggested I would wait outside, she told me she was almost ready and she didn't want me getting dirty.

"Have a little patience. I know you, Noble. You'll just wander off to the garden or the shed and get muddied or greasy. Just keep your eye on Baby Celeste. We're leaving in a few minutes."

The few minutes went on and on until I thought we would never leave. Maybe it was all Mama's illusion, fantasy. Even Baby Celeste grew bored and fell asleep with her head on my lap. I twirled her curly red hair in my finger and watched her eyelids tremble as she slept. Looking at her beautiful lips and soft cheeks, I wondered what sort of dreams she had. Were they serious prophetic dreams or dreams like I used to have, dreams full of candy canes and dolls, music and laughter? Was she the magical child Mama claimed she was or was she just a little girl, born into a world she might never understand?

Yes, I saw myself in her, but I saw Elliot, too, and I wondered how could it be that Mr. Fletcher could look at her, especially now that he was going to be an intimate part of our lives, and not see that as well.

Or had he seen that immediately? I suddenly wondered. The idea made my heart race.

Could it be that he did know, that this pursuit of him that Mama was so proud of, that Mama thought was spiritually directed and planned, was really just the opposite? She wasn't beguiling Mr. Fletcher for our purposes; he was beguiling her for reasons Mama did not see or understand. How dangerous was that? What could be the result?

As sweet and gentle a man as he seemed to be, he could be the very challenge to our world and our existence that Mama dreaded and about whom Mama warned. He could be that Trojan horse that Mama once accused Cleo, my dog, of being. He could be the dark shadow she feared was coming out of the forest.

And yet, how could Mama be so bewitched? And why wouldn't our family spirits have warned her as I thought they had warned me? Look how quickly and lovingly Baby Celeste had taken to him, I told myself. If she was the magic child, wouldn't she sense danger?

I was so confused. It made me dizzy. Should I be happy about Mr. Fletcher, happy we would have a man in our lives again, a father for Baby Celeste and even for me, or should I be terrified for all of us? If I showed that terror, Mama would only lock me away.

"I'm ready," I heard, and looked up.

I was sure she saw the surprise on my face. Mama wore her hair differently, swept to the back on one side. It made her look seductive, sexy. She had chosen a lipstick more on the pink tone, which matched her one-piece, sleeveless dress and her shoes. Was that an ankle bracelet? When did she get that? Or was it something she had always had but had never taken out until now? It was as if she were digging up one secret after another and astonishing me more and more with each revelation.

There was no denying she was so pretty, but instead of being proud of her and taking delight in her beauty, I suddenly felt that all too familiar pang of jealousy so strongly it embittered me and nearly tore me in two.

I gazed down at my calloused palms, my hard forearms, my jeans and clodhopper shoes, scuffed and worn. My toes curled unhappily within. A feeling of utter disgust and revulsion washed over me. It tightened my chest and squeezed my heart like a sponge squeezed in a fist. My stomach muscles stiffened. What am I, what have I become, I thought, that I would be so repulsed by the sight of myself?

"Don't tell me she fell asleep?" Mama said, finally taking note of Baby Celeste on my lap.

"You took so long," I accused, perhaps too sharply. I held my breath. She stared a moment, then shook her head the way she would shake off shower water. Mama accepted and denied things in a world within a world. She was always listening to voices, even as she spoke.

"Well, you'll just have to carry her to the car and strap her in her seat, Noble. I'm sure she'll become alert when we get to the shops."

Mama continued to walk into the living room toward me, wet her fingers on her tongue, then wiped my cheek.

"Honestly, you would go about all day blotched and streaked with grime. You haven't changed since you were four," she told me, but she smiled, too.

I looked up at her and she saw something in my eyes that caused her to take pause. I was angrily thinking that in her view of things I would always be her little boy. I couldn't even grow into a man, much less a woman.

"Are you all right? You haven't had any new problems, have you?" she asked quickly.

I shook my head immediately. If I had hesitated for a split second, she would have had me up in my room again, locked the door, put me on another fast, and gone off with Baby Celeste.

"Then let's get started," she said in a happier tone of voice.

I lifted Baby Celeste as gracefully as I could. She moaned but didn't wake up. When we put her in her seat, her eyes snapped open and she gazed around, realized she was in the car, and smiled.

"Ride," she said, and clapped her hands.

"There, see, someone is happy today," Mama said, pointedly looking my way. "Someone appreciates the great efforts I make for us all."

"I appreciate it," I protested.

"We'll see. We'll see."

Off we went. It was so rare that I left the farm these

days. As I sat and gazed out at the scenery, the homes and businesses we passed, I recalled how excited Noble used to be and how he longed so to be out in the world. His dream was to attend public school, to have lots of friends. His frustration, budding anger, and inconsolable misery had lured him down the dour pathway to his appointment with Death. Now that I thought about all that, it worried me that Mama hadn't understood, hadn't seen it all coming. She wasn't perfect after all. No one was perfect, except maybe Baby Celeste.

"I thought we would stop at Dave's drugstore today and visit with him awhile," Mama told me. "We're not being formal and all about announcing our engagement in the newspapers, but as you see"—she held her hand out toward me—"he has given me a ring and he's been telling the people he works with at the store and his regular customers, and you know how quickly news spreads around here. We'll be showing our faces at his store more and more often."

I couldn't hide my amazement at Mama's new outgoing personality. Aside from the people who came to her for herbal remedies, our attorney—Mr. Derward Lee Nokleby-Cook—some school officials when I was in the homeschool program, and Mr. Bogart, Mama had little or no contact with people living in what we always thought of as the outside world. She didn't need them; she didn't want them. It had been like this since Daddy's death, and even when he was alive, she was never eager to socialize, invite people to dinner, or go to restaurants. I remembered how Daddy had complained about their not taking advantage of their increased wealth, not taking vacations, going on trips, or shopping more for us and themselves. Before his death, those arguments were occurring frequently.

Why was she willing to be more sociable with Mr. Fletcher than she had been with Daddy?

Before we went to the drugstore, we went to the mall. It was a Saturday so it was busy. What surprised me most was how many teenagers and young people were there simply to hang about and socialize. I stole looks at them, feeling like a visitor from Mars. Could they see something different in me? Like Noble, I was so interested in everything about them, the way they talked, touched each other, horsed around, laughed, and especially what the girls were wearing.

I'm sure it was just my imagination, but it seemed that everyone was looking at us no matter where we went. Mama seemed pleased about the attention, which was another thing that surprised me. She used to complain about the "gawking eyes of stupid people" who saw us as a curiosity and whispered behind our backs. She never smiled back at anyone, not the way she was doing now.

We ran into some of her herbal-remedy customers, and as she had predicted, the news of her engagement to Mr. Fletcher was already a headline on the front pages of gossip. I saw the way women like Mrs. Paris congratulated her, her eyes mainly on Baby Celeste, searching for resemblances to Mr. Fletcher. As we walked away, I looked back and saw Mrs. Paris, Mrs. Walker, and Miss Shamus with their heads together, their tongues wagging. There was no doubt about what they were speaking. However, when I looked at Mama, she was beaming. Not only didn't it bother her, but it was obviously what she had wanted.

We bought Baby Celeste a new pink-and-white dress with a frilly hem and collar, light blue socks, and matching shoes. Mama wanted her to wear it all right now, too. After that we went to one of the bigger department stores and she bought herself a light V-neck sweater, another skirt, another pair of shoes, and a silk scarf. Then she had me get some new pants, a few more shirts, and a pair of the newer sports shoes so I would "look more in style." The salesman remarked about how small my shoe size was. I looked at Mama, but she didn't change expression, even when he went to shoes for much younger boys.

Afterward, she paused at the window of a more upscale men's clothing store and decided we should look for a suit for me to wear at her wedding. I was nervous trying on jackets with a salesman hovering about me, but Mama kept him busy finding matching ties, a formal shirt, and some socks. In the end she decided on a dark blue suit and told the salesman she would handle the alterations herself.

Once that was all done, we had some lunch, and then, as she had promised, she drove to the drugstore where Mr. Fletcher worked as the pharmacist. He was behind the counter filling prescriptions, but as soon as we entered, the store manager came over to us to congratulate Mama. His name was Larry Jones and he was no more than thirty or so. I wondered how he knew who Mama was, but the moment we approached the drug counter, I discovered the answer. There in a silver frame was a picture of Mr. Fletcher and Mama, a picture taken on their overnight trip. They were in the rowboat and he had his arm around her shoulders. She had a red rose in her hair.

I looked at her to see if she was displeased, but she was happy to see it there.

"Sarah," Mr. Fletcher called out as soon as he saw us. He mumbled something to an assistant and quickly came around the counter.

In front of everyone, customers, salespeople, the

manager, and me, he hugged Mama and kissed her on the cheek.

"What a wonderful surprise!" he declared loud enough for the whole store to hear. "Hi, Noble. And Celeste. Look how pretty you are."

Mama deliberately handed her to him and he held her in his arms the way he would if he were truly her father.

"We just came from the mall. This is a new outfit," Mama told him.

"She's beautiful," Mr. Fletcher said.

As if she had rehearsed her part well, Baby Celeste threw her arms about his neck and he laughed. The on-lookers now had no doubt that he was her father. Mama had pinned him to the bulletin board of scandal and rumor for all to see and prattle.

He reached onto the counter and got Baby Celeste a lollipop. Before he handed it to her, however, he checked with Mama. I thought she would say no for sure. We had no candy in our home and never had since Daddy's death. Once again, she surprised me by nodding her approval.

After he unwrapped it for Baby Celeste and gave it to her, he glanced at me and then at Mama, his eyes urging her to move away from nosy onlookers. She sensed something was wrong. Her eyebrows lifted.

"What is it, Dave?"

"Betsy," he said softly, and handed Baby Celeste back to Mama.

She immediately put her down and told me to watch her while she and Mr. Fletcher walked to the side to talk in private. I wanted to watch them and try to listen in, but a saleslady came over and began to talk with Baby Celeste. She took her to the toy section so I had to follow.

A few minutes later I heard Mama say, "We have to be going now."

She was standing behind me. Mr. Fletcher had returned to the pharmacy counter. He waved to me and I waved back. Mama already had Baby Celeste in her arms and was heading out the door. The way she was marching with her shoulders stiff and her head high told me she was upset. She said nothing until we had the baby in her seat and had driven away from the drugstore.

"What was wrong?" I finally asked.

"Betsy is coming home tomorrow." Mama turned to me, her face flushed. "She's coming home to talk him out of selling their house and marrying me, not that she can. The little bitch," she spit. "No wonder she has so many worthless boyfriends. Every time she's with one long enough, he dumps her. Of all the selfish . . ."

"What's Mr. Fletcher going to do?"

"Dave. Call him Dave. Stop calling him Mr. Fletcher!" Mama screamed at me. "He's going to be your stepfather."

"I'm sorry," I muttered, and quickly turned away from her raging eyes.

"You're sorry." She fumed a few moments. "What do you think he's going to do? I'll tell you what he's going to do. He's going to finally put her in her place. He promised me he would be more stern with her," she said, but not with as much confidence as I expected. "Oh, he's suffering from the usual guilty conscience, blaming himself for how she's turned out. She takes advantage of that guilty feeling he has. She's smart, the conniving little creature, and knows how to manipulate him. She's been doing it for years and years. He gives her whatever she wants, and if he puts up some argument, she wails about how he drove her mother

away, how he was too occupied to give her and Elliot
the attention they needed. She's good at it. I'm sure.
From the way he describes her, I can see she can give
Satan himself lessons. Wait until she's living in my
house. Things will change and quickly, too."

"She's going to move in with us?"

"What are you talking about? Of course she's moving in with us. I just told you she's returning after another disastrous love affair and I've told you how Dave
is selling his home. Once we're married, she will be
with us as well. Whether she likes it or not, she's going
to be part of the family. Believe me, I don't relish the
thought, but it is what has to be for now."

"What do you mean *for now,* Mama?"

She turned and gazed at me a moment and then
looked forward. "I would assume that someday she
will be on her own, that she might find some poor fool,
some idiot, to marry her, but until then, we'll have to
deal with the problem, for that is all she is to me, a
problem.

"Of course," she continued, "she blames Elliot's
death on Dave as well."

"She does? Why?"

"Same thing. He didn't provide enough attention,
take enough interest in him, left him in harm's way.
Whatever reason she can invent, she'll use. It's part of
what she does to manipulate him, only this time . . .
this time she is up against far more than poor Dave,"
Mama vowed. "It won't take her long to see that and
she'll change her tune."

The very thought of her coming to live with us
made me shudder. Too well I recalled the time Elliot
talked me into spying on her through a hole in the wall
in his room. It was something I did after he and I had
first met and he still thought I was going to become

one of his new buddies. I was afraid to resist the invitation, and at the same time I had to admit to myself that I had a great curiosity, a longing, to observe a girl like Betsy and see her during her most private moments.

At the time she was the sexiest girl I had ever seen. Buxom with pretty hair, she had a rounder face than Elliot with small, brown eyes and a weak mouth that drooped in the corners, giving her a habitual look of disgust when she was with Elliot and her father. However, I couldn't help being fascinated with her clothes, her makeup, the way she walked and spoke.

It was after I had seen her naked in her room, experimenting with her makeup and hair, that I had gone into Mama's room and first used her makeup. I recalled it now as if it were just hours ago when I had done it.

I had opened one of her lipstick tubes. It had looked all right so I had brought it to my lips and carefully traced along, pressing my lips together and then padding them the way I had seen Betsy do it in her room. The sight of bright red lips on my face made me smile. Encouraged, I had opened one of the jars of cream and rubbed it into my cheeks and under my lower lip, around my chin. My fingers were rough against my face, so I had to rub gently.

After that, I had opened one of the cakes of makeup and begun to experiment with color the way I had seen Betsy do it. Once I had finished that, I found an eyelash brush and started to darken mine. I was nearly finished doing that when I heard Mama's shrill scream. I had been so involved in it all that I hadn't heard her coming up the stairway. She was standing in the doorway watching me, her eyes wide with horror. She looked as if she might pull the hair out of her head.

Just like this recent event, she accused me of being

contaminated, and soon after that she decided it was Cleo's fault. Betsy Fletcher had brought me only bad luck. I had no doubt she would do it again. She had only disdain for me and I had no respect for her. How could we ever coexist in the same house? How could I ever pretend she was part of my family? Why wasn't Mama worried about that?

Sometimes, even now, when I recalled the sensuous way Betsy touched herself and gazed at her body, I would touch myself. The tingling I felt surging through me frightened and yet delighted me. If I longed for it too much, I pressed my face into my pillow as hard as I could. I would hold my breath while I chased away the images and visions. But just like what had happened after I had seen Mama and Mr. Fletcher kiss so romantically, it was impossible to stop the dreams, dreams in which I felt lips on mine, hands on my breasts, and dreams in which I recited pages and pages of wonderful romance.

Betsy would surely rekindle that in me.

"Her being with us won't be pleasant for me, Mama," I muttered almost under my breath as these thoughts flowed through my mind.

"It doesn't have to be pleasant for you," she retorted. She smiled to herself. "It just has to be. That's all. The rest will take care of itself."

Her self-confidence, which was normally reassuring for me, wasn't this time. If she saw any anxiety on my face, she ignored it, but I couldn't help thinking about all the responsibility I would soon be carrying on my shoulders. Betsy would snoop. Betsy would do her best to make us look bad to her father. Was this all just another great test?

I felt as if I were standing at the base of a mountain and an avalanche of unhappiness was tumbling down at me. I couldn't stop it and I might not be able to get out of its way.

Mama gazed into the rearview mirror at Baby Celeste, who still sucked on the lollipop.

"Wasn't she just marvelous all day?" Mama looked at me. "Wasn't she?"

"Yes."

"Yes." Mama nodded. "Yes. The looks on all their faces when they saw her was priceless."

The outing was obviously a big success for Mama, but I felt like someone waiting for the next shoe to drop.

9

Princess Betsy

♊

The second shoe drop came in the form of Betsy. Two days later Mr. Fletcher (I still couldn't get used to calling him Dave) brought her to the house. When I saw her, the look on her face revealed that he had practically dragged her. I saw them drive up and saw how she remained in the car until he opened the passenger side door and ordered her out. I was in the field where I had just put in some late-summer plants. I stood up and watched them walk toward the front door, Betsy lagging behind with her head down. Wiping my hands on a rag, I started for the house, too.

The afternoon sun had fallen behind some rather thick clouds the color of wood ashes. Shadows were cast over the house like a net woven out of darkness. I rolled my sleeves down as I walked. I was nervous about being face-to-face with Betsy, but I knew Mama would be angry if I wasn't there to greet our new "princess," as she had been referring to her the past forty-eight hours. When I stepped in, I found them still standing in the hallway.

Betsy had her head down with her shoulders hoisted and her arms crossed over her breasts. She wore a pair of ragged-looking jeans with the threads parting in the seat of it just under her left cheek, a faded blue T-shirt with the word *Dead* still legible, but the rest of it not, and a pair of what were once white tennis shoes, but were now more gray and scuffed. She wore no socks.

Mama was standing across from her, and Mr. Fletcher was on the other side looking at her hard, his eyes full of disappointment and anger. I had obviously already missed the opening blast of unpleasantness.

"I said," Mr. Fletcher punched out at her, "this is Sarah. You know how to say a proper hello, Betsy."

"Hello," she mumbled, then turned to look at me. Her eyes narrowed in a scrutinizing way that made me fidget inside.

She looked different from the last time I had seen her close up. Her face had thinned out and appeared longer, her nose sharper. She wore no makeup, not even lipstick, but her cheeks were flush, bringing a crimson tint to the area just below her hazel brown eyes. As she brought her arms down, she cupped them into fists and pressed them against her thighs. She wore no bra and her full bosom pressed her well-outlined nipples against the thin, worn T-shirt. Whatever she had been through to cause her to lose weight actually made her look more curvy and attractive.

She smirked and then softened her smug grin into a coy smile. "So this is my new baby brother, huh?"

"Noble is hardly a baby," Mama said. "He has many important responsibilities on the farm and he carries them out efficiently."

Betsy didn't look at her. She kept her eyes on me. I

felt like a deer caught in the headlights and looked quickly to Mama.

"Noble." She nodded toward Betsy. Her expression urged me to greet her.

"Hi," I said. "Welcome."

"Yes, that's right. We want to welcome you, Betsy," Mama said with a waxy smile, "and show you where your new room will be."

"New," she spit disdainfully. She gazed about her. "This is hardly what I would call new. It's probably older than the dump we have now."

"As a matter of fact it is," Mama said, undaunted. "And it has lots more history to it as well."

"Whoop-de-do," Betsy said. "We're moving into a museum. That's just great."

Her father was glaring at her with such anger and distaste, I thought he might just swing out and strike her squarely in the center of that disrespectful smirk. Instead, he pulled back on the reins of his temper and smiled at Mama.

"Showing Betsy around would be very nice of you, Sarah. Thank you."

"Why can't I just stay in our home until it's sold?" Betsy moaned.

"We've been through this, Betsy," Mr. Fletcher said through his clenched teeth. "I've got the furniture placed and I want the house kept immaculate for real estate showings. As a matter of fact, Sarah"—he turned back to Mama—"we've got a showing tomorrow. A couple from New York City who are looking for a vacation spot, weekends and summer. They are already interested from just riding by."

"Some vacation they'll have in that rat trap," Betsy said, and turned to me to get some agreement. I didn't change expression, which tightened her lips and sent her looking elsewhere. She folded her arms across her breasts again and looked as if she had planted her feet in cement.

"Well, we've all got to learn how to appreciate the little we have," Mama said. "What you think is a rat trap might look like a palace to the couple coming to view it."

"A palace?" Betsy laughed. "They'd have to be coming from a slum."

"Your father actually fixed that old home up very nicely," Mama insisted.

"So then maybe we should stay there," Betsy retorted. She was not going to be intimidated easily, not even under Mama's cold eyes and controlled fury.

Mama simply stared at her a moment, then turned and smiled at Mr. Fletcher. "Shall we take the tour?"

"Please." He reached out to take Betsy's arm, but she pulled back, glanced at me, and reluctantly followed them through the hallway, stopping at the living room.

"Who plays the piano?" Betsy asked.

"Sarah, and she plays beautifully."

"You mean Noble isn't efficient at that?" Betsy asked with a laugh.

No one responded.

"Daddy hasn't stopped talking about all you do," she told me.

"And none of it is an exaggeration," Mr. Fletcher said, nodding at me.

Betsy raised her eyes toward the ceiling "My father was always quicker at finding the good things in other people's children than he was in me or my brother."

"Betsy!"

"Forget it," she said with a shrug. "Let's continue the tour."

They looked in at the dining room and she complained that theirs was bigger and they at least had a nice big window.

"This is like having to eat in a railroad car," she muttered loud enough for all to hear.

"Hardly," Mama said. "And I'm sure you'll have better meals than you've had lately."

"I second that," Mr. Fletcher said. "I've had some of the best meals of my life here."

Betsy had no interest in looking at the kitchen, but they stopped there anyway before they headed up the stairs to the bedrooms. As they ascended, Betsy deliberately shook the balustrade, taking pleasure in how it rattled in places.

"Janitor boy," she called down to me, "you had better fix this efficiently or someone might just break it and fall, and we don't want any more accidents, now do we?"

I felt myself redden.

"Betsy," her father snapped, and she continued on, a laugh trailing behind her like a ribbon of disdain. When they all reached the second floor, I heard Baby Celeste call out. She had woken from her nap. It was as if a whip had been snapped right in front of my eyes. I hurried up the stairs, holding my breath. What would Betsy say the moment she set eyes on Baby Celeste? Would she see Elliot and therefore just assume as did the rest of the community that her father was actually Baby Celeste's father?

I reached the top just as Mama was carrying Baby Celeste out to introduce to Betsy. As always, Baby Celeste gave someone new a big, warm smile.

"Celeste," Mama said, "this is Betsy. She's going to come live with us and be your new big sister. Isn't that nice?"

"Betsy," Baby Celeste pronounced perfectly. Mr. Fletcher laughed.

Betsy simply stared at her, her expression unchanging. Then she turned to me and her eyes darkened for a moment. I was still holding my breath.

"Which room is mine?" Betsy asked Mama.

"You're right here, dear," Mama said, stepping to the right and opening the door.

I was surprised myself at how much Mama had done to the room. There were new white window curtains and the queen-size bed with the embossed rose on its headboard had a beautiful pink-and-white comforter and large, fluffy pillows. Unbeknownst to me was the placing of new dark pink carpet on the floor, part of what had been done while Baby Celeste and I were hiding in the turret room. I was actually somewhat jealous of the improvements. This room had a vanity table and a mirror as well. Mama had brought down standing lamps from the attic, and a large hickorywood chest stood at the foot of the bed. I had always wanted that chest in my room, but Mama had told me it had once belonged to her grandmother and the scent of her body powders was still in it.

"It's not the sort of furniture for a young man," she had said.

"Beautiful room, Betsy," her father said. "Much nicer than the one you have now, isn't it?"

"No. It's smaller, and besides, I'll be sleeping right next to a baby's room. I'll hear her whine all the time."

"Baby Celeste doesn't whine," Mama said sharply.

"Why do you refer to her as Baby Celeste instead of just Celeste?" Betsy demanded instantly. Actually, she pounced.

"It's just a habit," Mama said, obviously stumbling on her answer.

Betsy didn't seem to care what the answer was.

"Where's your room?" she asked me as if she thought I had a better arrangement.

"Right there." I nodded at the opened doorway behind her and across the hall.

She glanced at it and shook her head. "Where's that stairway go?" She nodded toward the short stairway that led up to the turret room. "That looks far enough away."

"That goes to a storage room," Mama replied dryly. "And it's not a place to loiter in, much less use as a bedroom."

"Who would want to loiter anywhere around here?" Betsy shot back.

Mama looked to be counting to ten. Then she smiled again. "Noble, would you take the baby out for a while. She could use some air."

"I'll bet. We could all use some air," Betsy remarked. "It smells in here."

"Betsy!" Mr. Fletcher cried.

"Well, it does. You burn that incense or something all the time, don't you?" she asked Mama.

"Yes, but from what I understand, you haven't been sleeping in the sweetest-smelling places anyway, dear. I'm sure you'll get used to it."

Betsy looked at her father. "Thanks a lot, Dad. I can just imagine the stories you've told about me."

I took Baby Celeste into my arms and started down the stairs.

"I'm going out, too," I heard Betsy say. She followed me down and out the door.

I set Baby Celeste down on the porch floor and she went right for one of her dolls she had left in the rocking chair.

"You're still not going to public school, right?" Betsy asked.

She went to the railing and sat against it, putting her hands on it and straightening her shoulders. It brought up her breasts. I glanced at her, then looked at Baby Celeste, who had climbed into the rocking chair and held the doll in her lap just the way Mama and I often held her.

"No, I got my high school equivalency two years ago."

"So what are you going to do, babysit for the rest of your life?"

"No. I don't babysit," I said sharply. "I help out once in a while, that's all."

"Sure. 'Take the baby out. She needs some air,'" Betsy mocked, then laughed. "You still don't have any real friends, do you?"

I didn't reply.

"What do you do for fun? Plant trees or something?"

"There is a lot to do here. I'm busy. And I read."

She shook her head. "This is really the boondocks."

"Why did you come back if you hate it so much?" I fired at her.

"I won't stay long. I have to warm up to Daddy a bit, you know. Be nice and cooperative until he gives me some money and I can leave."

"To where?"

"Anywhere but here. What did your mother do to get him to want to marry her, cast one of her spells over him or something?"

"She doesn't cast spells."

"Elliot used to believe she did. He told me about you."

The mention of Elliot brought the blood up my neck and warmed my cheeks so fast I had to turn away from her and look at Baby Celeste.

"Rock," she said. "Rock me, Noble."

I started to rock the chair gently and she hugged her doll and looked up at Betsy.

"How old is that kid?"

"She'll be three," I said.

"She has hair like Elliot. How long's my father been poking around this place?"

I didn't reply.

"Is she my sister or not?" she came right out and asked.

"No. She's my cousin. Her parents were—"

"Yeah, yeah, I know the fairy tale. I'm asking you for the truth."

"That's the truth."

"Fine." She looked about the farm. "I can't believe my father is actually going to go through with this. He wants to live here. He might as well check into a retirement home or something."

"This is a beautiful place to live."

She curled her lips and stepped away from the railing. "You have a cigarette?"

"No, I don't smoke."

"Right." She stared at me, then she smiled slowly. "I remember Elliot telling me about a time he brought some girls over to the house to smoke some weed and you ran away. Have you always been afraid of girls? Is that your problem?"

"I'm not afraid of girls."

"Oh, you have a girlfriend?"

"No."

"You go out on dates?"

"No."

"What do you do, make love to herbal plants?" She laughed when I didn't reply. "This is so crazy," she said, looking around, then turning back to me. "Do you know where I was just recently?"

I shook my head.

"I was living in New Orleans. Ever hear of it?"

"Of course."

"My boyfriend was a trumpet player in a place in the French Quarter. We had a lot of fun, partied almost every night until four in the morning, and slept most of the day."

"That doesn't sound like fun to me."

"I bet it doesn't to you. Your idea of excitement around here is probably a flock of geese flying north."

"If it was so much fun, why did you come home?" I asked, unable to hold back my anger.

Now it was her turn to be silent.

"I got bored," she finally replied.

"Did you get bored or did your boyfriend get bored with you?"

"Oh, you're so smart," she said, dropping the corners of her mouth the way I remembered she did. "Elliot told me how intelligent you were. He used to think you were something special. I don't know why he wanted to hang around with someone who hasn't been off the farm, but he did. You know, it was because of you that he drowned," she accused.

Her words seized my breath. "What?"

"If he hadn't been friends with you, he wouldn't have been around that creek, spending so much time in the woods. He would have been with real friends in town or something. I don't know how my father could want to be here for the rest of his life and want to be a father to you," she said sharply.

Tears were in her eyes, tears of sorrow, tears of disappointment, tears of self-pity—all mixed in with tears of rage and jealousy.

"That's not true," I said. "Elliot didn't die because of me."

"Right. Oh, what's the difference now anyway? He's dead and gone."

She sniffed and turned away.

"Betsy," Baby Celeste said. When she looked at her, Baby Celeste held up her doll.

"What does she want me to do with that?"

"Hold it. She likes to share."

"I haven't held a doll since I was her age."

Baby Celeste's smile was magical. Even Betsy couldn't resist it. She stepped forward and took the doll.

"What's her name?" she asked Baby Celeste.

"Betsy," she replied.

"Betsy? She named her doll Betsy?" she asked me.

"I guess," I said.

"When?"

"Just now. It means she likes you."

"Oh, brother." Betsy looked at the doll. It was one of the dolls Taylor had given Mama. Betsy pulled the doll's dress down off her shoulders and turned her around slowly. Then she held the doll between her breasts and smiled. "I guess we're proportionally the same, huh? What do you think, Noble man? Am I built as well as the doll? Is that what little Celeste here is trying to say?"

I shook my head. Why was she teasing me like this?

"Can't tell?" she asked, smiling.

I just stared at her.

"Maybe you need to look closer." She stepped toward me. I actually looked to the side to run off, but she stepped to my right to block me, then she slowly lifted her faded T-shirt to show me her breasts.

I couldn't swallow. I couldn't speak and I thought my heart had become stone.

The front door handle rattled and she dropped her T-shirt quickly.

"Later, we'll talk about it," she said, smiling, just as Mama and Mr. Fletcher stepped out.

"How are we all doing?" Mr. Fletcher asked.

"Just peachy keen, Daddy. Noble and I have been comparing bumps."

"Bumps?" He looked at me and I looked down.

"Yeah, Dad, you know. Who has flatter land, them or us?"

"What?" Mr. Fletcher looked at me and I looked away. "All right, Betsy. Enough. Sarah and I have decided to talk about our wedding plans now. You can either spend time with Noble or go back to the house."

"What would I do with Noble?"

"Maybe he would show you the herbal garden."

"Oh, wow, would you, Noble? You know what," she said before I could respond, "I don't know if I could stand so much excitement in one day. Do you mind if I pass today and do it some other day?"

I looked at Mama. Her eyes told me to stay calm and ignore Betsy.

"Anytime you're free, Betsy," I said. "We have an herbal tea that might help you be more optimistic about yourself."

Mama smiled.

Betsy grimaced, then spun on her father. "I'll walk back," she said, shoved the doll back into Baby Celeste's hands, and started off the porch.

"I won't be long," Mr. Fletcher called to her. "Don't go anywhere, Betsy, until I return."

"Where would I go, the local 4-H Club? Later, Noble." She started down the driveway.

"I'm sorry," Mr. Fletcher told Mama and me.

"It's all right, Dave. We both know how difficult it is for a child to adjust to a totally new home and family. It takes time, but I'm sure it will all work out well," Mama said.

"You're so understanding, Sarah. Betsy doesn't know what a gem she'll have for a new mother."

"Thank you, Dave. Noble, can you keep the baby occupied a while longer while Dave and I talk about the wedding plans?"

"Yes, Mama."

"Thank you."

"Thank you, Noble," Mr. Fletcher added, and they went back into the house.

"Betsy," Baby Celeste said, looking after her as she walked down the driveway.

"Yes," I said. "Betsy."

I took Baby Celeste's hand and led her down and we walked about the farm. I returned to the garden with her and gave her a small hand spade. She watched and imitated me as I planted and prepared the soil. I felt the hairs suddenly stand up on the back of my neck and turned slowly toward the forest. I saw nothing for a moment, and then I saw him standing there, leaning against a tree with that smug arrogance written in his smile, just the way it had been when he'd first come around to speak to me.

Baby Celeste was looking in his direction, too. Was it because she saw me staring at the trees or was it because she saw him?

"What is it, Celeste? What do you see?"

She looked up at me and smiled. Then she returned to her digging.

When I looked back, Elliot was gone. Would he haunt me forever and ever now? I wondered.

I heard Mama calling to us from the house.

"Come on, Celeste, we have to go in now," I said, and brushed off her dress and her hands. Then I carried her back.

"We've decided on a date," Mama told me as soon as we entered the house. "Two weeks from this Saturday."

"That soon? How will you get out invitations and get everything arranged so quickly?" I followed, not wanting to sound negative about it.

"We have a very short guest list. Dave has no relatives he cares to invite, and we certainly don't have anyone who needs an invitation," she said.

I looked at Mr. Fletcher. Did he understand Mama to mean that there would be relatives here, but in spirit, or simply no relatives we cared to invite?

"I have a few friends from the store," Mr. Fletcher explained.

"The ceremony will be simple and we'll have tables set up outside here," Mama continued.

"I'd like it if you would be my best man," Mr. Fletcher said.

I started to shake my head.

"Of course he will, won't you, Noble?"

"I don't know how to be a best man," I said, which I knew immediately was a dumb thing to say. They both laughed.

"It's not too difficult in this case," Mr. Fletcher said, smiling. "I'll give you the wedding ring to hold, and when the time comes in the ceremony, you'll give it to me to put on your mother's finger."

"We'd both like it very much if you would do that, Noble," Mama said.

"Okay," I said.

"Well, I'd better get over to the house and see what new crisis Betsy has created for me," Mr. Fletcher said. "She'll be better behaved tomorrow night. I promise. See you later, Noble. Bye, Celeste." He kissed her on the forehead. She smiled at him and he shook his head.

"What a personality this child has. I wish those cousins of yours were alive to tell me the secret. I could have used it with my children." He kissed Mama on the cheek and went to his car.

We watched him drive off.

"I know you're worried," Mama said as soon as I looked at her. "But don't be. Betsy won't be a problem for us. She won't be any problem at all." She took Baby Celeste from my arms and went into the house.

I wasn't sure why she had such confidence, but I had my first hint the next evening when Mr. Fletcher and Betsy came to dinner. I didn't know what he had said to her or threatened her with, but she was dressed nicely this time. She was wearing a bra, too, and a loose, light green blouse with a matching skirt and a pair of what looked to be brand-new shoes. Her hair was neatly brushed. She wore some lipstick, but nothing else. She was relatively sullen at the start, but she didn't make any sarcastic or nasty remarks. At what was obviously Mr. Fletcher's urging, she even offered to help serve our meal, but Mama told her she could be a guest tonight.

"After we're all living under one roof, we'll work out our responsibilities," Mama told her.

I could see it was on the tip of Betsy's tongue to come back with a smart remark, but she glanced at her father and then pressed her lips together like someone trying to keep from regurgitating.

Mama had made one of Mr. Fletcher's favorite meals, her meat loaf with garlic mashed potatoes. She had fresh, steamed string beans and homemade bread. For Betsy, Baby Celeste, and me, she had prepared fresh lemonade. She and Mr. Fletcher shared a bottle of red wine he had brought. Instead of serving family style as she usually did, however, she prepared each person's plate beforehand and brought it in.

Mr. Fletcher immediately began to rave about the food. Betsy pecked at it to start, determined to not appreciate anything, but even she was unable to not enjoy what she was eating and was soon eating more enthusiastically. Mama and Mr. Fletcher talked about their wedding plans as if none of us were there.

"I'm looking forward to you meeting my good friend Wyman Bogart," Mama told him. "He and I have been working together for some time. He's an old family friend, my oldest here."

"I have a surprise for you," Mr. Fletcher said, winking at me. "You talked about him and his store so much, I went over there yesterday and picked out a beautiful wedding ring for you. And," he said, tilting his head, "he told me you had already done the same for me."

"That was supposed to be a secret," Mama said, pretending to be upset.

"Our days of keeping secrets from each other ended very quickly," Mr. Fletcher told her, and they both laughed.

Betsy looked at me and dropped the corners of her mouth. Baby Celeste laughed along with Mama and Mr. Fletcher. They continued to talk about the wedding, Mama's plans for the dinner, and the music they would have. Mr. Bogart, who had found the minister Mama wanted, also had a musician who played the accordion.

"That's your music?" Betsy asked, finally speaking up. "An accordion?"

"It's just to provide music while we eat really," Mama said.

"Sounds like a terrific wedding," Betsy said, and scooped the last forkful of meat loaf into her mouth.

"It's simple, but it's full of meaning," Mama told her. Mr. Fletcher agreed.

Betsy said nothing more. In fact, she suddenly looked more than just bored; she looked tired, droopy. Her eyes closed and opened, closed and opened.

"Let's not worry about the dishes right now," Mama told Mr. Fletcher when he rose to help her. "Take everyone into the living room and I'll play something."

"Fine," he said.

Betsy looked confused when we all rose.

"We're going into the living room," I told her as I started for Baby Celeste, but to my surprise, she turned and reached out for Mr. Fletcher instead.

"Here we go," he cried, and lifted her out of her seat to carry her.

Betsy's eyes grew small with envy and anger before she rose and followed along. When we got there, she plopped into Grandfather Jordan's rocking chair and closed her eyes.

Before Mama came in to play for us, Betsy was asleep. Mr. Fletcher was too occupied with Baby Celeste to notice.

I looked at Mama and she raised her eyebrows and then smiled.

"She won't be a problem," she whispered, then went to the piano.

10

Elliot's Web

♊

Betsy didn't wake up until Mama stopped playing and it was time for her and her father to leave. It was as if Mama's music had kept her in a coma. She looked confused, even a bit frightened, at how much time had gone by and how much she had missed. She sat up, her eyes blinking, and vigorously rubbed her cheeks.

"Are you feeling all right, dear?" Mama asked.

"Yes," Betsy said quickly. "I guess I was just . . . bored," she offered, trying to climb out of her pool of embarrassment. Even Baby Celeste was staring at her as if she were some sort of freak.

"Bored? How could you be bored with that music?" her father asked.

"That kind of music puts me to sleep," she insisted. "It's elevator music."

"Perhaps you're just not used to a simple, gentle lifestyle," Mama said, keeping her irritation under a waxy smile. "In time I'm sure you will adjust and be very happy."

Betsy raised her eyebrows at me as if she expected I would offer sympathy and agree with her review of Mama's music. When she saw I wasn't going to come to her defense, she shook her head.

"I can't wait," she said. "Look at how much it's done for Noble man."

"I'd rather you didn't call him that," Mama quickly retorted, but still held on to her smile.

"Noble? You don't want me calling him Noble? I thought that was his name. Does he have a nick-name?"

I felt the blood rise to my cheeks.

"I don't want you calling him Noble *man.*" Mama looked at me. "He is a very noble man, but his name is just Noble, as yours is just Betsy and not Betsy *girl,*" Mama explained as pointedly and as carefully as she would explain to a foreigner.

"Right," Betsy said. "Fine. Noble it is." She really looked as if she didn't have the energy to put up any arguments. At her father's obvious urging, she thanked Mama for the evening and left ahead of him, showing how anxious she was to get out of our house.

"I'm sorry about her behavior," Mr. Fletcher told Mama when we all stepped out together.

"She'll get better," Mama assured him.

He shook his head and smiled at her never-ending optimism. "You're something, Sarah. Thank you for everything." He kissed her good-night. He patted me on the shoulder but gave Baby Celeste a hug and a kiss on her cheek.

"Bye-bye," she called, and he laughed.

"What a child," he cried back to us, got into his car, and drove off.

We stood there watching the car go down the driveway.

"You never told me about all the work that was done on what would be Betsy's bedroom, Mama." It had been simmering under my tongue ever since Mama had showed it to Betsy.

"Work was done on your room as well, Noble," Mama said, smiling. "We all love you and will never stop loving you."

"I know, but you never mentioned doing anything to that room. I was just surprised."

Her smile evaporated quickly. "You sound more envious than surprised. You wouldn't be either if you were trying," she accused, and went back inside with Baby Celeste, who was looking at me over Mama's shoulder with a similar expression of accusation on her face. Sometimes, she reminded me of a puppet when she was with Mama.

"Trying? What do you mean, trying? What haven't I done?" I asked, following.

Mama paused and turned slowly back to me. "You're not doing enough if anything is a surprise to you. Put out all the lights and go to bed." She started up the stairs to put Baby Celeste to bed. Rather than her rising above me, however, I felt as if I were sinking lower and lower with every step she took, shrinking until I might disappear into the floor.

If anything was a surprise to me? What was all that supposed to mean? What did she expect me to know?

I put out the lights and ascended the stairs, feeling almost as exhausted and depressed as Betsy. However, once again, as was too often these days, sleep was hard to capture. I tossed and turned, fretting in and out of dreams full of faces I'd never seen, voices I'd never heard. In between, I saw Betsy's smirking face and felt

her eyes crawling over my body like two spiders trying
to get into every opening.

She stayed away from our house all the following
week. Whenever Mr. Fletcher appeared for dinner, he
said she was either not feeling well or seeing some
friends. Both Mama and I knew he was making ex-
cuses for her, but Mama pretended it didn't matter or
upset her, while I was relieved not to be swimming
through all that tension.

The talk at dinner was always about the wedding
and what would follow. Mr. Fletcher and Mama still
had no plans for any sort of honeymoon, but they did
talk about trips we might all take in the near future. I
couldn't imagine Betsy being part of any of it.

Possibly because the gossip about us in the community was now so thick and curiosity about us so
overwhelming, Mama's regular group of customers
returned more often and new customers accompanied
them. No matter what remedies they sought, their
conversation always turned to Mama's impending
marriage to Mr. Fletcher. Everyone wanted to look at
Baby Celeste, who always enjoyed their attention. It
was truly as if she knew how to model and perform
the way Mama wanted her to perform. She'd smile,
talk, and let anyone who wanted to hug her, hug her.
If Mr. Fletcher was there at the same time, the visitors obviously considered it a bonus. Anyone could
see how quickly Baby Celeste had taken to him.
Heads would nod like those of the little toy animals
people put in the rear windows of their automobiles.
Off the busybodies went like hens clucking eagerly to
spread the news.

"People are talking about us everywhere," Mama
said. She called it "a symphony of wagging tongues"
and laughed as if she were the satisfied orchestra con-

ductor. Indeed, everything Mama wanted to happen seemed to be falling into place. Unlike me, nothing surprised her. She expected it all and her confidence influenced my own growing belief that higher spiritual powers were truly directing her every decision.

The crowning piece then occurred. Ten days after the New York couple had visited Mr. Fletcher's house, they made an offer. He countered and they settled. Everyone who visited us and learned of the relatively quick sale was astonished. From what I overheard them say, real estate apparently didn't move that rapidly in our area, and certainly not a house as old as the one the Fletchers had bought. Suddenly, instead of bad luck attending anyone who had personal involvement with Mama, good luck came. Combined with the positive results enjoyed from her herbal medicines and supplements, this new air of promise about Mama encouraged the gossips and meddlers to want to be in her aura, to shake her hand, to touch her or have her touch them.

One of Mama's strong beliefs was in fact a faith in her ability to transfer good energy into someone. It wasn't exactly the same as what people called the laying on of hands. She never claimed to have divine powers. Instead, she talked about an inner heat. Her body was simply blessed with the ability to capture the positive spiritual flow around all of us and channel it into people who needed and desired it.

How many times had I seen her place her palms on someone's temples, close her eyes, and hold her hands there until the client, as she liked to refer to him or to her, opened his or her eyes and declared the headache was gone? She removed aches and pains in shoulders and arms, legs and stomachs, and together with her herbal concoctions, she cured insomnia, indigestion,

arthritis, migraines, as well as sped up the healing of
operations and injuries.

I could still remember her soothing Daddy's tired
muscles and healing his aches and strains with merely
the massaging of his shoulders and back.

"I don't know if you have powers or not, Sarah," he
would say, "but I sure like your warm touch."

It brought a smile to my face to remember those
days, those happier times when Noble and I were
young enough to still believe in the promises of rain-
bows and miracles. Mama filled our ears with wondrous possibilities. It was truly like being in a special
womb, cared for and protected. The spirits that whirled
about our home and us were impenetrable, inviolate,
and most important, loving.

Although Noble did not care or pursue the spiritual
as much as I did, Mama's talk of it encouraged him to
have a faith in his own invulnerability. He could jump
from any tree, run as fast as he wanted, go as deeply
into the forest as he pleased, without the fears that accompanied most people. Warnings ran down his back
like raindrops on a windowpane. His own death must
have been a terrible surprise, a betrayal he never
imagined. I could never stop thinking about that moment, that brutal, ugly moment that changed all our
lives.

By the end of my musings and reveries, my vivid
recollections of those precious days, I usually had a
deep feeling of sadness and an even deeper sense of
loneliness. Once, Noble was the only friend I had in
the world. Now, I had none and the prospect of Betsy
being any sort of friend was slim and even frightening.

She had little or no interest in me anyway. Between
the time Betsy had come to dinner and the next time
she was at our home, she had spent time in the village

and malls, renewing some old friendships and making new ones. Mr. Fletcher complained that she could attach herself to a new boyfriend in hours. No sooner had she met someone who interested her than she was bringing him around and treating him like someone she had been with for months, even years. I understood Mr. Fletcher to mean she was intimate too quickly.

"I suppose it's my fault," he told Mama. He was always blaming himself.

They would sit together on the porch after dinner and talk, and I would be with Baby Celeste in the living room with the window open. I could hear their conversation.

"And why is that, Dave?"

"I never gave her the love and attention she required. She always had great needs, my Betsy, so she went elsewhere. She still goes elsewhere. We keep drifting apart. The truth is we're more like strangers these days."

"Perhaps we'll be able to change all that very soon."

"If anyone can help me do that, it's you, Sarah. You must have been a wonderful teacher. I'm sure the school was sorry to see you stop."

"I was a teacher here. I never stopped," Mama said as sharply as I had heard her say anything to him.

"Oh, sure. I bet. I mean, I know, and one can easily see what a wonderful job you've done with Noble. He's a fine young man, bright, polite, and very responsible. Why couldn't I have met you first?"

I knew Mama was smiling at him. The silence led me to believe they had kissed as well.

Sometimes, when I overheard them talk like that and when I saw the way Mr. Fletcher looked at Mama, his eyes full of admiration and love, I wondered myself if she hadn't cast some sort of a spell over him.

Was there an herbal concoction she had fed him, a love potion as many people believed, which she still fed him? Were there ways to do such a thing, and if you did, how could you feel the person really loved you? What would happen if you stopped feeding him, stopped the spell? Was it something he really wanted and something you merely showed him how to have, or was it simply trickery?

It was on the tip of my tongue to ask Mama these questions, but I was afraid, afraid she would somehow see it as a weakness or a failure on my part. How could I even think such things? she might ask, then narrow those eyes with suspicion and once again cross-examine me about who whispered in my ear. No, it was better to wait and have her tell me things, I thought. It was almost always better to do that.

Betsy never let go of the theory about some magic spell, however. She never visited with me without either coming right out and stating it or implying it. Whenever she returned to the farm, she would come up behind me in the shed or at the garden and rant.

"My father is very different," she would tell me. "I don't even recognize him anymore. It's Sarah this and Sarah that. He tells me I should try to be more like your mother. Imagine comparing me to someone who sells fake medicine and believes in ghosts."

"We don't believe in ghosts," I snapped back at her.

"*We?* Oh, is it *we?* You believe in it all, all this spiritual mumbo jumbo my father rants about? Energy in the air, a balance in nature?"

I said nothing. I didn't want to mention it, but I was sure I saw two of our cousins standing nearby listening and whispering to each other. They were wagging their heads, too.

"If you want to know the truth, it's this," she said,

stamping her foot to get my attention. "After Elliot died, my father told me never to set foot anywhere near this place. Not even look in your direction, and here we are, practically moved in already. How did that happen if she didn't do something weird to him, huh? Well?"

I wish he still believed we were bad and wanted what he had told you, I thought.

"People can change their minds, and people fall in love," I muttered instead.

"Oh, people fall in love. Look who's telling me, Mr. Plant Man whose only experience with sex is planting seeds in the ground. You're pathetic."

When I didn't respond to any of her baiting, she would get bored and leave me, mumbling all sorts of accusations and curses under her breath.

Some days before the wedding, her father began to bring her things over to our house. She was still being bitchy about the move and wasn't helping him carry the cartons, suitcases, and other things up to her room. Instead, I helped him.

"Reality for Betsy is settling in quickly whether she likes it or not," he told Mama. "The furniture the new owners didn't buy along with the house is going out the door tomorrow, and her bedroom set is part of that."

It didn't surprise me to hear it. The plan was for them to move in a few days before the wedding.

He thanked me for helping with Betsy's things, and we brought them all into the house and up to her room. Some of the clothing we simply laid over the bed.

"We'll just leave it all like that," Mr. Fletcher said. "It's her job to put her things away. That goes for unpacking the boxes as well."

When the boxes were placed on the floor, I could

see their contents. One box contained her undergarments and another was filled with blouses. Another had a few bathing suits.

"She doesn't throw anything away or give anything away," Mr. Fletcher commented when he saw how closely I was looking at it all. *"Charity* is a curse word to Betsy. God forbid she think of someone beside herself."

After I finished bringing things up with him, he took a walk with Mama and Baby Celeste. He had a late shift at the drugstore so he left soon afterward. After dinner, after Baby Celeste had been put to bed and Mama had retired to her bedroom, I thought about Betsy's things. I couldn't help it.

As quietly as I could, I went to her bedroom and looked at the clothing we had placed on the bed. Going to the boxes, I sifted through the undergarments, the bathing suits, and other things. Her clothing was of course quite different from Mama's. Mama didn't have skirts as short or skirts with slits on the side. I never saw Mama in a two-piece bathing suit, and she certainly didn't have such sexy, abbreviated panties or sexy bras.

I found an outfit I recalled Betsy wearing that first night when I'd played Peeping Tom and looked in at her, Elliot, and Mr. Fletcher. This was shortly after they had moved into the old Baer property. For years people believed Mr. Baer had something to do with my disappearance, and the nasty rumors and innuendos finally drove him to sell at almost any price.

I watched them having their dinner. Betsy wore this black-and-red-pinstripe, short-sleeve blouse with a black tie tied loosely around an open collar and a pair of matching black-and-pinstripe pants. I thought she looked more like a boy than I did except that her cleavage was prominent in the opened blouse and her hair was beautifully brushed down about her shoulders. Something about the clothing was fascinating, the way it turned out to be feminine. Was it only because she wore it?

Seeing this outfit again and recalling how she had looked awakened my interest in myself, in the me buried inside. What would I look like in it? I didn't have as big a bosom as she did, but I was as tall as she was. The pants would fit. Somehow, looking at her things—her bra, her panties, all of her clothes—like this was just like being a Peeping Tom again. It stirred me in places I had always tried to keep still.

Betsy couldn't possibly remember everything she had, I thought. In an impulsive rush, I scooped up one of her pairs of black, sexy panties and with the pin-stripe outfit in hand went to the door of her room, paused to be sure Mama was still in her bedroom, then tiptoed as softly as I could up the small stairway to the turret room. Once there, I closed the door softly. My heart was pounding.

Enough moonlight was coming through the windows to illuminate the room, but I knew one table lamp also worked. Under the subdued light in front of one of the antique-framed, full-length mirrors, I slowly began to take off my clothes. At one point I thought I heard the sound of footsteps on the small stairway and I froze to listen. The house creaked as it often did, but I heard nothing else and released my trapped, hot breath.

I took off the boy's briefs and put on Betsy's sexy panties. They were a little big, but the sight of myself in them fascinated me. They made my rear end feminine and my tight, hard legs somehow softer, more curvy than I had imagined they were. I turned and looked at myself from all angles before putting on the pin-striped pants and the blouse. I left it unbuttoned just the way I remembered she had. The blouse was also too big, but not terribly so. The pants fit well enough. Then I tied the black tie loosely around my collar and gazed at myself. Was I as interesting, as fashionable, as sexy, and as attractive as Betsy had been? Even thinking the word *sexy* made me shudder. For a long moment I stared at the sight of my cleavage. My breasts were perky, firm. Surely, I thought, I was more beautiful than she was. Young men would look my way faster than they would look hers.

I smiled to myself. Wouldn't it be wonderful to show her up someday? How quickly that smug arrogance would pour off her face. She would go and crawl up into a ball in some corner and she would deserve it. How many people had she hurt, driven to tears? Wasn't she trying to do it to me?

The definite sound of footsteps below sent me into a panic. I undressed as fast as I could, and as quietly as possible, I put on my own things again. Then I waited and listened. Hearing nothing, I went to the top of the small stairway. Sounds were coming from below. Mama was downstairs. I took advantage of the opportunity and quickly descended. I went to my own room and I shoved Betsy's things under an old suitcase on the floor of my closet. Then I undressed again and got into bed. And not a moment too soon, either.

Mama was at my door, white candle lit and in a holder in her hand.

"Are you asleep?"

I pretended I was, but it was always hard to pretend around Mama.

"You're not asleep, Noble, so stop acting like you are."

I turned and sat up. "What is it?"

"Something woke me. Something isn't right." She walked farther into my room. She lifted the candle so that the light from it would wash over the walls, into every corner and finally over me. "Do you feel it?"

My heart began to pound again. What should I say? Did some spirit tell her what I had done?

"No," I said. "I was falling asleep."

"But you weren't asleep. Something kept you awake. Well?" she demanded.

"I was just . . ."

"Just what?"

"Worrying."

"About what?"

"Betsy makes me nervous." That softened her shoulders. She lowered the candle and the shadow hooded my face.

"Oh. Yes. She could make anyone into a nervous wreck. She's done quite a job on her father. But I told you. She won't be a problem."

"She thinks you put a spell on her father." I thought that if Mama heard that, perhaps she would not be so eager to go through with the marriage. It would at least take her attention off me.

It only made her laugh.

"Of course she does. Three-quarters of the community believes that, I bet. Let them, let her think that. She'll be more afraid of me, and that's what a spawn like her needs to be, afraid.

"Poor Noble." Mama surprised me by sitting on my bed. She hadn't done that since I was very little. She brought the candle around to light up my face, then she reached out and stroked my cheek gently, running her fingers over my lips and under my chin.

"Would I ever let anyone, especially someone like that, harm you? Would our precious loving family stop protecting you? As long as you believe and hold on to your faith, you will be unassailable. She will see all this quickly and she will change or . . ."

"Or what, Mama?"

"Or be gone." She stood. She stared down at me, then she looked around again, slowly moving the candlelight about the room. "But there was something," she said in a whisper. "Something was in this house tonight."

She took a few steps toward my closet and for a long moment stood there staring at it. I held my breath. If she found Betsy's clothes, the panties . . .

When she turned away from the closet, I breathed easier. She looked down at me again.

"We've got to be vigilant, Noble, always vigilant. Remember, we have a precious person to protect. If ever you do anything or think anything that might endanger Baby Celeste, you hesitate. Understand?"

"Yes, Mama."

"Good. Good. Okay, try to sleep," she finally concluded.

She walked slowly to the doorway, turned, and lifted the candle one final time. Then she left, the light dragging behind her like a faded gold shroud being pulled into the darkness.

I lay back and stared into that darkness. I thought I heard whispering, but when I turned toward the wall, it stopped.

I've got to be good, I thought. There is nothing they cannot see.

I went to sleep promising I would.

The next day Betsy appeared with the remainder of her things. I helped her and Mr. Fletcher carry it all to her room, and then, without saying thanks or anything, she just closed the door in my face.

"She'll calm down," Mr. Fletcher assured me. "She

would always pout and sulk when she didn't get her way. My wife used to give in to it. I did, too, but those days are over now," he vowed, and smiled at me. "But let's not think of anything unpleasant, not at the start of a whole new wonderful life."

He put his arm around my shoulders. I didn't want to pull away, but it made me nervous.

"Maybe soon you and I will go up to the lake, huh? We'll take out a boat and have a real day together. What do you think?"

"Maybe." I knew I should have sounded more grateful and eager, but I couldn't.

"It's all right. We'll take it a day at a time. This is a big change for everyone. I appreciate that."

I helped him bring in his things next. Mama had just recently cleaned out her closets. For years and years, Daddy's clothing had hung there and had still been in the dresser drawers. As if it were part of some spiritual ritual, she decided to pack all that herself at night and bring it up to the turret room. I had offered to help her, but she said it was something a wife had to do alone.

Through the closed turret-room door, I heard her talking, and from what I heard, she was talking to Daddy's spirit. I wondered if she was apologizing, if it was a sad conversation, but I soon heard her laugh. "How wonderful!" she declared, then she became very quiet. I moved away quickly. I knew that if she ever caught me eavesdropping, she would be angry.

Helping Mr. Fletcher put his clothing away, however, was an entirely different thing. This I could do. He remarked about how much space was available to him.

"The closets in this house are much bigger than they were in mine," he told me.

Afterward, the four of us, Mama, Mr. Fletcher, Baby Celeste, and me, went out to plan where we would put the tables for the wedding feast and how we would arrange it all. Betsy was still up in her room sulking. Mama and I had created an arch for the wedding ceremony. I built it and she decorated it with vines and flowers. She and Mr. Fletcher then pretended to have a wedding rehearsal.

"This looks more like a stupid picnic," we heard, and turned to see Betsy watching from the porch. "What if it rains?"

"It's not going to rain," Mama told her.

"Right. You control the weather, too," Betsy chimed. "I'm going to town to see Dirk," she called to her father. "By the way," she added as she walked to Mr. Fletcher's car, "he's my guest for the picnic."

She laughed and got in. She drove off too quickly, spitting up gravel.

"I warned her that I wouldn't let her use my car if she drove like that," Mr. Fletcher said furiously. "That girl has gotten more traffic tickets. It's a wonder she hasn't been in a serious accident. I oughta cut off every gray hair in my head, put it in an envelope, and hand it to her with a thank-you card."

Mama laughed.

He looked at her and smiled. "I'm sorry, Sarah. I shouldn't add a single note of unpleasantness, especially right now, but that girl . . ." He looked after her.

Mama stepped up beside him and threaded her arm through his.

"She will change," she declared with such certainty, he had to look at her and smile. She nodded. "She will change," she promised.

The wind through the trees seemed to make the branches tinkle as if they were laden with tiny bells.

Baby Celeste heard it and looked that way. Her laugh turned Mama to us and the forest.

But Baby Celeste had turned completely around and was staring at the arch now.

When Mama turned to look that way, her smile wilted.

Did she see him?

I saw him.

Like someone waiting, like a spider who had spun his web, Elliot was standing in the middle, smiling gleefully at all of us.

11

A Down-to-Earth Wedding

♊

The following day, the Reverend Mr. Austin, Mr. Bogart's friend, came to our house to review the wedding ceremony with Mama and Mr. Fletcher. His wife, Tani, accompanied him. She was a pleasant, amiable, and talkative little woman, and I learned she was a close friend of Mrs. Bogart's wife's and knew quite a bit about us and our family history.

The reverend was a handsome man of about fifty with light brown hair and aqua eyes. He had a soft, gentle manner and touched your hand or your arm to reassure you whenever he said anything that might in the least way cause concern. He immediately made Mr. Fletcher feel at ease.

"When you had one marriage that failed, you naturally think it's your fault and you're naturally afraid of making another commitment," the reverend told him. They had taken a walk together, and I overheard it all while I was working in the shed, sharpening my chain saw with a chain-saw file.

Later, when we were all in the house, the reverend said he had a philosophy about marriage, a belief in the joining of kindred spirits.

"It's the fortunate man or woman who finds a soul mate," he said. "Too many of us are blind to the wondrous workings of the human heart, but I believe it is true that for everyone out there, there is someone."

"It was true for us," Tani said. She smiled at me. "And to inherit a fine young and responsible boy like Noble and a child such as Celeste to boot. You are truly a blessed man."

"I think so," Dave said. The references to me made me blush.

Mama prepared a nice lunch for everyone, then afterward, we all went through the steps of the wedding ceremony. Mr. Fletcher had somehow forced Betsy to attend, even though she would play no role in the formal activities. I thought she was there simply because she couldn't get her boyfriend to pick her up and take her away.

It took only two rehearsals for Baby Celeste to learn how to walk to the arch and hand Mama the wedding ring for Mr. Fletcher. She had such a serious expression on her face the whole time, too. It brought laughter to everyone's lips but Betsy's.

"What a beautiful and wonderful little girl!" Tani Austin cried.

Anyone could see how proud of herself Baby Celeste was, especially in the way she stepped back beside me, took my hand, and waited patiently for the rest of the wedding ceremony to continue. Betsy, on the other hand, let us know how bored she was by wearing earphones and listening to her music the whole time. I thought it wouldn't surprise me to see her do the same thing during the actual ceremony.

Mr. Fletcher ignored her and concentrated on Baby Celeste.

"She'll steal the show," he said. "But I'd enjoy being robbed by that sweet face any day."

Somehow, Betsy heard that over her music and paused to grimace smugly at him. She pretends not to care about her father's affections, I thought, but she doesn't hide her envy and jealousy when he shows how much he loves Baby Celeste. What good can come of all this? I continued to wonder. Why wasn't Mama afraid of it all? It wasn't beginning with any promise of hope and goodness.

In fact the first night Betsy slept in our home was a disturbing disappointment for Mr. Fletcher because she stayed away with her new boyfriend, Dirk, all day and called to say she wouldn't be at dinner that night. She was going with friends to New York City and would be home late. Before Mr. Fletcher could oppose her, she hung up. He came into the living room, shaking his head, and described the short conversation to Mama and me. I had the sense this was the first of many sessions like this to come.

"She speaks so quickly, I can barely manage to get a word in," he groaned. "And if I start to complain or ask a question, she speaks over me. Her mother used to do that. I'm sorry, Sarah."

I wondered if it was possible to estimate how many times over the next few months he would be apologizing to Mama for his daughter's behavior.

"Well, she knows her way home. We'll leave the door unlocked and the lights on," Mama told him without the slightest note of annoyance in her voice.

He nodded and dropped his defeated body into

Grandpa Jordan's chair. He smiled with delight, commenting on how comfortable it was and how at home it made him feel. It made me wonder if marrying Mama would give him the ability to experience the spiritual powers in our home. Would he draw strength from them as she did? Mama glanced at me, her eyes twinkling. To my amazement she still looked happy about it all, even the impending problems Betsy would bring into the house.

I didn't wait up for Betsy. I was sure that Mr. Fletcher did, however. He didn't go up to bed until late, sitting by the windows in the living room so he could watch for car headlights. Finally, Mama coaxed him up the stairs and into their bedroom. It was nearly morning when I woke up to the sounds of Betsy returning.

She did little to mask her entrance. She shut the front door hard enough to shake the walls, then stomped up the stairs, deliberately rattling the balustrade.

Mr. Fletcher had probably not slept at all. The moment she reached the landing, I heard him step out and whisper loudly, "Do you realize what time it is and how much noise you're making? You'll wake the baby."

"Why should I care what time it is? I'm not going to work tomorrow. I can't help it if that old, rickety stairway creaks. This place is just a big shack."

"Betsy," he said sharply.

"Well, it is. Tell everyone I would like to sleep all day and no one should bother me." She went into her room and slammed her door closed.

I heard Mama call to Mr. Fletcher. "Come on back, Dave. Get some rest. You're going to work in a few hours."

He muttered under his breath and went back into their bedroom.

No one tried to be any quieter than usual in the morning to please the princess. If anything, Mama deliberately banged doors and slammed dresser drawers. She spoke loudly to Baby Celeste and plodded down the stairs making more noise than Betsy had coming up a few hours earlier.

Mr. Fletcher smiled at breakfast and shook his head. "It won't matter if we set off a bomb down here. When that girl sleeps, it would take a crane to get her out of the bed."

Today was his last day to work before the wedding. He was taking the next day off and then they were to be married. He would take the following day off and then return to work, saving his vacation time for when Mama decided they should take the trip. They thought it might be fun someday to drive up to Niagara Falls, just because it was the old-fashioned idea for a honeymoon. He had gotten some pamphlets and had them on the table in the living room, hopefully to get Betsy interested. When he had mentioned it before to her, she had complained about driving so far.

"I get nauseous in a car, and besides, what would I do?"

She smiled at him and me and Mama and added, "Why don't you two go and leave us at home. We can care for the baby, can't we, Noble?"

The very idea of it, of being alone with her in this house, made me shake inside.

"You have trouble taking care of yourself, much less an infant," Mr. Fletcher told her.

She didn't get insulted. She just laughed that taunting laugh of hers and flipped one of the brochures.

"You can count me out of this," she declared firmly.

"I'll stay here and watch over the plants. You'd trust me with that, wouldn't you, Mrs. Atwell?"

She loved to taunt Mama by calling her Mrs. Atwell instead of Sarah. I had no doubt that even after her father and Mama were married, she would still call her that.

"I think it would be nice if you started to call Sarah *Mom*," her father told her, and she shot him a look so furious, he was lucky her eyes couldn't launch darts.

"She's not my mom so why should I call her that?"

"She'll be the best mom you ever had," he replied.

"I don't need a mother," she said, wagging her head.

"What do you need, Betsy?" Mama asked her softly, her face full of interest.

"Money," Betsy cried, unable to deal with Mama's calmness, "so I can get the hell out of here."

"So get a job," her father said. "I'll even help you find one."

She sat back with her arms so tightly crossed, she made the veins in her neck press against the skin until they looked embossed. She was soon in her sulk, and nothing anyone said or did would bring her out of it. It was better to just ignore her and go on to some other topic. What a happy home we're going to soon have, I thought.

As her father had predicted, the day after her New York trip Betsy didn't rise until it was already afternoon. We were having lunch, and when she came down, she unleashed a flow of complaints that seemed to nest in her mouth as comfortably as termites in damp, rotted wood.

"I can't sleep in that room! The bed is too soft and the windows sound like they're about to shatter when the wind hits them. I can't get the smell out of the room either. If I open the windows in there, mosquitos come through the holes in the screen. I need a fan or something."

"You seem to have slept well," Mama said, pretending surprise.

"I didn't sleep well. I slept. Why do the closets have that odor?"

"Mothballs," Mama told her.

"Mothballs? What are mothballs?"

"They keep moths away from the clothes so they don't eat holes through them."

"Ugh. Bugs live in the house? We didn't have many bugs in our old house."

"We don't have them either. That's why I have the mothballs," Mama said dryly.

I don't know if it was just my imagination, but sometimes when Mama spoke to her, she had a small smile on her lips.

"The whole house needs to be sprayed with something that will kill the odors, if you ask me," Betsy whined.

She started to search the kitchen cabinets and the pantry for something to eat and grumbled her grievances about the food Mama had.

"There isn't even a doughnut here."

"That's not a nutritional breakfast," Mama told her. "I'll fix you some toast and jam. The jam's homemade."

"Oh, brother. Can you drive me to town or let me use your car?"

"No, I can't let you use the car. Your father didn't give me permission for that, and I have things to do before I can go into town. Amuse yourself for a while."

"Doing what?"

"Why don't you help Noble," Mama suggested. I looked up at her quickly. Why was she putting Betsy on me?

"Doing what?"

"Noble, what are you up to today?"

"I wanted to start on gathering firewood, Mama."

"Firewood? It's still summer!" Betsy cried at me.

"The wood has to season and it needs to be split," I told her. I had deliberately chose work that she wouldn't be able to do.

"I'm not going to chop wood. You want me to have hands like yours, break my nails?"

I looked away. No, I don't want you to have hands like mine. *I* don't want to have hands like mine, I thought.

"You can watch. Maybe you can read. I'll give you a book to read to Baby Celeste, if you like. You should get her to know you better," Mama said.

Betsy stared at Mama, then glanced at Baby Celeste, who had just finished her lunch. "I still don't understand why you call her Baby Celeste and not just Celeste."

Mama had a way about her when someone other than me made her angry. She didn't like to show her rage, but because I knew her so well, knew every strand of her hair, every line in her face, I could see the subtle changes. Her mouth tightened slightly in the corners, her eyes narrowed just a bit and darkened, and the muscles in her neck stiffened before she formed a cold smile.

"If you must understand, I'll explain it. I once had a child named Celeste."

"I know all about her. My father talked about it enough."

"And so you know how I tragically lost her. My cousin graciously named her new baby after my lost daughter, Celeste, but we like to make a distinction for now. It's less painful. Memories can be like thorns in your heart," Mama said, moving closer to Betsy. "I'm sure you have painful memories of your brother, after the tragic loss you and your father suffered. It's not something to be ashamed of, but it's something you don't want to experience constantly, now do you?" Mama was inches away from Betsy now, hovering as if she could make that happen, make Betsy suffer constantly.

Betsy's anger and hardness softened under Mama's gaze. For the first time, I saw a glint of fear in her. She retreated a step.

"I'm not that hungry," she declared, seized a piece of bread, and charged out of the room. We heard her go outside soon afterward.

"Old habits die hard," Mama told me, looking in her direction. "She'll come around or be in even more pain than she is now."

I said nothing, afraid that whatever I said, Mama would take it wrong. Instead, I did what I had proposed I would. I went into the woods and began to cut firewood. Betsy watched me from the porch and then went into the house. Soon after she managed to get her new boyfriend to come out and pick her up. She didn't tell Mama he was coming or that she was leaving either. Later, she returned with her father, went directly to her room, and then emerged to go out on another date with her boyfriend. She came home earlier, but made just as much noise. This time, her father ignored it. I imagined Mama told him to do so.

The following day, because he was not working, Mr. Fletcher took Betsy shopping. He asked me if I wanted to go along. For a moment I was tempted to do so, but I glanced at Mama and then quickly shook my head and thanked him.

"What, Noble leave his precious plants and farm chores?" Betsy taunted. "He wouldn't know what to say to people unless they had leaves for ears and roots for legs."

I didn't defend myself. I wouldn't give her the satisfaction. She smirked and said she wasn't that keen about going shopping either. She didn't really want to buy anything nice to wear to the wedding ceremony and dinner, but Mr. Fletcher bribed her, promising her the use of his car the day after the wedding. Once we had all seen what she bought to wear, we realized he would have been better off if he hadn't.

"Make an effort, Betsy, please, for all our sakes," he cajoled.

I hated to hear a grown man beg his own daughter like that. Maybe if he had been firmer with her, things would have turned out better. Among the antiques in the turret room was a wooden plaque. Mama told me her great-grandfather once had it hanging on the wall in the hallway. It read, *Spare the rod and spoil the child.* She said her grandfather had bad memories of his father's harsh punishments, and once his father had died, he took the plaque off the wall and dumped it in the turret room. Mama wondered now if she shouldn't have nailed it to one of the walls in Betsy's room.

We didn't find out until the day of the wedding what Betsy had bought to wear. She wouldn't let her father see it either. He just gave her his credit card to use and she had it all in a box when she met him in the mall parking lot. The moment I set eyes on her, I knew she had chosen it for its shock value.

Twenty minutes before the wedding ceremony was to begin, she came downstairs wearing a navel-baring, stretch-jersey black dress with a skirt that was a good two inches above her knees. The material was so tight to her bosom that little was left to the imagination. She might as well have come out bare-breasted.

She had her hair pinned up and had enough makeup on her face to supply the entire cast of a Broadway musical. At least, that was what Mr. Fletcher told her. Her eyeliner was too thick, for sure, and with the heavy layers of bright red lipstick on her lips, she looked like a vampire who had just had a feeding.

Mama would not let her get the satisfaction of seeing her outrage. She flashed her a smile, then gave all her attention to our wedding guests, the most important ones for Mama being Mr. Bogart and his wife, as well as our attorney, Mr. Derward Lee Nokleby-Cook, and his wife, who was looking everywhere and at everything with a devouring hunger and interest. She had surely given herself the assignment of bringing back as much detail as possible to her friends about this wedding. Everyone was full of curiosity.

We knew that because Mr. Fletcher had come home with stories he was told in the drugstore. "They think we're getting married in some sort of weird ritual. Some people have pretty wild imaginations."

"What sort of things are they saying?" Mama asked.

"Oh, just ignorant, stupid things," he replied, obviously not wanting to describe them.

"Some of the people I met think you're going to sacrifice a goat first and then smear the blood on your faces," Betsy eagerly told Mama.

Her father gave her a chastising look, but Betsy shrugged. "I can't help it if that's what they think," she whined. "Don't blame me."

"I'm amazed they found out," Mama said with a straight face.

"Excuse me?"

"The goat is being delivered in the morning." Then Mama looked at Mr. Fletcher and they both laughed.

"Go on, make fun, if you like," Betsy said angrily,

"but that's the sort of thing people out there believe about you. And now they'll believe it about you, too," she told her father before storming out.

"Won't they all be disappointed?" Mama said, shaking her head.

They would have been. Nothing about the marriage ceremony was radical or unusual. No one wore a bizarre costume. The Reverend Mr. Austin came dressed in a dark blue suit, and his wife, Tani, wore a pretty, red, sleeveless dress. Joining them was the accordion player, Bob Longo, a stout, dark-haired man who looked as if he had borrowed his sports jacket from someone a good two sizes bigger and had black hair growing wildly down the back of his neck and curling at the ends.

The rest of the wedding party included the two managers from Mr. Fletcher's drugstore and their wives; another pharmacist, Larry Schwartz, and his wife, Joan; and the real estate agent who had sold the Fletchers' house, Judith Lilleton, and her husband.

A minute or so before the ceremony was to begin, Betsy's new boyfriend, Dirk Snyder, whipped his car into our driveway, throwing up a cloud of dust. He came barreling to a stop and leaped out as if he thought the car might explode under him. He was dark-haired, slim, with a pair of close-together brown eyes and a thin, crooked mouth that looked sliced across his face with a bent hacksaw. An unlit cigarette dangled from the corner of his mouth, and his sports jacket was tossed over his shoulder. He hurriedly put it on as he walked toward us. Betsy went out to greet him and whispered something in his ear that made them both roar with laughter. I thought I saw him slip her a pill.

I gazed at Mr. Fletcher. He had his head down,

standing by the minister, waiting for Mama to come out of the house. All eyes were on Betsy and her boyfriend as they took their places. Mr. Longo began to play "Here Comes the Bride" and everyone turned to look at the front door of the house, where Mama emerged, holding Baby Celeste's hand. I could hear people gasp with delight and amazement.

Mama had made Baby Celeste's dress out of the same material used in her own and styled her hair similarly as well. No one looking at them could think the child was anyone else's, and since she had inherited some of Mr. Fletcher's facial features, the foregone conclusion rested comfortably in the faces of our guests.

Mama and Baby Celeste came down the stairs and walked toward the arch where the Reverend Mr. Austin, Mr. Fletcher, and I waited. At the beginning of the short aisle we had created with chairs for our wedding guests, Mama released Baby Celeste's hand and knelt down to whisper something to her. She nodded and looked toward the rest of us with such a mature expression, everyone smiled. Mama continued down the aisle and took her place.

The ceremony began, and at the proper moment Baby Celeste walked down the aisle as she had rehearsed and gave Mama the wedding ring. Then she stepped back and took my hand. I exchanged a glance with Mr. Bogart. Something in his face told me he knew more than anyone else about us. His face was full of kindness, though. I felt no threat, no reprimand or accusation.

I heard Betsy's smothered laughter and glanced back to see her and her boyfriend giggling together. They looked drunk or already high on something. That was probably the pill I had seen him hand her. When the ceremony ended, everyone gathered around Mama and Mr. Fletcher to congratulate them. I lifted Baby Celeste in my arms and stepped back to watch.

"So, I guess this means I've got myself a new brother," I heard Betsy say, and turned to her and Dirk. "Whether I like it or not. Say hello to my brother, Noble man, Dirk."

"Yeah, hi," he said, and squeezed my hand hard. I didn't grimace and he laughed and then brushed Baby Celeste's hair. "Hey, you did a great job carrying the ring, kid."

She just stared at him the way Mama would, her eyes full of ice.

"Noble used to be my real brother's friend until he died, right, Noble?"

"Yes."

"Noble raises plants and chops wood all day."

"I'm going to go help bring out the food," I said.

"Noble's perfect. He's a perfect child and never causes his mother a moment's grief," Betsy told Dirk in a voice loud enough to follow me.

I paused and turned back to her. "If you want to help, follow me."

"Right," she said. "Just lead the way."

I started toward the house and heard them both laugh. Mr. Bogart's wife and Tani Austin were already inside preparing to bring out the food.

"I just love a down-to-earth wedding like this," Tani Austin said. "Too many affairs we go to are impersonal." She turned to Baby Celeste and me. "Your little cousin is simply the cutest child I have ever seen. I can see the family resemblances," she added, but not like a busybody.

"Thank you," I said, then helped bring out the food. Mama had prepared it all with her special herbal seasonings. We had turkey and roast beef, creamed onions, mashed potatoes, an assortment of vegetables, and homemade bread. Mr. Bogart had brought white and red wine, and Mama had permitted Mr. Fletcher to get the wedding cake from a baker who was one of his customers and who wanted to do something special. It had three layers with a chocolate trim around each. At the top were the two figurines under an arch created out of candy cane.

Before we began to eat, the reverend rose to make a toast: "There is no more magical word than *family*. It is truly a human garden in which the plants have to be nurtured with love and care. Both of you"—he looked at Mama and Mr. Fletcher—"have had more than your fair share of hardships, but somehow, through it all, you have endured and grown stronger. Nothing will make you both stronger than your union today, and nothing will be more of a blessing to your children than the love you bring to bear on them all. To your good fortune."

Everyone drank.

I glanced at Betsy. She wasn't laughing. She was staring with such anger and distaste at Mama and her father that it put a dark spot of terror in my heart. Then she turned to Dirk, whispered in his ear, and they both laughed again. They ate what they wanted and suddenly decided they were going to leave.

Betsy asked me if I wanted to join them. "We're going to meet some friends and party. Why don't you come along?"

"They haven't cut the wedding cake yet," I said.

"So what? It's just cake. Where we're going there'll be lots better."

I shook my head. "It's their wedding and it's not over."

"Oh, brother. What am I going to do about my new brother, Dirk?"

He shook his head. "Hey, if he's happy, let him be."

She stepped closer to me. "Are you happy, Noble? Should I let you be?" She deliberately brushed her breasts against my shoulder.

I looked about in a panic.

She laughed. "Don't worry." She took Dirk's hand. "I'll devote myself to helping you get over your shyness."

It sounded more like a threat than a promise. Trailing laughter, they hurried away to Dirk's car, not even taking the time to congratulate her father and Mama or tell them they were leaving.

Once again, Mr. Fletcher apologized for her, and once again Mama told him not to worry.

"I hope you will someday soon think of me as your new father," he said to me later. He had drunk quite a bit of wine by then and he looked a little sad, I thought. "I hope like me you will see all of this as a new start, a new chance for happiness."

I thanked him and then I looked over at Mama and saw an expression of great satisfaction on her face. She had taken the first important step in her plan to create a world safe and perfect for Baby Celeste, but would it be perfect and safe for me? I wondered.

Afterward, while everyone was enjoying Mr. Longo's music and relaxing, I had an opportunity to be by myself. I wandered up to the old cemetery and stood just in front of where I knew Noble was lying. Twilight had begun and it was that time of day when shadows nudged each other and began to awaken and stretch. When we were little, Noble and I thought night came about because all the shadows merged and blanketed the earth in darkness. The morning light would shatter them again and shrink them.

"But where do the shadows go in the daytime?" he always wanted to know. He asked Daddy, too, but Daddy didn't have a satisfactory answer for him. Daddy's answers were too scientific to satisfy a young boy with an active imagination.

"Where do shadows go?" he persisted, turning to Mama for the answers now. When Noble was curious about something, really curious, he was relentless. "They always come out the same way, with the same shape, don't they?" he pointed out.

It was a good observation, I thought, and even though I was satisfied with Daddy's answers, I looked forward to Mama's response.

"They go to sleep," she finally told him. "They sleep in the daytime."

"Where?" Noble chased.

"In the earth."

That wasn't a good enough answer either. If they were asleep in the earth, why couldn't he dig them up?

Did he still wonder about such things? Is a spirit curious or does a spirit know everything? When would I truly be like Mama and be able to have long conversations with our spiritual family and not just hear a few words and see them for seconds or see them like someone saw a mirage? Would I ever? Had it all passed me by and now, as she said, taken hold of Baby Celeste instead?

The voices of the wedding attendees were carried up to me in the soft, cooler evening breeze. Stars were beginning to emerge and twinkle above.

I looked toward the forest, but I saw nothing.

"Where are you tonight, Daddy?" I asked. "Are you here? Are you upset? Please come back to me," I begged.

There was the sound of laughter now and music again.

I turned and slowly walked back to the tables and the people. Mama was singing for them. She was singing "La Vie en Rose." The reverend and his wife, Tani, held hands like two new young lovers. Dave was gazing at Mama with such affection in his eyes.

I should be happy for her, I thought. She's so happy. Her voice is so full and perfect.

But when I looked up at the house and at a window that I knew to be one in my room, I saw the glow of the light from the hallway, and in the pane, silhouetted clearly to me, was Elliot. In the silvery glow of the starlight, I was sure he was smiling.

After all now, he was securely inside the house and not just inside my troubled heart.

12

Just You and Me Against
All These Females

♊

For a while I thought Mr. Fletcher might be right: this was a new start, a new chance for happiness for all of us, even Betsy. She was occupied with her new social life and surprised her father and us at dinner one night by declaring that she wanted to enroll in the community college.

Mr. Fletcher was so happy about it that he nearly leaped out of his chair to kiss her. "That is wonderful news, Betsy, just wonderful. If you do well at the community college, you'll be able to get into a four-year school and complete your degree. What are you thinking of becoming?" The words rushed out of his mouth so quickly it was like a dam full of hope had been broken. It made me think these words, this optimism, these ideas, had been held in escrow in his head for so long, they flooded over his tongue and nearly caused him to gag with enthusiasm.

"You know that you ought to seriously consider

teaching. Sarah can give you some pointers about that, having been a teacher herself. Or you could think of a career in the medical field. I could help you with that. You might even think of a business degree."

After his outburst, he sat there, smiling stupidly at her. Mama and I and even Baby Celeste just stared at Betsy, waiting for her to respond. Now she looked like the one who was overwhelmed. She glanced at each of us and then back at him.

"I don't know," she finally muttered. "Don't get so excited, Daddy. I said I was thinking about doing it. I didn't say I would definitely do it."

"I hope you decide to do it," he said. "Don't hesitate to ask me anything if it will help you. Sarah, as well," he added, turning to Mama.

"Of course," she said. "I'd only be too happy to help you with your future. It's never too late to think about it or too soon."

Betsy looked as if she had taken a step in a direction she didn't really want to go, but later, overhearing Betsy talk on the phone to some girl she had met, I learned the real reason for her considering community college. She had met another guy, Roy Fuller, who was attending the community college, was a star on their basketball team, and according to Betsy, was good-looking and sexy. Apparently, she had already dumped Dirk and was in serious pursuit of Roy Fuller.

Two days later she did enroll in the community college. Her father was more than willing to pay every expense, including buying her a late-model used car. After all, she told him, she had to go back and forth to the college and she couldn't put the burden on "poor Sarah, who has an infant to care for and an herbal farm to operate."

Whenever she was being nice or, in my eyes, con-

niving, she called Mama *Sarah;* otherwise, she re-
verted to addressing her as Mrs. Atwell, especially
when her father wasn't present.

"I'm no longer Mrs. Atwell," Mama would calmly
tell her. "Your father and I were married."

"Whatever," Betsy would say.

The following week, her father and she went looking for an appropriate car, and they returned with a
sporty-looking model in red.

"If you're nice to me, Noble man, I'll take you for a
ride," she told me after they had brought the car home. It
looked spankingly brand-new and had chrome everywhere and real leather seats. "I might even let you take
it for a ride. How would you like that?"

"Thanks, but no thanks."

She narrowed her eyes at me, then asked, "Do you
have a driver's license?"

I looked away.

"You don't, do you? How can you not want to have
a driver's license? It's the first thing anyone your age
wants, especially boys. You are weird," she charged, as
if I were doing her some sort of injury by not wanting
a driver's license.

"I want it. I just haven't gotten around to it," I muttered to get her off my back.

"Not gotten around to it! You're too old to be depending on your mommy to drive you around. What is
she going to do, pick up your girlfriend for you whenever you decide to have one? That'll be a scene." She
laughed at me. "You'll go parking and fool around in
the backseat while Mommy sits up front and waits and
maybe peeks at you in the rearview mirror."

"Shut up," I finally said. I had held back any sign of
temper until then.

"Excuse me? Shut up?"

"Just leave me alone," I begged, and hurried away from her.

"Freak!" she screamed after me.

Happily, she was so occupied with herself and her love interests and her new car those first few weeks of our new life together that she rarely paid any attention to me or to Baby Celeste. She wasn't around all that much, rarely ate dinner with us, and always slept too late for breakfast with us, so I didn't have to confront her often, but I could see that she was getting increasingly impatient and annoyed with my deliberate avoidance and disinterest in her and her affairs.

I was really surprised she actually went through with registration for the community college courses and bought the required books and notebooks. She had made promises to her father before and broken them. Why should this be any different? However, she went through with it and made a big show of it all, mostly to please her father.

I noticed Mama was noncommittal about Betsy's new college career. She said nothing positive or negative about it to any of us. When Mr. Fletcher praised Betsy for making an intelligent, albeit long-delayed, good step in her life, Mama sat with a soft smile on her face and occasionally shifted her eyes toward me. Her look gave me the eerie feeling things were still falling in place the way she wanted and the way a higher power had designed. I did not understand where it was all headed. I was happy about Betsy's decision because I thought it would mean I would have even less contact with her, but other than that, I didn't know what to expect.

Then, one night Betsy surprised us all at dinner, me especially, by suggesting I might follow in her footsteps.

"You could enroll just like I did. You have a high school diploma. You could be in the same classes as I am and I'd take you back and forth until you get your own driver's license. Well?" she demanded. "What do you think of the idea? It's a good one, isn't it?" She pushed me to say yes right then and there.

It threw me into a small panic. I looked at Mama, who sat like Buddha expecting me to come up with a good response and showing me no indication of what she wanted to hear.

"That really isn't such a bad idea," Mr. Fletcher said. "What do you think, Sarah?"

"When Noble is ready for it, he'll tell us," she finally said.

"Why isn't he ready for it?" Betsy challenged. She turned back to me. "You can't just hang around here for the rest of your life nursing plants and being a babysitter."

I didn't respond, which frustrated her. She shook her head and looked to Mama. "He's not retarded, is he?" she asked.

Mama smiled. "Hardly. In fact, I'm sure you'll be asking him to help you with your homework."

Betsy reddened. "Well, if he's that smart, why isn't he interested in doing something with himself?"

Mama looked lovingly at me. "Noble is a very special young man. He has more than just some book knowledge. He achieved very high grades on all of his exams and he knows he can do whatever he wants when he wants to do it, but he has something else, too."

"What's that?" Betsy inquired with a smirk.

"Wisdom. Wisdom. That's something you don't get out of books or classes or teachers. It comes from in here," Mama said, putting her hand over her heart.

"Oh, brother," Betsy muttered, shaking her head. "You see what a weird person you married and what a weird family you married into, Daddy?"

He turned crimson. "Betsy! That's a very inappropriate remark. I want you to apologize immediately," he snapped.

Ordinarily, she would have laughed in his face, I thought, but he was giving her money; he had given her a car and was going to pay the insurance for it. She was still working to keep on his good side.

"Okay, okay," she said. "I'm sorry. I just thought it would be nice if my new brother joined me at the college. We could share homework, study together, get to know each other more and more. What was so terrible about my suggestion?" she asked, her face full of self-pity.

Her father's face softened. "Well, those are all good motives, Betsy." He looked at me. "You just have to give everyone a little more time."

"Time? For what?" she cried.

"Time for relationships to develop properly. We ease into them slowly, carefully, if we want them to last and be worthwhile for all concerned," he lectured.

That was a lecture she never heard or cared to hear. I knew her well enough already to know she treated people, especially boys, like someone might treat a new flavor of the month.

"Okay, Daddy," she said sweetly. "I'll give it all time. Whenever you want to know anything about the college, Noble, just ask."

Mama kept that inscrutable smile on her lips. I could hear her laughing inside, however. That would be the day I ever needed to ask Betsy for anything or about anything, she thought. She wasn't all that wrong

Van Buren District Library - Antwerp Sunshine Library
24823 Front Avenue
Mattawan, MI 49071
269-668-2534   VBDL.org

Receipt - 12/28/2016

Van Buren District Library

Cambron, Martha

Items Checked Out Today:
Black cat
35101511542172   Due: 1/18/2017

Asylum
35101513591227   Due: 1/11/2017

CLOSED Friday Dec. 30 thru Monday Jan. 2
Happy New Year from your friends at VBDL!

to think it, and as Mama had predicted, soon after Betsy had begun her classes, she came to me to help her understand things, especially the math.

Up until then, she never came to my room. Now that she and Mr. Fletcher were living with us, I kept my bedroom door shut whenever I was in the bedroom. One evening she knocked on the door and then opened it before I had a chance to respond. I was lying on my bed reading.

"You're so smart," she began, "maybe you know what the hell this means."

Her forwardness with me made me uneasy, of course, but it also intrigued me. There was so much I didn't like about her, yet I couldn't help but be envious of the ease with which she met people, especially boys. She had no difficulty with little intimacies, making physical contact, holding hands, brushing her body against them, toying with them, capturing their eyes and interest. Did it come from a well of stupidity and recklessness, or a well of self-confidence?

She walked into my room and sat on my bed, slapping the math textbook on my lap. I raised my eyebrows and widened my eyes. She misinterpreted it.

"Oh, did I do some damage?" she asked flirtatiously. "Were you reading something erotic which made you excited? I know that could be very painful for boys. Was that it?"

"*No!*" I said too sharply and quickly. She laughed. "What do you want?"

She nodded at the opened book. "Look at that gibberish and tell me what it means. I'm supposed to do all those problems tonight."

I glanced at the pages. "Didn't your teacher talk about it in class?"

"I don't know. Maybe. I was busy." She smiled. "Roy sat right next to me, and you can put your hand under the desk. Know what I mean?"

"No." I really didn't.

"Maybe, if you're nice to me, I'll show you one day. So? What about the problems?"

I sat up and read the pages, hoping she didn't notice the way my hands trembled as I read. She was leaning over me, her warm breath reaching my face, the scent of her shampoo filling my nostrils. This was the way I could affect a boy if I were permitted to be who I really am, I thought. It made me nervous.

"It's elementary algebra," I began. "This is a college class?"

"Well, I guess so. I go to the college to attend it. I did take a test first and they did say something about remedial, whatever that means."

"Why is Roy Fuller in this class? Wasn't he a student there last year?" I asked, remembering some of the things I had overheard her tell her girlfriend on the phone.

"He isn't actually in the class. He just came to be with me."

"The teacher lets him do that?"

"I don't know. Yes. What's the difference? Who cares about that?" She stared at me a moment. "You know, your problem is getting very, very serious, Noble. You need to be with people your own age. You need a girlfriend."

Almost immediately, it threw me back to my time with her brother. He had told girls at school that he knew me well and he could get me to party with them. He used me to attract a girl he liked to him, and then, when I resisted, he went on and on just the way Betsy was.

"We could double-date," she said. "I have a girl-friend who would like to go out with you some-time . . .Well? Don't just sit there looking at me like that. You should be grateful, not dumbfounded."

"I can find my own friends."

"Yeah, right. Where will you look for them? In the forest? In the garden? The shed?"

"Do you want me to explain this or don't you?" I asked her sharply.

She shrugged. "Yeah, I suppose. I don't want to flunk out of anything the first week. Daddy would be very annoyed. And Roy would be very disappointed." She laughed.

I started to go through it. I couldn't help taking on Mama's teacher personality. It seemed to come natu-rally, but I could see Betsy's eyes moving over my face as I began to explain it as simply as I could. It was soon clear that she wasn't really listening or even slightly interested.

"Don't you shave yet?" she suddenly asked me. It sent a surge of electricity through my heart and down my spine.

"Yes," I said. "If you don't want to listen to me, why did you come in here and bother me?" I shot back at her.

"Relax. I was just curious. You're probably lucky you don't have a heavy beard or something."

She sat back, her hands on the bed, her body arched. How wonderfully free of inhibition she was, free of any self-consciousness about her body. When she looked at me, could she see the envy in my eyes?

"Roy likes to keep a two-day beard. He thinks it's cool or something. I guess it is sexy. I just don't like him rubbing his cheeks against mine. It burns. See," she said, nodding at me, "girls are going to like you.

You want me to talk to Fredda Sacks about a date? She'd like you, and believe me"—Betsy smiled coyly—"you'll have a good time."

"No," I said quickly and firmly.

She shrugged. "Okay, could you do me a big favor, then? Just finish those problems for me. I've got to get ready to go out. I'm meeting Roy at the mall. You could come if you want."

"If I do these problems, it won't help you. You won't learn anything."

"I'll learn it later. Thanks. Just leave it in my room when you're done."

She hopped off the bed and started out. "Once you have sex, you won't be so interested in your plants and things." She laughed. When she closed the door behind her, it was as if she had taken all the air out of the room with her.

Mainly to keep my mind off what she had said and done, I completed the math problems for her. She was already gone by the time I was finished, but I still knocked on her closed bedroom door before entering.

I hadn't seen her room since her father and I had moved her things into the house.

She had left all the lights on. The bed was unmade and clothes were tossed everywhere: over chairs, over the bedpost, and merely left in a pile on the floor by the closet as if the closet door were jammed. Her vanity table was just as much a mess, with open jars of cream, uncapped tubes of lotions, brushes, and hair clips scattered over it. What looked like a wet bath towel was draped over the back of the chair, and a stained washcloth was on the floor beside the chair. At the foot of her bed were three pairs of shoes, two lying on their sides, probably kicked off.

To get rid of what Betsy called a putrid odor, she

must have poured a bottle of cologne over the rug. It was so redolent that I couldn't imagine how she slept here. The window was shut and the shades drawn.

I looked about for a place to put the math book and the work sheet and decided to make a place for it on the vanity table. As I pushed things aside, covered some of the opened jars, I saw a container with dozens of tablets. Under each tablet was the name of each day of the week. I picked it up and saw from the label that they were birth control pills. I don't know why, but just holding the package frightened me and my fingers trembled so badly, I lost my grip. The container fell to the desk and the pills jumped out of their slots and flew off the desk, rolling every which way.

Panic dropped a sheet of cold ice down my back. For a moment my feet were embedded in the carpet. I couldn't move. My heart thumped with utter dread. I felt smothered. As quickly as I could, I started to gather up the pills. Some had bounced and rolled as far as under the bed. When I gathered up all I could see, I put them all back in the empty places, but there were seven places yet to fill, or, I wondered, were they empty to start? What day did the pills begin? I couldn't remember from my initial look.

I went back to my knees and searched the carpet even more carefully, inches at a time. When I found another pill, my turmoil intensified. If I had missed this one, I could easily have missed another and another. How important was it to finish all the pills and take them in the right order? What if I messed it up so badly she became pregnant? Was that possible? How I wished I knew more about this sort of thing.

With the tip of my nose practically brushing the carpet, I went back and forth as methodically as I could to be sure I didn't miss a spot. I knelt down and shoved my arm as far as I could under her bed and began to sweep my hand back toward me. Again, to my shock, another pill appeared. I hurried to put it in an empty space, then went down on my knees again.

"What are you doing?" I heard Mama ask, and looked at the doorway.

She was standing there with Baby Celeste, who somehow thought the sight of me on my knees was funny. I had left the door open, having no reason to close it. After all, I was just entering Betsy's bedroom to put the schoolwork somewhere. I was just going in and out.

"Well? Answer me, Noble."

I stood up and looked toward the vanity table. "I . . . helped her with her math and brought the book back."

"So why were you on your knees? What are you looking for, Noble?"

I started to shake my head and she stepped into the room.

"What is it?" she demanded.

"When I put the book on the table, I accidentally knocked something off . . . a container full of pills and some of them spilled out. I was just trying to find them all," I said quickly.

"Container?"

She walked to the table and looked at the packet. She glanced at me and then tightened her lips.

"I see. And have you found them all?"

"I don't know. I think I did."

"You shouldn't be in here, Noble, and you certainly shouldn't be touching any of Betsy's things."

"I just . . . she told me to put the book back in her room."

Mama continued to study the pills. She took the container in hand and then looked at me.

"Has everything been put back the way it was?"

"I think so. I'm not sure."

"Very good. Now get out."

I started away.

"Take the baby outside for some air," she added as I reached the door.

"For some air?"

"Yes, Noble. Take her for a walk. Go on," she ordered, and turned back to the vanity table. I wasn't sure, but I thought she was smiling.

Because it was a somewhat overcast evening, I didn't take Baby Celeste far from the front of the house. As always, she was curious about everything she saw. She wanted me to pronounce the name of anything she held or pointed at so she could repeat it and commit it to her memory. Recently, her vocabulary had grown impressively. She was putting together sentences and thoughts with the ability of someone years older. More and more when I looked at her now, I saw more thoughtfulness in her eyes and in her expressions.

I was proud of her and amused by her, but at times I was in awe of her. Did her quick study and obviously high intelligence mean she was as special as Mama believed, or was she simply a precocious child, just a bright little girl who could leap and bound over the challenges someone her age was supposed to master? I had achieved goals faster than they were normally achieved. Why make any more of it?

And yet, Baby Celeste did have something more in her eyes, something more in the way she studied everything and everyone. She could very well be the blessed child Mama predicted she would be.

"What will become of us, Celeste?" I asked her, half amusingly and half wondering if she could actually tell me. I was sitting on the steps of the porch.

She paused to look at me. She had a blade of grass in her hands and was trying to make a sound with it as I had shown her how to do. It was something Noble could do well. He played little tunes on blades of grass.

She hurried over to me and pressed herself against my leg as if she knew I wanted her beside me, to comfort me. Then she made the sound and laughed. I kissed her cheek. She had such light and delicate features, eyebrows that were barely visible, but long, beautiful eyelashes. If ever there was such a thing as someone with a delicious face, it was our Celeste.

She blew on the grass again, louder this time.

"You're getting as good at that as your uncle was," I whispered. I always felt I could tell her the truth, bring her close to that pool of revelation without endangering either of us much. She wouldn't understand and she never repeated anything I whispered. It was as if she knew what a secret was, knew it almost the moment she could hear one or see one.

Suddenly, she turned and threw her arms around my neck. I lifted her and kissed her cheek and she laid her head on my shoulder. The two of us sat there staring out at the darkness. I heard the distinct sound of branches cracking in the woods. My body tightened as I strained to see through the shadows.

"Deer," Baby Celeste said, and a moment later a small doe appeared.

It stood so still as it looked our way that it could have been a statue dropped in the night.

Baby Celeste slipped out of my arms and walked slowly toward the doe. It still didn't move. She lifted her hand and the doe lifted its head. Still, it did not flee. She took another step and another. I rose.

"Don't go too far," I warned.

She looked back, smiled, and walked forward. The doe's tail wove back and forth like a dog's. Baby Celeste lifted both her arms toward it, and to my surprise, the doe took a few steps in her direction. I held my breath.

And then the headlights of Mr. Fletcher's car cut into our driveway, pushing the darkness back.

The doe leaped to the right and then bounded into the woods, disappearing. I hurriedly scooped up Baby Celeste and watched as Mr. Fletcher drove up.

"Hey, Noble," he said, getting out. "What's going on?"

"Mama wanted me to take the baby out for some air," I said quickly.

"Yeah, it's a beautiful night. Still quite warm for this time of year." He paused. "Hi, Celeste."

She reached out for him and he took her into his arms and kissed her cheek.

"What have you been up to today?" he asked me.

"The usual. I'm getting pretty much along in the firewood." I said nothing about helping Betsy do her math homework.

He stared at me so hard, I felt a little uncomfortable.

"I've been thinking a lot about you lately, Noble. Betsy's suggestion that night at dinner wasn't all that bad, you know. Have you given it some thought?"

"A little," I lied.

"Well, no one has to rush into anything, fortunately, but I hope you don't think it out of line for me to give you some advice now that I've signed on to this family." He smiled.

I shook my head.

"You can't grow up helping your mother with an infant all the time, Noble, and doing simple farm chores. It's not a young man's life. You really do have to get out among people your own age, think about expanding your horizons, going further in your education, perhaps. Get a goal. I'd like to help you in any way I can."

I nodded and looked down.

He was living in a house of lies, and every time he spoke to me warmly like this, those lies danced in front of my eyes. He had accepted so much on faith, and so firmly, with such trust, that I had to wonder if he really lived under or within Mama's spell. What would happen when and if he confronted the truth? Would his heart simply burst?

"I also know how hard it is to grow up a young man with no father in whom you can rely and from whom you can get some advice, not only about things to do, but about yourself, your own emotional needs. I know we don't know each other as long as I'd have liked, but I want you to feel confident I will always respect your trust, keep any confidence you might want to place in me.

"After all," he said, bouncing Celeste a little in his arms, "it's just you and me against all these females here."

Oh, how my heart cried out for me to simply burst forth with the truth. No, I wanted to scream. You don't know me at all. You've never met me.

"Don't look so troubled, buddy," he said, running his hand through my hair. "I'm not pressuring you to do anything or say anything. All I want to do is let you know I'm here for you whenever you need me to be, okay?"

I nodded.

"Great. So," he said, looking about, "I see my daughter has gone somewhere again. She say where?"

I shook my head. "Something about the mall, I think."

"Hmm." He gazed back down the driveway. "She's there so much, she should get a job in one of the shops."

He turned back to me. "Just remember, Noble, little kids, little problems, big kids . . . you can fill in the blanks just watching me and Betsy. Going in?"

"Soon."

"Okay. I'll take Celeste inside. Cheer up, my man. Things are going to be just fine. We have too much going for us right now."

I smiled and nodded at him and watched him go into the house.

"What a fool," I heard, and spun around.

I couldn't see him in the darkness, but I was sure it was Elliot's spirit.

"You think he's stupid or just blind when he looks at Celeste and doesn't see himself?"

I studied the shadows and stepped forward slowly.

"Maybe he knows," he continued. "Maybe he's the one hiding the truth, living the lie. Ever think of that, Noble man?"

His laughter was carried off in the flapping wings of a spooked owl.

And in the wake I heard only the pounding of my own frightened heart.

13

The Problem with Betsy

♊

In the days and weeks that followed, Betsy's relationship to her new boyfriend grew more and more intense. Many nights she didn't return home at all and then showed up looking as if she had been up all night. She would sleep most of the day and walk about as if she hadn't yet gotten used to the miracle of being alive. She and her father would have frequent arguments about it and she would always threaten to move out. He and Mama discussed it often, and to my surprise she advised him to step back, give Betsy time to come to her own realizations and conclusions. Mama always seemed to be taking Betsy's side. If it was to get Betsy to like her more, it wasn't working.

In fact, I could see early on that one of the reasons Betsy was so determined to have her own romance was her disgust over her father and Mama's ever-growing-closer relationship. Mr. Fletcher, who now absolutely insisted I call him Dave, never entered the house, even a room, without kissing her. No matter what he was thinking beforehand or what sort of mood he was in when he returned from work, as soon as he set eyes on Mama, his face filled with sunshine. Every night after dinner when he wasn't on a late schedule at the pharmacy, they would take long, romantic walks together. He was forever buying her surprise gifts, and from what I saw him bring home, he had bought many things at Mr. Bogart's store.

Whenever he presented Mama with something in Betsy's presence or whenever he kissed her and Betsy was there, I watched her face. Her eyes twitched and she pulled in her lips. She looked away, and when her father asked her something, she either muttered a monosyllabic *yes* or *no* or simply ignored him. She always looked as if she couldn't wait to get out of the house and away from us, or should I say, *them*.

One night after Mama and Dave had left to go on one of their moonlit walks, Betsy, who was waiting for a phone call from her boyfriend, Roy, came into the living room where I was reading to Baby Celeste. She stood over us, her hands on her hips, and shook her head.

"God, how can you spend so much time with a baby?" she demanded.

"I enjoy how quickly she learns things. You would, too."

"Right. I just can't wait. Where are they?" she asked, gazing out the window. "Where the hell do they go out there anyway?"

"Just up the street, I imagine. There's a place where the road turns where you can go in a ways and see the creek at one of its widest points."

"Oh, really! Wow!" she said, turning back to me. Then she smirked. "I'm sure they're not going out there to look at the creek. They're probably necking under a tree or rolling in the grass."

"Why would they have to go outside to do that?" I asked, sounding simply curious.

"I'm sure they think it's more romantic or something. Maybe they see how the way they slobber over each other in front me makes me nauseous."

I just stared up at her. She narrowed her eyes and stepped toward me, her arms folded under her breasts.

"Doesn't it bother you to see your mother sleeping with my father, kissing him all day, holding hands and swooning over him like that?"

"Why should it? They love each other, don't they?"

"Please. Love." She looked away.

Baby Celeste could pick up on a tone of voice. She sensed the tension in Betsy's and stared up at her, her face so still, her eyes so full of interest.

"It's just embarrassing and disgusting for me to see, the way my father drools over your mother like that right in front of us. They act like . . . like teenagers. I can tell you I don't remember him being that way with my mother, and after she left us, he never went out on a real date with any other woman."

"So?"

"So I told you! It makes me sick to my stomach! That's what's so." Betsy paused and glanced at Baby Celeste. "Why is that kid looking at me like that?"

"She feels your anger."

Betsy smirked and shook her head. "She feels my anger? What are you, a child psychologist or something? Look at you, sitting there on the floor, reading a children's book. This is your idea of a night of fun. You really are pathetic."

Her words were like bee stings, but I refused to let her see how much they hurt.

"I'm going to have to help you with your vocabulary as well as your math," I said. "You need syn-
onyms."

"Oh, really? And what is that supposed to mean,
Mr. Genius?"

"It means you have to find other words to use when
you try to insult me. These are getting tired, worn-out."

She started to say something, then stopped and blew
some air between her lips.

"You know what I think," she finally managed, "I
think you're gay."

Just then the phone rang.

"Finally!" she screamed, and ran to it. I looked back
at the children's book.

"Tell my father I'm not coming home tonight," she
shouted from the hallway. "Not that he'll notice. His
eyes are too full of his new love."

I heard the door open and slam shut. Moments later,
she was in her car and kicking up gravel as she spun
around and drove down the driveway. I listened and
then looked at Baby Celeste.

"Betsy's sick," she said.

I laughed. "Yes, Betsy's sick. The thing is, she
doesn't know it and maybe she never will."

"Sick."

"Why do you say that, Celeste?"

She didn't reply. She looked at her book again and
picked up the story where we had left it before Betsy's
intrusion. Later, when Mama and Dave returned, he
was angry when I gave him Betsy's message.

"This isn't going to go on like this much longer," he
vowed. "I don't care how old she is. She has to show
us some respect here and take on some responsibilities.
With the light subject load she has at the community
college, there is no reason why she can't get a part-

time job and help support herself and especially that car.

"And she doesn't even ask if you need any help with the house and the meals, Sarah. You're too nice to her, letting her get away without doing more."

"I know, Dave," Mama said. "Don't get yourself all worked up again."

"I don't know whether I'm better off with her home or run off with some loser," he muttered. "I thought maybe if I provided her with a substantial home, a real family, a chance at some higher education . . ."

"She'll come around, Dave. They always do."

"I'm not as optimistic about it as you are, Sarah." He looked at me. "Sorry, Noble, I know she's not proving to be much of a sister to you or help with the baby," he added, looking at Baby Celeste. "Look at the smile on that kid. How can anyone refuse to take any interest in her? What goes on in that girl's empty head?"

"You have to relax, Dave. It's not good to go to bed with so much tension inside," Mama told him.

"Yeah, I know."

"Let me fix you something."

She made him a drink that she said would calm his nerves and help him to sleep. Like everything she prepared with a purpose, it worked, and soon afterward he was in bed, resting comfortably. After he was asleep, Mama came out of the bedroom and down the stairs. I thought she might be looking for me. Baby Celeste was asleep and I had gone out to sit on the porch. I felt that I was guarding the house.

She stepped out, sat in the chair beside me without saying anything, and stared into the darkness. Although she didn't look at me, I felt nervous, even a little afraid. Was she silent because she was angry at something I had done or said?

"You may wonder," she finally began, "why we have been alone these past weeks."

"Alone?"

She turned and looked at me. "Has someone been speaking to you?" she asked quickly.

I shook my head. I wouldn't tell her about Elliot, not now, maybe not ever.

"It's not because we've done anything wrong or because anyone is angry at us. There is evil in our house."

I held my breath. Did she know about Elliot after all?

"But it won't be here long," she vowed. She nodded. "Not much longer."

"What evil, Mama?"

"You know what evil. Don't start acting stupid again," she snapped.

I looked away, but watched her out of the corner of my eye. A moment later she smiled. "Baby Celeste is really becoming something, isn't she, Noble? You see it now, too, don't you?"

"Yes, Mama."

"Good. Then you understand why it is so important we continue to protect her and nurture her like some precious flower."

"Yes, Mama." I would do it anyway, I thought. After all, she was mine.

Mama rose. "Get some rest. We have difficult days ahead."

She stepped off the porch and walked slowly toward the old cemetery. I watched until she was swallowed up by the darkness, then I went inside and up to bed.

The difficult days she spoke of were filled with more and more tension because of the ongoing and sharper arguments between Betsy and her father. I could see the increasing wear and tear in his face, hear the growing strain in his voice. Whenever he set eyes on her, he would look troubled. He tried tying the money he doled out to her to work responsibilities in the house, despite Mama's advice to let that be. When he forced her to help with the kitchen and the dinners, she broke dishes or made a bigger mess in the kitchen. She couldn't set a table neatly, and whatever cleaning she did had to be done over anyway. He was always after her to clean up her room, but she never made her bed and didn't change linen until he forced her to do so. If she ate anything in the house, she left the dish wherever she had been sitting or lying. She dropped crumbs, spilled things, stained furniture. He was cleaning up after her more than someone would clean up after an errant puppy.

And all the while, Mama remained calm, understanding, still remarkably taking Betsy's side with the promise that she would soon change. The more sympathetic she was, however, the angrier Dave became at Betsy.

"Look at how nice Sarah is to you. How can you be so ungrateful and inconsiderate all the time?" he would chastise.

Betsy's reactions to her father's rants and raves were simply to look away, pretend she didn't hear him, or turn to me to ask a question as if he weren't even there. Frustration reddened his face. He looked more and more haggard, and when anyone asked him why he looked so tired, he would let loose with a catalog of problems he was having with his daughter. Mama and I were often witness to his speeches in the pharmacy because the sight of us would bring his vexation to a boil.

"That woman," he would say, nodding at Mama, "is

an angel. She's an absolute angel. What she contends with would drive anyone else mad. I don't deserve her, and Betsy certainly doesn't. Teenagers," he would spit, and people would nod in sympathy.

"She'll come around," Mama would say charitably. It never ceased to amaze me. From what trunk did she dig up all this patience and understanding? I knew firsthand what her temper could be like. Why wasn't she thinking of ways to change Betsy? Why was she so tolerant?

I couldn't disagree with Dave about Betsy being ungrateful. The nicer Mama was to her, the more she resented her. Betsy harbored all sorts of ridiculous suspicions, I thought.

"I know exactly what your mother's up to," she told me one afternoon after she had just had another argument with her father and Mama had interceded on her behalf. She came charging out of the house and found me stacking some kindling wood.

"What are you talking about now?" I took off my gloves and wiped the sweat off the back of my neck.

"I'm talking about how she makes herself look so good and pure to my father just so he'll hate me more."

"That's not true. She's just trying to keep him from getting sick over the things you do." I put my gloves back on.

"Oh, brother. You'd defend her no matter what. You know what?" she said, with her eyes as mean and cold as she could make them. I turned my back on her and started on the wood again, but she seized my shoulder to spin me around. "I said, you know what?"

"What?"

"People don't just think you're weird or gay. They think you and your mother have an unnatural relationship."

I wanted to reach out and slap her because it was as if she had just slapped me. I couldn't help the rush of blood to my face. It brought a smile to hers.

"Did I hit a sensitive area, Noble man? Is there some truth to the rumors? Maybe Daddy wouldn't be so devoted to your mother if he knew, huh?"

"Shut up," I snapped, and with the small hatchet in my hand I started toward her with such fury that she backed away.

"Don't you touch me. Don't you even think of it," she warned, but for the first time, from behind a cracked wall. "That's all you have to do. I'll make up stories about you," she threatened. "I will. I'll tell everyone you tried to rape me or something."

I shook my head and retreated. It restored her courage, so she stepped toward me again.

"You know, Elliot told me about the time he let you spy on me."

The blood that had risen to my face dropped to my feet. I kept my back to her.

"He brought you into his room and let you look through that hole in his wall. Go on, try to deny it. I'd like to hear what you say."

I continued to stack the wood. I'll do what she does, I thought. I'll pretend she's not there, pretend I don't hear her.

"I didn't care. I was actually flattered. Did you get a good eyeful? Did it make you excited? Did you fantasize about me and play with yourself? I like to think a lot of boys did and still do. Was I your first naked girl? What's the matter, the cat got your fat tongue? You're not so brave now, are you? Does your precious mother, who thinks you're so perfect, know about all that?"

Whatever angle I turned, she moved to stand in front of me.

"Leave me alone," I said, practically begged. Her smile widened.

"You can't believe he told me, huh? He did it to get even with me for something, and I surprised him by not getting angry about it. Who do you think is prettier, me or your mother?"

"That's a really stupid question."

"Oh, is that so? Why is it stupid? Because you can't appreciate any other woman? Is that the reason?"

"No!" I screamed at her. *"I can't!"*

She looked shocked. I hadn't meant to say that like that and she could never understand what it was I was saying anyway. How could she understand why I couldn't appreciate any other woman the way she expected I should?

"You are sick," she said, wagging her head and stepping back. "I'm getting out of here soon, getting away from all of you. You'll see. You'll all see and you can have Daddy to yourselves." She turned and marched back to the house.

Good riddance, I thought. The sooner you leave, the better it will be. I had no doubt she would leave and soon, but not before she was to wreak some more havoc on what her father had hoped would be a happy home, a new start.

It came first with the news that she had managed to get failing grades in every subject in which she had enrolled at the community college. My assistance in math hadn't helped her with the class because she didn't understand or try to understand any of the homework I had done. Her teacher knew pretty quickly that she was having someone else do the work, and like every other time she was exposed as a liar or a deceiver, she simply shrugged it off or made it look and sound like nothing of any importance.

Dave got the news first from one of her teachers at the college who came to his pharmacy for medication, and then he learned about her failures from the official college mailing that he read. His confrontation with Betsy over it came to a head in a storm of rage that threatened to blow out the very walls of our house. In the midst of that, I heard what people called the eye of the storm, the silence right before a hurricane resumes.

I had been outside most of the afternoon. I saw Dave return from work. He had gone into the store early and was off. He had the mail in his hands, waved to me, and went into the house. A little more than an hour later, Betsy drove in, her radio blaring as usual, the car spitting up dust as she tore up part of the drive-way and jerked it into the spot behind Dave's car.

It was late fall now. The days were shorter, the afternoons especially abbreviated. Years of experience in nature told me that the cooler breezes were foretelling an early winter. There were years when it actually snowed hard in October and the temperatures dropped to below freezing quickly.

I put all my tools away carefully and started toward the house. As I walked, I remembered my dog, Cleo, and how he had enjoyed following me about everywhere and how I enjoyed having him at my heels. He had filled the dark holes of loneliness and made my life here more than just bearable. Maybe I should get Mama to let me have another dog, I thought, but then I thought it would be heartbreaking if she came to harbor the same suspicions she had of Cleo.

I was really beginning to feel sorry for myself. Despite the brave and indifferent front I put up between myself and Betsy, her continual criticism, sarcasm, and challenges were having an effect. I could feel myself breaking down. I had come close to losing my temper a

number of times since her accusations about me and
Mama. I was tired of her lording over me, threatening to
do this and that to cause Mama to get angry. If anything
now, I was beginning to resent Mama's defense of her,
especially her understanding and tolerance. Why was
she closing her eyes to the harmful and damaging effect
Betsy was having on all of us, especially Dave?

Before I reached the porch, I could hear his shouting. I would quickly learn that he had rushed up to her
room after he had opened the letter from the college
informing him and her that she had been dropped from
the college rolls. None of us knew that she had been
dropped from two classes because she had simply not
shown up enough times, and apparently she had been
called into the dean of students' office twice to discuss
her situation. All the promises she had made, she had
broken.

I opened the front door and entered, listening to the
litany of charges and complaints Dave was shouting at
her up in her room. I closed the door softly and walked
down to the living room. Mama was sitting in the
rocker with Baby Celeste on her lap, her head against
Mama's breast, her eyes opened. She looked to be
listening as well. Mama didn't turn to me. She kept
gazing out the window, her face remarkably at peace,
actually caught in a beautiful glow.

Dave had left Betsy's bedroom door open so it was
impossible not to hear every word.

"Why did you even start this if you knew you
weren't going to do it properly? Just to get me to buy
you a car? Was that it, Betsy?"

"No," we heard.

"Then why? Why? To make a fool of me?"

"I don't have to do anything to make a fool of you.
You do enough yourself," she fired back.

There was a moment of silence.

Mama's smile widened. Why?

I thought he would just walk out and slam Betsy's door, but I didn't hear any footsteps.

"What do you intend to do with yourself now, Betsy?" he finally asked her, his voice quivering.

"I don't know. I have other problems, bigger problems."

What could they be? I wondered.

Mama turned her head slowly toward me and our eyes met. Baby Celeste was looking my way, too.

"What bigger problems?" Dave asked Betsy.

"It's not my fault. It's your fault!" she shouted.

"Excuse me? What are you talking about now, Betsy? What's my fault?"

I turned toward the stairway and listened hard.

"Those pills you gave me. They didn't work. They were probably old or something."

"What? You mean . . . are you talking about the birth control pills?"

"What other pills did you give me, Daddy?"

Another silence made the air in the house heavy.

"My God," Dave said finally. "Not again?"

"It's your fault!" she screamed. "You probably gave me samples or something that was no good anymore."

"You neglected them? You had unprotected sex and neglected to take your pills? Is that what you're saying?"

"*No!* Look," she screamed. "See, I followed directions. See, every pill I was supposed to take, I took."

I looked back at Mama. She was smiling now. The pills I had dropped, I thought.

"Mama?"

"Take the baby, Noble, and get her cleaned up for dinner. I have to get started on it," she said, rising from the chair.

I heard the door slam upstairs and a moment later Dave's footsteps on the stairway. He descended like someone going to his own funeral, his head down, his shoulders slumped. I took Baby Celeste's hand and started for the stairway. He paused and looked at me, and when he did, I saw such pain in his eyes, my own heart closed like a fist in my chest. His face was white with shock and agony. He just shook his head and continued down the stairs. He knew, of course, that we had heard the whole argument between him and Betsy.

Betsy's door was shut tight. I took Baby Celeste into the bathroom and helped her wash up and fix her hair. She loved to brush her own hair now and was very aware of how she looked, her clothes and shoes.

Betsy did not come down for dinner. Dave ate sparingly. Mama continually urged him to eat and not get himself sick over the situation.

"We'll do what we have to do, Dave," she said, putting her hand over his.

He nodded. "I'm sorry, Sarah. It wasn't supposed to be like this. I wasn't supposed to be bringing you new and bigger problems."

"For better or for worse," Mama recited. "In sickness and in health."

He smiled and looked a bit cheered. She threw me a glance that made me shudder a little. It was more like a conspiratorial glance. What did she think I knew or understood? I really felt sorry for Dave, and I was beginning to feel that I was part of some great betrayal. Even though I had no sympathy or love for Betsy, I hated seeing him so distraught and defeated.

After we ate, Mama prepared a dish and told me to take it upstairs to see if Betsy would eat.

"You don't have to do that, Sarah," Dave said. "She's old enough to know to come down if she wants something to eat. We're not going to cater to her any-more, not now."

"We won't," Mama assured him, "but we can't let her neglect her health, Dave, especially now, now can we?"

He had to nod, to admit she was right. "I'll take it up to her."

"No, Noble can do it. Besides, she might not open the door for you. She's in a funk. She's actually just embarrassed and feeling very guilty, and the sight of you only reminds her of her own failing."

"You're probably right about that, Sarah. Your mother is much wiser than I am, Noble. Maybe she does get good advice from a higher source."

Mama smiled and then looked firmly at me. I didn't want to have anything to do with Betsy, but I took the plate upstairs and knocked on her door.

"I have some food for you," I said when she didn't respond.

I expected she wouldn't answer and I would just turn and bring the food downstairs, but to my surprise, she opened the door abruptly. She was standing there in her bra and panties.

"You're just gloating, aren't you? You and your mommy," she accused.

I shook my head. "No, of course not. Why should we gloat?"

"That's all right. I've got a big surprise for all of you." She turned back to her closet. She plucked a blouse off the rack and slipped it on, turning to smile at me as she buttoned up. "You like watching a girl get dressed?"

"I came up here to give you this." I nodded at the plate. "Do you want it or not?"

She looked at the food. "I'm sick of the food your

mother makes. Nothing is normal. I bet you've never had a piece of pizza." She turned and found a pair of jeans to put on.

"So you don't want it?" I asked, tired of her quips and nasty remarks.

"You are bright," she said, sitting to put on her shoes.

I glanced to her right and saw a suitcase. "What are you doing?"

"What am I doing? I'm getting a life, getting away from this insane asylum."

"How can you leave?" I asked, more curious than happy about it.

"Watch me and you'll get the idea. Maybe someday you'll wake up, realize you're becoming weirder and weirder, and you'll leave yourself, although I have big doubts. After all, how can you stop reading children's books and talking to shadows?"

She smiled at the expression on my face. "Oh, you didn't know I overheard you whispering out there sometimes, did you? Or that I put my ear to your door and heard you talking to no one. You're crazy, aren't you? Do you see dead people?" she asked, laughing. "I know your mother thinks she does. Everyone knows about that.

"Which," she added, running a brush through her hair, "makes me wonder what the hell my father was thinking when he asked her to marry him."

"You just can't run away. You have a big problem to solve."

"Big problem?"

"We heard. We couldn't help but hear the way you were screaming at your father."

"Oh, so you're worried about me, Noble man? Well, don't," she snapped, and tossed her brush onto the vanity table. "I don't need your help or your mother's or my father's either."

She scooped up her suitcase.

"Where are you going?"

"Away," she sang.

"By yourself?"

"No, not by myself, stupid. I met someone who's fun to be with."

"You mean Roy?"

"No, not Roy. Roy is too in love with himself and his glory as a college star. He's not going anywhere."

"But . . . whose . . ."

"Baby? You want to know whose baby I have inside me? Well, that's for me to know and you to wonder about." She laughed. "Don't look so surprised. It makes you look even dumber than you are. Here, I changed my mind. Give me the food."

She reached out and with her free hand took the plate from me.

"This is what I think of your mother's cooking." She dumped it on the floor. Then she pushed past me and started down the stairs, her suitcase banging against the balustrade.

Dave came out of the living room and saw her descending.

"Where do you think you're going now?" he demanded.

"Away from here!" she shouted, and opened the front door.

I watched from the top of the stairway.

"Betsy, don't you dare leave this house," Dave warned. "I mean it. If you run off now with all these problems, I won't help you. I won't send you money. I won't—"

"*Don't!*" she screamed, her eyes bulging. "Stay here and die."

She stepped out and slammed the door so hard the house shook.

Dave lowered his head like a flag of defeat. I came down the stairs slowly and Mama came out of the kitchen, wiping her hands on a dish towel. She looked at Dave, who stood by the closed front door, and then she looked up at me.

She was smiling.

And that smile turned my blood to ice.

14

Dave Takes Sick

♊

Knowing that his daughter was pregnant and had run off with some new stranger she had met even after he had achieved what he thought was a new beginning for himself and her caused Dave to become as despondent as he had been the day he learned his son, Elliot, had died. He as much as admitted it to Mama.

"No matter what I do or try to do, I'm a failure as a father, Sarah. I've lost both my children. My whole family is gone. I feel like a man in mourning."

I wanted so much to tell him that all was not lost, that he was actually living with and caring for his own grandchild, but I had no idea what horrible things might come from such a revelation. It would lead to another and another, and our world would unravel like a ball of string. Only Mama could unwrap the secrets in our world. Only she knew what should be told and when something should be told. To defy her was to defy the spiritual family who protected and loved us. I would surely suffer some terrible punishment for it. I might even be sent to hell.

The tears I shed for Dave could fall only behind my eyes. I knew he was the kind of person who would worry more about my sadness than his own, and that would make me feel even worse, make me feel even more like a liar and a deceiver. Maybe the real reason Mama restricted the number of mirrors in our house was to prevent me from looking at myself, from seeing who I was and what I was. She was always worried about what my face revealed, even if only to me.

"You might as well be the front page of a newspaper, shouting the headlines, Noble. Stop scowling," she would say, or, "Stop pouting. And for God sakes, when we go anywhere, stop pressing your nose to the car window and looking out at everyone and everything with such desperate interest. Anyone would think you had been kept locked up in the basement all your life."

Would I dare tell her that I did feel that way sometimes? Did I have to tell her? Couldn't she see my thoughts scribbled over my face anyway?

Dave was certainly getting easy to read. The more forlorn he became, the more drawn and haggard he appeared, the more concerned I grew. I watched and waited for Mama to do more to help him, but she didn't appear to be worried. Was everything exaggerated in my eyes? Surely, she could see more than I could see, I thought. Yet I knew he wasn't eating well or for that matter sleeping too well. I heard him get up often late at night and walk softly downstairs to make himself a cup of warm milk, or, as I discovered one night when I came out and looked for him, to just sit in the old rocking chair and stare out at the night as if he were waiting up for Betsy, who had gone out on a date. Did he wake up thinking, hoping, all that had occurred was only a dream, only a bad dream? Go down and sit in the rocking chair, he told himself. She'll be home soon.

More and more he was drawn to the old rocking chair. He would even sit in it after dinner rather than sit on the sofa or the big cushioned chair. I wondered why he was drawn to it. Was he finally making a spiritual connection the way Mama often did with things in our house, things that had belonged to our ancestors? Did it give him relief or was he unable to resist it? Did it keep him trapped in his own depression?

Shadows deepened in every corner, walls creaked, and the chandeliers swung ever so slightly with every closed or opened door, sometimes their bulbs blinking like eyes. The whispering I often heard in the darkness grew louder and more frequent. Did Dave hear it, too? Did he think he was going mad? I saw a strange darkness in his eyes as he looked toward every sound. He was truly like someone who had stepped into a pool of depression, a quicksand of despair drawing him down, down, down.

He no longer rushed to ask Mama to take their famous romantic walks in the moonlight or starlight after dinner, and I noticed he would often drift into his own deep thoughts so quickly and for so long, he was even unaware of Baby Celeste pulling on his pants leg in an attempt to get him to pay attention to her.

"Dave," Mama would say.

"What?" His eyes would flutter as he looked about the room.

"The baby." Mama would nod at her sitting at his feet and looking up at him.

"Oh. I'm sorry. Hi, Celeste," he would finally say, and lift her into his lap, but his concentration was still directed elsewhere, lost in his thoughts. Was he thinking about his dead son or his errant daughter?

Weeks and weeks passed. Betsy didn't call or send any letters, which, according to Dave, was not unusual.

"Whenever she ran off like this, I would hear nothing or know nothing until the day she returned."

"Once she sees how much trouble she's in, she'll come hurrying back," Mama assured him, but he shook his head.

"Things are different this time," he muttered. "There's just too much resentment in her heart. I've made mistakes, many, many mistakes."

Mama assured him he hadn't, but he seemed inconsolable. During the next few weeks, he ate even less and less, lost weight, and developed dark circles around his eyes. He plodded along with his head down, his shoulders turned inward, going to work in a robotic, mechanical manner, and rarely brought home any interesting stories or told us about funny occurrences at the pharmacy.

"I know you're taking your vitamins," Mama told him, "but you need some of this, too." Periodically she had him drink one of her herbal mixes designed to restore energy. Only, this time it didn't seem to be working as quickly as it usually did for others, including me.

Eventually, Dave began to miss work. He would wake up with a bad migraine, take the medicine he dispensed to others, then sleep most of the day. Mama gave him her own remedies as well, and sometimes they worked rapidly and he was up and about and back to work, but more often than not, he remained lethargic and, in any case, never seemed to regain the glow of happiness and enthusiasm with which he had come into our lives.

Whenever he did show an interest in something, especially something he might do with me, I quickly agreed. I took rides with him to get things for the farm, had lunch with him at a fast-food place, even though Mama hated them, and willingly left whatever I was doing when he asked me to join him. I even went for walks with him in the afternoon. He would stop to look at his former home and tell me how he had felt when they had first moved in.

"It wasn't much to look at when we first moved in. Betsy hated it, of course, but Elliot seemed excited enough about it. He wasn't the great help on the property you are to Sarah, but he wasn't depressed or negative. After a while, he did seem to get along with his new friends. That's true, isn't it?" he asked me, as if he wasn't sure. "Eventually he was happy here, wasn't he?"

"I would say so, yes," I told him.

That pleased him, and seeing him smile about anything these days was a boon.

"I didn't have anywhere near as wonderful a place to roam when I was a boy, Noble. I grew up in Newark, New Jersey. We lived in a nice town house, but we had no yard as such. My parents weren't wealthy people, but we were comfortable. I could go to the parks or take rides to go hiking, of course, but to just step out your front door and have all this"—he waved his hand—"well, you're a lucky kid, Noble, a lucky kid. Your ancestors knew what they were doing when they settled here."

"Mama told us our great-great-grandpa Jordan's heart pounded the way a man's heart pounds when he sees a beautiful woman when he set eyes on this land. She said he fell in love with every tree, every blade of grass, every rock he saw and just knew he had to live here and work his farm here and build his home here," I recited. I had heard it enough times when Noble and I were growing up.

"Yes, well, I can understand the way he felt. I was

very happy to find that house and so cheaply, too. Of course, I didn't know the full story about the previous owner and what people thought he might have done to your sister, but I think I still would have gone forward. I'm glad I did." He smiled at me. "Otherwise, I wouldn't have met your mother and I wouldn't have met you."

We were on another late-afternoon walk. This time we had followed an old trail through the woods, one I hadn't taken for some time. I was reluctant to do it now, but he was insistent. The trail was overgrown, but not enough to hinder our walk. I knew where it would take us, and that set my heart to thumping faster. It wasn't long before we reached the creek, not far from where my brother had died. It seemed the stuff of dreams now, nightmares.

The creek wasn't as full as usual, but it was as clear as ever, the rocks beneath the water gleaming in the afternoon sunshine. We saw small fish swimming in what looked like maddened and frantic circles and a turtle struggling to get to the top of a rock.

"He probably thinks he's climbing Mount Everest," Dave said, then took a deep breath. "You can breathe here. You can feel alive. Yes, you were a lucky kid, a lucky kid," he muttered. "If only Elliot wouldn't have been as wild and reckless. We would have had some family, huh, Noble? You guys would have been brothers in the true sense of the word. Maybe together, you would have had a positive impact on Betsy.

"Oh, well," he sighed. "They say life's an accident and death is an appointment you have to keep. Some things are just meant to be. What do you think?"

"I don't know." I really didn't.

"Right. Why should you be so philosophical at your age? You have your whole life ahead of you."

He paused and put his hands on my shoulders as he looked directly at me.

"I'd really like to be of some help to you, Noble. Maybe I can do one thing right. Please don't hesitate to confide in me if you have any secret desires, wishes, ambitions. I won't laugh at anything, and if you want it enough, I'll do my best to help you, even if it means convincing your mother, okay?"

"Yes, sir."

"Dave, Dave. Call me Dave or call me Dad, but nothing else."

I doubt that I could ever get myself to call him *Dad*. Perhaps in that respect, I was like Betsy, who could never get herself to call Mama *Mother* or *Mom*.

I just nodded and we walked on, talking about nature, about the vegetation, the birds, the weather, anything and everything but Betsy and Elliot.

Mama was surprised at how much I was doing with Dave these days. At first she said nothing about it. I thought she would think it nice, of course. I was giving him some comfort, but when we returned from our long walk in the woods this time, she was sitting on the porch waiting and she looked upset and annoyed. Baby Celeste was taking a nap.

"Where have you two been?" she asked immediately, making me feel as if we had missed an appointment.

"Oh, Noble showed me some of the prettier spots in the forest and around the creek. There's quite a long, empty field southwest. I never realized how close we were to Spring Glen either. You can see the highway from a rise just after that field I mentioned. We saw quite a number of deer, too, didn't we, Noble?"

"Yes."

"Overpopulation, I suppose," Dave said. "Baby asleep?"

"Yes, she's taking a nap."

"Good idea. I think I might just do the same. It's been a while since I took a hike that long, Noble. Thanks for the walk."

"You're welcome," I said, and he went inside.

Mama looked at me and then stared ahead a moment. I turned to go to the shed.

"Noble," she called.

I paused and looked at her. "What, Mama?"

"Don't get too close to Dave."

"Why not?"

She didn't answer me. She just turned away.

"Mama?"

She looked at me again and I knew she would say no more. It frightened me. Why would she say such a thing? Was she afraid I would reveal all our dark secrets, betray her? For the remainder of the day, I would stop whatever I was doing and suddenly realize I was trembling so badly, my hands shook. I couldn't get her eyes out of my mind.

Dave slept right through dinner this particular evening. Mama said she had gone up to look in on him and decided not to wake him.

"I'll bring him something to eat later," she said, which was exactly what she did.

The following day he once again called in sick and did not go to work. He remained in bed with Mama bringing him things to eat and drink.

"What's wrong with him?" I asked before we sat at the table to have dinner. I hadn't seen him all day.

"He thinks he has the flu. You know pharmacists. They think they're doctors. He asked for it so I made some garlic soup for him. I don't think that's his problem, but I did it to humor him, and good garlic soup has other medicinal and nutritional value anyway."

"Maybe he should go see a doctor."

"Doctors," she muttered as if they were all charlatans. "He'll be just fine if he does what I tell him and eats and drinks what I give him and," she added pointedly, "stops thinking about that spoiled brat."

Mama always did wonders whenever I was ill. I couldn't deny it. I had never had some of the inoculations children were supposed to be given, but no one cared or checked to see if I had. I never attended public school where they might have checked.

The following day Dave did get up, dress, and come downstairs, but he looked much weaker and even much paler. We had our first real winter precipitation in the form of snow flurries. Although it had been cold, it was proving to be one of the driest winters on record. I made a nice fire in the fireplace and Dave sat near it, warming himself. He didn't seem able to rid himself of the chill. Mama made him wear a heavy sweater and gave him hot herbal teas and mixes, but he was uncomfortable all day.

Baby Celeste tried with more determination to get him to pay attention to her. He didn't want to ignore her or make her unhappy, but he was afraid he was coming down or had come down with something contagious and asked me to keep her from getting too close to him. His appetite was small at dinner, almost nonexistent. He picked at his food and tried to eat more to please Mama.

"Everything is very good, Sarah," he said apologetically. "It's just my stomach. It feels like I have a chain being tightened around it."

She nodded and told him not to worry about how much he ate, but I was alarmed. Why wasn't he thinking about going to a doctor at this point, especially with these symptoms? He should know enough to do so himself. When Mama wasn't in earshot, I asked him.

"Your mother's probably right, Noble. I probably have a touch of the bug. Her remedies are just as effective as anything I have at the drugstore for this, or anything else any doctor might prescribe," he insisted. "Thanks for being concerned."

When Mama returned from the kitchen, I turned away from him quickly and she looked at me suspiciously. Later, after Dave had gone to bed and she had put Baby Celeste to sleep, she confronted me in the living room. I was rereading Daphne du Maurier's *Rebecca,* a novel I knew Mama thought was inappropriate for me. She didn't come right out and say it. She would simply ask, "Why are you reading *that?*" She pronounced *that* as if it were pornography. It annoyed her to see me reading it again.

"If you're going to read that sort of book, do it in private. You should be reading something more . . . vigorous." *Manly* was really what she meant.

I closed it quickly and put it aside.

"Why," she continued, still glaring at me, "do you continually tell Dave to go see a doctor?"

"He doesn't look well, Mama, and he's missed so much work and seems so weak."

"His illness comes from places doctors know nothing about. I told you not to interfere."

"I'm not interfering. I just thought—"

"Don't," she said, snapping the word like a whip over my head. "Don't think. Things are taking place that are beyond your control, and mine for that matter."

"What things?"

She didn't reply.

"Mama, what things?"

She looked away and then turned slowly back to

me. "I was right about Baby Celeste. I even underesti-
mated her. She has been chosen. What we have done
for her is wonderful. You have, to this point, been a
great help, been of great assistance. Do nothing to ruin
that now, Noble. Nothing, do you understand?"

I started to shake my head and stopped.

It was better to nod, to agree.

"Will Dave get better soon?" I asked.

"It's not up to us."

"Who is it up to, then?"

She glared back at me. "Don't be insolent, Noble. I
don't like it, and it doesn't sound like you," she added,
the threat so heavy, I nearly choked up.

"Aren't you worried about him?" I dared to pursue.

She took a step toward me, steely eyed. "I am worried only about Baby Celeste, and you should be, too."

"I worry about her."

"I mean solely her. Everything else will take care of
itself or be taken care of, Noble."

What did that mean? Be taken care of? She saw the
question in my face and I knew it annoyed her.

"There was one thing that Betsy said about you that
I agree with," she continued, her voice suddenly more
pleasant.

"What's that?"

"I want you to go get your driver's license. I know you
know how to drive, Noble, but I am inclined to have you
run errands for me in the future, the near future. It will be
of some help for you to be capable of doing that."

I know I had my mouth open because she immediately said I would catch flies if I continued to sit there
staring up at her like that.

"Okay, Mama. Sure," I said, trying not to sound too
excited. "When?"

"Tomorrow."

"Tomorrow? But isn't this something that has to be done by appointment?"

"Your appointment has been made. You will take the driving test at two P.M. I'll bring you there myself," she said, then turned and walked away.

Been made? How long had she been planning this? Why had she waited until now to tell me? Why hadn't she let me practice more? Was it something she had still been debating and had only decided this very moment? What made her decide? It was so confusing, but I was too happy to utter a single complaint. Instead, I went out to our car and practiced parallel parking in our driveway. I could easily pass the written part of the test concerning all the driving rules and laws.

My mind was a jumbled mess that night, torn between the excitement of being able to drive myself and go places whenever I wanted, and the situation developing rapidly with Dave. While I was tossing and turning about all this, I suddenly became suspicious of Mama's real intentions. I had grown too fond of Dave to let him wallow in any sort of agony. He should at least take better care of his health, I thought.

But what more could I really do? Mama was right about my face: it told all, and I was never any good at keeping something secret from her long. The spirits that passed through my thoughts and saw everything in my head passed along and into hers as well. Spies were everywhere, even while I slept, even listening to and looking at my dreams.

In the morning Dave was excited for me when Mama told him what we were going to do that afternoon. He was still not feeling up to going into the store and decided he needed a day or so more of rest. I shifted my eyes from him quickly so Mama couldn't accuse me of anything, but he caught my look despite that and then declared that if he wasn't appreciably better in twenty-four to thirty-six hours, he would go see his doctor.

"Not that you're not doing everything you can for me, Sarah," he added quickly. "I appreciate and truly believe in your remedies. I might have something that really does require an antibiotic though."

She shook her head. "Do what you think you should," she said, making it sound like a personal affront to her and her reputation.

"We'll see," he said.

It sounded too much like surrender to me and it amazed me. His love for Mama was greater than his concern for himself. He worried more about hurting her feelings than improving his health. I glanced at her and thought maybe Betsy was right. Maybe Mama did have the power to put a spell over someone.

Before we left for the motor vehicle bureau, she prepared one of her drinks for him and had him go up to bed and rest. She had me do the driving to the bureau.

"As soon as you get your license, I'm going to have you do all our grocery shopping, Noble. I need to spend more time on my herbal supplements and remedies. Mr. Bogart is connecting me with another national health-food distributor and we'll have even more to do in the near future."

It all sounded good. I did look forward to my first experience alone in the shopping malls and stores. Despite all that I had been taught, seen, and heard, I couldn't help feeling like a prisoner about to begin a work-release program. The freedom was exciting and terrifying simultaneously, but that Mama was making it happen gave me confidence. I'd be all right. It would all be fine.

The driving license examiner was a short, balding

man with round, glassy eyes and a soft, pudgy pair of dull red lips that seemed habitually in a pout. His name, Jerome Carter, was on his name tag, and he nodded at it when he introduced himself with a perfunctory, timid handshake, the handshake of someone afraid he might be contaminated by touching someone else. From the things he said to Mama, he gave me the impression he would like to eliminate everyone less than twenty-one and more than sixty from the driving population. We had brought Baby Celeste with us and he did lighten up when he saw how she smiled at him. Mama and she waited back in the motor vehicle bureau lobby while I went out on the test.

Mr. Carter said nothing except when he gave me directions and commands. While I drove, he scribbled on his notepad and clipboard. I thought he was quite unsatisfied with my performance, and I resigned myself to being failed and having to reschedule, but to my surprise and delight, he told Mama I appeared to be a very responsible young man.

She looked more pleased than I was. I couldn't wait to get home to tell Dave of my success. He wasn't up and about as I had hoped, however.

"Isn't he sleeping too much?" I asked Mama after she had gone up to the bedroom and reported he was asleep.

"When you are in a healing process, you sleep. Your body needs the rest," she said, but without the kind of conviction I was accustomed to hearing in her voice and words. It troubled me, but I said nothing. Later that evening, apparently at Dave's direction, she called his store manager and told him Dave would not be in to work for the remainder of the week. I heard her say he was weak from his illness and it would be better for him to get good rest.

Afterward, she looked at me so hard, I had to shift

my eyes and pretend to be interested in something else. I didn't hear Dave get up at all that night and he didn't come down to breakfast in the morning. Finally, he rose in the afternoon, but he didn't dress. He wore his bathrobe and moved about in his slippers.

To me he looked dazed. Whenever I spoke to him, he didn't hear until I repeated it, and all he did when he rose was shuffle about the house, glance out the window, and then settle in that rocking chair, where he drifted in and out of short naps.

"He belongs in a hospital," I told Mama.

"What are you now, a doctor? The man is capable of deciding whether or not he needs to be in a hospital, Noble. He has had more medical training than the average person, hasn't he, and certainly more than you?"

What could I say to contradict that?

The following day my license arrived. Mama decided we should have a little celebration. Dave did seem to cheer up at the news, and she described her preparations of one of his favorite dinners, chicken Kiev. Naturally, she would make a rhubarb pie. Dave was so excited, he vowed he would shave and dress. He did look stronger. Perhaps this is the start of his real recovery, I thought. How fortunate that all these good things were happening simultaneously.

"Be careful, Noble," Dave called to me. "No speeding tickets, okay?"

"No," I said.

"As soon as I'm up and about a little more, I'll take a ride with you, okay?"

"Okay, Dave," I said, and he beamed back a smile that lifted my spirits.

With my new driving license in hand, I was sent out to shop for the foods and ingredients Mama needed.

Although driving off my property by myself would

seem like nothing to most people my age, it was the equivalent of being an astronaut for me. Full of excitement and adventure, I paused at the entrance to our driveway, took a deep breath, looked back at the house, then turned onto the road. I was sure no one was paying any special notice of me, yet it seemed to me that everyone I passed along the way, every person in every car that drove by or toward me, had shock and surprise on his or her face. It made me so nervous that I did almost run into the back of a pickup truck when the driver unexpectedly hit the brakes to make a right turn without any warning or signal lights. It brought me back to earth and I concentrated harder on what I was doing. What a disaster it would be to have an accident on my very first outing.

At the supermarket, no one took any particular note of my being there alone. Some of the employees recognized me from the times I had been there with Mama and Baby Celeste. They smiled or nodded. I filled the list Mama had given me and went to the checkout counter. The clerk was a rather chunky young woman with short, dark brown hair and small, dull brown eyes that looked to be sinking in her marshmallow face. When she looked at me, I looked down quickly and began to unload my groceries from the cart.

"Hello, Noble," she said, which surprised me. I looked up and read her name tag: *Roberta Beckman.*

She stood there with her arms folded under her large bosom, lifting it. The memories rushed back. She was the blind date Elliot had arranged for me years ago. She was heavy then, but she looked to have gained another twenty-five or thirty pounds. I had had a frightening sexual experience with her and actually ran away. Mama found out I had been with her and Elliot and a girlfriend of his, all smoking pot. That was the first time she had had any contact with Dave. She had gone to complain and revealed that Elliot and his friends had been smoking marijuana. Elliot hated me after that. I suppose I couldn't blame him.

"Hello," I finally said.

"You look like you don't remember me."

I shook my head and kept unloading the groceries. She started to process them.

"How have you been? I haven't seen you around anywhere," she said.

"I've been here."

"Oh, I just got this job. Lost my last job in a cutback. I was working at the mall in the chicken place. What have you been doing with yourself?"

"Same things." Unfortunately, all the groceries were on the counter and I had to face her.

"Terrible about Elliot. I really liked him. He was lots of fun. Harmony was quite upset for quite a while afterward, you know. She went to college. I didn't have the grades to go. She's in college in the Midwest. You never wanted to go to college? I remember you were very smart."

She continued to process the groceries. Then, she paused. No one was behind me waiting yet, so she had time.

"Of course, I know about your mother marrying Dave's father. Everyone thought it was so weird. How are they getting along?"

"Just fine," I said. "I'm in a little hurry."

"Sure." She rang it up and told me the amount. I handed her the cash Mama had given me and she made the change and then started to pack. Someone finally came up to the aisle, but she didn't work any faster. She won't have this job very long either, I thought.

"Maybe you and I can get together sometime," she said. "I'm not as wild as I was. Promise."

I nodded, but said nothing. The store manager came around and glared at her so she worked faster. I began to put the bags into the cart.

"Call me anytime," she said. "If you want, I'll come around."

"I'm busy right now."

She looked devastated, then flashed a weak smile. "If you find the time or change your mind, don't hesitate. Okay?"

"Okay." I put the last bag into the cart. I felt as if I were fleeing when I started out. I guess I really was, only she would never really understand why.

Meeting Roberta Beckman and having those memories return vividly put a dark spot on my joyful day. I had always been very conscious of coincidences. Nothing happened by accident in our world. Everything had meaning. Sometimes, that meaning was buried under other things, but it was there if you looked hard and long enough.

On good days, wonderful surprises always seem to occur, whether it be my discovery of a nest of baby hummingbirds or simply a magnificent and interesting new wildflower. I had learned from Mama that distinct rhythms of energy are going on continuously. Being able to tune in to them, sense them, and benefit from that knowledge was the special strength our family possessed now and would in the future.

Because this coincidence, meeting Roberta, was dark and unnerving, I was especially happy to get home safely. Mama wasn't downstairs when I entered to bring in the groceries. I called to her to let her know I was home. I wondered where she was and where Baby Celeste was. After I brought in everything and put away what had to be put away immediately in the refrigerator, I went searching through the house and upstairs. Mama and Dave's bedroom door was closed. I listened, heard nothing, and then knocked softly.

"Mama?"

A moment later she opened the door. I saw Dave in bed, his eyes closed.

"What happened? I thought he was starting to get better. I thought he was getting dressed to be up and about."

She stepped out and closed the door behind her softly. "We'll see. He was suddenly very, very tired, so I helped him to bed."

"Mama, this is terrible."

"Did you get everything on the list?"

"Yes, of course."

"Good. I'll start on dinner then."

"Where's Baby Celeste?"

"She was suddenly very tired, too, and fell asleep about the same time Dave did," Mama told me from the top of the stairway. She smiled. "It was rather extraordinary."

"What was, Mama?"

"The way she . . . reacted to Dave."

"What do you mean?"

"When he was happy, she was happy, and when he became low and tired, she did. Rather extraordinary." She nodded.

She turned and descended the stairway. Her words made me feel numb. What was extraordinary, exactly? Baby Celeste was always sensitive to the people around her.

I returned to their bedroom doorway and looked in at Dave. He was in a deep sleep. What had happened? He had been so energized about our little celebration. He had shaved and dressed and looked to be recovering.

He should go directly to the hospital now, I thought more firmly. I'd drive him myself if he would go. I hesitated a moment, listened to be sure Mama was not on the stairway, then I started into the bedroom, intending to wake him and tell him so. But the moment I set foot in the room, I heard Baby Celeste's horrible wail. It wasn't something she ever did. The scream was piercing.

In a moment I heard Mama shout and then start up the stairs. I retreated quickly and headed for the baby's room.

"What is it?" Mama asked.

"I don't know. She just screamed," I said, continuing into the room.

Baby Celeste was sitting up, her face contorted in fear. She had her arms up toward us.

Mama leaped ahead of me and embraced her, kissing her cheeks and stroking her hair as she reassured her. Celeste became calmer quickly. Then Mama looked at me with such accusation in her eyes, I stepped back and shuddered.

"What have you done?"

"Nothing, Mama. Honest."

Her eyes grew small, suspicious. "Something is wrong here. Something evil has frightened her. She's warning us."

I shook my head. Not me, I thought. Nothing to do with me.

"I don't know why," I said.

"Take her down and keep her calm," Mama said after a thoughtful moment. "I have things to do."

I took Baby Celeste in my arms quickly and started out.

"Noble," Mama called.

"Yes?"

"Be very careful. Very careful."

Careful of what? I wondered, but I simply nodded, glanced at her and Dave's doorway, and then with Baby Celeste in my arms, her arms around my neck, descended the stairs.

Behind me, I heard Mama and Dave's bedroom door close.

When I reached the bottom of the stairway, I looked at Baby Celeste. She wore an expression as angry as Mama's had been, and for reasons I didn't understand, I guiltily shifted my eyes away from my own baby's, my heart shrinking under the heat of my own pounding blood.

15

What Was Meant to Be

♊

I have seen flowers and plants wither and dry up when there wasn't enough rain, sunlight, or nutrition in the soil. For a brief moment, they look healthy, robust. Their future is optimistic, then reality sets in and they begin to degenerate. Their petals curl and their stems begin to bend.

Dave was like that.

When he first came to our home, he was so bright and hopeful, firm and full of energy. He was devoted to Mama and even to me, and he believed that his devotion strengthened him, strengthened us all. He bounded up the stairway, swooped down lovingly over Baby Celeste to scoop her into his arms and cover her with laughter and kisses. His optimism was contagious. Days seemed brighter; shadows seemed thinner. Our old home had a palpable new energy. Perhaps Mama had done a good thing after all, I had thought.

And then I saw that the roots of this new hope, like

the roots of a poorly planted flower, were reaching into places with nothing to help it, nothing to nourish it, nothing to keep it alive, especially after Betsy had returned. Now that she was gone, but had left in her wake so much sorrow and regret, Dave grew worse.

I felt so helpless standing by and watching him weaken, watching the light in his eyes continue to dim. Every morning, as soon as I woke, I would think about what I could do. At night I listened for my voices and I searched the shadows for Daddy, trusting he would have an answer. It had been so long since I had seen or heard anything from the spiritual world. It was like a curtain had been drawn closed. Was it my fault? Had my doubts and concerns driven everyone away as Mama had once implied? Was it because of evil once again in our house?

Dave's absence from work didn't go unnoticed. Mama's regular customers called and stopped by, all asking after him. Some had heard he was sick. They had been to the drugstore or whatever and knew.

"He's recuperating from a very bad flu," Mama told them. "I'm trying to build him up."

That a pharmacist had submitted himself to Mama's herbal remedies reinforced the confidence and faith Mama's customers had in her products.

"I'll bet the drugstore always worries he would tout their customers off them and their prescriptions and direct them to you," Mrs. Paris told Mama.

Mama just smiled as if it were something Dave had been doing, but something she couldn't discuss. I knew it was not something Dave would have done or would do. If Mama caught me listening in on these conversations, she would either give me a look that said, "Go away," or she would find something for me to do around the house.

Lately every day, in fact, Mama had something for me to get at the mall or shopping centers. She sent me on errands and sent me to make deliveries of her products to Mr. Bogart. Whenever I asked after Dave or volunteered to do something to help him, she found something else she needed done first. Some days I barely set eyes on him. One morning I heard the phone ring and overheard Mama tell his store manager that he was finally going to see his physician. She said she would let him know what transpired.

It cheered me to hear that, but the day went by, I completed more errands, and when I returned, she didn't mention Dave's having seen his doctor or planning to do so. I was afraid to tell her that I had earlier eavesdropped on her phone conversation, but I decided that if she didn't say anything about it in the morning, I would confront her.

That night I volunteered to take Dave's food up to him. She looked at me strangely, not angrily so much as curiously.

"Why would you want to do that, Noble?"

"I thought I would take part of the burden off of you, Mama."

She smiled. "That's very thoughtful, but it's no burden to me. It's better that you keep our Baby Celeste occupied." She took up the tray.

The past few days, she always kept the bedroom door closed. I couldn't even gaze in and perhaps wave to him or ask after his health. I knew better than to protest about it, and I knew I had to ask my questions as casually as possible. I was tiptoeing my words and feelings around her, afraid she would accuse me of something or another.

"How is he?" I did ask when she returned from bringing him his dinner.

"The same." It was all she ever said now, but I knew in my heart that it was not the same.

After dinner, after Baby Celeste went to sleep, I went out despite the freezing temperatures. It was cold enough to see your breath. I wore a sweater, a scarf, and my overcoat and gloves. I just wandered about aimlessly for a while, occasionally gazing up at the sky. The stars looked like beads of ice. Noble used to think they were, and when the sun came up, it melted them, and that was why there were no stars in the daytime. Maybe he was right, I thought.

I walked around the house and looked up at what I knew to be Mama and Dave's room. The light was on, but dimly, and the curtains were drawn.

"He's dying, you know," I heard, and turned to look into the darker shadows from which the words had come. "It's what she wants. She has no more use for him."

I said nothing. That voice was too familiar to me. I gazed into the darkness and gradually, gradually Elliot took shape from the shadows.

"I've poisoned the well. I told you I would and there's nothing you can do about it, Noble man," he said gleefully.

Was he there? Did I really hear him?

I stepped toward him and he retreated, falling back into the darkness more and more until he was indistinguishable from it. He's afraid of me, I thought. I am not helpless. I can still do something.

More determined now, I hurried back inside the house. Mama was in the kitchen cleaning up. I heard her mumbling to someone and for a moment that frightened me. The spirits were everywhere. The ones she could see and I couldn't see were surely watching me, watching every step I took, however Elliot's words rang and bonged in my head like a heavy church bell.

He's dying. She has no more use for him. He's dying . . . dying.

I ascended the stairway as quietly as I could, but the house was far more loyal to Mama than it was to me. The steps creaked even more loudly; the balustrade shook and rattled. I paused and listened for her footsteps. All I heard was a low, continuous murmuring coming from the kitchen. She was too involved in what she was saying.

I moved faster and then, again tiptoeing over the upstairs floor, made my way quickly to Mama and Dave's bedroom door. To me it sounded as if I were walking over a pile of loose rocks, no matter how softly I stepped. Once again I paused to listen, and once again I didn't hear her footsteps on the stairway behind me. Carefully, slowly, ever so slowly, I turned the doorknob and opened the door. The hinges, just as loyal to Mama as were the steps and floor, squeaked.

Only a small desk lamp was lit. It cast a giant shadow over the bed, a shadow that looked more like a shroud. Dave's forehead was somewhat illuminated. It looked as yellow as a slab of butter. As I drew closer, I saw that the blanket was up to his chin. A nearly full glass of water was on the night table with a small saucer beside it, a piece of old china rarely if ever used. In it I saw what looked like multicolored crumbs of some herbal substance Mama had created. The spoon beside the saucer indicated she had been giving Dave doses of it.

He was lying so still and staring wide-eyed up at the ceiling as if he saw something astounding. Whatever it was absorbed his full attention because he didn't hear or see me enter the bedroom. I approached the bed and stood beside it, looking down at him. His eyes did not move toward me, although he blinked.

"Dave," I said in a loud, careful whisper. "How are you doing?"

He continued to stare at the ceiling.

"Dave," I said, reaching down to touch his shoulder. Slowly, ever so slowly, he lowered his eyes and turned them toward me. He had no reaction. He looked at me like someone who wasn't sure I was there, who wasn't sure he had heard me speak. Maybe he thought I was one of Mama's spirits.

"Dave, it's Noble. Can't you hear me? What's wrong with you?"

His lips moved slightly and his eyes blinked.

"You've got to go to a hospital right now, Dave. You're very, very sick. Do you understand what I'm saying? I'll take you, okay? Dave?"

His head shook in tiny, almost incremental motions from side to side and his lips moved a little more, but he did not speak. I looked at the saucer, then lifted it and smelled the herbal medications. I had no idea what was in them, but when I looked closely at the glass of water, I saw that it, too, had something mixed in it, the residue of which lay at the bottom of the glass. Also on the nightstand were bottles and tablets of over-the-counter drugs and what looked like something someone would have to get with a prescription.

He had closed his eyes again. I shook his shoulder a little more vigorously.

"Dave, can you hear me? Do you understand what I'm saying? You're very ill."

He opened his eyes and turned a little more toward me, but his eyes showed no recognition.

I heard a laugh and looked across the room.

Elliot was standing by the window. "It's too late. Don't you understand? I told you, it's too late."

"No!" I cried back at him.

His smile changed to an angry look. "He thought you would be the son I wasn't, that you would take my place. He's dying a fool," Elliot said with satisfaction. "A fool."

I shook my head. "No, I won't let him." I stepped toward Elliot just as I had outside and he backed away. His laughter followed him as he sank into the wall and was gone.

Out of the corner of my eye, I saw Dave shudder as though a deep chill had cut through him like a knife.

I reached down and found his hand under the blanket. It felt cold, stiff. I had to make him understand what was happening to him. Desperation seized me. I had to help him.

"Dave, listen to me. Baby Celeste is really your granddaughter. I am not Noble. Noble is gone and has been for a long time. Elliot and I . . . we . . . I'm the real Celeste." Tears were streaming down my cheeks now. "Baby Celeste is my daughter, mine. Don't you see? Don't you understand what that means? You've got to get well. You haven't lost your whole family. You haven't."

He was looking up at me, but his eyes were still quite dull, his face unmoving.

I let go of his hand and slowly brought my fingers to my shirt. Although he continued to look confused and dazed, he didn't turn his head away as I unbuttoned it. Then I lifted the strapping that flattened my breasts and showed him my bosom. His eyelids flickered and his lips moved apart, but his tongue looked paralyzed. Then his eyelids closed.

"Dave!" I reached down to touch his face. His eyes didn't open. He didn't move. "Dave, are you all right? *Dave?*" I screamed.

"What are you doing in here?" Mama asked from the doorway.

I turned and looked at her.

"Why is your shirt unbuttoned?"

"Mama, he is very sick. He can't even talk. He looks like he's in a coma or something."

"I'm very well aware of how he is. I've made arrangements to take him to the hospital in the morning if he is not any better. Now get out and leave him be."

"But I think he should go right now." I looked down at him again. His eyelids fluttered and opened.

"He's taken something to help him rest. He decided to do it himself, so leave. You're disturbing his very needed rest. Leave, Noble, now!" she ordered. "You don't belong in here."

I hesitated.

"You're only making things worse for everyone. I don't like this insubordination, Noble. What does it mean? Who told you to come in here?"

"No one," I said, my heart pounding. I shook my head. "I was simply worried about him, that's all."

"If you're worried about him, leave."

I glanced back at him, and then I walked out, my head down.

She seized my arm. "Go to sleep. And don't come back in here unless I tell you to do so."

When I stepped out, she closed the door. I stood there in the hallway, torn between rushing to the phone and calling an ambulance myself or doing what she told me to do. If I made the call, I would be defying her more dramatically than I ever had. I had no idea what that would lead to, how it would impact our lives. Our world would surely come crumbling down around us and I might do irreparable harm to Baby Celeste.

I couldn't help crying, even though I managed to subdue my sobs. The tears flowed as I got ready for bed and even after I crawled under my blanket.

"Daddy, help us," I prayed. "Please, please, help us."

I waited and listened.

I heard Mama's footsteps as she went by and then down the stairs. A little while later, she returned, paused at my door, then went to her own bedroom. Emotional exhaustion finally lowered sleep over me and shut me up in my own tumultuous night of dreams. I tossed and turned and woke many times during the night so that when morning came, I was too groggy and tired to keep my eyes open. I slept much later than usual, but when I finally woke, I realized how late it was and practically leaped out of bed to wash and dress.

It was so quiet in the house that for a moment I thought everyone was gone. Could it be that the ambulance had already come and left? I couldn't have slept through something like that, could I?

Mama and Dave's bedroom door was closed as usual, but I hesitated outside my door, then decided that before I went down, I would check on him. I went to the door and knocked softly.

"Mama? Are you in there?"

I waited.

The sound of Baby Celeste laughing at something downstairs told me Mama had gone down. Once again, I went through a hard debate with myself. Should I just go downstairs, too, or should I look in on him as I had done last night? In the end I couldn't turn away despite her order and her warning. I opened the door and looked in. Dave was lying just as he had been, but I felt something different about him. I listened for Mama and then I went in and up to the bed.

He was staring cold-eyed at the ceiling. His lids were not flickering and his face was ashen.

"Dave?"

I reached down slowly and touched his face. The shock of deathly cold made it seem more like I had put my fingers in a candle flame. I literally jumped back and then brought my closed fist to my mouth to smother a scream. For a long moment, I felt that I couldn't move, that my feet had been nailed to the bedroom floor, but finally, I turned, rushed out and down the stairs.

Mama was sitting in the dining room having breakfast with Baby Celeste, smiling at her and laughing at something she had said. They both looked up as I came through the doorway.

"Well now, look who has decided to grace us with his presence this morning, Celeste," Mama said.

"Noble," Baby Celeste said.

"Yes, Noble. He just gets up and we're nearly finished with our breakfast, aren't we, Celeste?"

"Mama, I went in to check on Dave and . . . and . . . he's gone," I said, the words choking in my throat.

Mama nodded. "Yes, I know," she said with a nonchalance that took my breath away. She gave Baby Celeste another piece of toast and jelly, then leaned over to wipe her lips. She sat back again and looked at me.

"Mama, I'm saying Dave is dead."

"I think I know that, Noble." She leaned toward me, her eyes narrowing. "He was doing just fine. What made you go in there last night and do what you did?" she asked accusingly.

I shook my head and backed away a few steps.

"I didn't do anything. I wanted to help him."

"You're so pathetic when you lie. You didn't help anyone. You only endangered us all. There was a great swirl of displeasure about this house all night. I felt the anger and disappointment and I heard them mumbling.

I have a lot to do to make things right again, a lot to do."

"But, Mama, what about Dave?"

"It was what was meant to be. You are no longer to be concerned about it." She brushed some crumbs off Baby Celeste. "We'll need more firewood tonight. It's going to be a particularly cold evening. And I think you should clean out the roof gutters on the south side of the house. I noticed the old leaves and melted ice building up there, and you know that can lead to leaks in the roof."

"But . . ."

"It's all taken care of, Noble," she said sharply, and looked at me again. "I've called for an ambulance. You'd better have your breakfast. I'll be busy in a little while and you'll have to mind the baby. Don't just stand there looking stupid. Get cracking," she snapped.

I didn't want to eat anything, but I got myself a glass of water. Soon after we heard the paramedics arriving. Mama went to the door to greet them.

"Hurry!" she cried, and two paramedics rushed into the house. She showed them where to go. I stood back with Baby Celeste in my arms watching all the activity. A stretcher was brought upstairs moments later.

Could it be that he would be all right, that they had come in time to revive him? Give him CPR or some sort of electric shock that would bring him back? I wondered hopefully. I heard them emerging. The stretcher was empty. Mama followed, her head down. The two men glanced at me and then went out to their vehicle.

"What's going on?" I asked, breathless.

"The medical examiner is on his way," Mama said, her lips curled in the corners disdainfully. "It's considered an unattended death so there has to be an examination here. A lot of bureaucratic nonsense. Just take care of the baby as I told you. Dress her and take her out. Keep her out of everyone's way."

The medical examiner and a sheriff's deputy arrived shortly afterward. Since there were no signs of foul play, Dave's body was carried down and placed in the ambulance. I overheard them say there would be an autopsy, of course. All of the drugs Dave had taken and all of the herbal remedies Mama had created for him were carefully bagged and taken as well.

Baby Celeste and I stood off to the side watching everyone and all the activity. When the ambulance left and the sheriff's deputy and the examiner followed, Mama nodded at us and then went inside.

I followed with the baby. She was already sitting in the rocking chair, her eyes closed.

"What's going to happen now, Mama?" I asked softly.

She opened her eyes and looked at me. "Everything is going to be fine. Everything is going to be as it should be. Tend to your chores. You can leave Baby Celeste here with me." She rocked herself gently. "Just leave her with me," she whispered.

Later that day Mama began to make funeral arrangements. She called Mr. Bogart, who called the Reverend Mr. Austin. The date of Dave's funeral would depend on when the medical examiner released the body. Mama had a list of Dave's relatives, cousins and one elderly aunt. None of them had come to their wedding. He had explained he wasn't close with anyone, so Mama didn't anticipate any of them coming to the funeral. When she explained to the police that neither she nor Dave had any idea where Betsy would be, they said they would see about finding her, but that didn't lead to anything. Mama said they probably made the smallest possible effort, not that she could blame them. It wasn't, she reminded me and any of her customers, like searching for a kidnapped child.

The first day, we had no callers beside Mr. Bogart and his wife and the reverend and his wife, Tani. Some of Mama's regular customers stopped by on the second day. On the third day, Mama received a call from our attorney, Mr. Derward Lee Nokleby-Cook. He came to see her and they talked in the living room while I kept Baby Celeste occupied up in my room. Afterward, Mama told me Dave had made arrangements for most of his estate to be transferred to Mama and Baby Celeste, with a smaller portion going to Betsy. However, Dave, afraid of giving Betsy anything until she was more responsible, had left Mama as trustee of that portion. She was to dole it out when Betsy reached the age of twenty-five. Needless to say, Mama was pleased with it all.

Later that afternoon, the sheriff's deputy arrived with a copy of the report the medical examiner was making. He had ruled Dave's death accidental, but he had placed the cause on what he called "contradictions" between some of Mama's herbal remedies and prescription medications as well as over-the-counter drugs. The actual cause of death was described as renal failure, which led to heart failure.

A local newspaper reporter visited us the following morning to get a statement from Mama. People in what he called "the orthodox medical community" were up in arms about so-called healers like Mama who were not licensed by any respected authority and who endangered people with their herbal remedies because there was no warning about dosages and possible side effects when they were used in conjunction with prescribed drugs.

The irony of Mama accidentally causing the death of her own husband was not lost on the reporter. He tried to get her to say something more emotional, probably hoping to stimulate an argument between her and the medical community, but she only stated her regrets and her doubts that the medical examiner knew anything definite. Nevertheless, the news would undoubtedly have a negative effect on Mama's herbal-remedy business. It wouldn't be long before her regulars would dwindle to barely anyone.

She wasn't terribly concerned or at least didn't show it if she was. Her previous inheritance and now her inheritance from Dave were enough to keep us safe and comfortable. Mr. Bogart stood by her and told her he would continue to develop distribution for her herbal remedies. He had his sources outside the community, he said, and they were not influenced or dissuaded by the uproar in the medical community, which they distrusted anyway.

Dave's funeral was small. Mama had chosen a plain pine box for his coffin, in keeping with how much importance she placed on the spirit, and how little she placed on the body. The church, practically empty, echoed with the Reverend Mr. Austin's poetic elegy. He spoke about Dave kindly, but made it sound as if he didn't die, as if he were still among us, even sitting next to me and Mama. He smiled at us and nodded at Mama, who nodded back, as if the two of them knew a great secret few of the rest of us knew.

Beside our few friends and some of the more curious, there were some of his fellow employees from the drugstore and the manager. Mr. Derward Lee Nokleby-Cook was there without his wife. They attended the burial, too. It was a cold but clear day with barely a cloud in the sky, too beautiful a day for an interment. It was actually the kind of day Dave would have enjoyed, I thought. He loved the cool, fresh, crisp air.

Afterward, Mama had these people over. People had sent some nice fruit and candy baskets and Mama pre-pared some food. Tani Austin and Mrs. Bogart looked after the guests and cleaned the dishes and silverware. The people who came were all taken with Baby Celeste, who won their smiles and admiration with her rather serious and grown-up demeanor. She was call-ing Dave *Daddy* by now and told them all Daddy was looking after her from heaven. She actually lifted her little face toward the ceiling and smiled as if she could see him looking down at us. It brought tears to every-one's eyes.

As I watched Mama talking to people, sometimes holding Baby Celeste, sometimes just holding her hand, I realized how she had achieved what she had wanted. Baby Celeste had a real mother and father now. People were more than willing to accept and love her. What's more, she had the sympathy of strangers. I had never been deeper down in my grave.

Whether it had been Mama's plan or the plan our spiritual family had given her, it was all coming to pass. She had provided Baby Celeste with sufficient cover and she had maintained the existence of Noble, who could never be permitted to die. If Noble's death was ever validated, Mama would die herself, I thought. Never before had I felt as trapped, as locked away, as I did that day of Dave's funeral. So much was lowered into the ground with him, especially any hope that I would be resurrected, that I would be who I was.

I had dreamed and fantasized about my eventual revelation. In my mind it was to be a secret between

Dave and me, a secret he would keep until, he promised, he found a way to get Mama to accept it. I knew now just how much a fantasy that really was.

And so I didn't shed tears for Dave as much as I shed tears for myself again. I had done it so many times before, for so many different reasons.

In what did my hope lie now? Where was the new beginning Dave had promised? As I sat there thinking about all this, my front-page-of-a-newspaper face caught the attention of our visitors and mourners. They made a point of stopping to speak with me, to encourage me.

"Dave was a fine man. I'm sure you'll miss him very much," the store manager, Mr. Cody, told me. "He talked about you often. He was quite impressed with you, Noble."

"Thank you," I said.

"If you ever want to start working, come see me. I'll have a job for you at the store."

I couldn't even begin to imagine something like that, but I thanked him anyway and promised I would go to him if I did start looking for work off the farm.

Eventually, they all left and we were as alone as we were before Dave had come into our lives. Now it was almost as if that had all been a dream. In the weeks that followed, Mama donated all of his clothes, shoes, and hats to the local thrift shop, which gave its proceeds to charities. The darkness I had felt around us before Dave had come sweeping into our lives with his laughter and plans for our new future gradually returned. I could look out the window and practically see it seeping in our direction like a river of ink.

The only bright spot in our world now was Baby Celeste. Dave's death, the morbidity that followed on its heels, the funeral, none of it appeared to touch her as it touched me. Nothing gloomy could take hold of her. Her eyes continued to be cheerful, her smile soft and loving, and her little laugh and voice like the laugh and the voice of a cherub.

Mama was right about her after all, I thought. She is everything now. We are here for her and for what she is destined to do.

Weeks wove into months. I plodded with heavy footsteps about the farm, tending my chores, working hard to deliberately exhaust myself so I would sleep better at night. Mama, on the other hand, was as cheerful as ever, making her wonderful dinners, continuing Baby Celeste's early education, and playing her piano and singing as if Dave were still here, sitting beside us, listening and smiling with a face full of love.

Maybe he was, I thought, but not with any real confidence.

I watched time pass, and I waited like someone who knew deep in her heart that she had little or no control of what tomorrow would bring.

16

Betsy Comes Back

♊

It was late spring, only a few short degrees of rising temperature left before it would feel more like summer. Despite the loss of our local customers, Mama wanted to develop an even bigger herbal garden, perhaps to show her defiance. Mr. Bogart was more determined than ever to reinforce what he thought was her good work and answer her critics. He did find her more outlets. I didn't mind the added work; I still welcomed the distraction.

Baby Celeste worked beside me every day with her little hoe and rake. She mostly enjoyed inserting the seeds into the wet, prepared earth. I watched her do it. She focused so clearly and firmly on each seed as if she could easily envision the plant to come. Her soft, sweet lips moved with each planting, making it appear that she was reciting some prayer Mama had taught her. I had little doubt she might have done just that.

A little after two in the afternoon months after

Dave's funeral, we both heard the sound of a van turning onto our driveway. Pausing, we watched it approach the house. It was a quite beat-up, white van with a cracked windshield. As it drew closer, it rattled louder, then finally squeaked to a stop, the disturbed dust rising to encircle it, seemingly to keep it from coming any closer.

For a long moment, no one emerged. I moved to Baby Celeste's side and watched and waited. Finally, the passenger-side door opened and Betsy stepped out with a baby wrapped in a blue blanket cradled in her arms. She wore a red-and-black bandanna around her forehead and her hair was long and stringy. She was dressed in a one-piece, tie-dyed garment and wore a pair of sandals. The driver, a tall, thin man with a black ponytail streaked with gray halfway down his back, emerged, went around to the rear of the van, and produced two well-battered suitcases, one tied closed with a rope. He set them at the foot of the porch steps before returning to his van.

Betsy spoke to him, stood up on the balls of her feet to kiss him, then remained there watching him get into the van, back away, turn around, and drive off. She stared after him and waved as if she were watching the love of her life, her last hope, depart. Then, she turned and looked our way.

"Noble!" she cried. "Help me with these suitcases."

I looked at Baby Celeste. She wore the strangest expression, a mix of amusement in her eyes, but a tightness in her lips.

"C'mon, Celeste," I said, taking her hand.

"Looking at you makes me feel like I never left this place," Betsy said as we approached. "You're still in that stupid garden."

"You have a baby?" I asked.

She smirked and turned the infant, who was, remarkably, asleep.

"It's not a sack of potatoes. This is Panther. I named him myself, seeing as I gave birth to him in a motel called The Panther Inn. Fortunately for me, the owner's wife was a nurse. Even so, it was a filthy mess." Betsy moved the blanket off Panther's face. "Look at his hair. Black as the inside of a witch's heart," she said, laughing. "That's what Wacker said. He's the idiot who just brought me here. He believes in some of that hoodoo, voodoo junk your mother believes in, but he took care of me for nearly a month. Then he read his astrological chart and decided it was time we parted ways. Good riddance, I say. He was getting on my nerves anyway. Why are you just standing there with your mouth open? Take in my suitcases. Where's my father? Is he at work or what? I've got to show him his new grandson."

I couldn't speak.

"Oh, forget it," she said impatiently. She started up the stairs.

I reached for her suitcases and followed as she entered the house. Baby Celeste remained alongside me, just as transfixed on the events unfolding.

"Dad!" Betsy screamed when she stepped into the entryway. *"I'm back!"*

She woke her baby, who immediately began to cry.

"Dad!"

Mama appeared at the top of the stairway and looked down at her. I stepped up behind Betsy, Baby Celeste still right beside me, but now with her arms around my leg as if she were anticipating an earthquake. The suitcases weren't heavy so I continued to hold them. For a long moment, Mama just gazed at her. Then, she began a slow descent, speaking as she took each step.

"Why haven't we heard from you? Where were you?"

"Away," Betsy said, raising her voice over the baby's cries and bouncing him too roughly, I thought.

"Why didn't you ever call or write your father?"

"I ran out of stamps and small change. Where is he? Is he at work?"

"No, he's not at work," Mama said, reaching the bottom steps. "He'll never be at work again."

"What's that supposed to mean? Panther, would you wait," she told her baby, turning him and then cradling him in the crook of her arm. The moment Panther set eyes on Mama, his crying subsided.

"I got to feed him and I don't breast-feed. It spoils your shape," Betsy told Mama. Then she looked back at me. "I bet Noble was breast-fed. Maybe he still is," she added with a gleeful smile.

"I see your experiences have done little to make you mature and responsible," Mama said.

"Right. So where's my father?"

"Your father passed away months ago." Mama's words felt so heavy, even for me. Sometimes, death is so hard to take, it feels like an illusion. I couldn't count how many days, how many times during a day, I expected to see Dave appear and think all that had happened was just a bad dream.

"What? What's that supposed to mean? Passed away where?" Betsy looked at me and then back at Mama.

"Your father died, Betsy. He had heart failure. It shouldn't come as a shock to you, considering all you did to make him miserable, to put darkness and pain in his poor troubled heart."

Betsy shook her head, slowly at first, and then so vigorously, I could feel the pain in my own neck.

"You're lying. You're just trying to make me feel bad. Where is he?"

Betsy turned to me again and I quickly shifted my eyes to avoid hers.

"We'll take you to the cemetery, if you like," Mama said dryly.

Betsy stepped back, continuing to shake her head.

"No, you're lying." She looked at me. "She's lying, right? She's just trying to make me feel bad about not calling."

"I see you went ahead and gave birth. Now that you have a child, you had better think of changing your ways," Mama continued.

"He can't be dead. He can't!" Betsy said, stamping her foot. "Stop saying that."

"Not saying it doesn't stop it from being true. You won't be able to bury your head in the sand here. I'm sure your father's death wasn't a result of his having made such a choice, but it happened. Noble and I and Baby Celeste are still not recovered from the shock ourselves," Mama told her, still speaking in calm, measured tones. "He was a gentle, loving man. He should have had a long and happy life, but his troubles were too many and too deep."

"No," Betsy said in a loud whisper, her eyes large and full of fear.

"I did my best for him. Now," Mama continued, "if you have even an ounce of morality, an iota of a sense of right and wrong, and any sense of regret and repentance, you will try to be a mature and responsible person. Do you have bottles and formula for the child?"

Betsy continued to shake her head and, then, suddenly stopped as if the words had finally settled in her brain.

"You can't blame anything on me. If he was sick, it

wasn't until he came here to be with you, until you put a spell on him. It was your fault, yours!"

"Quite the contrary, I'm pleased to say. He had the happiest and best days of his life living here. When you weren't aggravating him, that is. If you have formula for the child and diapers, I'll see to him while you rest in your room. Later, we'll discuss how things will be."

"No," Betsy said, backing up farther until she was against the door. She turned slightly and put her hand on the doorknob, poised to bolt from the house.

"You can leave if you want to, but don't expect any help from us. Your father left explicit instructions in his will. I serve as the trustee of your inheritance, which will not be fully turned over to you until you reach the age of twenty-five. Until then, I will dole out money to you according to your needs and your behavior. Obviously your baby's needs will come under a different category. You and this child have a home here as long as you assume your responsibilities and do not create disturbances or any trouble at all. Nothing must be abused. Now, I repeat, do you have formula for the child? If not, I'll prepare something."

"*No!* I don't want you giving him any of your junk," Betsy cried, taking her hand off the doorknob and embracing the baby.

Mama glared at her. Then she turned to me.

"Noble, would you be so kind as to take Betsy's suitcases up to her room. Your room," she told Betsy, "is in far better shape than how you left it. I expect it to be kept that way. Do not leave your garments scattered about. Do not let the room fill with dust. Do not leave food in the room, and do be sure you wash your linen and your bedding once a week at minimum. You will set the table every night and you will clear it and wash the dishes. If you break one dish, even chip one, I will deduct the cost of it ten times from your trust fund.

"I want the kitchen floor washed every day and the furniture in the living room dusted and polished twice a week. We'll all, meaning you and Noble primarily," Mama inserted with a smile, "do the windows every weekend."

Betsy stared, her mouth moving but nothing coming from it.

"Furthermore," Mama continued, "we are not here to serve as babysitters for you while you go off rioting and carousing in the villages and towns. Should I so much as smell alcohol or see anything resembling drugs, I'll fine you a thousand dollars per incident to be deducted from your trust fund. And I especially don't want to hear any gossip or complaints about you while you're living under this roof.

"You're to invite no one here. I don't even want anyone driving onto this property. Is all this understood?"

Betsy didn't respond. She simply stared.

Mama nodded as if she had answered anyway. "Good. Now, I would once again suggest you give me the baby to feed and go take a rest, clean up, put on something appropriate and not something ridiculous like you're now wearing, and then, if you wish, we'll take you to your father's grave so you can pay your respects. If not, you'll set the table for tonight's dinner. Does this child have a name or haven't you had the wits to think of any?" Mama asked, nodding at the squirming infant.

Betsy looked more stunned now and not as defiant. She glanced at me, then she looked down for a long moment, deciding, I felt sure, whether to turn and run down the driveway or to obey Mama. The despair she felt, the loss of any real choice, and her own helplessness hammered down any residual defiance. Her shoulders sagged under the weight of her desperation and defeat and she bowed her head.

"There's formula and bottles in the suitcase Noble has in his right hand. It has all the baby's things in it."

"Good. Now what did you say the baby's name is?" Mama asked in an almost friendly, happy tone.

"Panther," Betsy muttered.

"Excuse me?"

"Panther. Panther!" Betsy shouted at her.

Mama shook her head. "Well, I suppose the pain of giving birth gives you the right to name the poor thing, even if it's a ridiculous name." She moved forward with her arms extended and waiting for Betsy to hand over the baby.

Betsy hesitated, then she nearly tossed him into Mama's arms before charging up the stairs, crying and sobbing loudly. Mama watched her, then turned back to me.

"Take the other suitcase up to her room, Noble. Put the baby's suitcase on the table in the kitchen first, however."

I nodded and did what she asked. Then I went upstairs and knocked on Betsy's door. She didn't respond. I could hear her sobbing so I opened the door and brought her suitcase to the closet door. She was lying facedown on the bed, her face buried in the pillow.

"Here's your suitcase." I turned to go.

"Wait," she said, catching her breath. "How did my father die?"

"He got very sick. We thought he had the flu at first. Mama did all she could with her medications."

"I bet she did."

"Your father wanted it that way. He took some medicine he had from the pharmacy, but nothing helped and he died." I made no mention of the cause being the contradictions created by the mix of cures. Let her learn it from someone else, I thought.

"Why did he put all that junk in his will? Why did he do this to me? Did she make him do it?"

"No. Actually, it came as a surprise to us." It had to me.

"I won't live like she wants me to. I won't and I won't be her little slave."

"For the time being, it would be better if you just did what she asks. It's not so terrible."

"Leave it to you to say something that stupid." She wiped the tears from her cheeks and sat up. She took a deep breath. "I'm not going to stay here long. I don't care. I'll find a way."

"What happened to your car?"

"I had to sell it. I ran out of money."

"I see. Well, don't you know who the father of your child is?" I really meant it as a way for her to get some additional help.

"I know what that's supposed to mean. You think I just sleep around with someone new every other day?"

"No. I meant that whoever he is, he should bear some of the burden and responsibility."

She looked thoughtful. "Well, I'm not sure. I think it was a guy named Bobby Knee or something. I met him at a party and it was after it would have happened. Bobby Knee was just passing through. I can't even remember whose friend he was."

"But I thought you were going with Roy then or . . ."

"Oh, you're so naïve. I didn't say I was going

steady with anyone. No one's going to own me. Ever!"
she cried. "Especially not your weird mother."

"You're lucky you have her helping you," I said angrily. I started out.

"I bet she killed my father somehow. I bet she did!"
she screamed after me, then she started to cry again.

I closed the door softly behind me. My own heart
was thumping. Despite her meanness and her bad behavior, I couldn't help but feel somewhat sorry for her.
And what sort of a future would that child she had
named Panther have?

When I went downstairs, I found Mama and Baby
Celeste in the living room. Mama was feeding Panther
and Baby Celeste was beside her, captivated by the infant's suckling.

"I brought up her suitcase, Mama."

They both looked up at me and smiled.

"I'm surprised at how healthy-looking and adorable
this child is," Mama said. "She certainly doesn't deserve a baby." She nodded at the ceiling. She looked
down at the baby again. "I'll have to watch him." Her
eyes slowly lifted toward me. "We'll have to be sure
nothing evil has settled within him and used him to
enter our world. There might be a reason why that hor-
rid girl returned to us just now."

The heaviness of her threat and warning surrounded
my heart like a sticky, murky mist. I looked at the unsuspecting infant in her lap.

"Surely he's too tiny, Mama, too new."

She laughed at me and glanced at Baby Celeste,
who looked to be laughing at me as well.

"It's especially when we are as helpless as he is that
evil has its way with us. I'll do what has to be done to
make sure it hasn't happened and won't, but as always,
Noble, you have to help me, help me and Baby Ce-

leste. It would be horrible if we exposed her to anything terrible, if we were negligent, would it not? Well?"

"Yes, Mama."

"Finish your garden work. We have a lot to do, a lot to do."

She turned back to the baby. I watched her for a moment and then went outside.

Just as I turned toward the garden, I heard Betsy's scream of frustration come pouring out of the opened window in her room.

It was shrill and desperate, but it was caught up in the breeze and carried off to die away in the forest where no one could help her.

For a moment I felt like screaming myself, like being some sort of relay runner, accepting her cry and carrying it forward. After all, I had been crying out myself, but containing it within my own troubled heart. I was caught somewhere between wanting to ally myself with Betsy and with being loyal to Mama. I took the hoe in my hands and began to work again. Don't think, I told myself, don't think.

Work.

Perhaps that was what Betsy finally told herself as well. Later, when she emerged from her bedroom and descended the stairs, she was wearing one of the clean, conservative dresses that had been hanging in her closet. She had bathed and brushed her hair, pinning it back. She wore no makeup. Dry-eyed and pale, she looked in on her sleeping baby. Mama had placed him between two large pillows on the sofa, and he did look contented. After that, Betsy went into the kitchen and began to bring in the place settings, the silverware, and the dishes and glasses for our dinner. She worked quietly, carefully, obediently. To me she moved like someone under a spell, walking in her sleep, but Mama was pleased.

"We'll make do with what we have," she declared at dinner. "We'll take care of each other and we'll make your father proud yet," she told Betsy, who ate methodically.

"How can he be proud if he's dead?" she asked Mama.

Mama smiled at her, smiled at me, smiled at Baby Celeste. "The dearly departed see us. The ones we love are always with us. Death dies the moment our hearts stop. It holds us only an instant."

Betsy smirked. It was easy to see what she was thinking, but she wisely kept it to herself. All she did was glance at me with some hope that in my face she would find some sympathy and agreement. Terrified that she might, I quickly looked away. Our first dinner without Dave passed with no further comment or question. Toward the end of the meal, we heard Panther cry and Mama told Betsy to see to him.

"He probably needs a diaper change."

"I know," Betsy quipped.

"Then you know to do it," Mama told her. "When you're done, see to clearing off the table."

"What about the baby?"

"I'll see to him," Mama said. "Noble, go upstairs to the turret room and find Baby Celeste's crib. Set it up in Betsy's room for her. I'll bring in the bedding soon and prepare the crib."

"Yes, Mama," I said.

Betsy shook her head at me and then went to change Panther's diaper.

"How lucky you are," Mama told her later, "that we have everything your baby needs here."

"Yeah, I'm the luckiest girl in the world," Betsy said dryly.

Mama smiled. "You don't know how true that is."

Betsy's first night back was difficult for all of us, although Mama never acknowledged it. No sooner had we all gone to bed than Panther began to wail. He cried and cried. I kept expecting Mama to get up to see to him, but she kept her bedroom door shut. Finally, I rose and went to Betsy's door.

"Is something wrong?" I waited, but all I heard was the baby's crying. For a long moment, I couldn't decide whether to return to my room or open her door. The baby's wailing didn't subside. Still, Mama didn't rise and come out to see what was wrong. I heard Betsy's groan, so I slowly opened her door and peered into the room.

Mama had put candles in both her windows. The glow of light spilled over the bed, where I saw Betsy lying with her hands over her ears. I stepped in slowly.

"Betsy?"

Panther did seem to be in some agony. I drew closer and finally Betsy looked my way and removed her hands from her ears.

"What's wrong with him?"

"What's wrong? Look at the stupid crib your mother set up."

At first I saw nothing, but as I approached it, I saw the greenish yellow layer over the railings and smelled the mix of herbs, the garlic, and lilac. Each scent in and of itself was tolerable, but the combination Mama had created was so acrid and sharp, I nearly choked on the smell myself. Mama had created her formula and then apparently painted it on the crib. I knew she believed that certain herbs had protective powers and could be used to exorcise evil.

"He can't stand the stink and neither can I!" Betsy screamed. "What did she put on there?"

I wasn't sure exactly, but beside the garlic, the stench and some of the recipes I recalled suggested some wintergreen, some toadflax, snapdragon, and tamarisk. Mama created her own formulas, always expanding and improving on what had been handed down to her, so it was truly impossible to determine it all.

However, it wasn't hard to see the baby was uncomfortable. He squirmed to avoid the odors that flowed over him. I looked back through the open doorway. Mama had still not risen and come out of her room. I couldn't stand by and watch this. The baby's face was contorted. I reached in, lifted him out, and brought him to Betsy.

"He'll quiet down if he sleeps with you," I told her.

Then I pushed the crib farther away from her bed, closer to the windows. One of the candles, as if in disapproval, flickered and went out. Throughout it all, my heart thumped and raced, pounded and knocked, with my fear of being discovered. Almost immediately, however, Panther stopped crying. His sobs ran down to a whimpering, and then in moments, probably out of exhaustion, he fell asleep.

"Thanks," Betsy said.

I said nothing. I just nodded and slipped quietly out of her room, closing the door ever so softly. Then I waited to be sure Mama hadn't seen me before I hurried back to my own room. In the morning at breakfast, Betsy let loose a torrent of complaints about the things Mama had done. Mama didn't stop her. Of course, I was terrified Betsy would mention what I had done, but she didn't, either because she didn't care to give me credit for helping her or she knew I would be in trouble. Mama didn't appear to be listening. She ate quietly and gave all her attention to Baby Celeste.

However, when Betsy finally stopped, Mama nodded, smiled, and said, "After you clean up the breakfast dishes, you can go upstairs and wash down the crib. It was only good for one night."

"What was only good? What was that stink?" Betsy screamed.

"It's not important for you to know. I doubt you would appreciate it anyway. I'm going into the village today. Would you like to visit your father's grave? I won't be heading in that direction often so you should take advantage of this opportunity."

"No," Betsy said. "What for? He can't hear me, and if he could, he'd be sorry anyway because of what I would have to say."

"Oh, he can hear you. And I'm sure he's already sorry. I'll pick up things for the baby."

"He's name is Panther, Panther. Call him by his name."

"Panther," Mama said with a smile. "You know, I'm beginning to like it."

She couldn't have said anything more annoying to Betsy than that. It was just too much for Betsy to accept that she had done anything to please Mama, and Mama seemed to know it. Betsy won't be any sort of match for her now either, I thought. She was already defeated, but she simply didn't know it or know how much. It wouldn't be long before she would understand that and then . . . what then?

Would she become one of us, or would she wither and die like her father?

We were all in a garden of one kind or another, I thought. Some of them were of our own choosing; some were places in which we found ourselves transplanted. In the end it was always the same: dust unto dust.

Betsy looked to me, her eyes no longer full of

anger, but now, perhaps because of my actions the night before, full of pleading. I could hear her crying for my help, but Mama's eyes were on me, too.

I returned to my work, and later Mama brought out Baby Celeste.

"I'm leaving now. Don't you dare do any of the work for that girl that I have assigned her. She carries her own weight around here or else."

"Yes, Mama."

"You're a good boy, Noble, and your goodness will so shine in contrast to her laziness and wastefulness, she can do nothing else but improve herself. Remember that."

"I will."

"Good. I'll be back in a few hours at most. Watch over our precious Baby Celeste."

I always do, I wanted to say, but I just nodded. Soon after Mama left, I heard and saw Betsy emerge from the house carrying a bag of garbage. She put it in the container and looked my way. I concentrated on my work, but I could feel her eyes lingering on me.

"Betsy," Baby Celeste said. I turned and saw she was approaching us.

"Why did you help me last night?" she asked—or more like demanded.

"I saw how the baby was unhappy. That's all."

"Sure. Have you met anyone since I left, since you got your driver's license and all?"

I shook my head.

"You just need to be introduced to people. I can do that for you if you help me," she said as a way of beginning some sort of negotiation.

"I don't need to be introduced to anyone."

"What's wrong with you?" she screamed. She stamped her foot. "Why does this child stare at me like this?"

I glanced at Baby Celeste, who was fixed on her.

"You amuse her, I guess."

"Oh. I amuse her. Don't I amuse you? Even a little?" she asked with a mix of hope and flirtation.

I kept working.

She reached out and grasped my arm to spin me around.

"Well?"

"What do you want me to say?"

She smiled. "When I think of something good, I'll let you know, and then you can say it. For now, thanks again for helping me." She leaned over and kissed me on the cheek, close to my lips, then deliberately brushed her breasts over my arm. "Um," she said with her eyes closed, "it's been too long."

To me it felt as if the whole world had stopped, everything—the breeze, the birds, all hearts in every living thing, were on pause.

"I'm so horny," she whispered, "I'd even consider giving you instructions. We can really help each other, Noble man."

I couldn't speak, couldn't make a sound. My throat had closed.

She laughed, then turned and walked away, pausing to look back at me flirtatiously. I hadn't moved a muscle since her kiss. Her laugh floated around me. What frightened me the most was that she had awakened my own sexuality. It stirred and stretched inside, tingling at my breasts, warming the inside of my thighs, making me feel weak. I trembled and closed my eyes.

When I opened them, I looked down and saw Baby Celeste gazing up at me.

She looked angry.

She looked like Mama.

And for the first time I wondered, was she really my child or was she somehow hers?

17

Unstrapped

♊

Nothing Betsy did was ever done well enough or properly in Mama's eyes. She trailed after her, finding dust where she had supposedly just dusted or found things that should have been put away. She didn't wash dishes clean enough and she always set the table poorly. Periodically, over the next week, Mama would burst into Betsy's room and find clothes that weren't hung or put in the dresser drawers, dust on her furniture, the bed awkwardly made, and the baby's things not in good order. When she saw some makeup spilled on the vanity table, she confiscated all of Betsy's cosmetics, telling her she would return them when Betsy learned how to care for her things and not make such a mess.

At the end of the week, Mama had her polishing the old silverware. Whenever she made her do something new, she held out the possibility of a reward, but that reward was always dangled at the end of a long pole, a pole far longer than Betsy's reach.

"Rub harder," Mama told her. "You should be able to see your reflection in the spoon."

"This silverware is so old nothing will bring it back," Betsy moaned. Then she turned and demanded money and the keys to the car so she could go into the village and buy herself sanitary napkins or Tampax as well as some other hygienic things. Instead, Mama gave her some of her own from her own bathroom closet where I would go monthly to get what I needed. It was an unspoken, unrecognized thing never mentioned or in any way noted. Frustrated, Betsy declared she would walk to town and she would finish the silverware later.

"And who is supposed to babysit for your infant while you do that?" Mama asked her.

"I'll take him with me," Betsy vowed. "I've got to have some time away from this . . . this hellhole."

Mama glared at her. "If you set foot on that highway without my permission, I'll consider it insubordination and fine you a thousand dollars for every step you take."

"You can't do that."

Mama smiled, turned, and opened a drawer under the kitchen counter to produce an index card.

"Your father's attorney and our attorney, Mr. Derward Lee Nokleby-Cook, is at this telephone number. Do you want to call him and ask him what I can and cannot do? He'll be very happy to explain it all to you clearly."

Betsy stared at the card, then looked away without reaching for it. She turned back after a moment.

"How much is in my trust? I don't even know that."

Mama put the card back in the drawer.

"Your father had two life insurance policies. He has assigned two hundred and fifty thousand dollars to you to be transferred completely when you reach the age of twenty-five, as I have already explained."

Betsy's eyebrows rose. "Two hundred and fifty thousand?"

"And it earns interest, so it will be worth more."

"Well, why can't I have some of that now?" Betsy whined.

"I told you that as you show responsibility and improvement, I'll give you the funds you need or want to use for sensible things. Your father had no idea about Panther, of course, since you never bothered to call or write about his birth, so he didn't include him in the will, but a portion of your trust will be used to fulfill the baby's needs. As he grows, he will require more and more."

"I should decide what he needs and doesn't need. I'm his mother."

Mama nodded. "Yes, you should. And you will when you show you are capable of making wise, mature decisions."

"I'm capable of that now!"

"I don't see that. I still see a high-strung, self-centered, irresponsible young girl. However," Mama continued with a smile, "I think in time you will improve if you carry out your duties in a responsible manner.

"Your father placed a very serious and heavy burden on me when he made me sole trustee of your legacy and clearly assigned me the task of helping you achieve maturity and evaluating that maturity. And I," Mama added firmly, "take my obligations very, very seriously.

"Now, it's time for Panther to be fed, and don't rush the food and make him gag like you usually do. You're not going anywhere today. After you finish the silverware, we have to air out our rugs, polish the living room furniture, and vacuum the entire downstairs."

Betsy said nothing. Her eyes were full of such hate and anger, they looked red.

"I'm calling someone," she said abruptly, and marched out to use the phone in the hallway.

Mama shook her head and looked at me.

Seconds later, Betsy came rushing back into the kitchen. "What happened to the phone?" she demanded.

"Use of the phone is a privilege in this house. I will decide when it can and cannot be used. I told you, if you want to call our attorney, you can do that."

"I'm not interested in the attorney. I want to call someone else. You can't tell me who I can and cannot call. My father didn't even do that. Where is it?" Betsy demanded.

Mama turned away and took a mixing bowl out of the cabinet. "I have work to do," she muttered.

"What if someone wants to call me?"

"I'll let you know."

Betsy looked at me, her face contorted in defeat and frustration.

"I told you to look after your child," Mama said as she opened a jar of sage.

Betsy stood their fuming for a moment, then made a mouselike sound, turned, and stormed out of the kitchen.

"Where is the phone, Mama?" I asked.

"The downstairs phone is locked in the hall closet, and the phone has a lock on it as well." She smiled at me. "Don't worry yourself about any of this, Noble. We have years of neglect and spoiling to overcome as regards Betsy.

"But," she said, running her hand lovingly over my cheek, "we have so much help around us. It's only a matter of time. Please go see if Baby Celeste has awakened from her nap." Then Mama kissed my cheek. It had been so long since she had done that. My heart filled with joy and hope.

Mama's so right, I thought. She's so right. After all, Betsy was about as spoiled as anyone could be.

Betsy heard me ascend the stairway. She came to her doorway, holding Panther in her arms. He looked awake, but still groggy.

"I know what she's doing," Betsy said. "She's stealing my money. I'll get help and she'll be in big trouble. You'll see."

"That's not true. Everything is proper and in order legally."

"I bet. God!" she cried. "Is this the way you want to live your whole life? Just working and never having any fun?"

"I'm not unhappy," I said, and went to look in on Baby Celeste.

She was awake, so I brought her down and we went outside. Betsy had walked down the driveway and stood near the road looking at it like someone looking through barbed wire. I could almost hear the argument going on inside her head. Run. Stay. To where would she run? What if she had to return? What if Mama was doing everything legally right after all and she walked away from more than $250,000?

Surely when she had returned, she had hoped to get a great deal of help from her father, now that she had an infant on her hands. With no money and with Panther to care for, she would not be able to do the things she had done in the past to get by. How many young men would want to take on an infant as well as her? No chain was around her ankle, but in her way of thinking now, there might as well be one.

She turned and walked back, her head down, her

whole body sagging like a flag of defeat. I took Baby
Celeste's hand and hurried away before she saw us.
Despite everything, I couldn't stand looking into her
eyes soaking in such agony. She was like some wild
animal trapped and contained, tortured by memories
and the sight of the world she had known and loved. It
was close, but just enough beyond her reach to torment
her.

When we went into the house later in the day, I saw
she was polishing furniture in the living room. Panther
was asleep upstairs in his crib. Betsy didn't look at us.
She worked harder, deciding I imagined, to do what
Mama wanted her to do so she could see if she would
be rewarded as Mama had promised. She went from
one chore to another without a single complaint.
Mama followed and inspected. She raised her eyebrows at me to indicate her approval and satisfaction.

"You did well today, Betsy," Mama told her at dinner. "You are capable of making a good change in
yourself."

"Can I have some money soon?" Betsy immediately
asked.

"Soon."

"How soon?"

"Very soon," Mama said, smiling. "Let's just be
sure this new change coming about is real."

Betsy's temper was a like a raging beast chained
down inside her. She didn't say a single nasty thing
even though her eyes could have served as launching
sites for nuclear missiles. She swallowed hard and ate
her meal. Afterward, she cleaned the table and washed
the dishes and finished polishing silverware. Even
though Mama hadn't told her to do it, she scrubbed the
kitchen floor and took out the garbage.

Afterward, she sat quietly in the living room holding Panther in her arms until he was ready for bed. She took him up and returned because she saw that Mama had let me turn on the television set. Betsy was upset that we could get only a few channels, but anything was better than nothing.

"You should both get a good night's sleep," Mama declared after an hour or so. "Don't forget tomorrow we do the windows, and you were going to put a new coat of varnish on the porch deck, Noble."

I rose and turned off the set. Betsy sat there staring at the dead screen as if she still saw the program we had been watching.

"Good night, Betsy," Mama said pointedly.

Betsy turned to her sharply. "Can I have the privilege of using the phone after we do the windows tomorrow?"

"We'll see," Mama said, and went to the stairway.

Betsy looked at me. "If she doesn't let me, would you ask after this boy I knew in the village when you go in on an errand? His name is Greg Richards."

"I'm not doing any errands tomorrow."

"Whenever you do!" she pleaded.

I listened for Mama's steps on the stairway, then I said, "We'll see."

I know I must have sounded exactly like Mama.

Betsy's face reddened. "Please," she begged.

"We'll see," I repeated, and quickly followed Mama up the stairway.

She was waiting for me just outside her bedroom door. From the look on her face, I was sure she had overheard Betsy's request. She smiled at me.

"Good night, Noble. Have a good sleep," she said, and went into her bedroom.

I was undressed and into bed before I heard Betsy come up the stairway. Since her arrival, I had taken to wearing pajamas/ and keeping my breasts wrapped even when I slept. I had no lock on the inside of my door. All the rooms in the house had the old-fashioned skeleton-key locks that could be turned from the outside or inside, but I had never had a key. Before she had run off pregnant, Betsy had often burst in on me. I couldn't help but be afraid she would do it again.

I had just closed my eyes and begun to drift off when I heard her scream. At first I thought it was the preamble to a dream. It was so muffled and quick, but then I heard it again and I sat up. She was in the hallway.

What now? I wondered, rose, put on my bathrobe and slippers and opened the door.

She was sitting on the hallway floor in front of her bedroom. Her head was lowered and supported by her hands with her elbows on her legs. She was in her bra and panties. Mama's door was shut. Betsy sobbed softly and gasped before looking up at me.

"What's wrong?" I asked.

"All my clothes. My nice things, my jeans and blouses . . . they're all gone. Go in there and look at what's hanging in my closet instead."

I looked at Mama's bedroom door, then I walked slowly across the hall, stepping past Betsy and into her room. Incredibly, despite the outburst, Panther was still fast asleep. The light was on and the closet door was open. I looked in and saw some of the dresses and skirts I knew had been stored in the turret room. They were faded, old garments with high collars, long hemlines, and bland colors.

"What did she do with my things?" Betsy asked from the doorway. She stood there with her arms folded under her breasts.

I shook my head.

"Now you can see for yourself that she's out of control."

"You can ask her in the morning."

"I don't want to wait until morning. I want my things back now." She turned toward Mama's bedroom door.

"Don't wake her. She'll be angry that you're waking her and Baby Celeste as well, who will surely wake up."

Betsy hesitated. "What will she do, fine me?"

"Maybe. You're doing so well. Don't mess things up. Soon, you'll get more privileges and—"

"What *more?* I don't have any!" she cried.

I looked at the clothes in the closet again. Once I had secretly put on a few of these garments up in the turret room, I thought. For me it had been exciting and wonderful.

"What is she trying to turn me into?" Betsy asked as she came back into her room. "She even took my shoes and put those ugly clodhoppers in my closet. Where does she get the nerve? Where does she get the ideas?" she asked frantically.

What was I going to say? What would I tell her that would make sense to her?

"I'm sure she's doing what she thinks is good for you," I replied instead.

Betsy shook her head at me. "Isn't there anything she does that makes you angry?"

"If she does, she doesn't mean it."

"Sure. Sure. She doesn't mean it." Betsy wiped the tears off her cheeks.

Panther whimpered.

"You don't want to wake the baby. You better get some rest," I said. "We have a big day ahead of us. The house has so many windows, and she likes to do the inside and the outside of each, as well as the sills and the frames."

"I thought I was doing what she wanted," Betsy told me, her lips quivering. "I gave up. I decided to do her stupid chores and do them well, but look what she did to me." She nodded at the closet. "This is my reward."

I said nothing. I started out of the room. She grabbed my arm and brought her face close to mine.

"I can't stand her," she whispered. Her fingers were squeezing tightly.

"Don't do anything you'll regret, Betsy," I warned her. "Please."

She released my arm and went to her bed. She lowered herself slowly and then just fell to her side. She made no sound, but her shoulders shook with her silent sobs. I stared at her for a few more moments and then walked out, closing her door softly behind me.

Mama was standing in her doorway.

She saw me come out of Betsy's room, but she said nothing.

Then she backed into her bedroom and closed her door, too.

I returned to my room and got back into bed. After my eyes grew used to the darkness again, I heard a rustling near the window.

He was standing there staring at me.

"Your mother is making it easier for me, you know," he said. "Easier for me to return."

I held my breath.

I couldn't see his smile of satisfaction as much as I could feel it.

The wind stirred around the house and was then reinforced with a gust from the north. He shrank and slipped through the window to ride it and go off into the darkness, leaving me behind to ponder the meaning of his words.

In the morning Betsy put on the skirt and the blouse that was the least distasteful to her. Some time during the night, she had stopped crying and feeling sorry for herself. I could see a hardness in her face. She was determined not to give Mama the satisfaction of knowing how deeply she had been wounded. More than that though, she had other purposes. She stepped up beside me and whispered in my ear:

"I know exactly what's going on here, Noble. Your mother wants me to get hysterical and run off. That way she never has to give me any of my money. But it's not going to happen," she vowed, and went right to her morning chores.

"I just knew those clothes would fit you well," Mama told her at breakfast. "They belonged to a cousin of mine who also had a baby out of wedlock."

Betsy looked at her with her mouth slightly open, her eyes suddenly brightening with some realization. "Is that why you thought they would fit?"

"Of course."

Betsy glanced at me. She wore a smile that was remarkably similar to her brother Elliot's. It put a chill in my heart. I looked at Mama to see if she saw what I saw, but Mama was already humming to herself and thinking of other things.

"She's crazy for sure," Betsy told me later. "I'll bring this whole thing down around her yet," she swore. "You'd better tell her to let me have my money."

Panic spread through my chest like a large caterpillar stretching into an awareness of its own existence. I could see the same sort of awareness and confidence in

Betsy's face. She began to ask Mama questions every chance she had, questions to draw out Mama's secret world.

"When I hear you talking and there's no one in the room with you, you're not really talking to yourself, are you, Sarah?" she asked Mama after dinner one night.

Mama looked as if she wasn't going to reply, but then, she smiled and said, "No, I'm not talking to myself."

"Who hears you then?"

"Those who love us. Love binds them to us."

"Do they love me, too?"

"No, not yet, but in time they might."

"What do I have to do?"

"Become a responsible, caring person," Mama said.

Betsy glanced at me, her eyes filling with satisfaction. Couldn't Mama see how she was baiting her?

"I'll try, Sarah. I really will. I'd like to be able to talk to people who aren't there."

"They are there," Mama said.

"No, I mean, who other people can't see. They talk back to you, too, right?"

"Of course."

"And that's how you know so much?"

"Yes," Mama said, her eyes finally smaller. Now she sees what Betsy's doing, I thought. "And if someone mocks them or in any way abuses them, they can be severe."

"Oh, I wouldn't mock them. Who am I to mock anybody?" She looked at Baby Celeste. "Does Baby Celeste . . . can she see and hear them, too?"

"Baby Celeste is very special. She sees and hears much more than any of us do or even could."

Betsy nodded. "Yes, she is special. She's so smart. I hope Panther is as smart as she is."

Mama didn't say anything. She smiled as if Betsy had said something very, very stupid.

"I'd like to learn more about the spiritual world," Betsy said. "I really would."

"In time you will," Mama promised.

"Good. Noble sees and hears them, too, I imagine?" Betsy gazed my way.

Mama smiled at me. "Noble does, and always will."

"Maybe I really am lucky to be here," Betsy declared, and began to clear off the tableware.

"I'll tell you what's really going to happen here," Betsy whispered to me later in the hallway. "Your mother is going to be committed and maybe you along with her, and then I'll get what's mine," she threatened, and went up to her room.

I wanted to run to Mama to warn her, but what would I tell her? Don't discuss the spiritual world with Betsy? Mama might think I was betraying her again. How could I believe anyone would think her mentally unbalanced for believing in our spirits? What difference could Betsy possibly make?

Much later, in the middle of the night, I was woken by the sound of my door opening and closing. I sat up and rubbed the cobwebs of sleep from my eyes.

"Who is it?" I asked the silhouetted figure.

"Who did you expect? One of your spirits?" Betsy said.

"What do you want?"

"Did you think about what I told you?" she asked, drawing closer.

"I don't know what you mean. Go back to your room. It's late and you'll wake everyone."

"I can't believe you're such a zero, Noble. My brother must have seen something worthwhile in you to have been friends with you."

"We'll talk about it tomorrow. I'm tired."

Instead of leaving, she sat on my bed. "I can't sleep. This is the longest I've gone without even a beer. You don't listen to any music. You don't want to go to a movie or hang out with people our age. She's got you crazy, too. You should be on my side. Why don't you suggest she babysit one night and you and I go to a movie? I'll look up some of my old friends and we'll have a good time. What do you say?"

"I don't need to be with your old friends."

"Sure you do. You don't know what you need and what you don't need. I've decided that's your problem. If you don't know what you're missing, you don't care. It's as simple as that, right?"

"No. Just go back to your room."

"You've been kept locked up too long, Noble. You're not an ugly guy. You're actually very good-looking, sweet. You have great eyes."

I shifted away from her and she laughed.

"I remember how shy I used to be, but after that first time, I waved good-bye to shyness forever and I'm happy I did. You don't stay young forever. This is the best time of your life and you're letting it all go by, Noble."

"I'm not unhappy. Just go back to your room. Leave me alone."

"You don't even know you're unhappy. I can make you happy."

"I don't want you to do anything for me."

She stood up. A cloud slid off the moon and the glow brightened, practically illuminating my room as well as the ceiling fixture. For a moment she just stared at me. I thought she would simply say something nasty like she always did and then leave me, but instead, she brought her nightgown off her shoulders and then, with a slight twist of her body, let it fall to the floor.

She stood there naked, the yellow glow washing over her full breasts and her stomach.

"Stop," I said, ashamed at how weak my voice sounded.

"No. I'm going to show you what you're missing, and maybe then you'll be more interested in having some fun with me and my friends."

"Get away," I cried, but softly, so as not to wake up Mama.

She saw that.

"If you don't behave, I'll scream and your mother will come in here and find us together. I'll tell her you invited me."

"Please, I don't want to be shown anything."

"I like it when you beg like that, Noble," she said, lowering herself to the bed. "It gets me more excited."

I thought I would leap out of the bed and rush out of the room. If I did that, Mama wouldn't think I had anything to do with Betsy coming into my room. I started to throw the blanket off me and turn to get out of the bed, but Betsy reached out quickly and put her arms around my neck, pulling me down and then bringing her lips to mine. She pressed hard and swung her left leg over me. I struggled to free myself, which only made her laugh and kiss me again.

When I twisted to my left to turn my body, she threw the blanket off me and, before I could stop her, shoved her hand between my legs. For a long moment, she was still and I was still. Her fingers moved like the legs of some big spider and then she pulled her hand back sharply.

In the glowing moonlight, I saw her face contort, her eyes go wide, and then she smiled, her lips twisted.

The realization exploded in her brain and she shot her hands out, tearing my pajama top apart, the buttons flying every which way. She gazed in awe at my strapped bosom.

"You're . . ." The words gagged her. Disgust washed over her face and she fell back on her haunches. "Take that off," she ordered.

I shook my head, my voice having fallen so deeply inside me, I was unable to raise it.

"Do it!" she ordered. "Or I will."

She started to reach toward me, so I sat up and undid the strapping. It fell away and my breasts, like two squeezed balloons, filled to their full shape.

"Holy shit, you're a girl." She laughed. "You're a girl!"

I brought the blanket up to cover myself, but she pulled it out of my hands.

"Look at you! You're so weird. I feel so weird. Why did you do this?"

I fell back to my pillow and stared up at the dark ceiling.

"Did my father know about you? I bet he was shocked when he found out, huh?"

She stepped off the bed and began to put on her nightgown.

"So what's this about? Does it have anything to do with the spirits? Your mother is making you do this?"

"No."

"No? What are you going to tell me? She doesn't know what you are?"

"I didn't say that."

"You're really nuts and so is she. You're both bonkers. I'll call that lawyer now. I'll tell everyone."

"Don't," I begged.

"Don't? Don't? No, I won't. I'll just continue to be a slave here." She turned to go out, then stopped and turned back to me. "Did my brother know about you? . . .Well? Did he? You might as well tell me all of it, the truth. Did he?"

"Yes."

She returned to my bedside.

"When did he find out?"

"I don't remember exactly when."

She continued to stand there and stare down at me. I could almost hear her brain clicking away. She glanced at the door and then she turned back to me.

"Whose baby is Celeste? She's yours, isn't she?" she said, answering her own question instantly. "And Elliot's. She's my niece. She's my father's grand-daughter. Well? Tell me!" she said, raising her voice.

My heart stopped. Mama could have heard her. If she came in now and saw this . . .

"Please," I begged.

"Please? Please? When I begged you to help me, what did you say? We'll see? Huh? You let her treat me like this, take away my things, keep my money from me, and you say *please?*"

I bit down so hard on my lower lip, I could taste blood.

Elliot was standing by the window watching and listening, a big smile on his face.

I shook my head at him and Betsy grimaced and then turned and looked at the window.

"What are you looking at?"

I tried to breathe, but my lungs were so full of heat, they wouldn't expand any further. I felt the blood pounding in my temples. I started to gasp and wheeze and it frightened her.

"What's wrong with you? Stop it."

I bent over, clutching my side. I thought I was going to start to vomit.

"Stop it!" she ordered. "Okay, okay," she said when I didn't stop. "I'll keep your stupid secret. Relax. I said I'll keep your secret." She pulled at my shoulder.

I fell back on the pillow. My breathing improved and my lungs stopped aching.

"You're a basket case." She stood there thinking. "Look," she said, stepping up to the bed again. "I don't really care what you and your crazy mother do to yourselves and even to that special child. You can swim in this madness all you want, but you're going to help me from now on, understand? You're going to get her off my back. You're going to take me to see my friends, and you're going to help me get my money, because if you don't, I'll have you committed as well as your mother.

"Now, when you get up in the morning, you find out where she put my clothes and you get them back to me immediately. And from now on, whenever she gives me a stupid chore to do, you do it. Also, we're going to town tomorrow night, so get that into your thick skull. You're driving me there. That's what you'll tell her and don't let her say no.

"Don't let her say no to anything I want ever again. Make her understand what will happen if she does. Is that clear? I want to hear you say yes or I'll just start screaming my head off in here. Well?"

"Yes."

"Yes. That's good." She smiled. "This might turn out better than I thought, even better than you thought. For one thing, you don't have to wrap up your boobs for me anymore." She laughed. "Now that we have more in common, I might be a better friend to you than ever." She walked to the door. "Good night, Noble. Or should I say, Celeste?"

She laughed again and slipped out of the room, closing the door behind her.

"I told you this would happen," Elliot said.

He crossed the room, and to my utter shock he got into my bed and lay beside me.

"Now we can be together again," he said.

He was gone in the morning, but all night long, I was sure I felt his breath on my cheek and my neck.

And his hand holding mine.

18

Betsy Turns the Tables

♊

Betsy was already dressed and waiting for me outside her door by the time I rose in the morning. She had Panther in her arms. His eyes were wide open, and in the morning light flowing through my bedroom windows and out my bedroom door, they looked like two shiny ebony stones glittering under the surface of the clear creek water. Unlike Celeste, Panther didn't usually smile at everyone he saw. Instead, he looked anxious. Most of the time I thought he stared with distrust and anger. I had to wonder how often he had been left alone, left crying his eyes out, hungry and uncomfortable.

"Remember, I want you to find my clothes and return them to me this morning so I can get out of this stupid costume," Betsy said, and started down the stairs. Mama was already downstairs with Baby Celeste.

Panic froze me. How could I do what Betsy wanted? How could I not do it?

I wasn't sure Mama had hidden her clothes in the

turret room, but I couldn't think of anywhere else.
When I went up to look, I discovered the door was
locked. I felt certain of it now because locking the turret door was something Mama did only when I was in
there with Baby Celeste and she didn't want us coming
out before the workers doing the rugs and curtains had
left. My mind was in turmoil. I was hoping to give
Betsy the clothes and then tell Mama she must have
found them herself. How was I going to get the key
away from Mama or talk her into returning Betsy's
clothes without getting Mama angry?

When I went downstairs, I found they were all already at the dining room table.

"What took you so long, Noble?" Mama asked. I
glanced at Betsy.

"Yes, Noble, why are you so late?" she teased.

"I just didn't realize the time, Mama." She held her
gaze on me, then turned back to fixing Baby Celeste's
cereal and fruit.

"So tell me," Betsy asked with her eyes mainly on
me as soon as Mama took her seat, "how long did you
try to find out what happened to Noble's twin sister,
Celeste?"

Mama looked up quickly from her mixed-grain cereal. She gave me just a slight glance and then turned
to Betsy. "We've never stopped trying to find out what
happened to her."

"Well, I don't understand it. Why don't I ever see
her picture on a milk carton or something? You should
be calling the police every week and asking what
they've been doing."

"What makes you think I didn't and don't still do?"
Mama countered.

Betsy shrugged. "You never talk about her, and
Noble here never says anything either."

"I think I told you once that it is very painful to re-live it all," Mama said.

"What was she doing that day? Weren't you with her all the time, Noble?" Betsy continued as if she was leading the investigation. Her impish smile wasn't lost on me, and the moment I shifted my eyes away from her, I could feel Mama pull herself up.

"That's enough. This isn't a topic I care to discuss with you or have you discuss at my dining table."

"I'm just trying to be more caring," Betsy said. "Losing a child at that age had to be devastating for you. I can't imagine how I would feel if someone just upped and took Panther one day. I don't think I'd rest a minute or do another thing until I had found him."

Mama glared at her. "I don't rest and she's never out of my mind, but I have many responsibilities," Mama told her, each word as sharp as a slap.

Betsy smiled to herself and nodded. She looked down and Mama relaxed her shoulders, but I knew this was not going to end.

"Here's what I really wonder, Sarah. You have such faith in your spirits, why haven't they told you where Celeste is?" Betsy looked up again. She made herself look as interested and as sincere as she possibly could.

I quickly swung my eyes to Mama. How would she answer such a question?

"The spirits that guide us, that exist among us, are only here," she said softly. "They do not wander the world like lost souls looking for a home and bring back news of the world. This is their home. We are their family."

"But—"

"That's enough!" Mama slapped her hand on the table so hard, a dish bounced. Baby Celeste's eyes widened and I looked down.

A long moment of silence passed. Mama began eating again.

"Whatever," Betsy said. "Noble has offered to take me and Panther into town today," she continued almost in the same breath. "I need personal things now, not later."

Mama looked at her and then at me. "Noble, did you tell her such a thing?"

Words twisted like rubber bands in my throat.

"He told me this morning, didn't you, Noble? I asked him to think about it last night, didn't I, Noble? When we had a nice chat, right, Noble?"

I felt as if the barrel of a pistol were pressed against my temple.

"Yes," I said, and looked quickly at Mama. "I thought, if she was finished with her work, we could just make a quick trip to the supermarket."

"No, it's the mall I need to go to, Noble. I told you that."

"Well, you're not finished with your work," Mama told Betsy. "I want you to clean out the pantry today, dust off the shelves, and then rearrange everything so it is all neatly set. The floor has to be washed in there as well. This is not a day to go anywhere. Besides," Mama continued like someone putting the finishing touches on a well-prepared response that anticipated Betsy's request, "I will be using the car today. I have to meet with Mr. Bogart and discuss our business."

Betsy's eyes radiated her anger, but she kept herself calm and smiled.

"Okay. By the time you return, I'll have all that done and then Noble can take me, right, Noble?" she hammered in my direction.

I looked at Mama. "Would that be all right, Mama?"

"We'll see," she said, pursing her lips. She was mad

at me, but I felt caught like a fly in a spider's web. Struggling only ensnared me more.

Afterward, when Betsy was in the bathroom, Mama asked me why I had promised her such a thing.

"She was so desperate and pleading and crying, I didn't know what else to tell her, Mama."

She considered. "Well, I don't mind your being compassionate, Noble, but you have to be careful with her. She knows how to take advantage of people and play upon their kindnesses. Look what she did to her poor father."

"I know, Mama, but I think things would be easier for all of us if she was given some rewards for the work she's doing. She's doing what you want her to do now," I emphasized.

"Hmm. Maybe."

"Can she have her own clothes back?"

"I don't see how that's possible." Mama started out to the car.

"Why not, Mama?" I dared to pursue.

She turned and smiled. "Because I had to burn them and bury them, Noble."

"You burned them?"

"Of course. Haven't I always taught you that fire is the most effective form of purification? Be careful. Don't give your trust and your good heart away too quickly. Take good care of Baby Celeste. I'll be home before dinner," she said, and left.

I stood there staring at the closed door, my heart pounding. Burned them? Buried them?

I looked at Baby Celeste, who had gotten herself ready to go out to the garden.

"Time to work," she said.

I started for the door.

"Where do you think you're going?" I heard Betsy

ask, and turned to see her standing in the hallway. "Get your ass in here and work on the pantry."

"But if I don't do what has to be done in the garden . . ."

"I don't care about that stupid garden. Did you find out where my clothes are?"

"Burned," Baby Celeste said.

I turned to look at her so quickly, a sharp pain shot through my neck. She looked so much older, her face firm and her eyes steady and dark.

"What did she say?"

"Nothing. I didn't get a chance to find out."

"Yeah, right. When your mother gets back, we're going to the mall, Noble. God, why do I keep calling you that? Maybe I'll just forget and call you Celeste, huh?"

I saw how much she enjoyed tormenting me.

Panther started to cry in the kitchen. She had left him in the bassinet.

"Oh, that kid is so cranky here. Actually, he's cranky everywhere. I'm too young for a baby. Look after him, too. I'm going to borrow some of your mother's makeup and see about my hair."

"You can't go into her bedroom!" I cried.

"Watch me. She took mine, didn't she? I want to do my nails, too. I'm falling apart in this house. You'll bring my lunch up to me later. I'll have an egg sandwich. I have to admit that bread your mother makes is good. She should be a baker and stop all this other nonsense."

Panther's cries grew louder.

Betsy put her hands over her ears. "It's all yours," she said, and hurried to the stairway.

I went into the kitchen. Baby Celeste followed; however, she looked unhappy about it. She waited while I calmed Panther, but she looked impatient.

"We have to go to the garden," she said.

"Not now. First we have to do the pantry."

"No," she said firmly.

"Just listen to me and do what I say, Celeste," I said irritably. Betsy was doing this to me, making me intolerant, but I couldn't help it.

Baby Celeste shook her head defiantly and started out of the kitchen.

"Celeste, don't you dare go out. You wait for me to finish in here first. You can help with the pantry."

"We have to go to the garden."

Panther started to cry again. What did he want? He had been fed and he didn't feel wet.

"Shh," I said, rocking him gently. He cried harder.

"The garden," Baby Celeste said, and stamped her foot. Then she turned to go out the front door.

I ran after her and, holding Panther in my right arm, seized her shoulder with my left and turned her back sharply. She winced but she didn't cry.

"You stay with me, Celeste. I told you we'll go to the garden later."

She glared up at me, then shifted her eyes toward the stairway as if she knew this was all Betsy's fault. Her eyes grew small and dark and her lips tightened. How much she looked like Mama, I thought.

"Help me with Panther," I said more gently. "Make him stop crying."

She thought a moment and then, with some reluctance, reached up to touch his hand. The moment she did so, he stopped wailing. His sobs wound down as he looked at her. She never shifted her eyes from his.

"See, he likes you. You can be a great help to me," I said, and returned to the kitchen. I put him back in his bassinet and placed it on the kitchen floor. Baby Celeste stood beside it and looked down at him. He reached up and she took his hand into hers.

"Thank you, Celeste," I said, and started on the pantry. Before I was finished, Panther had fallen asleep and Baby Celeste had curled herself up beside the bassinet and fallen asleep herself.

After I had taken everything off the shelves and dusted as Mama had wanted, I washed the pantry floor. Just as I finished, I heard Betsy calling down from the top of the stairway.

"Noble Celeste, I'm hungry. Bring me my lunch," she shouted. "Quickly."

Baby Celeste woke up, but thankfully Panther did not. I prepared the egg sandwich for Betsy and made one for Baby Celeste, too.

"We'll go out to the garden when you're finished with lunch," I told her.

I carried up Betsy's lunch and brought it to her room, but she wasn't there.

"I'm in here," she shouted from Mama's bedroom.

Slowly, anticipating something terrible, I walked to the bedroom. Betsy was sitting at the vanity table. She had almost every jar of cream open, powder splattered over the table, lipstick tubes open, and tissues everywhere. She had done up her face after much experimentation, but that wasn't the worst of it. She was also wearing one of Mama's pretty dresses, one that she had bought when she had first begun dating Dave.

"It didn't quite fit," Betsy said, standing, "but I fixed that."

She had taken a scissors to the hem and chopped it back.

"The bodice isn't bad. I'm surprised your mother wore such a dress and showed so much cleavage."

All I could do was think about what would happen if Mama returned and saw this.

"Well, is the pantry done?"

"Yes," I said, but shook my head at her and at what she had done. "You've got to clean up this room and you can't wear that."

"Oh, really? What will happen? Will I be fined? Will she take back some of my trust fund? Will she give me some new chores? Which we now know means she'll be giving them to you, Noble Celeste."

"Please put everything back the way it was. I have your lunch."

"Just put it on the table. And go look for my clothes. Find them before she gets back or I'll greet her at the door with headline news that will bust her gut."

I stood there, debating with myself whether I should tell her what Mama had told me and what Baby Celeste had almost revealed, but before I could decide, Panther's screams were suddenly so shrill, I practically threw Betsy's lunch tray onto the table and then ran downstairs.

When I reached the kitchen, I saw Baby Celeste standing beside the bassinet and looking down at him. His screaming continued.

"What's wrong with him, Celeste?" I asked, and approached.

His face was crimson, the crests of his cheeks as red as raw meat. Tears flowed down his cheeks so quickly, it looked as if he could drown in his own sobs. At first I had no idea what was wrong, and then I saw the black candle beside the sole of his left foot. The tip of the candlewick still glowed like an ember in a fireplace, and the heal of his sole was crisp and bright red. The shock of it sucked the wind out of my lungs.

Betsy had reluctantly followed me down, swaggering in the dress and holding half of her sandwich.

"What is it? Why does that kid cry so much?" she demanded, coming up beside me.

She looked down and for a few moments just stared at him and continued to bite and chew her sandwich. Then she saw the candle and slowly knelt to pick it up and looked at it closer.

"What's this?"

I shook my head.

Baby Celeste wore a contented, firm expression without the slightest hint of any fear of reprimand.

"It was lit. Look at his foot!" Betsy cried, seeing the burn on the heel of his sole. She turned to Baby Celeste. "Did you do that to Panther?"

She didn't answer. Instead, she looked up at me. "We have to go to the garden."

"The garden!" Betsy screamed. She threw the candle down and seized Baby Celeste's shoulders, shaking her. "Did you light a candle and put it in the bassinet? Well, did you, you little—"

"Stop it!" I shouted, pulling Baby Celeste from her grasp. "We've got to put something on that burn quickly."

Panther had been screaming so loudly, his voice was strained.

"Why would she do that? She's crazy, too. You're all crazy!"

I went quickly to Mama's herbal closet and found an extract of witch hazel that I knew she used for burns. I began first by applying an ice cube to relieve the pain, and then dried the spot and applied the remedy. We rocked the bassinet and eventually Panther closed his eyes and fell asleep from the shock and excitement.

Betsy stood off to the side and watched, not making any effort to help soothe her own child and comfort him.

"This does it," she said when I finished. "You get me my clothes and we get your mother to give me my money. I'm out of here. I can't wait to get away from you lunatics."

"I can't get you your clothes," I said in a quiet, defeated voice.

"Why not?"

"My mother said she burned and buried them."

"That's what I thought that monster said before," Betsy replied, looking at Baby Celeste. "You'd better keep her away from Panther. Otherwise, whatever happens will be your fault."

Betsy went back upstairs.

I knelt down and took Baby Celeste's hand in mine.

"Why did you do that, Celeste? Why did you burn little Panther?"

She shook her head.

"Why? Tell me," I demanded.

"Clean him."

"Clean him?"

She had seen Mama use fire too often to drive away evil, I thought. This happened because of the things Mama had told her?

"That was bad, Celeste. You were bad."

"No." She shook her head and pulled her hand out from mine.

"You were. You must not do anything like that again," I said sternly.

"You're bad, too. We have to work in the garden." She turned and ran out of the kitchen.

Betsy was mean and selfish, but maybe she wasn't so wrong about all of this, I thought sadly. Baby Celeste wasn't growing up right. I lifted the bassinet and carried it and Panther to the living room where Baby Celeste had curled up on the sofa. She had her thumb in her mouth and her back to me. I set Panther down gently, then went to the sofa and stroked Baby Celeste's hair.

"We were going back to the garden, but you shouldn't have hurt little Panther, Celeste. That's not the way to clean him."

She shook her head, kept her thumb in her mouth, and closed her eyes.

"Do you understand me? He's just a baby. What did he do to make you want to do that to him? Tell me."

She didn't answer. She held that thumb in her mouth. A thought came into my mind, a thought both terrifying and intriguing. I turned her slowly to me.

"Did someone tell you to do that, Celeste?"

She nodded.

"Who? Who told you?"

She pointed toward the doorway, but I saw nothing.

"Was it a man?"

She nodded.

"What did he look like? What color was his hair?"

"My hair." She touched her head. Then she turned her back to me again and closed her eyes.

I sat there, unable to speak, unable to move until I heard Mama drive up.

The moment she entered the house and looked in at us, she knew something was wrong.

"Why are you in here on such a beautiful day, Noble?" she demanded before I could speak.

I felt a great exhaustion, a deep emptiness. I didn't have the strength to find answers that would soothe or please Mama. This sense of helplessness made me numb. All I could do is stare back at her. She stepped farther into the room, looked at Panther in the bassinet, and then at Baby Celeste, who had turned and sat up to look at her. Her eyes moved from one face to another.

"What happened here?"

"When I wasn't watching, Baby Celeste lit one of your black candles and put it in the bassinet under Panther's foot to burn him."

Mama looked at her and then back at me.

"Why weren't you watching?"

"I was upstairs."

"Doing what?"

"I brought something to Betsy."

"Did she do her chores? Is the pantry finished?"

"Yes, Mama." Why wasn't she more concerned about what Baby Celeste had done?

Her eyes widened and then she fixed them on me. "Where's that girl? Why wasn't she watching her own child?"

Betsy had heard her enter the house and had come down the stairway quietly. She was still wearing Mama's dress and all the makeup.

"You think you're going to blame it on me?" she said, spinning Mama around. When Mama confronted her, she gasped at the sight of her in the dress and with all that makeup on her face. "It was all your precious special baby's doing." Betsy smiled. "I'm sorry, I mean your cousin's baby."

"What is the meaning of this? Why are you in that dress and where did you get the makeup?"

"Don't you recognize the dress?" Betsy said, twirling. "Oh, I'm sorry. I needed to make some alterations. I hope you don't mind."

Betsy's audaciousness stunned Mama. She stood there staring at her and then turned to me.

"What's going on here, Noble?"

"Yes, Noble, what's going on here? Your mother has a right to know. Tell her."

"Stop it!" I snapped.

"Stop it? That's exactly what I intend to do," Betsy fired back at me with her hands on her hips.

"I don't know what you're up to now, Betsy, but you have put yourself back months with this behavior. I couldn't justify giving you a single penny of your father's trust," Mama told her.

Betsy held her smile. "Oh, you're going to give me a lot more than that, Sarah. Isn't she, Noble? Or should I say, Celeste? What should I call you? Sarah, what should I call her?"

Mama gasped audibly as her hands lifted and fluttered like baby birds to the base of her throat. She took a step back and shook her head.

"What are you saying? What is she saying?" Mama asked me.

"Tell her what I'm saying."

"Stop, please," I begged. "I'm doing what you asked me to do."

"It's not enough anymore. I haven't got the patience for any of it. You listen to me, Sarah," Betsy continued, heartened, encouraged, and strengthened by Mama's signs of retreat. "The whole world is going to find out what a sick thing you did here, making her behave and act like a boy. And the whole world's going to know about your precious Baby Celeste, who is just as sick as the two of you.

"Unless," she continued, now merely a foot or so from Mama, "you turn over all my money to me immediately. You go to that locked-up phone and you call the attorney and tell him to have my check ready tomorrow. Hear me?"

Mama shook her head. She couldn't speak.

Betsy smiled. "What actually happened here, Sarah? If that's really Celeste, where's Noble? . . . Well? Tell me!" she screamed into Mama's face.

"No!" I cried, and lunged forward to pull Betsy away.

Baby Celeste started to cry and that woke Panther, who joined her in a chorus of screams and wails while I struggled to pull Betsy away from Mama.

"You go make that call, Sarah. You go do it now. I'm warning you!" Betsy continued, waving her fist at her face.

Mama continued to shake her head, then she hurried to the stairway.

"Where are you going, Sarah? You better be going to make that phone call," Betsy shouted after her.

Mama didn't look back. She climbed the stairs, pausing at one point to steady herself with the rickety balustrade. She looked about to faint.

"Mama?" I cried up at her.

She turned and stared down at me with such hateful accusation in her face, I felt my heart shatter like brittle china under my breast. It brought tears to my eyes. I shook my head and whispered, "Mama, please."

"Call!" Betsy screamed. "I want to get out of here tomorrow!"

Mama continued up and disappeared.

"How could you do that? I was doing everything you wanted," I bawled.

"Oh, stop it. You should be grateful and thanking me on your hands and knees. You won't have to pretend to be a boy anymore, but you better see to it that she does what I asked her to do. You go impress her with my determination, hear me? And I want some money and the keys to the car right away. I'll give you ten minutes. Go up and get it and come right down. Do it!" Betsy ordered, pointing her finger at the stairway.

I looked at Baby Celeste, who was clutching herself and sitting on the sofa. Tears streaked down her cheeks

almost as fast as Panther's had. Panther was crying so
hard as well that the bassinet rocked.

"The children," I said.

"Oh, they'll live. Just do what I said." Betsy gave
me a shove toward the stairway. "Now."

I started up the stairs slowly.

"Move it, Noble Celeste. You were a freak after all.
I was sure you were gay. Maybe you are." She
laughed, then turned and shouted at the children, "Shut
up! Shut up, shut up, shut up!"

I hurried the rest of the way, hoping to get the
money and the keys and get her out of the house as
quickly as I could. At the moment that seemed to be
the only solution there was. Mama's bedroom door
was open. I stopped in the doorway and watched her
clearing off the vanity table slowly and putting things
away. She moved as if she were walking in her sleep.
Betsy had thrown garments all over the room.

"Mama, I'm sorry. She came in on me at night . . .
Mama . . ."

I heard something, and at first it confused me, but
as I entered the bedroom, I understood she was humming to herself. I recognized it immediately, a song
she often sang to Noble and me when we were young.

"Mama?"

Instead of answering me, she started to sing.

*"If you go out in the woods today, you're sure of a
big surprise . . ."*

"Mama, please listen to me." I touched her arm.

She turned and smiled.

"If you go out into the woods today . . ."

"Mama?"

" . . . you'd better go in disguise."

She turned away, continued to clean up, and returned to humming.

I watched her for a few moments.

"Noble Celeste!" I heard Betsy shout from the foot of the stairway. "I'm not waiting here all day!"

I looked around and saw Mama's purse. While she was distracted, I opened it, took out her car keys and some money, then closed it.

She was singing again.

I hurried out and down the stairs.

"Did you get it?"

"Yes." I flung the keys at her. She caught them and smiled. "What about the money?"

"Here's all I can find." I handed her the bills.

She counted them quickly. "Okay. This will do for now. When I come back, she had better have made that phone call. Otherwise . . ."

She let her threat hang in the air.

"Children," she said, turning to Baby Celeste and Panther, who was dozing again, "I now leave you in capable hands. Have a good night.

"I'll be thinking about you, Noble Celeste," she said, and walked out.

The moment the door closed, Mama's scream pierced my heart and fell like thunder from above.

19

Almost Over

⚎

When I rushed back up the stairs to her bedroom, I found Mama collapsed on the floor. Her body was folded awkwardly, twisted with her right arm out and her left under her torso. When I knelt beside her, I saw that she had fallen hard and scraped the left side of her forehead. A tiny trickle of blood emerged from the wounds. I rose quickly and retrieved a wet washcloth to first clean the scrapes. Fortunately, she wasn't heavy. In fact, I was surprised at how I hadn't realized her thinness beneath her clothing. I could feel her rib bones as I lifted her gently and laid her on her bed. I put the cold, wet washcloth over her forehead and rubbed her hand.

"Mama, wake up. Please," I moaned.

Below, Panther was still crying loudly, but Baby Celeste had come up behind me and was standing in the bedroom doorway looking in with concern.

"We have to work in the garden," she said, as if that

were the solution to everything. In a vague place deep in the bottom of my mind, I wondered if it was, if working in the garden was magical and somehow roused all the good spirits who would come to our aid.

I shook Mama's hand. She groaned.

"Mama, wake up. Please," I begged.

Her eyelids fluttered, opened and closed, and then fluttered again.

Baby Celeste drew closer. "The garden."

"Celeste, please. Don't you see Mama's not feeling well!"

She looked at Mama and then at me, her face full of accusation, I thought. I could almost hear her thinking, *This was your fault.*

Mama groaned again, then her eyes opened. She looked at me, but she didn't speak.

"Mama, are you all right? What should I do?"

She stared and still did not speak. Then her eyes shifted away. I wiped her scrapes clean and went for some healing balm. When I returned, Baby Celeste was gone, which put some more panic in my chest and made me feel as if my nerves had broken into tiny little marbles rolling and bouncing inside me. I could take only short, little breaths and hurried to care for Mama's scrapes. All the time, she kept her eyes fixed on the wall and avoided looking at me. I begged her to listen and talk to me, but she didn't utter a sound.

Concerned for Baby Celeste and especially for Panther's welfare now that I had seen what Baby Celeste had done to him before, I reluctantly left Mama's side and hurried downstairs. Panther was in a deep sleep again in his bassinet, but Baby Celeste was nowhere to be found. I stepped out and saw her working in the garden.

"Celeste!" I called. "Why did you go out without me?"

I charged off the porch, anger like a wind carrying me to the garden where she was bent over, digging with her small spade and ignoring my cries. I ripped her away from the soil.

"Didn't I tell you to wait for me? Didn't I?"

She glared at me sullenly.

"First, we have to see to Mama and then we'll come out here, Celeste. The garden is not important now."

"We have to work in the garden," she chanted.

I carried her back, struggling and screaming in my arms.

"You're being very bad," I told her. "You know what happens to people who are bad in this house."

I marched up the stairway with her and put her forcefully down on her bed.

"You take a nap," I ordered. "I need to tend to Mama."

I left her glaring at me and closed her bedroom door, but I was worried she would sneak out again. In the top right dresser drawer in Mama's bedroom, I found the skeleton key that opened and locked all the doors in the house. Before this, I would never dare touch it or look for it without Mama's permission. I returned to Baby Celeste's bedroom door and locked it. The second she heard that, she wailed and pounded on the inside of the door.

"Take a nap!" I shouted.

Then I calmed myself, went downstairs to bring Panther up in his bassinet, and put him in his crib in Betsy's room. He moaned and squirmed a little, but he didn't wake up. How many days like this had he already had in his life? I wondered, but I didn't have time to think about all that now. I had to return to Mama.

She was still lying flat on her bed, her head turned toward the wall, her eyes opened, the eyelids blinking slowly. I sat beside her and held her hand, hoping she would eventually turn to me and tell me what she wanted me to do, but the afternoon light dwindled into twilight and she hadn't moved an inch or said a word. In fact, her eyelids closed and she fell into a deep sleep.

I rose, feeling exhausted myself. The children were quiet; the house was dark. I had to see to dinner, I told myself when I looked with longing at my own bed. I was tempted to fall asleep and dream that none of this had happened, but I descended the stairway slowly and went into the kitchen to prepare something for all of us to eat.

My early days as Celeste, a daughter who often stood side by side with her mother in the kitchen, returned to my memory. As Noble, I had done little in the kitchen, but remarkably, all I had done with Mama years and years ago was vivid. I prepared her wild rice and prepared some eggplant with her herbal breading. Then I set the table. I heard the grandfather clock bong and listened expectantly for the sounds of Mama rising. She would be pleased at what I had done, I thought. She would be restored.

But when I went up to see her, I found she was still in a deep sleep. I hesitated, wondering if I should wake her anyway. She should eat something, I thought. If she doesn't wake up soon, I'll feed Baby Celeste and Panther, then bring up some food for her. She'll still be pleased.

I unlocked Baby Celeste's door and found her curled up on the floor beside it. She sat up, rubbed her eyes, and looked at me furiously.

"If you behave now, you can come out. Are you going to behave?"

She nodded, but did not speak.

"Come on then. I've made us dinner. We have to get Panther and feed him, too."

Panther was squirming uncomfortably in his crib and alternating between sobbing and coughing on his tears and pain. I put another dose of balm on his burn and brought him down to sit in his high chair at the table.

"Help me bring everything out," I told Baby Celeste. She did so, but not with the same excitement and joy she had when Mama asked her to do it.

Afterward, she sat quietly and ate, watching me feed Panther and eating something myself as I did so. I couldn't stand the way Baby Celeste glared at me. It was Mama's angry face transposed on her face like some mask she could take off and put on at will.

"We've got to behave ourselves," I lectured, "and help Mama. She's not feeling well, and not behaving will only make her feel worse, Celeste."

Her normally sweet lips tightened in the corners, but she didn't say, "Okay," or anything. She finished eating and then, without my telling her to do so, began taking things back into the kitchen.

Panther ate, but he was uncomfortable. I wondered what Betsy was doing and when she would return. Until I had a good talk with Mama, there was little I could do to make Betsy happy and keep her from making trouble for us, I thought. I settled Panther in his crib and then I looked in on Mama. She had turned her head and had her eyes open, but she was staring at the ceiling.

"Mama, how are you? Are you hungry? I made some dinner for you."

She didn't reply.

"I'll bring it up," I said, thinking that when she saw it, she would be pleased and begin to speak.

Baby Celeste followed me about, but was as silent as Mama, not responding to anything I said or asking for anything. I fixed Mama's pillows so I could sit her up. She was limp and did nothing to help. Even after I put the tray before her, she just stared in silence.

"You've got to eat and drink something, Mama. You have to." I began to feed her.

She looked at me and she chewed slowly.

Good, I thought, she's coming around. I fed her as much as she would take and made her drink as much water as I could, but then she just turned her head and closed her eyes. All the while Baby Celeste sat on the floor listening and watching. I adjusted Mama and her pillows again, then carried out the tray.

"Let's go downstairs, Celeste," I told her. "I'll read with you."

I continued down the stairs to the kitchen, my mind reeling with worry and confusion. It took me a few minutes to realize Baby Celeste hadn't followed. After I had taken care of the dishes and silverware, I went back upstairs, expecting she had remained in Mama's bedroom. She hadn't. I looked into her bedroom, and to my surprise I found she had prepared herself for sleep and was in bed. It was truly as if she was tuned in to Mama's every mood, every feeling. Suddenly, that frightened me. Instinctively, I thought that wasn't good.

I attended to Panther, talking and playing with him for a while until he, too, drifted off to sleep, then I went downstairs and sat in Grandfather Jordan's chair and waited with a trembling heart for Betsy's eventual return. It was like anticipating a tornado. The silence was ominous.

"Daddy," I whispered at the darkness outside our windows. "Come to me. Help me. Help us."

I held my breath and listened and waited, but I heard nothing beside the pounding of my heart, thumping like a distant drum.

For some strange reason, I began to hum Mama's song.

Then I sang it softly.

"If you go out in the woods today . . ."

I sang myself to sleep and didn't wake up until the whole house shook with Betsy's laughing, drunken entrance, slamming the front door. She stood in the hallway looking in at me, her body swaying. I was about to speak when a young man with dirty-blond hair, dressed in a dark blue athletic shirt and jeans, stepped up beside her and put his arm around her waist. He had tattoos over both his forearms. They looked like snakes twisting into what looked like chain links.

Betsy had gone directly to a clothing store and bought herself a new blouse-and-jean outfit with a pair of pink and white shoes. The blouse was half-open, revealing her breasts almost down to the nipples.

"There he is, my stepbrother," she said, and laughed.

I was holding my breath in expectation. What had she told this stranger?

"Hi there," he said, waving and then laughing.

"This is . . ." She turned and looked at the young man. His eyes were set close above a thick nose that looked as if it had once been broken. "Was it Brad or Tad, I can't remember," she said, and laughed.

"Tad." He lifted his right hand to wave at me again.

"Brad is with a rock-and-roll band called . . ." Betsy looked at him, her eyes turning in her head like loose marbles.

"The Hungry Hearts."

"Yeah, the Hungry Hearts. They're good. Maybe I'll

take you to hear them one night when you're not working in your garden or chopping wood or painting poles." She laughed again. Then she seemed to sober up instantly and step a bit forward. "Did you get what had to be done, done?" she demanded.

"Yes," I lied. I thought, under the circumstances, it was the wisest thing for me to do.

"Good. Good. Noble here is perfect," she told Tad. Then she tugged on his arm. "C'mon. We'll use his room tonight. You don't mind, do you, Noble? I don't want to wake up you know who," she said in a conspiratorial tone.

I looked away and shook my head. She probably hadn't told him that Panther was her child.

She laughed again and pulled Tad to the stairway. I listened to them giggle and navigate their way upstairs, wondering if they would wake Mama. I almost wished they would. At least she would speak and move again, but apparently they didn't. Once they were in my room and had shut the door, the house returned to its ominous stillness.

I closed my eyes and made silent prayers.

When I opened them, Elliot was sitting across from me.

"It's almost over," he said. "The whole thing . . . it's almost over."

I simply stared at him. He no longer frightened me or surprised me. I could see that bothered him.

His smile softened to a grin of confusion. Then he shook his head.

"You're happy about that, aren't you? You wanted all this. You wanted me to succeed."

I said nothing.

I closed my eyes again, and when I opened them much later on, he was gone.

And in his place there was nothing but emptiness, a deep, dark emptiness that had settled comfortably in my heart and wrapped itself snugly around my very soul. There was nothing left for me to do but sleep, surrender to it like a soldier who had fought his best and settled regretfully but willingly into a bed of defeat.

At first light, I was woken by a tug on my hand and opened my eyes to see Baby Celeste standing there and looking at me.

"Celeste!" I cried, and scrubbed my cheeks with my palms. "Is Panther awake, too?"

She shook her head.

"Did Mama wake you?" I asked hopefully.

Again, she only shook her head.

"C'mon then, let's see how she is." I started up the stairs. She didn't follow. I looked back at her standing at the foot of the stairway. "Don't go anywhere now, Celeste. We're going to make breakfast in a minute."

She didn't reply. She just continued to stare up at me. I hurried to Mama's room, taking note as I passed my own bedroom that the door was shut. It would be quite a shock for Mama to see that Betsy had dared bring someone to our house like this, I thought.

Mama was awake, but she had the same distant look in her eyes. What frightened me the most, however, was seeing that she had wet herself like a baby.

"Oh, God, Mama," I cried.

She didn't look at me; she didn't in anyway acknowledge that she had heard me. For a moment I just turned in circles trying to think of what to do first. Then Panther began to cry. I anticipated Betsy rising to see about him, but the door of my bedroom never opened. I didn't know what to attend to first.

"Mama, you have to get up. You have to change and clean yourself. Please," I pleaded. "Mama!"

She closed her eyes, then she opened them and looked at me. I held my breath.

She smiled.

"Mama, oh, thank you, thank you," I moaned to every spirit that dwelled in and about our home.

"Noble?"

"Yes, Mama, yes. It's Noble. Now listen. You have had an accident. Please get up. We need to change the linen on your bed and you need to clean yourself."

"An accident?" Finally she realized what she had done. "Oh. I'm getting older, I guess."

Panther's cries grew louder.

"Who's crying?"

"It's Panther."

"Panther? Who's Panther?" She started to prop up on her elbows.

"Betsy's Panther, Mama. Betsy's baby."

She looked at me and shook her head with confusion.

"Okay, Mama. Can you get up and get yourself out of these clothes? I'll look after the baby, okay?"

"Baby? Baby Celeste," she said, remembering.

"Yes, she's downstairs waiting for us to make breakfast."

Mama nodded. I guided her to her feet. She wobbled and then steadied herself. I directed her toward the bathroom, then went to look after Panther. He had to be changed. I tried to make as much noise as I could to wake Betsy, but I thought even if a bomb went off at the bedroom door, she wouldn't waken. Even if she did, I realized, she would be of little help.

Baby Celeste was already in the kitchen trying to get breakfast started. She had taken juice out of the refrigerator and found her little bowl for her cereal. I smiled at her efforts and then got Panther situated in his high chair. I prepared his breakfast, put up some oatmeal for Mama, and toasted some of her homemade bread.

Betsy had still not risen even after I had accomplished it all. I went up to check on Mama and found her sitting in the bathtub naked, but without any water. She was wiping a washcloth over her arms and body as if there were water and soap. The sight made me feel as if I were melting from top to bottom, my body sinking into a puddle at my feet.

"Mama . . . there's no water in the tub."

She looked at me and smiled. "You come to wash my back?" she asked.

It was something she had often had Noble do when he was little. It was the one thing other than his imaginary games that he took seriously. She offered me the washcloth. I lowered my head. What was I going to do?

The sound of Betsy's laughter spun me around. She was in the hallway.

"Noble!" she screamed. "Where the hell are you?"

I looked at Mama, then I hurried out to see what Betsy wanted.

She was standing in my doorway, holding a pillow against her naked body.

"Bring us coffee and toast us some of that bread I like with that blackberry jam. Don't take all day either," she ordered. "Afterward, you and I will have a talk about things. Where's the queen?" she followed as an afterthought.

I thought I heard the sound of bees around my head. I looked back through Mama's bedroom door and then at the stairway.

"Oh, don't act like such a jerk," Betsy quipped. "Just do what I ask."

"Hey!" I heard her new boyfriend call. "Where the hell are we?"

Betsy laughed. "You're in herbal heaven," she cried, glared at me, then backed into my bedroom. "Hurry it up," she ordered, and closed the door.

I returned to Mama's bathroom. She was out of the tub and wiping herself with a towel. I had to see about the children. They had been left alone too long.

"I'll be right back, Mama. I made oatmeal for you."

"You did? How sweet. But," she said, lowering her head and raising her eyes at me, "did you make it or did Celeste?"

"Celeste," I said softly.

"Thought so. That's all right. I know you wanted to do it yourself, Noble. And that's what counts the most." I watched her go to her vanity table still naked and begin to brush her hair. She moved the brush ever so slowly.

She'll be occupied awhile, I thought, and rushed out and down the stairs.

Panther had thrown his food off the high chair and, using his spoon, heaved his eggs all over the table and even the walls. I looked at Baby Celeste, who was sitting there finishing her cereal and watching him.

"Why did you let him do that, Celeste?"

She looked at me, a tight, small smile on her face.

"You're still being bad. I'm not letting you outside today. You're going to spend the day in your room."

I wanted her in there anyway. I wanted her away from all that was happening.

She looked unconcerned. I made a quick attempt to wipe Panther's face and body and some of the mess he had created, and then I put up coffee and cut the bread to make the toast Betsy wanted. Before I was finished, Celeste brought in the breakfast dishes, even Panther's, and placed it all neatly on the counter by the sink. Then she shot me a look of disgust and went out and up the stairs to her room.

I heard Betsy banging on the floor of my room and shouting for service. After I prepared the tray, I looked in on Panther, who was occupied with his remaining food. He had a fistful of scrambled eggs, enjoying the feel of it. Betsy screamed again. I carried the tray up and knocked on my bedroom door.

"Enter," I heard, and managed to open it.

She was in bed with Tad and sat up immediately. "Put it right here, Brother."

Tad smiled, one eye closed.

I set the tray down in front of them.

"Oh," she said, "draw me a warm bath and throw in some of that herbal bubble-bath crap Sarah makes. It looks like it is good for your skin. Right, Brad?"

"Tad," he said.

"Tad. Isn't my skin smooth?"

"Like a baby's rear end," he said, and they both laughed.

I started out.

"Close the damn door," Betsy screamed.

"Gladly," I muttered, and did so.

When I looked in on Mama, I saw she had put on her nightgown and was about to crawl back into bed.

"Mama, what are you doing? We have to change the sheets, and you don't want to go back to bed anyway."

"I'm tired, and it's late. You should go to sleep, too."

"No, Mama. It's morning. Get up. Get dressed," I urged.

She shook her head and, despite the messed sheet, crawled under the blanket again.

I just stood there for a moment. I had to call someone, I thought. I needed help. The only one I could think of was Mr. Bogart and his wife, or perhaps the Reverend Mr. Austin's wife, Tani. First things first, I thought. Mama wasn't going anywhere. I had to deal with Betsy and settle that.

I looked in on Baby Celeste, who was sitting in her chair in her room looking at the pictures in old family albums. She was quiet so I left her and started Betsy's bath. Then I ran downstairs, got Panther, and brought him up to wash and change him into one of his outfits. Before I was finished, Betsy came into the room and closed the door behind her.

"Your bath's going to overflow," I said.

"I'll look after it. Don't you mention that kid being mine, hear me," she warned, nodding at Panther. "I told him he's your cousin, too. When do I get my money?"

I put my hands over my face.

"Well?" she screamed.

"Mama's not right," I said, lowering my hands. "What you did put her into a . . ."

"A what?"

"A bad mental state. She's in a daze, confused. I'm very worried. I might have to get help."

Betsy stood there thinking. "Don't call anyone just yet. We'll handle it. I'll think of something. After my bath, I'm going into town with Tad and buy the things I'll need when I leave here. I'm going to need more money, credit cards. Get all that from your mother. You know where she keeps her checkbook. Write out a check for as much as she has in the account. When I return, we'll see about the rest. Understand? Well? Don't just stand there staring at me."

"I'll do what I can."

"Do more than you can," she countered, turned, and left me with Panther.

After I dressed him, I brought him down and put him in the playpen we had set up for him in the living room. He cried about being left alone, but there was nothing I could do. I returned to Mama's bedroom. She was asleep again, so I looked through her things, found more money, her checkbook, and two credit cards. I've got to keep Betsy happy enough not to make us any more trouble, I thought.

There seemed to be a balance of $2,400 in the checking account. I wrote out a check for $2,000 and made it out to cash. Then I brought everything to Betsy, who was soaking in the tub.

"I have to hand it to her," she said, hearing me come in. She had her head back and her eyes closed. "This herbal bubble bath really feels good."

She sat forward and looked at me. "Well?"

"I have a check for two thousand dollars for you. You should go to the bank to cash it. If they call here, I tell them it's all right. These are the only credit cards we have, and there's about four hundred dollars in this," I said, showing her the roll of cash.

"That's a start. Good for you. You're being smart, Noble Celeste. How's the queen?"

"She's just sleeping."

"She better get well enough to make that call to the lawyer soon," she warned. "Hand me the towel."

I did so and she got out of the tub.

"You see," she said, turning toward me to show me her breasts. "Still firm. If you should ever become the woman you are, don't breast-feed."

I rushed from the bathroom, her laughter chasing after me. When I reached the stairs, I heard the piano.

"Mama?" I called.

The music was different though. I found Tad in the living room playing.

"This thing is badly out of tune," he said. He nodded at Panther, who was sitting quietly and looking at him. "Kid likes rock and roll." He laughed and continued to play.

I went into the kitchen and cleaned up. I had no appetite whatsoever and just sipped a little coffee. Soon after, I heard Betsy come downstairs.

"We're off," she shouted from the entryway.

I stepped out and looked.

"I'll be back this afternoon, and then we'll do our business. You understand?"

I didn't say anything.

They left and the house was quiet again. Panther called after her. I walked slowly down the hallway and looked in on him. He was standing in his playpen. Being deserted was not a new experience for him, I thought. This wasn't the first time and it would surely not be the last.

Suddenly, I felt so trapped, so enclosed, it was as if I were in a playpen myself.

I stepped outside quickly and took deep breaths of fresh air. The sky was partly overcast, but there was enough sunlight to give my dark heart some respite from the shadows that were dancing around inside me.

I looked to the woods, and suddenly I was sure I saw Daddy. He stepped out and started toward the house, but something stopped him and he was back in the woods again. I watched.

He stepped out and started toward the house. Again something stopped him and he was back in the woods.

"Daddy!" I screamed, my tears lifting over my lids and sliding over my cheeks.

He started for the house but stopped and shook his head.

He was back in the woods.

He can't come here, I realized.

I looked about. Shadows were moving everywhere and stopping.

They're all locked out.

Something was terribly wrong, and until it was made right again, we were alone.

We were all deserted.

20

A Dance of Death

♊

Sleeping didn't help Mama. If anything, she appeared to fall further into some abyss of madness. She babbled incoherently when she was awake, then drifted off. I tried to get her to drink some water, but it ran out of the corners of her mouth. Her tongue was like a plug keeping anything from going down her throat. I knew that she couldn't last long like this, but I kept hoping that somehow I would get her sensible again.

I spent my day looking after Panther. Baby Celeste remained sullen and angry. Finally, when Panther was taking a nap and Mama was asleep again, I tried to satisfy Baby Celeste by going out to the garden. She did seem pleased, but because we couldn't stay long, she returned to her sulking, ate little, and ignored me. Finally, she went up to her room and closed the door. When I looked in on her, she was asleep in her bed.

Late in the afternoon, Betsy returned alone. She had bags and bags of clothing, shoes, cosmetics, everything she had lacked and wanted. I had to help her bring it all in and up to her room. It took me two trips. She didn't even look at Panther or ask after him. All she did was babble about the wonderful new clothing she had gotten. I tried to be as interested and excited about it all as I could, just to please her. Finally, she stopped and asked about Mama and our attorney, Mr. Derward Lee Nokleby-Cook.

"I've decided to join Tad's band," she told me. "I'm going to travel with them and be their manager. One of the first things I'm buying with my money is one of those buses with a bathroom in it. We're going to paint the name of the band on the sides. Everyone's excited about it. Well?"

"I'm trying to do what you want. But Mama's still asleep."

"What do you mean, still asleep?" she cried, grimacing. "That's just a bunch of crap. She's pretending. And I can tell you it won't work."

She threw down her new blouse and marched out of her room.

"Betsy!" I cried after her. "Don't."

She forged ahead and burst into Mama's bedroom. Mama was still in bed, of course, her eyes closed. Betsy charged right at the bed. I ran after her, but she got there first and started to shake Mama.

"Wake up, Sarah. This pretending won't work with me. I want my money and I want it right away. Wake up, damn you!" she screamed, and shook Mama so hard her head bounced back and forth.

I grabbed Betsy's arms to stop her, but she was so determined, she broke free of my grasp and shook Mama again. Mama's eyes opened, but she didn't speak nor did she look at Betsy.

"Stop pretending to be in some sort of a sick daze!

You do what I asked and do it now, damn you!" she screamed.

Mama didn't speak, didn't even utter a sound in defense or protest. Her eyes closed again.

"If you don't do what I want, I'll go downstairs, boil water, and throw it on your face," Betsy threatened.

Mama's eyelids fluttered, but didn't open. Betsy flung her back to the bed and pillow, turned, and glared hatefully at me.

"I'm sick of you. Sick of her. Sick of this place. She's not getting away with stealing my money!" Betsy bellowed.

"She's not stealing it," I said as calmly as I could. "Your father wanted it this way."

"He did not. She made him do it." Betsy pointed at Mama. "She had him hypnotized or something." She glowered at Mama. "You're not getting away with any of this anymore, Sarah," she shouted.

"She can't help it. She's not well. I can't even get her to drink water."

"Oh, stop. I know what she's up to. She probably thinks her spirits will save her, but not this time. You're not the boss this time, Sarah. You're not telling anyone to do anything anymore. I want my money!"

Mama's lips moved slightly but her eyes remained closed.

"She's not pretending. You'll have to wait until we get her well again."

"Is that right, Noble Celeste? I have to wait?" Betsy said, smiling madly. "Me? I'm the one who has to wait for my own money?"

"Can't you see how she is?"

She turned back to Mama. "I see a phony, a lunatic. That's what I see. Okay, you want to play hardball,

Sarah, we'll play hardball. I'm going down to boil the water."

She spun around and charged past me, pushing me aside as she went by and out the bedroom door. Mama moaned, but she didn't open her eyes.

"Please, Mama," I said, "let's get her the money and get her out of here for good."

Mama didn't open her eyes, didn't move her lips. I touched her face lovingly and called to her, but she didn't react. She doesn't hear me, I thought. It was what I had always feared. Facing the reality of Noble's death drove her down so deeply, her own body had become her coffin and she was about to close the lid on herself.

"Oh, Mama," I moaned, lowering myself to press my cheek to hers, "can't we live happily as we really are? Can't I be your Celeste again? Please, Mama."

My tears rolled off my cheeks and onto hers, but she didn't open her eyes. I felt the vibration of a moan within her, a vibration that sounded like a long, hollow *Noooooooooo!* Then I stepped back, looked at her, and waited to see if she would react before I left the bedroom. I had to go. I had to calm down Betsy and figure out some sort of solution until I could get Mama some help. Perhaps I would call Mr. Bogart, I thought. He would know what to do. Or I could call the Reverend Mr. Austin and his wife, Tani. They were so nice, so understanding. They would help us.

I'll tell Betsy my plan, I thought. It will calm her down to see I'm trying to do something.

When I went looking for her, I did find her in the kitchen. She had put up a pot of water and brought it to a boil. She heard me behind her and turned.

"Has the queen decided to play ball? Is she up and ready to make the call?"

"No, Betsy. I told you. She's not pretending. I've

decided to call Mr. Bogart or the Reverend Austin and ask them for help. They'll know what we should do."

"Oh, is that your solution? Call her herb distributor or that silly reverend, who'll probably come here and make wonderful speeches about how lucky we all are to be together? Maybe she isn't pretending. Maybe she is crazy, but I'll snap her out of it. I have everyone waiting for me. Tad is getting it all together. We're leaving tomorrow after I get my money. Time's up." She put a pot holder around the pot handle, lifting the boiled water off the stove.

"You can't do that. She won't even know you're threatening her."

"Oh, she'll know. I'll let a drop or two fall on her face and she'll suddenly see the light," Betsy said, her eyes wide with excitement. "Get out of my way or I'll throw it all on you." She brought the pot back and up, poised to cast the water at me.

"Please. Just give me the chance to get us help. It's the best way."

"Move!" she shouted.

I had no doubt that she would throw that boiling water at me. I stepped aside and she walked quickly out of the kitchen with me following and cajoling her to be reasonable, to give me an opportunity to do the things she wanted.

She didn't respond or pause until she was halfway up the stairs. "If this doesn't work, then we'll go to your plan, but I think it's going to work. Trust me." Then she continued up, stopping about three steps from the top.

Baby Celeste had come out of her room and was standing glaring down at her.

"Get that kid out of my way or I'll scald her."

"Celeste, get out of her way," I screamed, and hurried to catch up.

Rather than get out of Betsy's way, Baby Celeste held her arms out to prevent her from going past her and, to my shock and surprise, stepped down toward her, practically challenging her to attempt to go farther.

"She's as crazy as your mother," Betsy said, and brought the pot back to cast some of the boiling water at Baby Celeste.

I charged up the few steps that separated me from Betsy and seized her right arm.

"*No!*" I shouted, and wrenched her back. She missed a step, but the force of my pull sent her flying against the wall on my left. She hit it hard with her forehead, spun like a ballerina in the air, and then came down two steps below, her legs crumbling under her weight, sending her head over heels down the remaining steps. The pot of boiling water seemed suspended in midair for a moment, then came crashing down behind her, the water leaping out of the pot, some of it splashing on her legs. She landed at the bottom of the steps, her body twisted awkwardly so that her torso was going in one direction, but her head in the completely opposite. The pot clanged on the floor and rolled to a stop.

Betsy's right arm was turned and bent all the way back at the elbow. Her left arm had slapped against the step so hard, I could see that it had broken at her forearm, the jagged bone actually piercing the skin and starting a trickle of blood. I stared down at her, astonished at the strange ballet I had caused, a ballet I realized almost immediately was a dance of death.

I stood there in shock, not realizing for a good minute that Baby Celeste had come down the steps and taken my left hand into hers. She was staring at Betsy, too.

"Oh, my God," I said. "I think she's dead."

Then I realized Baby Celeste was there and I looked at her. She was as still as a statue, intrigued with the sight before her. I lifted her into my arms and slowly descended toward Betsy's broken body. Her eyes were still wide open, but had already taken on that glassy appearance of two marbles, no longer bringing any information into her head. They were now two snuffed candles, not even smoldering. Darkness had entered her and quickly drowned every thought, every memory. She was filled with silence.

"What are we going to do?" I moaned.

Baby Celeste stared down at her and then turned to me, her little eyelids blinking rapidly.

"Put her in the garden," she said.

The shock of her suggestion truly hit me like a bolt of lightning, but instead of making me feel hot, it drove the blood into my feet and turned my heart to ice. Still carrying Baby Celeste in my arms, I turned and ascended the stairway. Mama will know what to do, I thought. Mama will tell me. She has to wake up now. She has to help me.

I entered the bedroom as quickly as I could and went to Mama's side, lowering Baby Celeste to the floor. She stood there beside me looking at Mama. I took Mama's hand in my two hands and went to my knees, lowering my head like someone in prayer.

"Mama, a terrible thing just happened. I tried to stop Betsy from throwing boiling water at Baby Celeste and coming up here to throw it at you, and I made her fall down the stairs. I'm sure her neck's broken. I'm sure she's dead, Mama. She's dead. What should I do? Please, Mama. Please wake up and help me, help us. Please."

I waited, but she didn't move, nor did she speak. Nevertheless, I remained there and pleaded with her. I don't know how long I was there on my knees, but darkness fell around the house and my knees suddenly stung and ached. Baby Celeste was gone when I turned to look for her, and I could hear Panther crying. He sounded hoarse so I was sure he had been crying awhile and I had just not heard.

I pulled myself up and looked down at Mama. She had her head turned a bit to the right. Panicked, I felt for her pulse. It was there, but so very slight. She was running down like some old windup toy, I thought.

I'll make her something to eat. I'll prepare one of her many cereals with honey. If I get her to take in some food, she'll get better, I decided. Yes, that's all I have to do: get her to take in some food.

And I have to look after Panther and Baby Celeste as well, I thought, and rushed out. First things first, I told myself. After I've done everything that has to be done, I will sit in the living room in Grandpa Jordan's chair and I will wait to be told what I should do. That's it. They'll tell me. Things will be fine. I should have thought of that before. How silly of me. They won't let anything bad happen to us.

I went directly to Panther and changed his diaper first. Then I soothed him and calmed him and carried him down to feed him. He looked at Betsy's body with some curiosity, but no emotion. He didn't call to her or reach for her. Instead, he tightened his little arms around my neck.

"There, there," I said. "It will be all right. We'll all be fine."

Baby Celeste was in the kitchen nibbling on a graham cracker.

"Hungry," she said angrily.

"I know, Celeste. I'm going to make us all dinner right now. Keep Panther occupied while I do it." I put him in his high chair. I gave him one of the crackers Baby Celeste was eating, and like a good girl she sat with him and talked to him while I worked on our dinner.

We are going to be fine, I thought. I fed them both, then I took the bowl of food with a cup of herbal tea up to Mama. She hadn't moved a muscle, changed her position one inch. I fixed the pillows and propped her up, but her head fell forward. I lifted it gently under the chin.

"Mama, please try to eat. I have something very good for you." I spooned some cereal into her mouth, but her jaw didn't move. The cereal remained on her tongue.

Maybe I can wash it down with water, I thought, and filled a glass. I held her head tilted and poured it in. She gagged and spit it up along with the cereal, but her eyes didn't open.

"What am I going to do?" I asked her silent face.

I stepped back and looked at her, then I walked out slowly, my head bowed, my shoulders sagging under the weight of such defeat. My thoughts were like Ping-Pong balls bouncing back and forth, pieces of this idea, pieces of that, but nothing sensible, no two sentences being completed. I was in a daze myself by the time I reached the bottom of the steps and avoided Betsy's broken body.

I put Panther in his playpen. Baby Celeste sat beside it and opened one of her books, and I sat in Grandpa Jordan's chair and waited with my eyes closed. I know I fell asleep because when I opened them again, Panther was asleep in the playpen and Baby Celeste was lying asleep on the sofa. The house was dark and silent.

It was then that an idea came to me. It came to me

so vividly and firmly, I was sure it was coming from
our spiritual family. It brought a smile to my face. Of
course, I thought. I should have thought of it before. I
got up and looked out the window, and sure enough,
there they were, all of them gathered together, looking
at the house and talking. Daddy was there, too, but
someone was missing, someone I had to bring out as
well.

I glanced at the children and decided they were fine.
Then I hurried upstairs, not even noticing Betsy this
time, and went directly to Mama's bedroom, opened
the dresser drawer, and got the door key. Mama was
still propped up as I had left her to feed her, but her
head was down and her arms limp.

"Everything will be fine soon, Mama," I said. "Just
wait and you'll see."

Excited, I ran up the small stairway to the turret
room and opened the door. I knew just where to go and
what to get. It took me only a few minutes to do that
and be out and downstairs again. I went back to
Mama's room and stripped naked. Then I went into her
shower and scrubbed myself well, luxuriating in the
lather of her perfumed soap. As soon as I was out and
dried, I began to brush my hair differently. I sat at her
vanity table and put on my makeup just the way I had
experimented with it some time ago. Buoyed by what I
saw in the mirror, I put on the bra, the panties, and the
dress I had chosen long ago as my favorite during one
of my secret visits to the turret room. I slipped on the
shoes and I looked at myself in the mirror.

"Oh, Mama," I cried, "I am beautiful. Look at me.
Look at me once and see me, really see me," I pleaded.

I was sure she raised her head and looked, and then
she smiled. I was sure of it.

I smiled back.

"Celeste." I was sure she said it. "My darling Celeste. You've come home."

"Yes, Mama, I'm back for good." I hugged her and was sure she hugged me.

Then I hurried out and down the stairs. I had to show everyone. That was very, very important.

I stepped out of the house and walked to the edge of the porch.

"Look at me!" I shouted.

They all turned.

Daddy was smiling. "My left arm!" he cried.

Off to my right, a shadow lifted from an unmarked grave. Everyone turned to look. The shadow came out of the little cemetery and slowly made its way down toward the house. When it drew close enough, we could all see. It was Noble, and he, too, was smiling.

"My right arm!" Daddy cried.

Noble went to him and Daddy put his arms around him. I stepped off the porch and they both approached me and embraced me.

We three turned and looked up. That was Mama looking out and down at us. I was sure.

"How wonderful," Daddy said. "We'll all be together again."

"Yes, Daddy," I told him.

"And you'll play with me?" Noble asked with suspicion and doubt.

"Yes, I will. I promise," I said.

He looked at Daddy and smiled.

"We can all go in the house now," Daddy said. "Lead the way, Celeste."

I held his hand and he held Noble's hand. Behind us, our family members clapped and cried out in joy. I opened the door and Daddy and Noble went in ahead of me.

When I turned, I looked toward the forest where I saw Elliot, his head down, making a quick retreat into the darkness from which he had come and to which he would return forever. Then I went in, and with Daddy and Noble beside me, I undressed the children, got them into their pajamas, and put them both to bed. I fixed Mama as well to make her more comfortable.

Daddy sat beside the bed and held her hand, and Noble sat with me on the bed. We talked softly late into the night until my eyes wouldn't stay open.

"Go on to sleep," Daddy said. "I'll stay with her."

"Me, too," Noble said.

"Okay," I told them. I kissed Mama's cheek and then went to bed.

I fell asleep in my clothes.

I slept late into the morning. Panther was up but he was occupied with some of his toys and apparently didn't cry out and scream as he usually did every morning. It was Baby Celeste who woke me with a scream.

I rubbed my eyes and sat up. She was standing in the doorway staring at me.

And she was crying.

"What's wrong, Celeste? Why are you crying?" I quickly got up to go to her.

She backed away from me as though she was frightened of me.

"What's wrong, honey?" I asked, smiling at her.

"I want Noble."

I tilted my head. "Noble?"

"I want Mama."

"Mama. Yes. Let's go look in on Mama." I reached for her hand, but she pulled away and ran to her room, slamming the door closed on me.

"Celeste, what is it?" I cried after her.

That child is a handful, I thought. She always will be.

I went to Mama's bedroom and looked in on her. She was exactly as I had left her, only when I drew closer, I saw she was pale, her lips blue. I rushed to her side and felt her face. It was cold. Her fingers were stiff.

Mama's gone, I thought. Mama's gone. They took her last night. Daddy and Noble took her with them.

I didn't cry. Mama wanted to go, otherwise she wouldn't have gone, I thought. She'll be back anyway. They'll all be back. In the meantime, I had a lot to do. It would be the last time I would work so hard in the garden.

It all kept me so busy, I forgot about the children. By the time I looked in on them, Panther had fallen back asleep, probably exhausted from crying. Baby Celeste was curled up with her thumb in her mouth. She looked absolutely terrified. I practically dragged her out and down the stairs to get something in her stomach.

"You can be silly and childish afterward," I told her. "For now you have to eat something."

I prepared food for Panther as well and went back upstairs to him after I looked after Baby Celeste. He was awake again and hungry. I had no trouble getting him to eat everything. I changed him, dressed him, and brought him downstairs.

Baby Celeste still refused to speak to me, but she at least went into the living room to occupy herself with her books and toys.

"I've got a lot of housecleaning to do," I told the both of them. "I want the two of you to behave yourselves while I work. If you're good, I'll give you both some ice cream later."

Baby Celeste looked up at me skeptically. Panther

jumped up and down in his playpen, energized and remarkably happy, I thought.

We're all going to be fine, I told myself again, and
went right to work.

Late in the afternoon, I heard a car pull up to the
house and moments later a knocking on our front door.
I had just finished putting all of Betsy's clothing in
the turret room and was halfway down the stairs. Baby
Celeste came to the living room doorway to see who it
was, too.

"Noble," she said hopefully.

I shook my head. "No, Celeste. It's not Noble.
Noble doesn't have to knock on the door to be let in."

I opened the door and saw Tad standing there. He
was wearing a jeans jacket, no shirt beneath it, and a
pair of torn jeans and sneakers without socks. His hair
was unbrushed, the strands in revolt and trying to escape from his scalp in every direction.

"Is Betsy here?"

"Betsy? No. Betsy's gone."

"Gone? Where did she go?"

"I don't know. She didn't say. She just packed her
things and left."

He raised an eyebrow. "Who are you?"

"My name is Celeste."

"Where's what's his name? Noble?"

"Noble isn't here now. He's fishing."

"Fishing?"

Just then Panther let out one of his shrill screams.

"One moment please," I said, and went into the living room. He wanted Baby Celeste to give him her
crayons, but she had wisely refused. He would have
tried to eat them. I picked him up and out of the
playpen. When I turned, I saw Tad had come into the
house and was standing in the doorway.

"Well, she must have left some information for me. I'm Tad. Didn't she mention me?"

I shook my head. "No, I'm sorry. She didn't mention you or leave anything for you."

"Do you live here?"

"Of course, I live here," I said, smiling.

"Well, where were you the other day when I was here?"

I shrugged. "Maybe I was in the garden."

"The garden? You couldn't have been in the garden all the time."

"No, I'm not in the garden all the time, but I'm there often."

"What, were you just in it now?"

"Pardon me?"

He nodded at me and I looked down at my mud-stained dress.

"Oh," I said, smiling. "I've been doing a lot of cleaning today."

"Must have been a pretty dirty house," he remarked dryly. He turned and looked up the stairway. I could see he didn't believe me and wanted to shout for Betsy.

"Go on," I said.

"What?"

"Shout her name if you like. Call her."

He stared at me a moment, then turned and bellowed, *"Betsy!"*

Her name echoed, at least in my ears. He stood there waiting a moment, then turned back to us. Baby Celeste was staring at him so hard, he looked at her and then at me.

"Something smells fishy here. Betsy was very excited about going with me and my band. She would have called me or something."

"Betsy is very unreliable."

He thought a moment. "Did she get her money?

"What money?"

"Her inheritance."

"Oh. You didn't believe that, did you?" I laughed.
"There's no inheritance."

He stared. "Where's this Noble, you say?"

"He's at the creek, fishing. It's about a half mile
through the woods."

He smirked. "Half a mile through the woods."

"Yes. I'm sorry we can't help you."

"Yeah, me, too," he said, and walked out.

I went to the window and saw him get into a car, in
which sat another boy about his age and a girl. He
spoke rapidly and with great animation to them, then
he started the car, shifted, and spun his wheels to turn
around and drive away.

"I don't think they'll be back," I muttered.

Baby Celeste shook her head in agreement. Then I
returned to Grandpa Jordan's chair and she returned to
her books and toys and Panther played quietly in the
playpen.

We're fine.

Everything is just fine, I thought.

Epilogue

Forever at the Farm

♊

Mr. Bogart was the first to come. I hadn't realized almost two weeks had gone by. He said he had been calling every day and had become concerned.

The day before he arrived, my whole spiritual family joined me in the living room and we discussed the near future. To my surprise there was disagreement. Some thought things were fine the way they were, but most thought the house had been irrevocably contaminated. Auntie Helen Roe, who was in her wheelchair, thought it had to be cleansed and should be set afire. Grandpa Jordan was so outraged by the suggestion, he looked as if he could burst a vein in his neck, even though I knew such a thing was no longer possible. Daddy said nothing. He just smiled and shook his head at Mama while they all argued. I knew what he was thinking. *You have a crazy family, Sarah. I always told you so.*

Mama was the one who decided that if I went

through the house thoroughly with two white candles and washed the walls with candle smoke, it would suffice. That threw them all into a discussion about the number of candles needed and if any had to be kept lit in the rooms. Mama relented and said, "Okay, after she washes the walls, she'll place candles in all the rooms and light them and leave them for two days and nights."

Aunt Sophie said it should be three nights. Three was, after all, a magic number.

Mama, although she didn't look as if she believed that, agreed. I think she agreed just to end the discussion.

Grandpa Jordan was happy that a solution other than setting the house afire had been found. They all embraced me, kissed me, and wished me good fortune before they left, and then I went ahead and followed their directions.

Mr. Bogart noticed the lit candles right away and asked me about them. I explained just why I had done it and he nodded, and then, after inquiring about Mama, he went upstairs. I followed him up. He saw the lit candles even in the hallway and nodded at me. Then he went into Mama's room, and after a few moments I heard him go to the phone in her room to call the Reverend Mr. Austin. After that Mr. Bogart and I looked in on the children. Then we went downstairs to wait for the reverend, who drove over as quickly as he could. The moment he walked into the house, he grimaced as if the odors put him in actual pain.

When he turned to me, he smiled in confusion and looked at Mr. Bogart. "Whom do we have here?" he asked.

"This is Celeste," Mr. Bogart said. "It always was."

The reverend's eyes widened, but he didn't say anything unpleasant.

"I'll explain it to you later," Mr. Bogart said, which satisfied the reverend.

He then asked after the children.

"They're both taking naps," I said.

"They're fine," Mr. Bogart told him. "We'll talk about them afterward."

Mr. Bogart wanted to take the reverend up to Mama's room. While they were up there, Baby Celeste had woken and called out to them. Mr. Bogart had her in his arms when they all came down, and she had a dreadfully angry look on her face. The reverend look stunned and confused.

"Where's the downstairs phone?" Mr. Bogart asked me.

I explained why Mama had locked it up to keep it away from Betsy, and then they asked me where Betsy was. I told them she had gone off, but Baby Celeste, glaring at me, told them she was in the garden.

"In the garden?" the reverend asked. "I didn't see anyone out there when I drove up."

He and Mr. Bogart looked at each other and then they went out to the garden, Mr. Bogart still carrying Baby Celeste. While they were out there, Daddy, Noble, and Mama came into the living room to wait with me.

"It's all right," Daddy said. "You've done just fine."

"Of course she has," Mama said. "The house is sacred again."

"When you're finished here, I want to play knights and dragons," Noble told me. "You said you would," he reminded me firmly.

"I will," I told him, but he sat there looking as impatient and distrustful as ever.

The reverend and Mr. Bogart returned, the reverend looking pale. He kept pulling on his collar as if his neck had thickened and he was choking. Mr. Bogart set Baby Celeste down and she went directly to the sofa and sat with her hands folded in her lap like a polite little lady.

Mr. Bogart said everything would be all right, everything would be just fine, and I smiled.

I knew that even before they had come. He went back upstairs to Mama's room to use the phone.

Not long afterward, two police cars drove up and the policemen met with Mr. Bogart and the reverend outside. Baby Celeste and I watched them through the window. They talked and the reverend pointed toward the garden and then pointed at the house. The tallest policeman took off his hat and shook his head. He returned to his car and used his radio microphone. Then they all walked out to the garden.

"A lot of turmoil over nothing, if you ask me," Grandpa Jordan said. I hadn't realized he was in the room with us until that moment. He nodded at me and went out to see what they were all up to. Mama sat beside me.

"It's all right," she said, and she held my hand.

Not long afterward, another car appeared, and a short, bald man in a suit and tie stepped out with a woman dressed like a nurse.

"She is a nurse," Daddy said, looking out with me. It always amazed me how he could hear my thoughts.

"What's a nurse doing here?" Auntie Roe asked with her lips curled in disapproval. She rolled her wheelchair up beside us and peered out the window, scrunching her nose and turning her eyebrows in toward each other. "Too many strangers sticking their noses in our business."

"Amen to that," Great-great-uncle Samuel said, coming up behind her. "Everyone's a nosybody these days."

The policemen and the man in a suit and the nurse

spoke for a while outside just before another car appeared and another woman and man in a suit appeared. This woman was in a gray jacket and skirt with a white blouse and had short brown-and-gray hair. They conferred as well, then they all came into the house.

"Hi there," the bald man in the suit said to me. "I'm Dr. Levy. And who's this beautiful little girl?" he asked, looking at Baby Celeste.

"I'm Celeste," she told him with a serious and grownup expression on her face.

"Well, hello to you, too," he told her. "This is Mrs. Newman. You can call her Patty," he continued, introducing the nurse. "She's here to help you, too."

"Help us do what?" I asked quickly.

"Oh, get you organized, comfortable. We have to take you to my clinic," he told me, "so I can help you get back on your feet."

"I'm on my feet." I stood up to show him.

He smiled and looked at Patty Newman, who smiled and shook her head.

"Where is the other infant?" the woman in the gray suit asked, and stepped forward. She looked impatient. The reverend was in the doorway behind them. He told her Panther was upstairs in his crib, and she put her handkerchief over her face and hurried up the stairs.

"I need you to come with me now for a while," Dr. Levy told me.

"I can't leave the house and the children."

"Oh, they'll be well taken care of," he promised. "And the police are here now. They'll be sure the house is protected."

"The house is always protected," I said, smiling. "We don't need the police for that."

"I'm sure it is," he said, raising his eyebrows. "And I'm very, very interested in how you know that."

I looked at Mama, who was shaking her head. She was sitting on the sofa.

"What should I do?" I asked her.

She didn't reply.

"You've got to go with them," Daddy said. "It will be best for the children, too."

"But she promised to play with me," Noble moaned.

"I have to play with my brother," I told Dr. Levy.

"Tell him to come along," he said. "I have lots to do and play with at my offices."

I looked at Noble. He seemed intrigued. After all, it wasn't often he could leave the grounds.

"Are there other young boys and girls there?" I asked, knowing he would want to know that.

"Oh, yes." Dr. Levy turned to Patty Newman. "Patty helps to take care of them as well, don't you, Patty?"

"Absolutely," she said. "You'll have lots to do."

I turned back to Noble. He was nodding with much more enthusiasm.

"Okay then," I said slowly, "but I have to be back to make dinner later."

"I understand," Dr. Levy said. He turned to Patty. "Mrs. Newman, shall we help the children move along?"

"Come along, dear," Patty said. She reached for me. I looked at Mama.

She was looking down at the floor. Daddy had his arm around her.

"She'll be fine," he said. "They'll both be fine."

We started out of the house. The woman in the suit had Panther in her arms, and the man who had come with her was kneeling in front of Baby Celeste and whispering. She was looking past him at me. She was still angry at me, I thought. Maybe this would help.

She nodded after something he said and he looked pleased.

"You're a very bright little girl," he told her.

We stepped out onto the porch.

Did I say how beautiful it was? I don't think a cloud was in the sky, and the blue was a cross between deep aqua and turquoise, with the turquoise more toward the horizon. Shadows were shimmering in the forest and the world was so still and quiet, I thought I could make out the distant gurgling of the creek as the water navigated around and over rocks. A large black crow lifted off a tall branch and soared toward the sun.

Noble and I got into the backseat of Dr. Levy's car. Noble was excited. It had been so long since he had been in a car.

I looked back and saw Baby Celeste and Panther being placed in the other car. In the garden two policemen were digging. I hoped they wouldn't harm any of the plants.

Before we started away, an ambulance arrived and two paramedics got out with a stretcher and headed toward the front door of the house, where another policeman was waiting for them. I saw he was directing them upstairs to Mama's room.

Patty Newman got into the backseat with Noble and me, and Dr. Levy got behind the steering wheel and started the engine.

"Are you all right, dear?" Patty asked me.

"Yes," I said. "I'm fine."

Noble fidgeted. He was never good at sitting still and he was impatient about our getting started.

A long time ago when I was Noble's age, Daddy decided he was going to take us to see something special he had discovered on a lot upon which he and his partner were constructing a new home. Mama didn't come with us, but that wasn't unusual. We often went places only with Daddy.

When we reached the lot, we got out and he walked us to the rear of the foundation his men had recently laid. He brought us to a large fallen tree trunk under which a hole had been dug and around which some dried grass had been placed with obvious care. Inside the hole were baby field mice, still pink and blind. They were feeding off their mother. Noble wanted to pick one up, but Daddy told him it would alarm the mother. We should just stand back and watch for a while.

"Not long from now," he said, "they will see and they will be old enough to go off on their own."

"What will happen to their house?" I asked.

"It won't be important anymore. They'll each create their own homes later, and the females will have their own babies in them."

"Why don't they just come back here?" I asked.

"They want their own," Daddy said. "Sometimes, we have to move on and find ourselves. We're all a little different and we need something that's ours, not something that belonged to our forefathers, but something that we create ourselves."

"You create homes for people."

He nodded. "Yes, so you see, if everyone stayed in the home he was brought up in, I'd be out of work."

"Mommy wants us to stay forever at the farm," Noble said, his eyes small like Mama's.

"I know," Daddy said. "But someday, someday you'll leave. It will just be in you to do it. And you mustn't be afraid."

"I don't want to leave," Noble said petulantly.

"We'll see," Daddy said, his voice dripping with wisdom. He winked at me.

Where would we go, Noble and I? I wondered.

I looked out then toward the mountains in the distance.

I was doing that now.

And I was smiling and thinking about Daddy holding our hands and walking us back to the car, the breeze lifting the beautiful strands of his hair, his eyes full of hope for all of us.

And I knew in an instant what he was saying.

We would leave our home someday perhaps.

But we would never leave each other.

Never.